I0636013

Arbitrary Nonsense

(or the Pendulum Rift)

a novel
by
Virgil Blackwell

ARBITRARY NONSENSE
A Swift-Tuttle Paperback Novel

Published by
Swift-Tuttle Press
New York, New York

This is a work of fiction. Names, characters, places, and incidents either are a product of the author's imagination or are used fictitiously. Any resemblance to actual persons, living or dead, events, or locales is entirely coincidental

ISBN: 978-0-9855180-1-1
Published in the United States of America

For Jack

~

Arbitrary Nonsense

(or the Pendulum Rift)

Between Here & There

In the doorway stood a stranger, the ghost of an old man who'd appeared out of nowhere, or so it seemed, trapped in the shadowland of an antique mirror that fit him like a coffin. He lingered there in an evening robe with knee-high socks and fuzzy slippers, looking like a rumpled wizard that had just been struck by his own lightning. Tufts of white hair stuck out from his head in shock, his wrinkled face clownish, his eyebrows wiry and untamed. His green eyes blinked in surprise, baffled by the image of himself, staring back, alive.

A stranger, the old man thought. He didn't even recognize his own face. How long had it been since he last met himself eye to eye? Had he grown old overnight? Possibly, quite possibly... he always did feel lighter when he awoke from his strange dreams, as if he'd shed the years in his sleep.

The old man crept toward the looking glass—naturally wary of shadowlands, strange vortexes, and other cosmic phenomenon in his old age—and covered it with a sheet.

Back when he had the courage to the bizarre thing, the antique mirror had reflected every corner of the room: under his bed (where it warped his dreams), behind his bookshelf (where every book opened a portal to another universe), beside his oak desk (cluttered with scribbled notes, books, and bird feathers) until he vanquished the foe by masking it with a sheet in the broom closet.

The mirror was a temptation, a ritual, an attempt to conjure up memories and make sense of his past. He tried his best to remember. He was once a professor of philosophy. He knew this to be true. He would lecture his students for hours on the great thinkers of Western Philosophy—Plato, Aristotle, Plotinus, Descartes, Rousseau, Nietzsche, Hegel. He couldn't remember much else. Events were jumbled, memories melting like broken icebergs in the Arctic under the midnight sun. He could never quite fit the pieces together.

There were two wars (one heroic, the other not-so-heroic), a dozen burials, six weddings, and a car crash in there somewhere. He'd buried his wife but couldn't remember her face. He'd buried his son but couldn't remember how he'd died or why he didn't cry at the funeral. The memories were foggy at best, with the exception of a few imagined ones such as his abduction by the aliens of Xeno Genius and running for governor of the great state of South Dakota.

Now in his old age, he dwelt on little more than confused nostalgia, fantasy, and bizarre dreams. On most days, the three blended into a comfortable delirium, a delirium that had now been soured by the vision in the mirror.

The reason he'd decided to unmask the mirror had slipped out of mind, lost forever in the ether. He fetched his mahogany pipe from his desk and gummed the thought over, unable to recall what had compelled him to do something so foolish.

He paced about the room that defined him. White walls, glaring white, peeling white, each layer flaking off to whiter white, riddled with holes where pictures once hung, now forever bare. Or did he by presence define the room? he wondered. And what's in a definition—*a word*—besides the breakdown of infinity into the world of things as the Great Moltarius once said?

Perhaps he thought too much, he thought. Perhaps there hung the crux of his existential quandary. The wheel of his brain cranked round and round, as if pedaled by a gerbil with insomnia. New thoughts bounced off the walls. Questions chased answers chased questions as he chewed his pipe. Fresh air, he decided, that's what he needed to clear his mind. He slid open the glass door to his balcony.

Under a moody twilit sky, a metropolis loomed out of the

dark, illuminated by lightning veins that streamed madly through the concourse. Taxi cabs sputtered their guttural cabspeak, roaring down avenues, past billboards—those giant postcards of a better life—while the skyscrapers jutted up (and up) to reflect, with silvery sheen the carnival of life below. Parades of people, the millions, walking A to B, waiting at C for D, talking to J and M, while N and L flirted famously on brownstone stoops. The whole human comedy juiced and squeezed.

The old man saw none of this as he shivered out on his balcony. To him, the world looked cold, barren, dead. To him, life below was just trivial noise and motion over which the full-bellied moon, his only companion, lay gloomy among a conspiring sea of stars.

"It's just you and I tonight, Luna," he told the moon, "Listening to whistles and bells."

Truth be told, these twilight communions were his only contact with the world outside his roost. Always at sunset, he'd wait for the sky to fade out and for the projected universe to show itself behind the illusion so he could talk with the moon.

He soaked in the dusk, cinching his robe tight. He looked out over the city. He thought back to the days of his youth—this alone he still remembered with clarity—when there had been a spark in his eye, when life, love, and happiness still retained some humor, when he and his two friends Addie and Norman had reveled in the nonsense and hijinks of adolescence.

The nefarious trio had grown up together in the small town of Warren, a western suburb of the city. Small as any, same as anywhere with apple-blossom groves and birch trees for lovers' initials winding in consummate rows by scarred tar roads and old colonial houses.

On any given day, they could be found up in the trees shouting obscenities/absurdities or downtown by the coffee shop singing with trashcan percussion late in the evening, ranting nonsense philosophies about immoral fish and heaven as a giant cup of tea. Although the neighbors generally frowned on such silliness, their antics might have been ignored were it not for the constant pranks.

During their reign of terror, they had spray-painted I HATE VANDALISM on the stucco of town hall, added bubblegum tentacles to cartoon figures on Slow Children signs, faked existential seizures in Englewood Park with shaving cream and torn pages of Sartre's *Nausea*, held protests against political activism, and similar acts of ironic stupidity which inevitably aroused public scorn and suspicion.

But they didn't care. They were young, wild and alive. Ready for whatever adventure lay down the road, no matter how ludicrous or stupid. They were reckless but passionate in their absurdity. And nothing mattered because nothing mattered and that was a beautiful thing.

It was painful to think about, the hopeful innocence of his youth when time was blessing instead of a curse. The moon cast a maudlin glow as the sky darkened with his mood.

"Oh, you and your gravedigger's gloom, Luna," the old man told the moon. "Do you hear me? Damned to speak, let alone sway the tide."

The moon remained silent and slowly rose above the city, spiked through by a skyscraper like an olive on a toothpick.

"Got you too, did they?" He shook his head. "The bastards… who would dare lance the moon?"

He turned away and went back inside. The room's unearthly silence welcomed him. He slid the glass door shut. Had he always been here? It didn't feel like home. What belonged to him seemed borrowed from another man's life. His desk and handwritten notes, the sleigh bed (two feet too small), the piles of books and collection of empty birdcages. Where had the cages come from after all? And who had let loose the birds? He wasn't even sure the birdcages had been there when he'd awoken last.

These were the dangers of sleep. Whenever he'd drift off, even for a second, the room would rearrange itself and he would be forced to relearn it all. This was why he paced to the rhythmic echo of his thoughts. To unravel some part of the mystery before it was erased from record.

He could hardly recall his own name. He'd written down someplace, several places, he was sure of it, so that he would remember. He knew it began with an M...

Marcus! Marcus! Marcus!

A black sparrow cawed, soaring out from the rafters in a spastic, manic flight about the room. The bird flapped its tiny wings in desperation and banged against the walls.

"Out with you!" The old man flung open the glass door and scolded the bird with a pointed finger. "Be gone!"

The sparrow flew down and perched itself on his wagging hand. The old man's anger cooled when he realized the reason for the bird's clumsiness. The poor creature couldn't even open its eyes. The blind sparrow pawed on the grooves of his hand and ruffled its black wings. The old man slowly curled his fingers so he could cup the bird and ferry it outside. The moment his fingers grazed its feathers, the sparrow vanished on touch.

He stared at his empty palm. He closed and opened his hand over and over, as if he could make the bird reappear through some ritual of improvised magic.

Gone. Vanished. Another phantasm. They came in waves, always after sundown in the bewitching hours of twilight. Phantom objects would materialize out of thin air—framed photographs on the walls, a grandfather clock with a Glockenspiel chime, a wooden mallet, an hourglass of ashen sand, and then there was the stranger outside the mirror, a man in a hooded black cloak who never spoke and only watched.

He rushed over to his desk, saddled into his armchair, and pick up one of the bird feathers. He dipped its pointed tip in an inkwell and scribbled on a piece of paper: *Marcus... remember your name is Marcus.* He knew the name was his, or once his, yet it had lost its meaning. All his aspirations and his failings forgotten. Like the reflection in the mirror, it evoked an image of someone he couldn't reconcile with his fractured presence of mind.

He continued scribbling: *Nothing makes any sense here. I am bewildered by this place. I am and I am not, with only fleeting memories to anchor myself in the curious sea of time.*

The old man paused when he realized he'd attracted an audience. A grey-haired mouse scurried out from behind a stack of books, wandered over the chessboard, and sat down beside the white pieces. The mouse nudged a white pawn forward with its black nose and looked up at him, expectant.

The old man hooked his knight out, swiped the pawn, and returned to his writing: *If everything is nonsense, then perhaps that's the key to solving the riddle. Transmute reality into its sparkling facets like sunrays through a diamond and study the prismatic shards of light.*

He leaned back, embraced by the arms of his chair. He was exhausted, but he dared not fall asleep. Who knows how old he'd be when he awoke next? He reached into his evening robe and pulled out his pocket watch. He unclasped the silver lid. He held the clockface in the palm of his hand, staring at the ticking seconds to stay awake.

The hour and minute markers didn't move at all, stuck at the three o'clock and thirty-six notch, while the seconds marker still made its rounds. He focused on the pocket watch, though no matter how hard he concentrated on the ticking, his eyelids soon drooped and surrendered. There, in the roomy darkness of his scattered mind, he saw the black sparrow again, swooping blindly through the void.

He jolted his eyes open and refocused on the watch. The broken hands of the dial inexplicably moved forward, then clicked back into place when he strained his eyes. Shadow obscured the round edges of the pocket watch, swelling out from its circular face until there was only the silver watch and his palm suspended in the darkness within darkness.

Then the seconds compelled the minutes compelled the hours, the time-hands spinning faster and faster, casting a blinding light that dispelled the dark and silenced the ticking.

Part One: The Art of Arrival

Welcome to Oblivion. The fabled beginning and end from whence all things come and go. The bull's eye in the dartboard. A pinpoint explosion where being and nothingness mate. The hole behind the Big Bang that tunnels infinitely in all dimensions.

In the deep sleep, it's a simple trip—a slip down the dark tunnel of the subconscious into the endless sea of the great unconscious where Oblivion swirls like a sinkhole, creating tides of existence. And who's behind this mighty force, you might ask? Who's turning the crank, ruffling the ripples? That's anyone's guess really, and those brave few explorers who've tried to map its tangled corridors have all fallen short on the paradox that the doors always change their destination.

They say you can never step in the same river twice, and the same goes for skinny dipping in the collective unconscious of Oblivion. It is alive. And for the dreamers and the dreamed caught in between, there is nothing more dangerous...

CHAPTER ONE

Lost Souls, the Well, and a Poem for Marcy Kean

Fall in the town of Warren. A magical time of shuttered windows, sweaters, and autumn nostalgia in remembrance of those lost days of childhood. A time of reflection when the trees combust with that last gift of life, when the leaves loft and tumble, one by one, like silent thoughts of the canopy which only the thrush hears clinging to a limb.

There is no death, only the uneasy quiver of stripped trees dowsing the sky.

Cloistered by naked woods, the forgotten schoolhouse of Warren Elementary sat dark with its memories of spitballs and arithmetic, abandoned for bigger, more sterile school in the center of town. Ivy crawled up the worn brick walls. Wind whistled through its cracked windows. The arched doors to its checkered halls stood forever locked. And down a hill of long brown grass in the schoolyard, Norman and Addie patiently waited for nothing to happen.

Norman sat on the head beam of a swing set with his legs dangling off. Addie rocked beneath on a wooden swing. Their conversation teetered back and forth, syncopated to the swinging chains.

"No, you can't have it both ways," Addie said, kicking up the mulch and fallen leaves as she rocked on the swing. "You either believe in the concrete world or you believe everything's an illusion. I don't give a damn what the shamans say."

"They are not shamans. They're Buddhists," Norman hollered down. "Think about an onion."

"What about an onion?"

"You peel off layer after layer after layer and what have you got? Just a little stem. So the question is: what is the onion? The little stem or the layers?"

"What does that have to do with anything?" Addie said. "I peel the onion, it's real. I peel off the layers, maybe cry a little, maybe my fingers smell afterward. It's still an onion. I chop up the onion and make a salad. Still real. Tastes like onion. If it were all an illusion, couldn't I just imagine the onion tasted like a tomato? Couldn't I convince myself it was a tomato? Then what would a tomato taste like? What kind of demented salad would I have then?"

~

Across the schoolyard, young Marcus walked in circles beside a wooden fortress of cargo nets, bridge planks, and winding metal slides. A brown suede jacket flapped at his hips, his coattail trailed behind. A paperback copy of Plato's *Republic* was tucked under his arm, dog-eared and half-read, although he didn't remember reading a page.

Marcus paid no attention to the pseudo-intellectual argument unraveling nearby for he believed such conversations were best left for rooftops. Thankfully he was distracted, looping on a thought. He removed Plato's *Republic* from under his arm and propped it on his knee. He sprawled out a paper napkin so he could quickly scribble down—from the tip of the tongue, the top of the brain—a nonsense poem:

By the river stream, I heard him scream, little Charlie Bean. He waded his feet, in the water too deep, and so began to dream. As he started to sink, I heard him think... in a turquoise world, nothing's pink and everything's not as it seems.

At first, Marcus felt satisfied with the fate of Charlie Bean. On second read, he disagreed with the way he'd crossed the T's, crumpled the poem in a ball, and tossed it under the jungle gym.

~

"But you can't negotiate with tigers," Addie said, grounding her sneakers in the mulch to slow down the swing.

"Well, not in a point-for-point debate on why it shouldn't eat you," Norman said. "Tigers may be tricky, but if you were to trust your instinct, you'd probably have a fifty-fifty chance of outwitting it. See, that's where reason loses out. It may tell us why a pot of water boils, but our obsession with reason has put us out of touch with our primal instincts."

"Maybe, but without it, we wouldn't have rifles which are a failsafe way to negotiate with tigers," Addie said. "The progress of humanity has always been reason's triumph over instinct. That's why we don't live in the jungle anymore and don't have to have these domestic disputes with tigers."

"But without instinct, without intuition, there is no inspiration," Norman protested. "When reason says no, the dreamer's heart defies logic and imagination sets flight. We are both capable of outstanding reason and a massive imagination to suspend all disbelief. That's what makes the impossible possible. That's what brought us out of the jungle to begin with."

"This conversation is pointless," Addie said. "Anything can be argued and picked apart until it's meaningless, until it's a bunch of arbitrary nonsense."

Marcus wandered out of the dark. "Since when was nonsense ever arbitrary?" He drew a pack of Trenton Reds from his jacket, flicked his zippo, and lit a cigarette. He exhaled and watched the smoke mingle with the low mist that shrouded the night.

The brooding poet leaned against the swing set, smoking. Addie hopped off her swing. Norman hung down from the top beam like a monkey, shuttled hand-over-head to the side post, and shimmied down.

"There he is!" Norman said. "I told you he'd show up. Didn't I tell you?"

"Yes, many many times," Addie said, annoyed.

Norman brushed off his hands. "May I have a ciggy?"

Marcus shuffled out a cigarette from his pack and handed it over. He then shifted out another piece of contraband from his suede jacket, took a healthy swig, and passed the flask of whiskey to Norman.

The brooding poet had always been the rebel, the corrupter, the unnamed leader of the trio, although not only for his deft skill at stealing whiskey from his father's liquor cabinet or cigarettes from Bucky's Cornerstore. He held a confidence to be admired, complemented by an insatiable lust for danger. It was Marcus who let loose the neighbor's pit bull to practice lasso. It was Marcus who convinced Addie and Norman that they could and would stop at nothing to build a rocket ship. It was Marcus who jerry-rigged a fuse to the propane tank behind an abandoned train depot, although it was Norman who lit the fuse, and inevitably Addie who ran screaming and stamped it out in the nick of time.

"Where were you?" Addie asked. "We've been waiting here for over an hour."

"I lost track of time," Marcus said.

"You alright? You look pale."

"I'm fine. I feel a little strange, that's all." Marcus passed the whiskey to Addie, hoping this would stop the questions.

Addie slugged from the flask and winced. "Like how?"

"Don't know really. Everything feels kind of surreal, like I'm here but not here. Or like this has happen before? It's bizarre."

"Talk about bizarre." Addie handed the flask to Norman. "Wait till you hear who we met today."

"Who's that?" Marcus asked.

"A time traveler," Norman said and lit his cigarette.

"Hold on," Addie said. "Let me tell the story."

"True, you've earned it. You did kill the dog."

"I barely hit it. It's fine. Besides, if the brakes actually worked on your car, I wouldn't have hit it at all."

"You killed a dog?" Marcus took the whiskey back and drank.

"We hit a dog," Addie corrected him. "It ran out in the road and I swerved, but yeah we clipped it and the poor thing ran off whining. But we're responsible people. I mean, we didn't drive off and pretend it didn't happen. No, we stopped the car and got out. The dog must have gone into the woods or something. So we go knocking on doors trying to track down the owner and we come to the last house on the block, a rundown shack with tires on the lawn, and we ring the buzzer and out comes this guy... who'd you say he looked like?"

"Burt Reynolds," Norman said.

"Yeah, like a retired cowboy," Addie said. "And he's like 'Oh yes, that's my dog' and invites us in for tea."

"I think he was French," Norman said.

"Definitely foreign. Weird guy. He sits us down in his living room and starts brewing a pot of tea, which we politely accept, and then tells us not to worry, that once he gets his passport re-approved, he'll simply travel back in time and make sure the dog is safely in the house."

"Tell him about the pink phone," Norman said.

"In a second," Addie said. "Anyway, the guy was obviously nuts and starts telling us about how he traveled back in time to study pigeons because of their immunity to certain diseases, and about how his future wife is a waitress at this diner and how they'll meet on the train in 433 days or 344 days, I forget. But get this: Norman is so into it, bullshitting on the finer points of time travel, that the guy's convinced that Norman is a fellow time traveler in disguise and tries to get him to punch the secret numbers into this oversized pink phone on the coffee table so he can hitch a ride to the year 3046."

"So we left," Norman said.

"Smart thinking. Never trust a time-traveling Frenchman," Marcus said.

"We should have gone looking for the dog," Norman said.

"I know, it's not like I don't feel bad about it," Addie said. "The guy said he'd go back in time and save it anyway."

"Oh, isn't it convenient to believe in time travel when it gets you off the hook for dog murder," Norman said.

"That's the trouble with not having a soul," Marcus added. "Total lack of conscience."

"That's not funny," Addie said. "I have a soul."

"No remorse..." Norman shook his head. "Dog killer."

Marcus and Norman finished their cigarettes and stomped them out together. They never missed an opportunity to tease Addie about losing her soul. During one of their poker games, Addie had made the mistake of betting her soul against Marcus's first-born child. Addie lost, of course, to three Jacks and a pocket ace, and forfeited her soul to Marcus on a grocery receipt signed in blood.

Besides her paranoia over the condition of her soul, Addie almost always maintained a level perspective. She was a nervous kid with big-rimmed spectacles and an abnormal appreciation for black turtlenecks. Addie knew more about backgammon than any 17-year-old really should and felt painfully compelled to deconstruct every situation right after it happened. The great accident of humanity weighed heavily on her heart, as she, day after day, tried to come to terms with the fact that there were holes in the universe and no one seemed the least bit concerned about plugging them up. She was fiercely intelligent, and therefore shy, anxious, and overwhelmed by existential dread.

"Why do we always hang out here?" Addie asked.

"On the playground?" Norman said.

"Yeah, are we trying to reconnect with some happier time in our childhood or do we just want to ruin the past with our nihilistic irreverence?"

"Both," Marcus said.

"Nostalgia is a kind of escape, right?" Norman said. "It's healthy."

"I wouldn't call smoking cigarettes while dwelling on the tragic loss of our innocence healthy." Addie adjusted her glasses and looked at her wristwatch. The dials were stuck at 9:31. "That's weird. My watch stopped."

Their conversation lulled into silence when a scraggly cat with black and white splotches moseyed by across the playground. After a day of prowling in the woods, the cat was returning home to the abandoned schoolhouse. It was not amused to find the three young hoodlums trespassing in its backyard. Tail flailed, the cat studied the intruders standing in a circle, drinking from the flask, and stalked off, uninterested.

"Look, a cat," Norman said.

"Yeah, I see it," Addie said. "There are a lot of strays around here."

"It's not a stray," Norman said. "It has a collar. See?"

Its collar twinkled silver in the moonlight and then lost its shimmer when the cat wandered under the jungle gym. Norman hopped after it, in quick pursuit. The cat climbed on top the wooden fort to keep its distance. When Norman came too close, the cat simply leapt off and scurried over the mulch, through the long grass, and into the bushes that hedged the brick schoolhouse.

"Norman, don't chase the damn cat," Addie said. "It's probably rabid." She stole the whiskey from Marcus and noticed the copy of Plato's *Republic* under his arm. "You're still reading that, huh?"

Marcus pulled the book out and flipped the pages. "I'm picking my way through."

"What's it about?"

"It's hard to say. It's really just this old guy arguing about justice."

"Oh fascinating."

"It's the foundation of Western thought."

"An old guy arguing about justice?"

"Yeah."

"Sounds captivating."

"Socrates is kind of a grifter. He makes these rhetorical statements that he poses like questions, which make sense at first and then go off on wild tangents. And then by the time he finally gets to the answer, you forget the original question."

"Great, remind me not to read it. There's nothing I want more than to be gaslit by some ancient Greek dude who's been dead for thousands of years."

~

In the hedges beside the elementary school, Norman was having a fantastic time poking through the brush for the cat and its shiny collar. With his head and one arm inside the bush, he tried to scare the cat out of hiding. He relished this primal moment—the hunter vs. the hunted—especially since it combined two of his favorite pastimes: chasing things smaller than him and the collection of shiny objects.

His fascination with all things shiny verged on obsession. Norman couldn't resist inspecting every tiny piece of metal or glass that happened to be shining in the road or grass or train track. It was indeed an odd and spontaneous affliction that Marcus and Addie often joked would someday lead him into grave trouble. Yet in every joke, there lies some cryptic truth.

The collar shimmered with a touch of moonlight and made itself known to Norman. He could see the shape of the cat, its yellow eyes piercing out from the dark, unaware its hideout in the bushes had been betrayed by its shiny collar.

On the count of three, one… two… Norman didn't wait for three.

"What's he doing?" Addie asked.

Norman dove headfirst into the hedge.

"Ah, he's just getting in touch with his animal nature,"

Marcus said.

"He's an idiot, that's what he is," Addie said and walked over to the bushes. A gust of wind rustled the maples and oaks in the schoolyard yet not the slightest twitch came from the bush. There was no sign of Norman besides some snapped branches where he'd jumped in. She spread apart the hedge.

In the same instant, Marcus lit another cigarette and saw the sky turn black, as if every star had imploded into nothingness at once, the plug pulled. In turn, the moon opened up in night sky, or what he assumed was the moon until he saw its giant pupil staring back. The giant Eye blinked out of the sky as quickly as it had appeared and left of no evidence of its peeping in the sheer black night.

"I think the moon just winked at me. Did you see that?"

Addie, however, saw none of this since she was otherwise occupied yelling at the schoolhouse hedges.

"Norman? Stop screwing around. It's getting late."

No response.

"Hey Marcus," Addie hollered across the playground. "He's gone."

"What do you mean gone?" Marcus sauntered over to inspect the hedge. He sparked his zippo and cautiously lowered the flame into the twined dark of the bush. "He must be somewhere in here. It's hard to see. Wait... there's a hole."

"A hole?"

"Yeah, like an open manhole or a well." Marcus forced his head into the hedge. "Norman! You down there?"

Still no response...

"It's just like him to pull a prank like this."

"Do you think he's hurt?"

"Depends how deep the hole is."

"What a moron."

"I'm sure he'll come up for air once he's done playing in the sewer." Marcus handed his friend a cigarette. "Want to steal his car and go grab a cup of coffee or something?"

"Sure. Why not?"

Marcus stuck his head in the bush again. "NORMAN, we're going to get a cup of coffee. We'll be right back, alright?"

While their friend tumbled to some unknown demise, Marcus and Addie smoked their worries away and headed for the parking lot. Among a fleet of retired school buses was Norman's car—a smashed-up red Mazda with a cracked rear window, its metal bumper strapped on with a bungee cord, its rusted tank dripping a puddle of gasoline onto the pavement.

The car was Norman's lone possession and prized piece of junk, although he rarely drove it himself. It was common ritual to steal his car whenever possible, solely because he would leave his key in the ignition all the time, and they would feel obligated to do so in light of his stupidity. And so Marcus and Addie would take the car and cruise about blasting grungy rock 'n' roll on the stereo, revving the decrepit 1993 Mazda to its breaking point, crawling halfway out the window so they could howl with the traffic.

This would piss Norman off and he'd swear never to let them drive the car again. His anger, however, often frizzled after a couple minutes, and he would forget the whole transgression. That is, until the next time.

Addie hopped on the hood to finish her cigarette while Marcus went around to the driver's side of the car.

"Now I remember why I don't smoke. These things are really disgusting," Addie said, discarding the half-smoked cigarette to a slow death on the pavement.

Marcus opened the car door. "Hey, toss me the keys."

"Oh yeah, sorry." Addie searched her pockets. "Wait, I think I gave them to…"

They glanced back at the silent hedge.

"The one time Norman actually takes the keys and now he's gone and fallen down a well."

"I thought it was a manhole."

"Same difference." Marcus got onto the hood with Addie and flicked away the glowing remains of his cigarette butt.

"Well, I guess we'll just have to wait for Norman then," Addie said. "I'm sure he's okay, right? Probably just having a laugh at us, splashing around down there."

A plan began to hatch in Marcus's brain, a rescue mission down the mysterious hole. What dangers lay in store, what beasts may be down in the belly of that hole growling for more fresh meat, he didn't know nor did he care. He ripped the bungee cord off the car bumper and thrashed it like a whip.

"I'm going down there to get him," he said.

"I don't know if that's such a good idea," Addie said. But she was already speaking to the wind. Off Marcus went, like a secret agent with a death wish, storming toward the hedges.

Addie stayed on the car hood, in no rush to join Marcus in his mission to find Norman. Instead, she sat there in silence and admired the night. The peace, the quiet, the cosmic serenity of the completely black sky.

"Marcus, what happened to the stars?" Then smoke. She smelled smoke. Her nose flared in all directions until she spotted disaster. Directly where Marcus had thrown the end of his cigarette, a small fire smoldered in the grass.

"Dumbass, your stupid cigarette started a fire," Addie shouted from the car.

"Well, put it out," Marcus said. He mangled the branches and hunted for the best point of entry into the hedge.

Addie, enraptured by the peaceful night, was more amazed than alarmed at first by the small fire that seemed to dance for her amusement. The flames happily ate the grass, almost making spiral patterns as they set fire to the fallen leaves and then turned their attention to the mulch-laid playground.

Fortunately for the fire, the mulch had been sprayed with a highly flammable lacquer that was experimental during the

1970s and was supposed to preserve wood chips for hundreds of years. Unless set on fire, of course.

"Marcus!" Addie leaped from the hood. "Fire! You started a goddamn fire!"

The flames caught an inviting trail of engine oil that had spilled off the paved lot and followed the fluid back to its source.

"Just stamp it out with your foot," Marcus said as he crawled out of the bush. "What's the prob—"

The red Mazda exploded into air and somersaulted on its back next to the swing set. The metal roof buckled on impact, the windows smashed out, and the hulking wreck came to rest upside-down on the mulch, tossing bits of metal and fire like flaming piñata.

In a flash, the playground burst into flames. The fire spread across the mulch and fallen leaves to the jungle gym where it feasted on the tire swings, ropes, the wooden bridges between turrets. It spread up the brown grassy hill to cook the brick walls of the elementary school and then down again, blazing every blade of grass and shrub in its path.

Addie's heart raced, looking to Marcus for an answer, a plan, a solution to this god-awful fix. They'd been in trouble before. There was the terrifying chase by the butcher-knife wielding sous chef at Café del Mer who'd failed to see the humor in luring a gang of seagulls into his kitchen with a kite smeared with fish guts. There was the time they'd decided to hatchet trees in Mr. Thompson's orchard, but incorrectly predicted which way the trees would fall, and countless other moments of impending doom that Marcus had both instigated and saved them from with his quick wit.

The flames surrounded the bush in a ring of fire that encircled Marcus and Addie, dumbstruck by their own makeshift hell. Marcus batted down the inferno with the book of Plato's *Republic*.

"I told you to put it out, but you wouldn't listen, would you?" Addie said. "You never listen to me, never!"

"We need to stay calm here. This fire is problem number two. We need to deal with these things one at a time," Marcus said. "I'm going down that hole after Norman. You can do what you want. Dance in the flames or whatnot." He threw the book over his shoulder and hunched on his hands and knees beside the hedge. "Ah good, there's enough room to crawl in."

"Wait, hold on. Let's think this about this a second."

Marcus scrambled into the bramble like an enormous snake and made his way slithering through the underbrush. Curiously, the hedge seemed like an endless mess of branches inside. Soon all he knew was darkness and heat and sharp twigs and that the hole was somewhere ahead. Still, he crawled onward, trying not to panic, trying not to think about the flames that nipped at the bush outside, trying to not to think about how he would repel underground with only a bungee cord, and found the hole.

It was an abandoned well, he could see now. The limestone rim was chipped around the edges and slimy from its years in the undergrowth. He listened for Norman but could only hear Addie's complaints nearby.

"We're screwed. We should get out of here. I'm getting really claustrophobic right now. Marcus, are you there? Hello?"

"The hole is right up here." Marcus sparked his lighter to illuminate the well. "There's a ladder, looks kind of rusty. Okay, I'll go first. Are you coming?"

Addie scuttled to the light. "Yeah."

"Alright then, let's go," Marcus said. He shouldered over the edge and lowered himself in, clinging valiantly onto the rusty ladder. He whistled up at the flames above to keep his mind off the descent, and noted how the fire created a hellish hallo around Addie's terrified face.

The impromptu tune faded into a droning dum de dum as Marcus himself faded into the darkness below. Addie climbed down the grimy ladder rungs after him into the pitch-black hole. She gazed upward at the well entrance, aglow with angry flames, and then down into the deep dark unknown.

Chapter Two

The Fall (or Subterranean Folly)

Down the well, Norman fell, down, down, down the hollow chute until it widened into a cavernous pit. However it didn't feel as if he were falling at all. After the first hundred feet or so, gravity slowed and what had been empty darkness before attacked him in a symphony of color and luminance. Spirals of yellow, green, and violet burst out of a blinding vortex. He drifted through the chaotic light-spritzed void, entertained by the marvelous swirls of color, light, shape, pattern, motion.

The vortex expanded into a hungry mouth that sucked everything (and pseudo-thing) into its vacuum. Gaining speed, he hurdled through lucid hues, knocked against ephemeral shapes, and, in a jolt, felt the sudden jumbled ecstasy of a metaphysical death. The entirety of life compacted into a dense moment. Rushes of nausea, mania, hunger, fear, anxiety, paranoia, depression, anger, joy, pain, orgasm, thrill, objectivity, subjectivity, supersubjectivity, and finally the calm, the zenith of Zen, a shuddering tranquility and oneness with the eternal all.

The vortex spit him out as fast as it had sucked him in. Gravity immediately became relevant again. Suspension in space and then splash into an ocean of subterranean jelly. He struggled to stay above the surface, bobbing and flailing, and gasped madly for what he thought would be his last breath.

The jelly slurped him under. His lungs filled with jelly, involuntarily sucking in the slosh until his chest felt as if it would explode from the pressure. He choked and gagged on the gelatinous water in frantic gulps, then slowed his breathing in amazement. His lungs relaxed. The pressure subsided. He inhaled the goo again and blew out bubbles, practicing slow rhythmic breaths underwater as he sunk deeper and deeper into the subterranean abyss.

Shelves of rock emerged. Crags and cliffs made the faces of an awkward cavern. A collection of items bobbed in the gorge like a floating junkshop. A chair here, a bowl there, a wheel, keys, a television, reading glasses, a book of poems, a pair of pants, a stove, a greek pillar, a quill pen and ink jar, a satellite and telescope in tandem. No two items were the same and each specimen was so immaculately crafted that their sublime form shined in the murky deep like an underwater exhibit of human ingenuity. Off behind a salient jut in the rock shelf, he swore he saw an airplane float past a microwave and a bowling ball.

Norman processed all this with the innocence of a child lost in the woods. An unchartered territory of strange and wonderful things. He snatched a light bulb when it drifted by. It sparked alive with a dozen tiny radiant fish swimming inside. He let go of the light bulb, which drifted off and smash into a rock ledge, emancipating the living sparks.

That's when he became aware of the odd fish that swam through this yard sale of invention like an obstacle course. There were fish of every hue, every bizarre mutation, with hawk fins, bright-striped gills, reflective black eyes. He couldn't identify any of the species by name, though they resembled the exotic fish he'd seen lurking in photographs of forgotten ocean depths. He even spotted a black shark when the predator nosed out of a finely rounded length of pipe next to a piano off in the jelly waters.

The fish were in no way alarmed by his presence, since they assumed he was either a distant cousin or a piece of furniture. Norman remained perfectly calm, despite the obvious dangers, soothed by the water's tingling sensation as he sunk deeper into the cavern.

The floor of the jelly ocean came into view, with odd craters and hairy pits from which clumps of giant kelp waved in greeting. He pulled his knees up to his chest like a parachuter coming in for an unexpected landing, dodged a bicycle and a can of tomatoes, and hit the spongy ground.

He breathed in the goo, grateful to be on solid footing again. He blew out more bubbles, which floated over his head into the amalgamation of scientific marvels, curios, and appliances. How did all this garbage end up down here? he wondered. It then occurred to him for the first time that he was no longer in the comforts of his old home, that all facts added up to one obvious conclusion. That he had, without a doubt, passed on to the world beyond the world, or underneath it as the case may be.

He was rather indifferent to the revelation, his mortal concerns subdued by fascination since it was immensely entertaining to simply watch the layer of junk hover there and single out various novelties. Gazing up through a floating window at the golden horn of a suspended phonograph, he became cognizant of a low humming that radiated through the jelly. His mere acknowledgement of its existence intensified the sound. It was a conversation, or rather a multitude of conversations that overlapped one another. There were no distinct words, only mumbles, yet he sensed messages in the verbal undulation. The more he listened for it, and speculated as to where the sound might be coming from, the louder the chatter became. He looked away from the bobbing inventory and the noise dropped out.

Norman meandered about the bottom of the subterranean cavern with mindless admiration until he noticed a peculiar spectacle rooted in the ocean floor ahead. From out of a crater, a giant tree sprouted as high as he could see into the dark jelly waters above, its massive canopy so large it cast a shadow over the entire cavern, its roots outstretched like fingers groping the spongy ground.

When he wandered over for a closer look, two doors slid

apart in the gigantic trunk to reveal a hollow hidden within. Inside, an elevator boy tipped his red cap. "Going up?"

"Is there any other way to go?"

The elevator boy gave a blank look. "That's a stupid question."

Norman walked into the hollow tree, which somehow created a bubble that prevented the jelly from flooding inside. The interior of the trunk was furnished in the style of a grand dame hotel. Gold fabric walls, indigo buttons, a numbered dial over the door frame. He wiped a heavy film off his clothes and shucked it on the floor, drenched but happy to be out of the goo.

The elevator boy adjusted the funny red cap on his head. "What fathom, sir?"

"Fathom?"

"Of Oblivion, sir," the boy replied, pointing toward the dial overhead.

"Oh, I see," Norman said, even though the response answered nothing. "To the top then."

"The 1st fathom, sir? Do you have an invitation?"

"Of course, I do. Do I look like an idiot?" Norman said and ran his fingers through his wet hair to straighten his appearance.

The elevator boy smiled wanly and pulled the lever.

The doors of the tree shut, the elevator boy pressed a button. The floor lifted and Norman watched the dial rise. 1312, 1300, 1293, 1250, 1224... the elevator ascended faster and faster until they were traveling at a hundred fathoms per second. In a splinter of that second, he screeched in and out of existence. He blinked and there was no elevator, only his body rising. He blinked again and he was back in the elevator, being smiled at by the boy in the funny red cap.

BING. The needle struck '1'. The jaws of the elevator released, as if pried open by the hands of God himself. A hall cast out in front of him, straight forward into infinity.

"Your floor, sir," the boy said.

Norman thanked him and stepped out of the elevator. The boy cleared his throat and rubbed his thumb and index finger in a less than subtle gesture.

"Oh yes, of course, sorry," Norman said and scrounged through his pockets. He dug out a jellied glob of spare change and slapped it in the boy's hand. "There you are. Thanks again." The elevator boy smiled politely, while waiting for the doors to glide shut, and flipped him the bird as soon as he'd turned away.

The trip, thousands of fathoms up or down or wherever they had traveled inside and outside of time, had left Norman with a hemorrhaging case of vertigo. Convinced he was standing on the ceiling, he lunged out at the wall for something to hold onto and stuck there like a wad of gum. He unstuck himself once the vertigo had passed and looked back to see no sign of the elevator, nor any button to call it in case he changed his mind.

He peered down the endless hall, no doors to be seen, grey and seamless and absorbed in a muted incandescence. No exit. A singular melodic tone, angelic and seductive, rung soft like a struck tuning fork but so powerful the hall trembled from the vibration. The accord of all sound separated from the deep tone when it swam into his eardrums, a harmony which enveloped him from the inside out. And as the tone lulled him in a catatonic state, he felt summoned, drawn away from the wall and propelled through the hall till it ceased to be.

He disintegrated. Soon Norman and the hall were no more than fragments in his mind. And there he existed, without body, without space, without color, without flesh, a pure entity of consciousness. But where was he? A moment of nothingness resided... A door came into being that he saw without eyes, with a vision beyond sight. He contemplated a knob, and it was; he contemplated a hand, and it was.

His translucent fingertips grasped the knob, and for the first time since the fall, he was afraid. A tremendous, all-consuming fear. Of what? Of the unknown, that there was nothing left to discover, except further nothingness? Does the beautiful beyond still remain infinite? he thought. Or has it become finite by the ravenous minds of time?

With a turn of the knob, the door burst open in a wild scream. Beyond the threshold, a crowded ballroom pulsed with a primal rhythm, swinging to the loud and funky sound of nine-piece lounge lizard band up on the mezzanine over a sweaty menagerie on the main floor. Mobs of monkeys danced the rumba in a flurry of limbs. Gigantic fish shook their tailfins flamenco. A couple iguanas swapped tongue in a dirty tango under the sinister red glow of a giant octopus suctioned to the ceiling like a chandelier. Possibly there was reason to be afraid.

Norman sauntered in, awestruck by the jungle party underway, and began to wonder if he'd gotten off at the wrong floor. But if one's going to crash a ball, best to do it with confidence and style, he thought. And so he made his way through the mob, past the giraffe drinking out of the punch bowl, past the walruses in the corner sipping highballs, over to a whale in a bowtie behind the bar. He ordered a martini just to be social.

CHAPTER THREE

Curious Apparitions

Approaching at a rapid clip, the grey expanse rolled like a vast ocean, as if the waves had frozen to accept her death, her eyelids whipped open by the velocity as her end scream into view. Even after she'd made impact, a moment or two passed before Addie realized that she wasn't dead nor drowning in the ocean. Her face and arms were buried in black sand, so icy cold against her cheeks that she rose in alarm, coughing violently in uncontrollable fits.

She shook the debris out of her hair and wiped off her face. Blurry-eyed and frantic, she thrust her hand into the black sand and miraculously found her spectacles on first try. The glasses weren't even broken really, aside from a few dents in the frame and a slight crack on the left lens.

She rubbed her burning eyes and put her glasses on. A sea of dunes rolled back to every horizon. A never-ending desert.

This must be wrong, she thought. How was there a desert at the bottom of a well? Was she hallucinating? What was in that whiskey anyway? She knew she should have never trusted Marcus. In fact, the last time something like this happened, she was sure she'd made a note never to trust Marcus again.

She retrieved her trusty notebook diary from her jeans and leafed through. She did. A week ago. Damn, she thought, I always write stuff in here and forget to look at it.

A brisk chill snapped her out of her neurosis. She shivered. The desert was cold. It spoke of death. The sky that whirred around her was starless black, not even a moon to light her path. The blackish sand gave off a pale glow, which painted the desert shades of ghostly grey. The wind that carried the black dust in wisps whispered in her ears. Soft shrieks, the voices of the long dead.

She ran her fingers through the charcoal-grey sand, smooth and airy, curiously smooth. It felt like… the revelation shot her up from her haunches like a dog on fire.

"Ash," she said out loud to no one but the rolling dunes.

Yes, a desert of endless ash and the black horizon, the desert of Alcazara to be exact, buried in the limbo of the 193.74th fathom of Oblivion. Although the nightmarish landscape seemed all doom and gloom, Addie was actually quite fortunate for the starless night and bitter cold of the desert. Had it been the Light Season in Alcazara, when the searing sun scorches the ash and the skeletons come alive and tremendous giants roam the desert scavenging for bones to munch, she surely wouldn't have lasted for very long.

"There must be a rational explanation for all this," she said quietly to herself, so as not to rouse any poltergeists from the ash. Her heart throbbed in her chest, beating in 6/8 time with an accent on the upswing. She scooped up a handful of the black sand.

"It feels real, but it can't be," she said, trying to calm herself down, trying to rationalize. "Perhaps the fall knocked me out and I'm simply dreaming. Yes, of course. This is a perfectly archetypal dream. Perfectly normal. Lost in the desert. No escape. What would Freud say? The dry bleak desert, less than lifeless. Cold like my heart, dead like my non-existent libido. Bleak like the fate of humankind due to my lack of interest in the shameless proliferation of the species. Doomed by apathy, by hopelessness, by a post-atomic reality. All the struggles and conflicts of the world amounting to nothing more than a proverbial tautening of the wire, a constriction of the thread that weaves and binds the universe, restraining it from spiraling off into utter chaos. And what then, when it snaps?"

She looked about the dead Sahara. "Ashes, ashes, everywhere."

Her thoughts turned to bonemeal, cremation, the world in

an urn, the Apocalypse, hell after the fire's petered out, death, death, a thousand corpses burning on a pyre, teeth and skulls under her toes. Her throat clenched thick, as something slithered up her gullet, its slimy body sliding out her mouth, the head first and then the tail. Before she could cough it out, the tiny lizard leapt from her mouth on its own and nuzzled around in the desert soot.

Addie stared at the lizard. The lizard stared back. Neither seemed quite sure what had just transpired. The lizard blinked upward with its tiny beadlike eyes and wagged its tail. She hunched down beside the lively creature and stuck out a finger. The nervous lizard scrutinized the huge fleshy digit wiggling playfully in front of its snout. It escaped between her legs, racing in circles around her feet, making ellipses in the dust, until it abruptly stopped and burrowed under her left shoe. She jerked her foot away, just before its tail slipped under the soot.

She dug through the ash in search of the lizard. Instead of a scaly tail, her fingers grazed something cold and metal. A chain, a thin chain. She attempted to yank it from the ash. It tugged back. She pulled harder.

There came a loud snap from underneath, which released the chain and sent Addie lurching back in a puff of soot. Once the black dust had settled, she inspected the treasure in her hand. A round locket dangled from a gold necklace, glinting in the dim glow of the desert.

She popped the latch to discover the notched points of a compass, scarred and sooty. The needle wobbled left to right with uncertainty. A pinch of ash swished under the glass.

The compass wasn't the only thing she'd yanked from the dust. Half a bone-hand had been unearthed, its fingers flat out, the ones that were left at least. Its skeletal middle finger had broken off and its thumb was cracked by a fissure straight through the palm bone. Addie didn't know whether to laugh or scream at the funny white bones that stuck out of the ash as if to say hello.

"Ha, you scared me there for a second," she said, clutching the compass tight in her fist, worried the skeletal hand might lunge from the black dust and try to steal it back. She disregarded the bones and apparent corpse under the ash. She shut the thought out of mind along with her grave-robber's guilt. She secretively examined the stolen treasure in her cupped hands. The fine markings of its notched face, the painted points, the strange weight of the compass.

The black starless firmament rippled and folded faintly in the glass reflection, as if a mouth behind the curtain of night were mawing its way through the infinite darkness from the other side. There was no sign of disruption in the starless sky when she looked away from the compass. Yet in the reflection from the compass glass, this phantom mouth of darkness widened, rolling back the lids of a giant Eye that stared from the center of the compass points.

She clasped the lid shut and turned toward the sky, expecting to dismiss it as a hallucination. But there it was, the Eye, big as the moon and twice as bright. It peered down at the lonesome traveler stranded among the ashen dunes, bathing her in the blinding light of its stare.

Addie could only gaze at the curious apparition for a few seconds before an intense pain forced her to look away and shield her own eyes. And then in the next instant, it was gone. The only evidence the Eye had ever blinked out of the black sky was the desert ash, which glowed fierce in its aftermath.

"This is only a nightmare brought on by head trauma," she reassured herself. "I'll just... I'll just walk this off. A nice stroll, through the cursed desert. I need the exercise anyway, even though it's not real. Nothing's real, of course. But I'm sure if I walk for a little while here, I'll feel more refreshed when I do wake up."

She aimed the compass into the desert while shifting from

left to right until the needle rested confidently on North.

"No time for lizards or corpses or eyes in the sky," she told her compass. "Let us see what's over that dune yonder, eh Wally? Mind if I call you Wally?"

The compass remained silent.

"Good. Off we go then."

For countless hours, she trudged on across the desert of ash, rising and falling with the dunes, only pausing on occasion so she could check her compass Wally. Although it made no difference which way she headed, she maintained a northbound trajectory. The illusion of progress. The compass's bobbing arrow acted as both her navigational and psychological crutch. All hope hinged on Wally. That and the promise of an end to this nightmare somewhere north.

Her wristwatch, in an inexcusable act of irony, had magically started ticking again. Addie tried not to dwell on this. In fact, she tried not to dwell on anything as she made her pilgrimage over the wind-sculpted dunes. Like any reasonable person does when confronted with something that doesn't fit into their belief structure, she denied the whole confounded situation as impossible, and therefore not worth worrying about.

She checked the compass, out of compulsion, every seven minutes exact so that she could measure the distance traveled, in hopes this would keep her sane. To pass the time, she confided in Wally her darkest secrets—the accidental murder of her hamster, her prepubescent obsession with disco, how she sometimes fantasized about flamingos in flagrante.

She had just finished confessing her sixth-grade crush on her teacher Mr. Nevins, when the Eye blinked open in the starless night again and rolled its fire-bright stare over the dunes, soaking the ash with its luminance. She ducked behind a dune crest and dodged the blinding light when the Eye roved over and promptly disappeared. Although the curious apparition had once again left no mark in the sky, she still felt watched, self-conscious in her desolation amid the desert nowhere. And so she decided it best to stop her confessions.

The pervasive gloom of the cold desert began to wear on her psyche. Her nerves were jostled. Strange thoughts lagged in her mind. Convinced that the only way to defeat the nightmare was to prove that she wasn't afraid, she shucked off her shoes, peeled off her socks, and threw them over her shoulder to walk barefoot in the black ash. Nightmares only work if you give into the fear, she told herself. She'd read this somewhere. She was sure of it.

This has gone on far too long, she decided. Was this punishment? Purgatory perhaps? Whose ashes were these? Was she walking among ghosts? Was this dead land the land of the dead? Could be a coma, she thought. Lousy fantasy to get stuck in if it was. Then again, she hoped it wasn't a coma. Everyone would think they were burned alive in the fire. Who would ever think they'd be crazy enough to climb down that stupid well?

She noted the time on her watch when the minute hand rounded out for the seventh time. She checked her compass. The needle pointed South. This can't be happening, she thought. Damn you, Wally. What's this supposed to mean? The only way... the only possible way was that she'd passed the middle somehow, that this was the middle. The middle of what? What? What? she panicked. Wait, I could start again, I could keep a record, a mental map, start East or West, maybe...

A song drifted to her ears, a murmur out among the deadened waves of ash. She climbed the highest dune in sight and searched for the source, squinting through the cracked lens of her spectacles. There, off in the distant dunes, a black horse trotted along the horizon line.

"Must be another hallucination," she told herself. "It's natural, you're tired. You're not going crazy. Right, Wally?"

The compass twitched to the Southwest.

"Right. Okay."

The black horse sang on, disappearing and reappearing at the desert's edge. But what if it was real? Addie livened with hope. She imagined herself, riding gallantly on the mystery horse, through the desert, heading East, West, South, whichever way she chose. The horse mounted under her legs, the wind through her hair, the black night blurring as she galloped in steed.

She pointed the compass in the direction of the singing horse. The needle wobbled East. Yes, new direction. New chances. She waited for her watch to round out before venturing off barefoot after the horse. Carefully, carefully. I wish I had a lasso or something, she thought. Maybe I'll cough one up soon. A horse. This was it. This was her way out. Ride to horizon's end.

And so she headed east over the ashen dunes, with newfound courage and delusion, on the hunt for the phantom horse, determined to walk this nightmare off, trying not to think about the Eye or the other skeletons undoubtedly buried in ash and whether or not they would come searching for her, crazed by the smell of living flesh.

CHAPTER FOUR

The Gnarled Hands of Fate Knock Thrice

Marcus opened one eye first, then the other. The room curved, serene in its blue perfection, the phantom color originating from a bluish light that wafted up from under three doors like vapors from a kettle and crept up the walls, up into the darkness from whence he'd fallen.

Flat on the ground and still in a daze, he examined his scraped hands and the barlike scars seared into his palms. He remembered the fall in flashes, the moment of panic when Addie slipped and grappled onto his leg, the pain as he gripped the rusty ladder for dear life, the burn before he let go. There was no pain anymore. The scrapes on his hands were merely evidence of the fall. Marcus picked himself up and brushed off his brown-suede jacket. There was a slight tear in the right sleeve. He fussed with it a second.

In all honesty, he was somewhat disappointed with the antechamber between worlds where he now found himself, what he assumed was the gateway to the afterlife. He'd expected more fanfare, angels trumpeting from the clouds or fire demons screeching (depending on wherever he sat on the scale), or possibly a bearded man cross-legged on a stone dais who would divulge the true meaning of life and how he went wrong. The room instead had the same weight of limbo that had hung over his old life above ground like a fog.

Three doors led out of the circular room. Left, right, and behind. Wooden signs were riveted to each and engraved with block letters. To the left, the sign read: PHILOSOPHER, to the right: POET, and behind: FOOL. Three doors, three walks of life… three destinies? Perhaps this was the end and the beginning. He'd never given much thought to reincarnation, but it made as much sense as any of the other harebrained ideas about life after death.

He read the signs again and mulled over his options. He assumed the doors were either passages into the beyond, the everafter so to speak, or passages to a new life, a life reincarnate. The logic of latter seemed to correlate with the signs. But perhaps not. Maybe there were different afterlives he could choose from. Or maybe he needed to choose the right one. Or maybe this was a puzzle, in which the signs were possible answers to an ancient riddle.

Confused but curious, he headed for the first door, the left door, the PHILOSOPHER door and knocked. Silence… nothing but an echo. That's philosophy for you, he thought. He reached for the doorknob and found none. Had it ever had one? He pushed the door. It didn't budge. He then got on his knees and attempted to stick his fingers underneath so he could give it a tug. Jammed. He stepped away, furious, and gave the door a kick. It didn't ever shudder.

He might have waited for the door to move on its own had he read *The Moltar* and been privy to these guiding words from the Great Moltarius, the wholly forgotten prophet for Absurdism: *Philosophy moves for no man who decants the world in a test tube. It is only the metaphysical mind that can breach the doors of new knowledge. Either that or a very large sledgehammer painted in mystic symbols and gypsy curse…* But he hadn't read *The Moltar* and instead moved on to the right door, the POET door, in hopes of better luck.

The POET door did have a knob, as well as a bolt and three horseshoe locks to boot. A small sign tacked beneath the main sign simply stated: CLOSED FOR RE-INNOVATIONS. He pushed, bashed, banged, pounded, kicked, slammed against it. When this failed, he resorted to swearing expletives in a variety of languages, recalled from a dirty little dictionary he'd once read entitled *How to Insult the World*. The door wasn't even offended. He spat at it, as was his habit, and walked away.

As luck or fate would have it, the last door, the backdoor, the FOOL door had an abnormally large doorknob affixed to it, slightly off-center. He snuck toward the door, frightened that the knob might run off or disappear completely if he were too hasty. He crossed his fingers, said a prayer, and then gave the knob a yank with both hands. No such luck.

He checked to see if either of the other doors had mysteriously opened while he wasn't looking. Nothing had changed except for the smoky curls in which the blue light vapors drifted out from under the door frames. No movement, no sound beyond Marcus's breathing in the silent limbo of the circular room.

"What is this all about?" he cried up into the shaft of darkness. "Is this some kind of cruel joke?

Perhaps the doors would all swing open at once if he acted like he didn't care. Perhaps it was his desire to leave that held him hostage there. Whatever, he thought, it's useless. If I'm stuck here, so be it. He was too tired to think, too tired to care. He slumped down on the floor and leaned against the FOOL's door in defeat. It sheepishly gave way behind him. Marcus stood up and straightened his jacket before the exit ajar. He pushed the door inward.

Darkness. A pale darkness. A ring of blue fire flickered somewhere below, powerful enough to cast a weak light on the stairs that descended into the cavernous room. Trespassing deeper still, Marcus could faintly discern a circle of candles laid out along the edge of a rounded floor. He noticed two other staircases that likewise arched out of the dark like spider legs.

The candles marked the outer circle of a spiral design that resembled a checkered tortoise shell, the floor dissected into big black and white scales that spiraled inward from the light and shrank in size as the tiles wrapped round a triangular marble table at its center. A black kettle sat on the table, as if expecting company.

A number of theories on what this strange cave might be competed in his mind. Could be used for human sacrifice, in which case he hoped he'd been invited to witness the ritual and not partake. Or for a séance to breach tunnels into parallel universes. Or perhaps the cave was a simple setting for afternoon tea in the afterlife, and when he'd finished, he would move on to pre-dinner aperitifs and parlor games.

He arrived at the bottom and noted how the three staircases aligned perfectly with three wooden chairs tucked into the sides of the triangular table.

"This seems inviting. I can play this game," he said loudly, in case the Fates happened to be listening. He strutted across the spiral design to his geometrically preordained seat and sat down.

The kettle rattled on the marble and let a breath of vapor out its spout. A porcelain cup clinked into existence on the table. Marcus picked it up and poured himself a cup of what smelled like chamomile tea. He leaned back in his chair and indulged in another sip, savoring the taste.

Halfway through his cup of tea, he spotted someone coming down the staircase on the left. A tall someone, abnormally so. A man, he could see in the darkness, a man of awkward familiarity, seven feet tall, lank as bamboo, who walked with his head tilted back like a broken cattail.

It took Marcus a couple sips before he recognized the face, even though it was his own. The features were nearly identical except wrenched and stretched like taffy in odd directions. His cheeks sagged and his chin drooped, elongated much like the rest of him.

A tall and twisted doppelganger.

This came as no real shock to Marcus since he'd long defended an elaborate theory on doppelgangers. In summary, he'd always believed he was being hunted by his evil twin like a shadow stalks the sunlight.

His theory hypothesized that everyone's doppelganger was just beyond the next bend, that flitting face in the crowded street. He would be charming and suave, just like Marcus. Debonair and cunning, just like Marcus. He would wait for the day when Marcus would be unprepared and then appear out of the shadows to challenge him to that final duel: ten paces where they would then turn fast and stare with intense concentration, trying to force the other to implode into a marble. Marcus assumed that day had come.

Much to his disappointment, the tall gentleman showed no sign of malice when he noticed the visitor at the table and gave a kind smile. "Why, hello there! A little early, aren't you?"

Marcus shot up from his chair, teacup in hand.

"Please, don't get up," his towering twin said. "Sit down, sit down. Starting on the tea without us?"

"I'm sorry?" Marcus said.

"No need to be sorry," he said. "We weren't expecting you so soon, that's all."

The tall gentleman strode down the last of the stairs in a single bound. He stepped onto a black square in the spiral design and made a swooping bow. Marcus was so stunned that he couldn't even muster up the words for polite conversation such as 'Nice weather we're having' or 'Good day to you, too, sir' or 'What a pleasant cave you have here.'

His towering twin bent over the ring of candles and waved his finger through the flames. "The Old Du Mo'or is still burning, eh? Fancy that."

The tall gentleman stretched his leg the length of the spiral design and arrived at the table. There then came an AH, OW, WHOOPS, OUCH off somewhere in the dark of the cavern. Marcus and his towering twin turned toward the noise to see a small man hopping clumsily down the right staircase. At first, Marcus thought maybe the man only seemed tiny from the distance. But when the man tripped and bounced down the stairs like a human basketball, swearing and flailing his little arms, it became immediately clear that this second visitor was, without a doubt, a dwarf. And not just any dwarf... a doppelganger dwarf.

The dwarf landed his rump square on a square, a white tile in the design, and sat there, huffing. "Look who decided to drop by? It's the master! Hoy hoy!"

"Get over here. You're late." The tall gentleman gripped the table edge and lowered himself into his chair, awkwardly with his knees peeking up. The dwarf jumped onto his stubby feet. He tottered over to the last seat and vaulted up onto it.

"Relax, old friend," the tall gentleman told Marcus. "Please, sit down and join us."

Marcus did as he was told. He sat down again and sipped at his tea to remain calm.

From across the wide triangular table, the dwarf tried in vain to grab the kettle out of reach. The tall gentleman snatched the kettle with his long fingers and poured his tiny twin a spot of tea. "You simply have to ask, you know?"

Marcus panned between the dwarf and the tall gentleman. Double doppelganger, he thought, I'll have to fight them one at a time. Or perhaps they would fight each other. Perhaps this whole scene was being played out for his amusement. But, alas, this fantasy of an epic duel was a loss since the twins seemed more intent on drinking tea than engaging in a telekinetic battle. Or perhaps...

He slammed the teacup on the marble and rose from the table so fast he almost knocked it over. "It's poisoned, isn't it? You knew I couldn't resist a cup of chamomile tea? Clever, very clever."

"Don't be foolish. Relax, my friend. We mean you no harm."

"Yes, relax," the dwarf and the tall gentleman sipped at

their cups in unison.

"Look, you can stop with the charade," Marcus said, posing like a boxer, ready for a fight. "I know what's going on here." He locked eyes with his dwarfish twin, figuring he'd be easier to implode first because of his size, and strained to make his tiny head and arms suck into his body through the concentrated power of his mind. The tall one would prove a challenge, he thought.

"What's he doing?" the dwarf asked, the teacup trembling in his hands.

"He's trying to implode you into a marble."

"Oh," the dwarf slurped at his tea. "Well, that's not very nice, is it?"

Marcus put his fists out and refocused to force mind over matter. "You may have me trapped and outnumbered, but I won't surrender easily."

This one-sided standoff went on for several minutes, during which time neither of his odd twins imploded into marbles and instead patiently waited at the table enjoying their tea until Marcus gave up and sat down.

"Okay, so maybe you aren't doppelgangers. Shape-shifting cave ogres, is that it? You've drugged the tea and are waiting for me to pass out so you can haul me into your lair and eat me alive."

"He really doesn't remember us, does he?" the tall gentleman looked at the dwarf to share in his disappointment. "Has it been that long?"

"It has been a long long time," the dwarf said.

"A long long time? It seems like a short long time, doesn't it?" The tall gentleman turned back to Marcus. "Let's start over, shall we? As I was saying, welcome."

"Yes, welcome, welcome," the dwarf reiterated. "Time again, once again."

"Does somebody want to explain what's going on here?"

Marcus said. "If you aren't shape-shifting ogres, then who are you?"

"We are the practical and irrational counterparts of your psyche."

Marcus remained nonplus.

"It's very simple," the tall gentleman said. "He's the tiny madman and I'm the old wise crow. Have you forgotten us already? That really hurts."

"I apologize if my memory is a bit foggy right now," Marcus said in anger. "So am I dead or what? Is this the afterlife or is there another door around here somewhere?"

"Dead? That depends on what you mean by dead. It's a very relative term, you know. Let's just say you're neither here nor there. Between here and there, rather. It's hard to explain."

"Well, you better try. I'm in no mood for guessing games."

"Oooh," the tall gentleman said, taken aback, "Seems our boy has grown some bite since we last saw him."

"I've had enough of this," Marcus said, pushing back his chair. "I'll find my own way out of here, thank you very much."

He rose to leave the table, and the tall gentleman rose with him. The imposing stature of his doppelganger, its colossal shadow cast by candlelight, its slanted eyes fierce and fiery, its mouth further twisted in a vicious scowl, paralyzed Marcus with sudden fear.

"You will sit back down and finish your tea," the tall gentleman told him. "This is no laughing matter, my boy. You will listen to what we have to say."

Marcus feigned as if he weren't frightened in the least, and knees shaking, sidled into his seat at the table again.

"There's nothing to be worried about, master," the dwarf consoled him. "Drink some more tea. It's very good. Very good, right? Pour a cup of tea on your head, or guzzle straight from the kettle if you'd like. Make yourself at home. You used to come here all the time when you were younger. It's been such a long time, we thought you'd lost your screevy."

"My scurvy? Excuse me?"

"Screevy. Your ability to perceive the impossible as possible, yin as yang and the paradox as the box," the tall gentleman said.

"Oh, not the paradox again," the dwarf complained.

"Would you like to explain it to him then?"

"No, you have the stage. Make your pretty speech."

"Alright," the tall gentleman started, "What you must first understand is that everything exists in relation to the mind, while not exclusive to your own mind. You are part of and inseparable from a collective mind, an overmind or undermind or throughmind, depending on your perspective. And the world from which you've come is one of many many worlds that ripple from the collective unconscious of this overmind, an island in a great sea, your mind one small circle in a greater sphere. That said, the actual ability for your mind to wander, so to speak, usually comes from death's release, or from breaking through the illusionary paradox that keeps the mind captive in its conscious world. Or from complete insanity. Are you starting to understand?"

"Not really." Marcus lifted the teacup again, enticed by the smell. "So I'm stuck here."

"We are all only passing through," the dwarf snorted with a twitch of his fat nose. "This is Oblivion, master, from whence all things come and go. A blank page of which we are only one picture, the plane of all that is possible and impossible and probable and otherwise. It is as infinitely deep as it is finite in its exact fathoms. Don't dwell on it. It's only a fancy explanation for something that really can't be explained. Anyway, like we said before, simply consider yourself somewhere between here and there, completely lost and beyond the point of no return."

"Well said, and entirely unhelpful," the tall gentleman

remarked.

"Thank you." The dwarf smiled.

"May I ask you both a question?" Marcus said.

The dwarf looked up at the tall gentleman, who in turn looked down at the dwarf, and then across the triangular table. "Sure."

"Where am I?"

"Well, my dear friend," the tall gentleman said, stretching his fingers and cracking his giant knuckles, "This is our meeting place. Your meeting place, burrowed in the deepest recess of your mind, where the circles cross with the great unconscious. Thus here we are."

"Servants come to bid the call of their master," the dwarf added. "And we are your pitiful monkey puppets."

"Ahem, I would rather consider myself counsel at the lord's court," the tall gentleman said. "As for this place, this is where in times past you have come to converse with us. Sometimes you'd come to ask us questions or consult with us on certain matters, or often, when you were a young boy, you'd come to simply chat."

"Ah, you were such a nice boy then. So dangerously imaginative, so full of life," the dwarf said wistfully.

Marcus crossed his arms like a child. "I still am."

"Oh, my poor delusional friend," the tall gentleman leant over the table and said with great sadness in his towering eyes. "Listen and listen close. You are not as young as you pretend to be. In fact, you are very old and very bitter, aged beyond your years. Fading. Trapped in a box, looping on thoughts that never quite show their faces. You are lost, that's why you are here. Perhaps you've come to pass. Or perhaps you'll return to your room in the starry sky, with its bare walls, books, and birds. Regardless, we have come to heed you a warning. As we speak, your mind is splitting, running tangents, winding through Oblivion. The next time you awake, who knows where you'll be or who you'll be. Be careful, that's all we ask. One can get into a lot of trouble, haphazardly wandering the tangled corridors of Oblivion."

"Thank you for your concern," Marcus said. "But I think I can fend for myself."

"Do you now?" the tall gentleman smirked. "What do you think?"

"We've said what we've come to say," the dwarf said. "There's no use pestering the master."

"Right you are," the tall gentleman resigned. "Let us propose a toast then, shall we?" He held his teacup high into the air and the dwarf did the same. Marcus didn't know what to think or who was thinking for him. Although he felt frustrated and thoroughly confused, he raised his cup over the kettle with his doppelgangers.

The dwarf glanced up at the tall gentleman. "Shall I?"

"You shall."

"To minding the mind's mind," the dwarf said. With a swoop of fine china, the three clinked their teacups. The kettle rattled on the marble once again and coughed out another breath of steam. Marcus brought the tea to his lips and vanished with one last sweet sip.

CHAPTER FIVE

Crashing the Jungle Bash

Nobody likes to be *that guy* at the party. That silent guy in the corner leaning self-consciously against the wall, posing like James Dean. The guy who gives a plastic smile and nods to you across the room, even though you've never met him before. The guy who suckles one beer the whole night and can't remember who he came with. The guy who concentrates a little too hard on the music while clapping at inappropriate moments. The guy who you can't tell whether he's thinking about grabbing another beer or sneaking off to the bathroom so he can quietly pass out in the tub. The guy who inevitably eats all the hors d'oeuvres.

Norman, of course, couldn't help being *that guy* since he was the only guy, or human for that matter, at the Jungle Bungle Bash. He grabbed his third helping of delicious breaded canapés and thanked the tuxedoed camel who strutted off, carrying the tray balanced on its hump.

For once, Norman felt he had finally arrived, immersed in this scene of pure animal debauchery. This was life unbridled. No rules. No inhibitions. Just animals being animals, with cocktails. He thought about how foolish humanity was for repressing their primal instincts, their urges to be free and unleashed. In short, to be feral. That's what it means to be alive, he thought as he quietly ridiculed all the nameless countless philosophers who'd tried to give life a civilized meaning. Licking his fingers and sipping his martini, he made sly eyes with a sexy lemur out on the dance floor but couldn't tell whether her looks were carnal or predatory, then wondered what the difference was.

The stares were inevitable. Every now and then, he'd catch an alligator sneering, or a bunch of hyena snickering his way as he loafed about the ballroom, still wet with goo from his swim in the subterranean jelly. He was more flattered than embarrassed by all the attention. A human debutante at the animal ball. He only wished that he'd re-materialized in a clean shirt.

Oh well, he thought, it's only a matter of time before I'm transformed into a tortoise or parrot or whatever and invited to take part in the great cycle of life. I mean, why else would I be here?

He went back for another martini to pass the time. An orangutan and a ferret were leaning on the bar and arguing rather obnoxiously over the music.

"You only say that because you're next down on the evolutionary chain."

"No, Fred. Think about it. It's the natural process. Adapt and survive. It's obvious nature had something to do with the humans."

"But it misfired, Bernard. I'm telling you it was an accident. All of humanity is one great accident. Big brain stuck in a dumb animal. Sometimes evolution screws up. Why else would mother nature create an animal that would slowly destroy it?"

"Because that's the way it works. It's not nice, it's not pretty, but that's life as we know it. That's the ugly side of nature. The big guy screwing over the small guy."

The ferret was about to retort when he noticed the human standing right next to them at the bar. "Um, excuse me? What are you doing here?"

Norman tipped the whale bartender. He lifted his martini with delicate grace, slightly baffled by the confused faces of the orangutan and the ferret. "Getting a martini."

"Why don't you ask the human?" the orangutan told the ferret.

"Me? What about you?" the ferret said.

"Fine, fine," the orangutan said. "Um, excuse me?"

Norman sipped at his drink. "Yes. We've met."

"Do you consider yourself evil?" the orangutan asked. "I mean, not you specifically, but humanity in general?"

"I don't believe in good and evil," Norman said and walked off.

The ferret shook his head and watched the human disappear into the jungle bash. "Well, it's decided then," the ferret said. "What an asshole."

Norman, pleased with himself for having honorably represented humankind, waded back through the festivities. The brief repartee made him hungry for some odd reason. An exasperated appetite for meat, and only meat. Thick bloody flesh. He could taste it on his canapé-caked teeth. He lapped it with his tongue on the underbelly of his mouth. He had to restrain himself from a rabid desire to tackle certain ballroom guests and tear into the prey—the wild boars that snorted tumblers of bourbon, the rabbits that copulated under the stairs, even his monkey brethren on the dance floor.

He repressed this hunger out of politeness and heard his stomach grumble in protest, or what he thought was his stomach until he realized the throated purr was coming from elsewhere. Under the mezzanine, under an archway that led out into a courtyard, a tiger was apparently sizing him up from afar. Norman considered introducing himself and engaging in small talk as a way of taming the threat, but swiftly decided against the idea. You can't negotiate with tigers, he reminded himself. Just keep moving.

On the hunt for more hors d'oeuvres, he hit an impasse in the crowd and almost tripped over a semicircle of intellectual squirrels. They chittered away, engrossed by something blocked out of view.

"He's absolutely spectacular."

"A true passion for art."

"He is. It is. Life is. How poetically simple."

"I dig, I dig."

In the middle sat a single squirrel, curled and silent, a motionless ball of fur.

"What's he doing?" Norman whispered to a nearby squirrel.

"Performance art," the squirrel responded. "He's a nut."

Norman sipped at his martini and noted the faint taste of apricot. "Well, that's fairly obvious. But why is acting like—"

"Shhh!" she scolded. "You'll break his concentration. It took him three hours to transcend into this nuttery."

He apologized and observed the squirrel artist and its nut mimicry in silence. Somebody or something tapped his leg.

"Hey man, I think you got the wrong room, dig?" squeaked a nasal voice from below. A penguin in dark sunglasses stood at his waist. "I say, you dig?"

"Sure, I dig," Norman said. "What am I digging again?"

"Ain't your scene. Don't know how you got in. Somebody must have mistaken you for a chimp." The penguin dipped down his shades so he could have a good look. "Easy mistake. It's all good. I'll get you where you need to be."

It took a few rounds of the notion cycling through his head before Norman finally came to terms with the fact that he was indeed being pestered by a hipster penguin who seemed intent on kicking him out of the party. He was about to tell the penguin to get lost when he glanced over at the corner bar. A python was slowly swallowing the ferret alive while the weasel persisted to argue with the orangutan. He took this as his cue to leave.

"Great party, love the music," Norman said.

"This is the Jungle Bungle Bash, baby." The penguin pushed through a gang of dingoes playing craps. He pointed off with his flipper toward a fountain courtyard under the mezzanine where the party spilled out for drinks and conversation alfresco. "This is just our little breather from the life cycle. Eventually everyone gets a little too drunk or bored and end up in the pool out there to be reborn again. Reincarnation is a crapshoot, though that's the only downside of being an animal in my opinion. We choose this life. At any time, we could fill out an application to become human again, but what's the point? Humanity is a drag, man. Gotta tie your shoes all the time, wipe your ass, file taxes. You know what I'm saying?"

"Oh yeah, sure," Norman said. "I've always felt more at home with animals anyway."

He reached out for another hors d'oeuvre as one of the caterer camels passed.

"You really don't want that," the penguin said.

"Why?" he said, already munching away. "These are great."

"Because it's probably made with man flesh."

Norman spit out the hunk of breaded human and gargled the rest of his martini to kill the taste.

"It's a dog-eat-cat-eat-squirrel world, man. You have your foie gras and we have our cucumber and pickled human sandwiches. You, my friend, are a delicacy here. Over this way."

Drunken sloth clogged the stairs up to the mezzanine balcony. The hairy slobs, slugging champagne bottles with their three-toes, whined and drank and complained about the speed of the music. At the top of the stairs, a flock of ostriches hung their necks over the banister, spying down at the wild scene.

Norman shoved through the feathers so he could catch up with the penguin who was already down at the far end of the mezzanine. A red curtain hung along the wall, draped as a backdrop for a lizard lounge band on a main stage over the grand fete.

"Slow down," he shouted over the music. "Where are we headed?"

"Relax, ain't no trip. We're almost there." The penguin drew back the curtain with his flipper. "You first."

Norman slipped outside. Space. A terrace in space. The stars sparkled and gleamed with a divine luster there in the high heavens, frozen in cosmic silence, no noise whatsoever escaping from the wild jungle party behind the curtain. A railed walkway extended from the terrace, winding through the void like a ribbon.

"Beautiful, eh?" the penguin said and started out along the walkway. "Ain't nothing like nothing to make you wonder about it all."

Norman, guided by the railing, cautiously stepped out onto the path, suspended by nothing but space. The walkway curved and bended until it came to a fork. A second path diverged from the wonky walkway and swung up to a platform where a large arrow sign that read 'Humans Only' pointed to a hole ripped in the fabric of space and time.

"That's the shortcut to eternal teatime for you humans," the penguin whispered. "Nothing but serenity the likes of nothing you've ever experienced. And really really boring. Straight on goes to the Genius of Creation. He's a bit difficult to understand, talks in riddles if you know what I mean, but he's a nice enough guy. Maybe he'll enlighten you. He just gave me a headache. Strange old dude. Slightly senile, you dig?"

Norman ascended the path to the platform, keeping a safe distance from the cosmic hole through which he spied on the heavenly tea party. Billions of children danced in circles, with laughter and sunbeam smiles, holding hands and prancing around an enormous tea saucer. A chorus sang in jubilation atop clouds of steam: "God is good. God is great. Let us thank him for this fate. An eternity without any fear. Strike up the band and let's give a cheer, for the Father-all-powerful-Genius-of-Creation." And so on.

The Almighty wasn't without his usual sense of humor in his creation of the human everafter. The big joke here was a great glowing red sphere that floated aimlessly about the heavenly realm. Upon entering the celestial tearoom, all of God's children had been warned not to touch the sphere, however curiosity gets the better of everyone, eventually. Then poof, and the next thing they knew, they'd wake up hatching out the belly of a cockroach.

Norman snuck away from the cosmic hole and returned to the penguin. "I believe I'd like to meet the Genius of Creation."

"Alright, you do what you want. I gotta be cruising back and digging that crazy scene before my eternity is through." The penguin turned and waddle away. "Stay loose, baby."

Norman wanted to wish him a similar farewell, like 'Right on, dude' or 'Catch you on the flip,' or 'Thanks for digging me up to this here rooftop,' but by the time he turned to say goodbye, the penguin was already gone and he found himself all alone on the winding path in the Great Nothing.

CHAPTER SIX
The Specter Returns

The devastation carried on for miles and miles. Swathes of jagged char marred the plains. Here and there, a crumbled stonewall, half a schoolhouse, the markings of a city square were laid waste, looking more like shadows than ruins in the afternoon sun. In stretches throughout the wasteland, a strange heather waved like fine hair when the train brushed by and whisked the ashes of the old world into a low dusty fog.

It was a stark reminder of what had come before, what had been purged in the fast fire of 2317 A.P. Leaning against the windowsill, Zander watched the wasteland scroll by mile after mile and imagined what it would have looked like. Whole cities swallowed by fire and smoke, a necessary vengeance against an evil unseen but heard in the compounded screams of the millions who threw their arms to the godless sky in surrender, pleading for salvation. A sacrifice for the future—yes, although a secret guilt plagued the new world, just as the old had been plagued. They would have wanted it this way, they'd said. Not genocide; euthanasia. The terms redefined to justify their crimes.

Zander sunk back in his seat. He knew it was only right to remember. He knew that sheltered behind the Republic's great walls, thousands of people went about their lives without the faintest grasp on the weight of such a tragic history. They would never see the wastelands. Not even the slightest doubt would ever cloud their hearts, purified by the love of society reborn. If at any time unanswered questions began to gnaw at their consciences, they would simply take the red pill and recite the mantra ingrained by the Academy: *'It is not for one to dwell on time past, only to understand and give energy to the future.'*

None of the other passengers in his train compartment

paid any attention to the ruins outside the window. Facing him, a balding man, buttoned up in tweed, sat upright in his seat, stroking his mustache. Every now and then, he'd stop and pull out a golden pocket watch from his jacket. He'd unlatch it, read the glass face with the same stunned affection. Then he'd wrap it up in its chain loop by loop and tuck it back in his inside pocket. Seated beside the clock-watcher, a lady in a blue dress browsed the headlines of the *Republican Guard*. Across from her, a young man in a blue peacoat drooped in and out of sleep.

The scorched fields of ancient sacrifice outside were no concern of theirs. They thought only of home, happy for their safe return to the Republic.

Zander studied the rubble of their ancestral civilization outside, forgotten in the dusty fog. Years before, it had been his duty to catalogue artifacts from the catastrophic events that had destroyed the old world and birthed to the new one: The Phasing, The Trials of the Inoculation, The Revolts of 2325, The Antriac War. He had been one of a dozen archivers assigned to piece together and revise the passages of time in the musty Office of Preservation. In the end, it was all fiction, the inconsistencies ironed into a fabled history, which the commonwealth purported as truth under the Law of Accord.

The archivers sifted through mountains of yellowed documents, tattered tomes and dated periodicals, recording anything of note. It was never clear why they were compiling the written scrap of the former world. It's for the records, they were told. Still, their duty was guarded with the utmost secrecy.

He had considered himself privileged at the time to be immersed in the spoils of writings hundreds of years old. Day after day, he'd leaf through medical books, travel magazines, telephone directories, ledgers, legal documents, old newspapers in search of clips of information that might corroborate the Republic's history of how the pre-plague societies came to such a cataclysmic end. He'd delighted in stitching together the censored mystery of what had come before.

The scorched wasteland thinned to vague piles of debris. A fine heather rose and reclaimed the plains. Abruptly, the train entered a tunnel and left the passengers in darkness. On cue, the tube lights flicked on overhead. The balding man unraveled the lengthy chain and peeked at his pocket watch again. The young man beside Zander snorted and yawned awake. The lady in blue neatly folded up the newspaper in her lap.

Zander pulled out his own pocket watch: 14:41. Right on time. Oh how the Republic loved their palindromes.

"You were worried too, weren't you?" the balding man said.

Zander stuffed his watch back in his pocket, "Worried?"

"We were a minute off a few miles ago. Thought we'd never make the tunnel on time. Ridiculous to think such a thing, but I guess I'm just extra cautionary. Never been late, have they though? I keep checking, but never, never. Not that I would want to be off-time, glory knows I'd never want that. But I check to check. Extra cautionary."

"No harm in that," Zander said in hopes this would end the conversation.

"Name's Raymond." A frail hand thrust out of the tweed jacket in his direction. "And you are?"

"Devan," Zander lied, ignoring the hand.

Raymond pulled his hand back, checked it front and back to see if it was dirty. He rested it on his knee. "You, ah, had business in Elseboro?"

"I'm a researcher for the Collections," Zander said. "I had a number of samples to collect for the Institute. It's very confidential. I'm forbidden to talk much about it. My apologies."

"Hmmm... yes. Oh, no need. I didn't mean to pry. Just making chat." The balding man sniveled and scratched his mustache. "I myself overlook labor operations in the foundries. Also very private. My apologies."

"None needed," Zander said.

"I make this transit often. This time of year is very busy for us, even busier with the Centennial. Much to be done. How long have you been away if you don't mind me asking?"

"Several months," Zander replied and immediately regretted doing so. "I've been far too busy to keep track of the days. It's been a fair amount of time, though. Far too long."

"It always feels that way, doesn't it?" Raymond said. "I can't stand being away for more than a couple days. I become unnerved. But such anxiety is natural, is it not? After all, who would want to be outside the Republic? I can't understand how Smiths can live and work out there in the middle of a wasteland. I'd be in perpetual fear for my life. The territory is improving, little by little, but still very savage."

The man's fatherly guise troubled Zander. His candor seemed phony, suspicious even since it didn't fit his hard-grooved face, his squat nose and that stern mustache, the mark of high rank among the Hero breed.

"Ah, to be back in the arms of the Republic, behind those glorious walls where all is settled and sane. You are returning for the Centennial, yes?"

"As is proper. It is also the end of my tenure in Elseboro."

"Well, glory good." Raymond slapped his knee. "Have you been following the trials at all?"

This is front, Zander reminded himself. Pay attention. This man is full of half-truths. He's trying to shake something out of me, taking mental note of my every reply. Tread carefully here. Keep the game short.

"I don't pay much attention to the circus of rumors."

"Yes, of course not. Neither do I. But it is a joyous

occasion, is it not? Always is, always is. Very exciting, these times they are exciting, don't you think?" Raymond crinkled his eyes and studied him. "You know, I must say you do look familiar? Have we met before?"

Zander had been waiting for this question. He'd seen it stew in the old man's mind.

"No, I don't believe so."

"You sure? Did you ever spend any time at Reinstock?"

Reinstock was the only social establishment in Elseboro, a ramshackle watering hole of questionable reputation. Back in the beginning of the reconstruction, and subsequent salvage of abandoned Elseboro flats, the decrepit warehouse had housed bins of scrap metal and raw materials for shipment back to the Republic. Once Elseboro developed into a full-fledged colony, the warehouse was converted into an after-hours gathering place for the Smiths who worked hard labor in the Outer Yard.

"I had little time to socialize," Zander said. Whatever the true nature of this interrogation was, it eluded him. Have the guardians been alerted to my return? he thought. Surely his face must have been forgotten by now, with so much time to wash it from memory.

"Perhaps I'm just getting old," Raymond gave in. "The older you get, the more the memories all meld together."

Something seemed menacing in the crook of his complaisant smile.

"Perhaps," Zander said.

The train intercom saved him from more of the inquisition: *BEEP BEEP BEEP Attention! BEEP BEEP Attention! TRANSIT 1033 is closing in for arrival. Please remain seated while the inspectors verify all passenger credentials. Thank you for your patience and cooperation. Approximate arrival time is gauged at fifteen minutes on 15:00 chronology.*

Raymond whipped out his watch again and gave it a self-conscious glance.

"14:54. Excellent. Such punctuation never ceases to amaze me."

BEEP BEEP Attention! Please remain seated until the inspectors have reviewed all passengers.

Zander slid a briefcase out from under his seat. He spun the dials, snapped it open, and pulled out his transit papers. Raymond kept his grinning eyes fixed on him and fanned himself with his credentials. The young man stretched upright in his seat, his papers ready in his right hand. The lady in blue rummaged through her purse and retrieved her transit papers.

The doors to the train compartment swished open. Two inspectors in zippered yellow jumpsuits marched in. They surveyed the passengers before the taller one spoke.

"Transit credentials, please."

The young man beside Zander handed over his papers. The first inspector scanned the barcode and passed the credentials to the second inspector who punched the numbers into a palm-sized digital ledger.

"Your name, purpose, and IDR, please," the first inspector said.

"Harlan Smith, auxiliary relief engineering, L23B10DS19." the young man said with pride.

"He's green," the second inspector told the first.

Zander offered his transit papers before the inspectors could ask.

"Your name, purpose, IDR."

"Devan Saint, artifact collections, S31B15DK22," he told them. He maintained his composure as the inspector inputted the information. Zander had known this was a gamble from the start. No guarantees. His life in the hands of thieves and madmen, a delicate matter involving men of delicate tempers. The only question he'd asked was: how much?

"Green."

The inspector turned to Raymond, "And you?"

Raymond gingerly laid his papers in the inspector's hand. "Raymond Hero. Primary supervisor of energies, reference H259C09Y32"

"Green again," the inspector announced after a moment's computation.

The lady then passed over her transit papers. "Glenda Saint, assistant archive director, S210J53PK50."

Zander turned flush when she said this. His throat swelled, his palms sweated. How had he not noticed her before? Glenda, Row D3, Console 9825. She had sat behind him for years, rifling through papers at astonishing speed, never pausing to let her fingers rest, tap, tap, tap, tap, tap. During his eight years in the Office of Preservation, they'd never shared a word aside from the cordial hello and goodbyes. She'd spent her breaks at her desk, whispering to herself.

And there she was, a ghost from his past, sitting across from him, giving the inspectors her most disarming smile. Zander felt sick. This was disastrous, she was a living breathing disaster. Had she recognized him? No, not yet at least. She'd be too shy to say anything anyway, he reassured himself.

"She's green."

The inspector reviewed the data on his digital ledger.

"Thank you all for your patience," he said, and with this, the inspectors promptly exited the compartment.

Zander stole a glance at Glenda. One word and he'd be finished. All the suffering, the stowings, the deception, the miserable nights in dank cellars, dodging raids, always on the move, would have been for nothing. He angled his face toward the window, the hollow of the tunnel howling outside, the train carving through the darkness. He checked his pocket watch again, 14:55, and sweated through the minutes till the train horn blew.

Zander shuffled on his brown suede jacket and lagged

behind the others as they filed down the train corridor. Through the side windows, he watched the passengers disembark. He kept an eye on Raymond and Glenda as they filtered into the swelling crowd on the station platform. He imagined the two would converge at any moment, steal away to some secret rendezvous and radio their surveillance report to Control 6 together.

You can't let the paranoia take hold, he told himself, whatever the reality or unreality of the situation is. Keep your cool. Keep focused. Remember why you're here.

He stepped off the train with the briefcase tight in his hand and exited into the terminal. The station was a massive dome of cambered steel beams that soared up and over in a crisscross fashion and made the trains seem like mere toys in comparison. The whistle blew three times to announce the departure of Transit Henderboro, which then rumbled and huffed down the tracks, precisely five minutes after Elseboro arrived, as always.

Under the apex of the dome, in the middle of the terminal, a huge green-glass sculpture of a hand held an almost comical clock in its grip. The crowd of disembarking passengers warped round the clock sculpture and split into five separate queues, which branched off down a series of arched hallways. Zander's heart fell at ease when Raymond and Glenda took their allotted places in different queues. His anxiety softened to an uneasy nostalgia, which made him pause before the enormous hand-clock.

The sculpture's huge translucent fingers curled over the round top and crushed into the clockface. An inscription on the sculpted wrist read: *'Without the measure of time, reason has no bind,'* a reverent statement of time's dominance over the majestic power of reason. How many revolutions had the hand-clock made since he'd last marveled at the sculpture? Time had been insignificant in Elseboro. The workforce stopped and started at the horn's blow opposed to the punch of the buzzer or the clocktower chimes.

What an odd notion it was that, while he was hiding away in the wasteland, the Republic still ticked, the turbines turned, the Smiths mended, the Saints tended, and the Heroes defended. Rise, clean, work, rest, work, rest, sleep—or stated in Chrono—07:07, 07:15, 08:08, 13:31, 14:14, 17:15, 21:12, as divined from the Standards for Productivity, circa 2362.

Every life in the Republic was intricately aligned, contributing to the great purpose. Every duty methodical in executed cause-effect, every mind-body-hand in sync, feeding off one another's efforts and energies. A fully autonomous machine like the clock with its gears that wound round forever in the hollow encasement of the glass hand.

Somewhere in the machinery of the commonwealth, she still lived and breathed with the rest. Leyna Saint with her black hair and fervid hazel eyes, Zander's longtime friend and confidante. The night before he'd stowed away to Elseboro, she'd given him a damning farewell in the bunker tunnels where Phaedrus and the other rebels were preparing for the next day's diversion.

"This is suicide," she'd warned him. "Even if you make it there, you'll never be able to come back. You know that, don't you?"

"It's a risk I must take," he'd told her.

"But you don't have to leave."

"I'm a danger to everyone if I stay. It's better this way. The future of the resistance depends on it."

"Forget the resistance. You have a choice, Zander, a say. This is your life on the line. Listen to me. Do you really think they care about what happens to you?"

"Please, don't fight me on this. This is my choice. No one else's. You don't understand what's at stake here."

"If you've made your decision, then there's nothing left to

say. But don't expect me to shed one tear for you. Don't expect me—"

"Leyna, please. Come on. Be reasonable."

"Just go," she'd said, covering her face. "Leave me alone, okay?"

Although he didn't see her the next morning nor during the mayhem that followed, he could have sworn he felt her eyes stinging his back when he snuck onto the Elseboro Transit and made his escape, hidden in the mechanical underbelly of the train's cargo hold.

The glass clock read: 15:23. Zander had less than an hour till his rendezvous with Weber. Perhaps she'd be with him. He headed for the terminal corridor marked 'S' in accordance with the initial letter of his counterfeit IDR.

Guardians watched over the arched entrances. They were just boys, he could tell by their young faces, recent graduates of the Academy. They stood tall in grey waistcoats, crossed on the chest with the Hero's insignia, a yellow serpent straddling a sword-shaped syringe. Their small hands hung nervously at their sidearm holsters. So young yet so stoic, so cold and so proud. They understood neither life nor death, yet were ready to stand in judgment, to kill or be killed for whatever the Republic deemed as justice.

A series of black doors along the corridor swung open and shut, swallowing the passengers. The line again divided into separate smaller queues at each door. Zander moved into place at the door labeled '3', in accordance with his second IDR digit, and waited his turn. Soon he was behind the black door in a bright oval-shaped room with a lanky man in a labcoat.

"Take a seat," the doctor said and adjusted the legs of a medical chair. Zander sat down in the blind of twin spotlights that protruded from the wall like portholes.

"My name is Dr. Voss Saint and I will be your inoculator on this juncture of 5.03.2433." The doctor snapped on a pair of plastic gloves. "How are we today? Had a pleasant transit, did we?"

"Well, sir. Yes, sir."

"Glory good," he wrung his hands. "Your name and reference, please."

"Devan Saint, S31B15DK22."

"Have you been away long?"

"Approximately fourteen months."

"I'm surprised you didn't grow horns," the doctor chuckled at his own joke. "Any health trouble?"

"None really."

"Let's have a look at you," the doctor said. "Please remove your jacket, brother."

Slipping off his jacket, Zander caught an intense glare from the wall lamps and rubbed his spotty eyes. The doctor stuck a stethoscope in his ears and gently probed Zander's chest and lower abdomen.

"Everything sounds like it's in working order." The doctor gave him a short smile. "Any abnormal heart palpations, shortness of breath?"

"No, sir."

The doctor walked around to the back of the chair, "Bare your forearms and lay them out straight, please."

Zander laid out his arms on the armrests. The doctor held them tight against the chair as he strapped on leather constraints. "And your mental health? Any dizziness, confusion, headaches, toxic thoughts?"

"No, sir. None, sir."

The doctor picked two glass vials off a shelf—one clear yellow, the other a turbid green. He shook them vigorously, one at a time. He unsheathed a long syringe from a metal rack on the counter.

"You are pleased to be home?"

"Very much so."

"Good," the doctor said and gently tightened the straps. "The Council has authorized a slight recalibration of the boosters. Some people feel a tingling sensation and soreness afterward. Try to remain relaxed." He pricked a vein with the needle and eased in the plunger. Zander felt a dizziness slowly overtake him. He shook himself awake. The doctor sucked the green liquid from the second vial. With remarkable precision, he injected the needle into the same puncture wound.

"And… there." The doctor plucked out the syringe and clotted the wound with gauze. He removed the arm constraints and helped Zander out of the chair.

"Hope you enjoy your leave, Devan," The doctor handed him an inoculation verification receipt. "Will you be returning to Elseboro in the near future?"

"That all depends on the whims of the commonwealth," Zander said, slightly dizzy from the shot.

"As does so much." The doctor smiled back. "Glory be the Republic."

Part Two: The Republic

It may be a shock to most twirly bearded philosophers that the whole of human existence is confined to three fathoms of Oblivion, namely the 335th, 336th, 337th. The majority of questioning humanity bounces between the 336th and 337th fathom, unaware of the fluctuation, while those enlightened enough to fully involve themselves in the lower 335th fathom are primarily devout monks and piano tuners.

In 2433 A.P. of 336.84th fathom of Oblivion (where we find our wayward traveler), there is little left of humanity and its earthly conquests, beyond the small pockets of civilization that survived the devastation. Who was to blame for the last measure is unclear, for the sudden white flash that blackened the sky with orange clouds and blotted out the sun.

Before the fallout, the world had been tightening at an exponential rate. Most of the southern hemisphere had become inhabitable due to extreme heat, forcing millions of immigrants to seek refuge in the north. Meanwhile, the northern countries shut down their borders while they fought over the dwindling supply of natural resources through proxy wars using everyone else as pawns.

As a result, the world teetered on the verge of a great war. A war that would never happen. The plague would serve to destroy everything that war might have and far more, as if exterminating mankind before it had a chance to do so itself.

The first cases were discovered at a port town on an island

in the South Pacific. They called it the Fisherman's Flu. Dockworkers fell ill with a fever so severe that it made their bodies overheat, their lungs fill with fluid, their skin turn jaundiced and scaley. The unlucky few who didn't die in a matter of days went mad with fever.

Travel was restricted from any port in a hundred-mile radius of the epicenter. Sanctions were imposed on imported and exported goods from the infected nations. After a series of humanitarian missions and a coordinated euthanasia of all infected parties, it seemed they had defeated the virus. Then five years later, cases sprung up in major cities around the globe.

There was no time to react. In metropolitan areas, the plague spread like wildfire. No one was safe, inside or outside the quarantine zones. The air was contaminated, the water supply tainted. Emergency rations were air-dropped to the sick. When this failed to contain the plague, there came an international consensus to cut off the quarantined regions and purge the virus like a cancer.

They firebombed entire cities and provinces, yet still the plague kept spreading, and in its wake, chaos. They tried in vain to control the problem through martial law and slaughtered millions in fear of spreading the disease. Then the killing became less scrupulous. Anyone who refused to obey the emergency directives was shot dead on sight and hauled to the pits. And so from plague came violent unrest as governments collapsed around the world. It was only a matter of time before the button was pushed, out of paranoia that someone else would press it first.

By the time the scientists at the Renvock Institute had formulated a vaccine, there were few left to save. The scientists, after almost two years in isolation, were ill-prepared for the desolation outside their sterile fortress. The scorched ruins and stony rubble, the thick sulfuric air, the skeletal remains half-buried in a layer of grey dust and debris.

Their mission became to cross the barbed streets in the nearby city of Pravijk in search of survivors, inoculate one victim at a time, and return them to the Institute, while others guarded the compound. This went on for months in which time the scientists garnered a small army of inoculators. Their objectives changed once the survivors outgrew the Institute. Food, clean water, housing. The basic necessities that had for so long been firsthand in the world were now scarce.

The inoculators eventually found no more victims to be saved. Only bodies to be buried. An uneasy calm settled on the city. And from this tragedy rose a leader among the group, Dr. Edgar S. Benedict, whom many regarded as a saint for his contribution to the cure. It was he who spoke to the refugees, it was he who spoke from the balcony of the Institute to the scared survivors at the world's end. It was he who spoke these words, on the third month of the third day of 2333 AP in the 336.84th fathom of Oblivion.

"Today we stand at a pause, a still moment in time, in disbelief. A testament to humanity, charged with this great task," he said, "Not to resurrect the world that's perished, but to boldly charge anew into an unknown future and prove we are worthy to have cheated death."

Boy, was the old man a poet…

CHAPTER SEVEN

Rendezvous in the Café

Swirl...

"So I tell the guy I'll do it myself. I mean I can't be wasting time teaching this kid the simple two-turn-and-bind when I got eight guys down the line counting on me. And what does this punk do? I turn my head for a second, and what does this kid do? He goes and gets Kendrick."

"No kidding. What'd he say?"

The drop unfurled clouds, full stratus of cream, swirling like an underwater storm in the black drink.

"You know Kendrick. He doesn't say anything, he just comes over and grumbles something about us being behind schedule and that he doesn't have time to deal with it. Well, the kid's miffed and he's complaining and moping right next to me. Meanwhile the buzzer blows and we get a last-minute line of radio watches pumping down the chute and he's doing such a sloppy job I just can't take it. I tell him to switch places with me and just do the winding, which he's fumbling at just the same."

Zander stirred his coffee at a table nearby while eavesdropping on the Smiths rehashing stories at the café bar over a couple pints of bootleg grog. He spread out a newspaper and pretended not to listen to their conversation.

The headlines of the *Republican Guard* were nearly all about the Centennial—CONTENDERS ANNOUNCED FOR THE TOURNAMENT... NEW CURFEW IN ORDER FOR EVE OF... PRODUCTION UP 3.4 PERCENT IN... and so on. On the back page, the names and statistics of the Academy's graduating class were listed in columns along with the selected contenders for tomorrow's tournament.

"And then…" the Smith laughed under his breath before talking real low to his friend on the next stool. "And then, well, I pull a number on him. I mean, I guess it was kind of childish, but the kid's gotta learn somehow, right? Without him seeing, I unscrew the cinch bolt in his hose while showing him how to hold the winder right. And you should have seen it. He clicked the button, off went the hose like wild snake twisting round and spraying steam and nearly throwing him on the belt. It was hysterical."

The Smith chuckled so hard he almost fell off his seat. His friend joined in, more reserved in his laughter, and downed the rest of his pint.

From behind the newspaper, Zander's eyes wandered from the bar and surveyed the rest of the basement café. In a corner, a greasy-haired man and a young woman were animated in a conversation about the annual Trials, judicial proceedings held in public to capitalize on crimes committed against the commonwealth and give solidarity to the Republic's unique notion of justice. A scruffy man across the café scribbled in a journal, pausing only to bite his pen in thought.

The hands of a clock were tied at 13:33 on the wall, the second hand forever pushing—tick, tick, tick—without success. This was a clear crime under the Laws of Accord, although in the dingy basement that was the Café Obscura, the guardians were more concerned with the rabble of regulars than any broken clock.

Zander flipped out his own pocket watch and checked the time: 16:25. Weber was now twenty minutes late for their rendezvous. He wouldn't let himself speculate as to why. He discreetly patted the briefcase under his chair to make sure it was still there. He opened up the newspaper again. He sipped at his coffee and waited.

The café was exactly how he'd remembered it. Same slate tables, same greasy lights hanging low from the patchwork ceiling, same staff at the bar. Even his coffee tasted the same. Nothing had changed yet everything was different now. This place was no longer his safe harbor. The café and all its familiar faces were drowsy memories of how his life used to be.

Every decision has its consequences, he told himself. Things will change and change again. Still, he felt cheated out of a quiet life.

"Your check, sir," the waiter said and left a metal tray with a slip of paper on his table.

"Thank you," Zander said without looking up. Once the waiter had left, he lifted his head to find a man sitting at the table across from him, likewise absorbed in the day's paper. The newspaper hid his face, and he held it conspicuously this way with two fingers tapping the page as he read.

Zander picked the bill out of the tray and noticed something written in small letters at the bottom: *The air is not clean in here. Get rid of the luggage and meet me outside.* Two eyes peeked out over the newspaper—two brown eyes behind a pair of square spectacles that bobbed on the bridge of a hawkish nose—and ducked back down. The lines in his forehead collected beads of sweat like an abacus.

In the mirror over the bar, Zander caught sight of his old friend's profile hidden behind the newspaper. Weber looked much the same as he did the day they'd met many years ago at the Ceremony for Progressive Achievement, a particularly boring affair where the Republic's finest Saints—researchers, educators, and scientists alike—were awarded for their excellence. Weber had been honored that night with a platinum pocket watch for his work teaching the youngest pupils at the Academy. After a brief conversation at the ceremony, he and Zander found they shared a similar intellectual curiosity, a desire to seek out forgotten knowledge from the distant past.

They became quick friends and began to frequent the

basement cafés together in their leisure time to conspire over chessboards, talk poetics, speculate past and future, calculate the course of history, the struggles, the triumphs. It had all been an intellectual exercise back then. A way to pass the time. And even when they did voice some criticism of the commonwealth, they'd round out their critique with equal praise for good measure. Only later would their conversations take on a much more serious nature.

Nose in the newspaper, Weber tapped his fingers at a more rapid pace on the outside page. Zander grabbed his briefcase from under the chair. He gave a sly glance around the room and headed for the restroom in the backend of the café.

Zander entered the restroom and locked the door. He waited and listened, then checked the stalls to make sure he was alone. He laid his briefcase on the sink and snapped it open. Its contents: a series of folders with fabricated identification forms that verified his alias. He unhooked the latches of a secret compartment underneath. Inside, an antique revolver lay on top of a leather satchel.

There was a subtle knock on the door. Zander ignored it. He lifted out the pistol and checked its chambers. Four bullets. He stuck the revolver in his belt, under his jacket flap, and tried not to think of the fate delivered by the missing pair. He stuffed the leather satchel in his inside pocket and snapped the briefcase shut. Another knock on the door, louder and more insistent.

"Just a minute," Zander said.

"Collie in the yard," a voice whispered through the door.

When he returned from the restroom, the café was hushed. The couple in the corner had brought their conversation down to a dull murmur, chatting about what they'd watch that evening on the tube. At the bar, the Smiths wiped their mouths and folded their hands. A newspaper was abandoned on the table, his friend nowhere in sight.

A door upstairs creaked open and silenced the basement café. Footsteps clanged down the steel-grate stairs. A tall man in a guardian's uniform entered the café. He cast his steely eyes around the room and accounted for every head bent down in an attempt to look uninterested. The guardian approached the barkeep and asked him soft questions, too soft to hear.

Avoiding eye contact, Zander returned to his table and put some money in the bill tray. The bartender pointed across the bar, across the café, in his direction. The guardian turned. Zander folded his newspaper, tucked it under his arm, and in the same motion, tugged out the revolver from his belt.

"Stay where you are. Let's not cause any trouble here."

He pulled the hammer to cock his revolver, then let it drop back into place when the guardian walked right past his table, over to the Smiths at the end of the bar.

"Is there a problem, sir?" the first Smith said.

"Clint Smith," the guardian said. "You are under arrest for the attempted sabotage of manufacturing plant Sector 366."

"Wait a minute, hold on here," Clint said. "There must have been a mistake. I've been working in that plant twenty years and given nothing but—" He stopped short when he saw the guilt unfold on his friend's face. "You... how could you?"

His friend couldn't bring himself to look him straight on. "I'm sorry, Clint. I really am. You've got to understand. These are delicate times, and you know what you did was—"

"You've been radioing me this whole time? Where is it?"

Clint grabbed his friend's wrist, spotting a red light under the sleeve, and twisted it to smash the radio watch into the bar counter. The guardian wrenched his arms away and cuffed his wrists behind the stool.

The instant the cuffs shackled on, Clint's eyes bulged as an electric surge sent 700 volts through his nervous system and numbed him out. The cuffs were designed this way. Zander had seen this same scenario played out a hundred times before.

One shock would zap the suspect into compliance—the light flashing green on both bands—then another and another if the suspect didn't keep his cuffed hands close enough together. This guaranteed cooperation.

The guardian wrestled Clint out of his seat and leant the frazzled man on the bar. He scanned his retina with a digital ledger.

No one in the café said a word. No one even looked up from their private tables at the arrest, the fidgeting body of the Smith, his eyes bulging in absent recognition of the guardian who promptly put a black hood over the prisoner's face to hide unsightly effects of the electric shock.

Zander subtly made sure his revolver was concealed under his jacket and rose from his seat. He nodded to the bartender, passing the commotion at the bar. He calmly walked out of the basement café, up the stairs and into the world outside.

Chapter Eight

Father-all-powerful-genius-of-Creation

Since the beginning, God has been fairly misunderstood, probably on account of his title: the Father-all-powerful-Genius-of-Creation. While it is only right to credit him with the glory of all creation, there's still one question (a common question in the fan mail) that even God cannot answer. What's the meaning, the purpose behind it all, the reason for existence? The secret truth of the matter is that God interviewed for the position. The conversation went like this:

Two voices in the dark. God, stuttering nervous about the job offer, and the voice of the Great Unknown.

"GOD."

"Hello, yes, hello. It's dark. I can't see you. I'm here to interview for the…"

"Yes, I know."

"Of course, you do. Silly me. So ummm… so…"

"Calm down and tell me about yourself."

"Sure, sure. I know it may seem like I've had very little experience with this sort of thing, but I'm a hard-worker and long eternities are no big deal for me, and I really appreciate that you're willing to grant me this interview."

"Pleased to hear it. You have my full confidence in this job. Just don't screw it up. It's a six day a week gig with overtime omniscience, but you do get Sundays off."

"And benefits?"

"There's unparalleled power, unending praise, and a cushy retirement package when you're finished with the manual labor. However, you will still be responsible for administrative oversight."

"Great. Thank you so much. It's an absolute honor. One question, though, what exactly is it that you want me to do?"

"Fix Nothing."

"Oh, I didn't know Nothing was broken."

"It isn't. Nothing is Nothing. That's the problem."

"Right, so… how do I fix Nothing?"

"I'm sure you'll think of something."

"Got it. But why? If nothing is Nothing, why does it need to be fixed?"

The question fell on absent ears. The Great Unknown did not respond, nor did God and the Great Unknown shake hands, primarily because they had no hands to shake with. In the brink of no time, God stood alone in the midst of unending nothingness, before time, before space, contemplating how he could fix Nothing.

In the same nothingness, billions of eons later, Norman now contemplated life, death, and the haze in between. The walkway roped through the vast void, the only thing that gave it any form or definition. A white door stood suspended in the nothingness after a series of stairs at the end of the path. A glamorous 'G' glittered on the door, embroidered with sparkling gold and silver filigree and strung with a dozen colored lights that lit up like Broadway.

He ascended the stairs, step by step. Heart pounding, Norman arrived at the top of the stairs and marveled at the tacky Las Vegas excitement of the door. It was shiny.

The door swung inward.

God sat with his feet up on a large mahogany desk, his back slouched in a leather swivel chair.

"Oh, hello there. Come in, child. Don't be afraid."

The office was simple, the massive desk conquered half the room, occupied by stack after stack of manila files, with more stuffed in black filing cabinets against the high walls. A panoramic window behind the desk looked out onto the void through diamond-checkered glass. Norman walked inside and wracked his brain for something to say to the Father-all-powerful-Genius-of-Creation. There was an awkward and extended pause.

"Nice door," he said finally.

"Thanks." God said. He swung his feet off the desk, knocking off some files onto the floor. "You must be Marcus, am I right or am I right?"

Norman stopped, thought, and tried to remember his name, which he knew wasn't Marcus. Why did that name sound so familiar? He briefly recalled something about a hole and a cat with a shiny collar, but he couldn't flush out the memory, as it often is when one travels thousands of fathoms in less than a heartbeat.

"No, I'm Norman, sir."

"Which one of us is omniscient here, Marcus?" God chuckled, playfully swiveling side to side in his chair. "You must be a bit confused. But I assure you, everything is okay. Except that you're dead." God said, smiling and swiveling. "Well, you must have a lot of questions, having just died and all. Take a seat."

Norman sat down in a tiny red chair, which was no more than two feet high. He twiddled his fingers like a misfit who'd been sent to the principal's office. He shivered. A draft. It's a chilly, he thought. Probably from being so high and mighty.

"I am God, as you must already know, though you can call me the Father-all-powerful-Genius-of-Creation if you'd like. That's how everybody addresses me up here anyway. I've never been much for grandiose titles, but who am I to complain?" God said. "I bet you're wondering how I created such a beautiful, flawless universe of infinite splendor."

Norman looked up from his fiddling at the Almighty. "Not really, but—"

"That's all right, most people are too nervous to ask," God pressed on. "It really is a funny story. You see, I was just sitting here... of course, this was before I created this chair, desk, room and whatnot... anyway, I was sitting... or was I standing? Yes, that's right... I was standing in the midst of nothingness because, of course, something hadn't been created yet. I was just sitting..."

"Standing," Norman corrected.

God glared wildly. "How would you know? You weren't there... or were you? No, you weren't there, because nothing was still nothing. Can I continue with my story?"

"Sure. Go ahead."

"Now, where was I... okay, I was standing amidst nothingness when I started to think, 'Hey if I exist why isn't there anything else which exists?' So I mused on that for a bit, contemplating myself and everything and then thought, 'What if,' those are the magic words, I'm telling you, 'What if something existed instead of nothing?' Then straight out of the blue, or nothingness or whatever, something existed. I forget what it was... Oh yeah, this weird flaming rock. Well, I was content with me and this rock of fire, existing together, heck of a thing to look at it, let me tell you, this colossal flaming rock, but as you could imagine, rocks aren't very good conversationalists. So I say to myself, 'God,' that's me, 'What if something else existed that could carry a decent conversation, or at least make idle chit chat.' So again, bing bang boom, I create a fish. The grandest fish the universe had ever seen, or the first at least."

So I chatted with this fish for an eternity or so, and he had some wonderful ideas about what I should do with my newfound powers. He talked of space dimensions and cosmic energy through which an outer universe could be constructed. A genius after my own heart. He suggested that this universe be shaped like a giant fish, but I told him about my ideas of an infinite void for the self-expansion of the cosmos, and he seemed to dig it.

So we arrived at a mutual agreement for how this universe

of ours was to be created, or universes I should say. We took the concepts of space, energy, matter and lit up the void with a big bang from which a cosmic multiverse could extrapolate. Once creation had begun, I added minor direction here and there. The duplicity of light, the sanctity of water, more rocks, life and the evolution kick, which guaranteed plenty of fish to appease my fishy friend.

And that was that. I set myself up in this celestial palace and made heaven, hell, purgatory, and the trivia of life. And that's how I keep myself occupied these days. The game of life is endlessly entertaining."

He swiveled around in his chair to face the window behind the desk. Diamonds of stained glass made everything queerly distorted outside.

"Come here. Don't be afraid of little old me," God said, motioning for him to come closer. Norman stood up and went to his side. God tapped on the window glass. "This, my friend, is the checkered pane of objectivity where I gaze with a watchful eye upon all my little creations. Through every diamond pane of glass, another immaculate universe to behold. Absolutely beautiful, isn't it?"

Norman nudged in beside the Almighty so he could peer out and beyond. At first, the darkness outside appeared empty and devoid of light. Looking closer, galaxies, stars, planets flashed into rapid orbit. Closer still, time slowed down, the blue marble of the Earth in focus. Focusing, the ocean and continents populated by a noise—a noise which he heard now, the fish in the sea, flocks of birds soaring across the Atlantic, the beavers gnawing at logs, panthers in the jungle and the electronic hum coming from all the tiny lights shining back. Behind those lights, the human civilization, he could feel it, its beating heart, a unified pulse of love and compassion disrupted by pangs of fear and greed.

For the first time in his entire conscious existence, it sunk in. It was no boast nor exaggeration of the Creator. The universe was beautiful, life was beautiful, the reaches and depths and fathoms of infinity were beautiful. He smiled, God smiled, because they knew it was good.

"But I've been talking too much. Anyway, talk, my boy, talk," God said with his arm slung over his shoulder. "So how do you like the afterlife so far? Is this one heck of a good time or what?"

"Very nice."

"Nice?"

"I mean peaceful. It's kind of cold but still pleasant."

"Oh, well, my apologies," God said. "I get a bit fed up with all the complaints, you know. 'Oh no, my hair's falling off,' 'Oh no, I lost my job,' 'Oh woe is me, my son died in a car crash and my sister was eaten alive by vultures,' 'Dear God, how could you be so cruel?' Really. Give me a break. I work my ass off day in and day out to keep the world from falling apart, and this is the thanks I get? What a bunch of whiners! I give them the miracle of life and all they do is complain about how bumpy the ride is."

Norman wandered back to his seat so that God would have some room to vent.

"And the prayers. Night after night, listening to these people prattle on about the weather and their dying mothers and may their dinner parties be ever successful..."

His body gave an involuntary shiver. The Almighty turned with an icy stare.

"You gotta admit it is chilly in here," Norman said. "It might be a draft coming from the window."

God let his anger rip through his holy larynx. "Would you rather it be broiling hot? I can arrange that."

He pushed aside the clutter on his desk—nifty trinkets, bobbles, cards, dice among scattered files—till he found what he was looking for. There, in the middle of the muddle, an oversized red button protruded with one bold black word on it: HELL. His hand hovered over the button. He stopped short of pressing it when Norman's eyes widen with a childish look of fear.

God chuckled again. "You are a funny little man."

"I wasn't complaining," Norman said.

"Oh, I know, I know," God smirked. "So tell me about yourself. Tell me about your life."

"There's not much to say, really," Norman said. "I lived well, I think, for my short time on the planet. I did my best to keep myself amused and not get upset about much."

"And your mother? You were kind to your mother, yes?"

"Oh, yes. I was kind of weird as a kid, eating paste and counting stars, though I don't think it bothered her. My father was an engineer, worked long hours…"

God's fingers did a little dance across the messy desk.

"…once we went to this fair in Sonoma…"

"You've never committed adultery, have you?"

"Never married, although I once kissed this girl Miranda by the pond in fourth grade…"

"Good." God arched an amused eyebrow. "Ever steal anything? Rob old ladies? Maybe filch a six-pack from a convenience store?"

"Oh no, I wouldn't," Norman said and stumbled over the words when the memories bobbed back. "… Never. Not that I recall, at least. A lot happens in a life."

"Never…" God said. "Never killed anyone, did you?"

"Kill anyone? Of course not."

"Not even a dog perhaps?"

A flood of memories hit Norman like a sledgehammer to the forehead. The car, the road, the black labrador, teatime with the time traveler.

"Never hit a dog with your car?" God asked. "Maybe it ran out into the road. Maybe you couldn't swerve away in time?"

"No…" Norman sweated. "Wait a minute here. That was Addie."

"Addie, huh? And who is Addie? You never chopped down any crab apple trees in Mr. Thompson's orchard then, did you? I supposed that was someone else, too."

"Hey now, that was Marcus. I was only pushing the tree so it would fall the other way."

"Marcus? Yes, of course. Marcus. Who you are not, right?" God's hand lingered near the HELL button. "And what about chasing a poor innocent cat down a well? You're going to deny that one, too, are you?"

Out of nowhere, a black and white cat hopped onto the desk, weaved through the stacks of files, and nuzzled the shoulder of the Father-all-powerful-Genius-of-Creation.

The cat meowed as God petted its fur.

"Is this the guy?" he asked.

The cat narrowed its yellow eyes on the visitor, then flared its tail and hissed wildly.

"Yes. That was my fault," Norman said. "But hold on, you've got everything mixed up."

"It seems like you have quite a record, Marcus or Addie or Norman or whoever you think you are." God retrieved a manila folder from the stack of files. "Must I go on?"

"Wait, please God. Hear me out."

"You see, there's no need to hear you out," God said, flipping open the file and running his finger over the facts. "I know everything you are going to say or ever could say in your defense. And besides you've already said enough."

The Almighty looked Norman sternly in his eyes. He narrowed his brow, his hand positioned over the button of damnation.

"Goodbye, Marcus. Ta, ta. And please don't scream for mercy, because frankly I don't have much left and I certainly wouldn't waste it on the likes of you… dog killer."

God pounded the red button with his fist like a judge at the gavel. In response, the mouth of Hell tore open underneath the tiny red chair, igniting its wooden legs as it collapsed through the burning floor, devouring the chair and its occupant in a sloppy lap of fiery tongues.

CHAPTER NINE

The Clockwork

It was the end of the workday and Anderson Boulevard, which cut south at a right angle through the commercial district toward the heart of the Republic, was busy with the rush-hour bustle. Wary of the congested sky, the Heroes, Saints, and Smiths strolled down the boulevard under umbrellas, in the shadows of the towering offices and shops selling wares from the Great Factory. The Saints, free from their ties and labcoats, walked side by side with the Smiths, hair greased and fingers black under the nails with factory grime. The day-shift Heroes, stiff and upright, marched down the road on leave for their eight hours of R&R, still armed and suspicious of everyone.

Zander watched the people pass from a narrow side street outside the café. Everyone appeared much the same out of their work clothes. The men wore blue wool peacoats, top hats, and grey slacks. The women were dressed in flowing skirts, their fair hair wagging all the way down to their hips like horse tails, never to be cut, a symbol of the Republic's prosperity. The citizens strutted along in uniform stride, chatting with their neighbors and unwinding their pocket watches on occasion to check the time. Happy for another day done, another step forward. Clomp, clomp. Tick, tick.

Through the umbrella parade, Zander spotted Weber on the opposite side of boulevard. They converged onto the road and met in the middle of the bustling crowd.

"Good to see you, old friend," Weber said, moving along with the pedestrian traffic.

"And you as well," Zander said. "Busy day."

"Indeed," Weber said. "Believe it or not, we're safer talking out here than in our old haunts, I'm afraid. Much has changed since you've been gone."

The sun, diffused through the gauzy sky, shimmered off the boulevard bricks and gilded the road ahead. The commercial district in every sense had the feel of the post-modern metropolises that lay in ruin outside the city walls, from the flat red streets to the steel buildings that jetted into the sky, to neon messages that scrolled across high-rise sheets of black glass.

Zander felt like a child, marveling at the sloping boulevard and streamlined architecture with new eyes. Everything that had once seemed commonplace, now seemed alien. How small such a place could make one feel? He gazed up at the staggered heights of the plemetic buildings that pressed the boulevard and climbed like stairs into the cloudy sky. Their cold windows reflected green in the dim sunlight, blue in the shade. Electrical conduit pillars fortified their sides, aligned across the boulevard as the road traversed through the commercial sector.

"Has Phaedrus been behaving himself?" Zander asked.

"More or less. He has his moments of idiocy. There's been more talk, too much talk," Weber said. "It's evident they know of us by now. They don't know who we are, that's clear, but they know of us."

"But that's the way we've always wanted it. Or am I mistaken?"

"Yes and no. We've always wanted a presence. The difference is we've only wanted them to know, what we want them to know. Nothing more, nothing less. Rumors pass down these dusty streets like garbage rolling in the gutter."

They descended the hill with the parade. The skies broke over the umbrellas in showers, the grey thinning but never dissipating as the clouds swelled over the city. The skytrack hummed overhead, on which monorail trams looped from one sector to the next.

At the bottom of the hill, a canal separated the gleaming

high-rises from the Old Quarter across the bridge, where the citizens of the Republic headed en route home. The remnants of pre-war monuments on the other side had been grafted in new stone and steel. The scarred faces of former plazas, arcade markets, and municipal buildings had been given a polished look. Crows cawed from atop the old churches charred all the way to the top of their steeples, evidence of the inferno that had once consumed the city in a high fire.

To think back from then until now—from ruin to civilization, from darkness to the lampposts that spotted every city block, the cubbyhole storefronts, the seamless stonewalls and steel towers, the arabesques that graced the crescent buttresses and arches, so small, so intricate, as though they had been etched by children's hands—it all seemed a bona fide miracle.

Here was a civilization that had reinvented man—as if one could separate the man from the monolith—that had risen from the ashes, triumphant. That had trudged stone, rebuilt cities, reestablished and reinvented itself. That had seen the end, shivered through the plague, carried mankind from the brink of extinction. That had vanquished the demons of old society and persevered against all odds, only to be reborn, eternal immortal, forever amen.

And here they came. The progeny of the blessed, citizens proper of the Republic, marching to the beat of the rain pitter-pattering on their umbrellas. Electronic chimes jingled whenever they would dip in and out of the little shops and boutiques. Blinking animations played over and over on the digigraph awnings, a chopping butcher's knife for the meat market, a pair of scissors for the barber, the figure of a lady curtseying for the dress shop.

The ground quaked when another tram passed over the boulevard, through a gap between twin high-rises. In its wake, Zander felt oddly displaced. He continued searching for something that would reconnect him with his past, in the shop windows, in the bright faces of the young, of the old, of the women with their painted smiles and the proud men, and then back to Weber, his oldest friend, but nothing could deliver him to his former self.

The more he searched, the more he felt disjointed. It was a feeling he knew all too well, augmented now by time and proximity. He'd thought that, upon his return, he would regain the vigor he'd lost when he pulled that trigger three years ago, a rite of passage punctuated by the shot. He'd assumed he would once again be charged by the passion, the conviction that had driven him to forsake his peaceful life for a fool's dream. A dream of the Republic undone.

Maybe it had always been this way, he thought. Maybe he had joined the resistance for the sake of drama itself. Perhaps it was out of boredom, and not altruism, that he fantasized revolution.

How plain the Republic seemed, how colorless. It was like a black 'n' white schematic of life contained. During his time at the Offices of Past Parlance, he often read of "zoos" and how captive animals adapted to their artificial habitats. The citizens of the Republic were no different in his opinion. Cattle fed and cattle bred. Yet to look at their faces, it was as if they knew no greater joy than to do what was asked of them. It rosied their cheeks, quickened their gait.

"Where's Leyna?" Zander asked. "I'd expected her to be with you."

"We don't know," Weber said and left the statement to linger.

"What's that supposed to mean?"

"She had an argument with Phaedrus about a week ago and we haven't seen her since. But you know how they get along. She'll be back."

"You think she's betrayed us."

"No, no, listen to me. No one thinks that," Weber said, though he could tell by Zander's expression how transparent the lie was. "Sure, some people said a few things in the heat of the moment. But you must understand the pressure we've been under. Since you left, there's been a slow unraveling. We've all been awaiting your return."

"As well you should have been," Zander said. He could sense there was more to the story of Leyna's vanishing act than what he'd been told. He swiftly dropped the subject when a passing Saint tipped his top hat and squeezed by along the boulevard, along its final approach to the riverbank of the canal.

Obelisk posts fenced the canal bridge into the Old Quarter and its grand plaza, Concord Square. Between these posts, armed guardians in regal grey uniforms stood sentry on the bridge, still as statues, unmoved by the rainy-day parade. Their surveillance was aided by the Orbservers, the mechanical watchers of the Republic. The spherical drones zoomed by on patrol over the canal, over the crowded bridge, scanning retinas.

Zander and Weber hung close and moved under the cover of umbrellas.

"I don't like this at all," Weber muttered half to himself, half to Zander, once they were safely past the guardians. "Too much activity today."

"There was a man on the train," Zander began. "A Hero, a supervisor of energies, or so he said. He asked a lot of questions."

"What about?"

"About nothing in particular. But the whole interrogation was rather odd. He had a queer look in his eyes, as though he were hunting for some hidden meaning in my answers."

"There have been too many strange happenings lately. It doesn't bode well."

Once on the opposite side of the canal, they made their way through Concord Square, where stages for tomorrow's festivities were being raised. Smiths punched in nails, fastened bolts, and secured the planks with remarkable speed and precision. Others dressed the platforms with garland, colored bands, and pennant flags, while teams of Saints negotiated how to wire the electronic video screens that would broadcast the Centennial tournament throughout the Republic.

At the eastern end of the square, an audience had gathered under their umbrellas to watch the tick-tock of a clocktower that chinned out from the high gothic walls. Three concentric circles traced the clock's face. Six hands pointed in disparate directions to record the year—the month, the day, the hour, the minutes and all the ticks in between. A colossal pendulum drooped underneath the clock face like a wagging tail and swung over an arched passageway that led into Kensington Plaza. Through the archway, the Arch of Truth could be seen, and beyond it, the canal bridges surrounding the Citadel.

Saint Benedict, founder of the Republic, had been amazed to find the clocktower still standing amongst the rubble when he and his scientists came probing the dust after the Antiac War. He had interpreted its survival as a sign, that time goes on just as life goes on. In the face of war and pestilence, the pendulum still swings, strikes the petal, turns the gear, turns the crank, moves the thin hand, the long hand, the short. Every internal twitch working toward the movement of Time. During the Plemetic Reconstruction, he'd ordered the clocktower be secured as a centerpiece in the acropolis of his new republic, a statement of undying devotion to the forward evolution of society for *he who observes time observes the progression of mankind.*

As the six o'clock hour approached, excitement buzzed through the crowded square. Everyone counted down the seconds with their necks craned back, galvanized under the tick tock trance. And what were they waiting for? Why did the loyal citizens of the Republic flock every evening to hear the clocktower chime as the crows cawed from the ramparts?

The truth was they were waiting for the clock to stop. No matter how practiced their smiles, they all secretly humored the same dark thoughts. A skepticism paired with an obtuse guilt for having survived. They waited to see if, in a single stroke, their great Republic would be swiped from them like some ethereal dream.

Zander stared up at the clocktower with Weber by his side in the crowd, and wondered why these people who fashioned themselves as the embodiment of reason would choose to live by superstition. These people who rose by the buzzer—never before and not a second after—and slept by the pill; who combed their hair, shined their shoes, waxed their ears with immaculate precision; who calculated passing numbers in their head to make sure they didn't add up to 13; who scrubbed their fingernails over and over, afraid the slightest speck of dirt was the germ of the next plague waiting.

It was truly a madness, swinging as the pendulum swung, between neurosis and utter bliss, between moments of unbearable friction and the indescribable joy of connection when the numbers fit, when their collective movement became a fluid ballet, when the clocks chimed on the hour, always on the hour.

A thrilling hush settled over Concord Square as the minute hand quivered a notch before twelve. It trembled like a drunkard's unsteady hand, then twitched forward. Bong. Bong. Bong. Bong. Bong. Bong...

CHAPTER TEN

Ashes of Time

It weighs upon one. The hours that pass, unmeasured, unchanging. Dead time. Dead as the dunes that undulated to every horizon. Still as the black eternal night of the cold desert. Overwhelmed by the stark infinity of endless dunes and endless ash, Addie felt as though she were sinking, as if the farther she walked, the deeper she waded, soon to be buried up to her neck and become a dune herself.

Barefoot and broken, she dragged her toes slowly through the bonedust, over the ashen dunes. Her legs had liquefied long ago; the muscles turned to jelly. The dry desert air tasted like wallpaper. Her throat felt like a sawmill. The thought of water made her tongue tired.

It had been more than seven hours since she'd last seen the black horse, and with every passing minute, her psyche unraveled another loop. East had changed West without any warning several hundred dunes ago, and to make matters worse, her compass would spin wildly every time the wind would surge or whenever the giant Eye would blink in the starless sky. Still, she was determined to beat the desert at its own game, whatever that game was. She'd given up trying to measure the distance traveled and instead began looking for paranormal signs in ash, patterns in the dunes, traces of the Eye to navigate by. Which is why she'd ripped off the sleeves of her turtleneck to draw a map of the desert in black ash on her forearm. In short, she'd gone completely nuts.

I must stop counting, she thought. It knows I'm counting. Perhaps the compass was a trick, put there to throw me off course. It surely hadn't done its previous owner much good. Maybe if she started digging... Maybe there were trap doors underneath the ash... yes... trap doors that Wally was trying to lead her to… She couldn't have been wandering aimlessly all this time. There must be some undiscovered purpose. This was destined to happen. She was getting somewhere. She simply needed to follow the map.

A sudden gust of wind swirled the ash into a dusty storm. The compass went haywire again. Addie accordingly drew an X southeast of her wrist and tried to make sense of the pattern on her forearm, which now resembled a doomed game of tic-tac-toe. She laughed at this, laughed in manic desperation, laughed out at the never-ending desert and huge dunes ahead. She laughed as the wind howled in ghostly shrieks. And then she felt a light at her back.

"What do you want from me?!?" she turned and yelled at the Eye, which had once again torn a halo of infernal light in the night sky, shining its radiance down upon her. The compass twirled until the needle struck North again, pointing at the blinding apparition. She held the compass into the fierce light, not sure what to expect, its circular shape eclipsed the fiery stare.

"Is this what you want? Is it?" She dropped onto her knees and dug into desert with her bare hands, deeper and deeper, trying to heave out the black sand quicker than it could slump in. She buried the compass in the ash. "You can have it. Good riddance."

The storm died down. The voices in the ash died down. A garbled sea shanty murmured in the calm, as if in a lullaby:

> *Dum de dum… gruesome fate…*
> *… dum de dum de dum…*
> *Dum de dum… rusted sword…*
> *… dum de dum de dum…*

Addie cursed at the buried compass, "Shut up, Wally."

> *Years and years… dum de dum…*
> *… sailed the lonesome seas…*
> *Never lost a fight… dum de dum…*

... weakened in the knees...

"Quiet, Wally. Shut up, shut up. SHUT UP." When she turned toward the sky for guidance, the Eye had already vanished. She rose from her knees in horror. "No! Come back and show me the way. I'm ready."

> *Dum de dum... drink and swear...*
> *... dum de dum de dum...*
> *Dum de dum... caught in the sway...*
> *... dum de dum de dum...*
> *Dum de dum... ... rued the day...*
> *... dum de dum de dum...*
> *... fate of... dum de dum de dum...*

The song was coming from somewhere else, she realized. She chased after the song, up the spine of a dune that seemed to climb and climb forever into the starless firmament. The horse, she thought, of course, the goddamn horse had returned. But why was it singing?

When she reached the dune's summit, she adjusted her broken glasses and realized that she'd been fooled. There was no singing horse, there never was, she could see now. Rather, what she'd believed to be a horse showed itself as simply two men carrying a rectangular box.

Addie crouched behind the dune crest and observed from afar as they passed by. The men wore the same drab costume, white collars and white cuffs peeked out from black sweater-vests, black slacks, bowler hats tipped on their heads. A coffin swaggered between them. Maybe they're morticians? she thought. This must be a sign. Even if it were all an illusion, even if they disappeared into the dust, this must be a sign. The Eye was trying to show her the way.

The mortician, who held up the front of the casket with his hands bent behind him, kept his head bowed in the somber march. The second mortician, who buoyed the rear with one hand while sipping from a canteen with the other, jerked forward when he walked due to the dead weight of a peg leg. He sang this shanty out into the empty desert as they plodded along:

> *"Oh now the gruesome fate*
> *of old poor Johnny Voord...*
> *Took them down one by one*
> *with his rusted sword...*
> *For years and years,*
> *he sailed across the lonesome seven seas...*
> *Never lost a fight, took a smite,*
> *never weakened in the knees...*
> *Would drink and swear and spit and slit*
> *Until the early morn...*
> *But in that fey caught in the sway,*
> *he rued the day that he was born...*
> *Oh now the gruesome fate*
> *of old poor Johnny Voord..."*

It was pure torture to watch the singing mortician drink from the canteen between verses. Addie could almost taste the cool water on her tongue, almost feel it wet the inside of her dust-covered mouth and trickle down her scratchy throat. The sensation was so painfully visceral that her thirst soon became unbearable.

"Ho there!" the singing mortician cried out when he spotted Addie running toward them in a blind puff of soot, "Stay where you are! Fie, fie, keep back! Francis, recite your mumbo-jumbo!"

"It looks like a girl, Gulliver," Francis said.

"I can see that, Francis," Gulliver said. "That don't mean she ain't dangerous."

Addie arrived, hot-faced and out of breath, and threw herself at the morticians' feet.

"And who are you?" Gulliver barked at her.

"Looks like a live one," Francis said.

"You never can tell, never can tell. Who are you? Come on, speak."

But Addie could only pant and drool and jab at the canteen in the mortician's hand.

"What is it? You dumb or something?" Gulliver tipped another drink. "You want a sip, do you? Well, I suppose you've earned it if you're out here."

The mortician handed the canteen over. Addie clasped her hands around the cool metal, pressed it to her lips, and gagged at the sickly sweet taste that coated her throat.

"Aghh, that's not water."

"Well now. She does speak," Gulliver said. "No, m'lady. That's wine. Now would you mind giving back my canteen?"

"You're drinking? Are you crazy?"

"No, I'm drunk actually. We're in mourning, you see?" Gulliver rapped on the coffin.

"But how…" Addie said. "Where did you come from? Is there a town nearby? Where'd you get those hats?"

"We came…" Gulliver said with an absent gaze toward the starless sky. He thought hard on the question, and then decided not to answer it. "…We came from far away."

"How far and where are you going?"

"We could ask you the same question, but I think the answer would be just as unsatisfactory," the mortician said. "Let's just say we've come to bury an old friend. I'm Gulliver and this is Francis. Say hello, Francis."

Francis studied Addie up and down with disinterest. "We really don't have time for this."

"Oh don't be silly. We have as much time as there is bone in the ash," Gulliver said and then noticed the pattern drawn on Addie's bare forearm. "Ah, that looks like a treasure map. Are you hunting for treasure, m'lady?"

"I'm hunting for a way out of here," Addie said. "I'm… a little lost."

"So are we, to be honest. Not lost, per se. Just wandering. Searching for something, you see? Searching for a proper place to bury our dead captain here, Johnny Voord. An old soul as they say, but ah well, ah well. *Oh now the gruesome fate of old poor Johnny Voord,*" Gulliver sang wistfully. "Walk with us if you'd like."

The somber march resumed across the cold desert. The morticians brooded, one in song, one in silence. A swig of the canteen, a shed of a tear.

"*Oh now the gruesome fate of old poor Johnny Voord... Took them down one by one with his rusted sword...*"

Addie didn't know what to say. She still wasn't certain if the morticians were real or if she were suffering from another delusional episode. Nevertheless, it felt good to have company, even the company of two morticians and a corpse.

She wondered how long they'd been carrying the casket. It looked heavy, a lovely carve of oak with twin handles on either side and two on the head and foot. A shovel lay strapped on top, bound several times over with rope. Where had they come from? she wondered. And how did they end up parading this coffin across the vast expanse of ash?

She dared not ask any questions, though. Death, after all, is a sensitive subject.

"Life..." Gulliver began, "Life is something more than the obvious. A spark in the eye, a skip in the step. Warm blood, you know? Many die many times before their final day of rest. But not old Johnny. He lived like few knew how. Yes, he was mean, often uncouth and unkempt, you must be to sail the unchartered waters. The open sea weathers a man like nothing else. Johnny commanded the universe, arched leg up on the bow with a scowl and a smile. And when he hollered with the hoarse wind, you had to leap to life. Oh Johnny, forgive us. Forgive us for our lack of fire."

Gulliver spat at the sand and made a sign of the cross. The

funeral procession continued across the desert.

"*Oh now the gruesome fate of old poor Johnny Voord. Took them down one by one with his rusty sword. Would drink and swear and spit and slit until the early morn. But in that fey caught in the sway, he rued the day that he was born.*" Gulliver sang sweetly maudlin. "Poor Johnny. You know how he died? How he met his grizzly end?"

Addie shook her head.

"Well, it be a long tale, though I'll keep it brief," the mortician told him. "Old Johnny Voord came from nothing, a bastard child of poverty and ill circumstance. He took to the sea one day as a deck swabber for the notorious Captain Wheelock, the sort of captain who would toss a sailor into the choppy waters if he didn't like the look in your eye.

"For years, he sailed under Wheelock, pillaging and swashbuckling and the like, till that fateful night hunting for the treasure of Sid Righteous. Legend had it that the treasure was buried somewheres on Robins Island, though no one knew exactly what it was, only rumors of a hidden cave filled with chests of gold bullion, jewels, pearls, sapphires, and diamonds by the plenty.

"Wheelock never lived to find out what the true treasure was. On the night before the Bobbing Bulfinch was to set shore on Robins Island, his first mate Randall Dreadknought decided he was tired of being second in command and cold-murdered the captain in his sleep, dumping his corpse overboard.

"There were no witnesses to the fact. Dreadknought told the crew the next morning that Wheelock had tumbled off the starboard trying to fix a bridle. But that story didn't wash with Johnny Voord, no surey. It stank foul and Johnny had a keen sense for the smell of mutiny. Dead set in his convictions, he challenged Dreadknought to a duel in Wheelock's honor. When he declined, Johnny did what any respectable sailor would do. He lassoed a rope round Dreadknought's neck, hoisted him up the mast till he confessed to the crime, and then snapped it with a yank. Johnny never was much of the forgiving kind.

"Johnny Voord became captain of the Bobbing Bulfinch without any squabbles. He was hard to please, but kind to his crew when he so chose. There was liquor at every port and a lot of it, all provided by their gracious captain. There were few complaints and those complaints there were, Johnny would patiently listen to the whiner before cutting out their tongue. He never did return to Robins Island in search of Righteous's treasure. That was Wheelock's dream which Johnny left untouched for him to fancy in his sleep of death."

Lost in the fish tale, Addie walked alongside the pirates-turned-morticians as they escorted the coffin through the desert. The canteen passed back and forth while Gulliver regaled her with Voord's adventures on the high seas. This will make the time fly by, she thought, I'm sure this guy has a thousand stories. We'll just go bury the body and then off home, wherever that is. She hoped they wouldn't need her help… she would politely refuse if they asked. No harm done.

For the moment, she fell at ease. The liquor, it seemed, was slowly starting to bring her back to her senses, or at least dumb the panic receptors in her brain.

"…Voord had a way of sleeping with his eyes open and would often dose off behind the rudder wheel for days without anyone noticing. But never did he stray course, not once, tearing through storms, shallow waters, Royal Navy fleets with cannonballs flying," Gulliver said. "And all went swimmingly for seventeen years about the seven seas until the day that Johnny Voord met the North wind of Lessex. It was a dark and terribly stormy night. Johnny had spent from sunrise to sunset surveying the angry waters. Soon it grew so dark, he couldn't tell between crag of rock or crest of wave. That is, until his ship collided with black stony death.

"The blow breached the hull and the Bobbing Bulfinch began to flood. Johnny scuttled about from bow to stern, from drowning belly to crow's nest. He cursed the stormy deep and growled at his crew to scully the water out faster, faster. But with the ship topsy-turvy at the mercy of the sea, the crew could barely stand, let alone save the ship from sinking. Then in a moment of dangerous clarity, Voord had a solution. 'Pull closer and drop anchor,' he ordered. The crew did as he bid. They knew better than to argue with the captain, even if they knew their lives were in danger.

"So the leaking Bobbing Bulfinch pulled up to the rock that had struck it minutes before, and on the captain's word, the crew heaved the anchor off into the dark waters. The ship reeled back when the anchor hit bottom, lurched forward when the gales battered the sail with a vengeance. The crew wheeled in the chain and held it taut to restrain the ship from another scrape as the Bobbing Bulfinch whipped side to side like a mad dog on a leash."

Francis stopped fast and brought the march to a halt.

"Here," he said and pointed at the desert floor. There, out of the ash, a chrysanthemum had mysteriously grown in a pale bloom of yellowish green. The morticians laid down the coffin for a closer look.

"Do you think it's a sign?"

"A sign? Bloody hell, it's a sign." Gulliver stroked its tentacle petals. "I'll be damned."

"We all are," Francis said. He flicked out a knife, bent over the coffin, and cut loose the shovel, "Shall we?"

"We shall," Gulliver said.

"Do you need a hand?" Addie asked.

Francis thrust the shovelhead into the ash. "Oh we need much more than that."

Gulliver swiftly hit him with the flask.

"Ouch, damn you."

"Quit your whining and start digging."

"Why do I have to dig?"

"Cause I'm talking to the girl," Gulliver said.

Francis looked as if to protest, then resigned. He grumbled under his breath as he made his first dent in the desert.

"Where was I?" Gulliver asked the wind and dunes. "Ah yes... the Bobbing Bulfinch was thrashing like a mad dog in the storm, tethered to the guts of the sea by its anchor. Without a flinch of fear, Johnny Voord ventured out onto the wagging bow with a lug of rope over his shoulder. In a leap of sheer courage, he hopped onto the crag so he could tie off the ship. He bore wind and wave, frantically looping and tightening the rope. Once the Bulfinch was secure, he braced himself to jump back, waiting for that exact moment when the ship would swing in front of the rock. But alas, the waves were quicker than his feet and off they lashed him into the cold hungry sea.

"The crew rushed to the starboard and hung their heads over the rail to search the choppy waters for any sign of their captain. Just when they'd judged him as dead and drowned, Voord roared out of the sea, hoisting himself up the slack from the rope he'd tied off to the crag.

"The crew watched in disbelief as their captain climbed onto the bow of the ship, screaming profanities and taunting the ocean at the top of his lungs. He heaved himself over the rail, and collapse there on the deck, surrounded by his crew, shivering and spitting and yelling, 'It will take more than that to kill old Johnny Voord.' He then felt weak and held out his hand for help. But no one offered him a finger. 'Help me up, ya bastards,' he scorned, but then he got a good gander in their eyes. Cold as the ill-tempered sea.

"His first mate Caleb answered his request by drawing a blade and snapping his fingers to the rest of the crew. Mutiny. They'd had enough, you see. Enough of the mad conquests, the endless days at sea in search of phantom treasures. The crew held poor Johnny Voord to the slippery deck and bound his hands, tied a length of rope to his ankles and carried him to the plank.

"With the waves slapping the boards and the swaying Bobbing Bulfinch anchored by the rock yonder and the hook undersea, Johnny was told to give his last words. 'May God spare no mercy on your souls,' he'd said. They then slit his throat and shoved him off. For three long hours, the wails of poor Johnny Voord could be heard howling with the wind as he dangled upside down by his feet, bleeding the last drops of life into the open sea. And when the moans finally died out, they cut him loose to bob forever on the lonesome waters. Oh now the gruesome fate of old poor Johnny Voord."

An involuntary tear trickled down Gulliver's cheek at this point in the story. He paused to wipe it and then continued.

"And so you understand now why we are mourning. We were two in the crew of Johnny Voord, just boys though. There was nothing we could do to stop the mutiny. Caleb waited the storm out, anchored to the silt and tethered to the rock, while we patched up the ship, then sailed the Bobbing Bulfinch to the nearest shore.

Francis and I never took to the sea again after that. I became a scholar of sorts and Francis here became a priest. As it turned out, Caleb never sailed again as well, for two days after we returned to harbor at Van Dyke, he got his skull cracked wide with quarter bottle of Skunk's whistle in a bar brawl."

"Tragic," Addie said.

"Yes. A tragedy for sure," Gulliver said. "And so it is that we have come so very far to put poor Johnny to rest."

"But that still doesn't explain how you ended up here? And how…" It was the sight of a hammer snug in Gulliver's belt that then alarmed Addie. Who needs a hammer in a desert? It just didn't make sense. And because it seemed so unneeded, its presence, hanging at the pirate's hip, somehow immediately seemed suspect.

"How if…" She started again trying to form the thought and found the wine had made her drowsy. Staring at the coffin, she stumbled upon a serious knot in the fish tale. "If… if the body washed out to sea, then what's in the coffin?"

"You are quick, m'lady. I'll grant you that," Gulliver said. "Have a look for yourself."

Addie weighed her curiosity with grave trepidation. Surely, this is some sick joke, she thought, it's obvious these morticians have a depraved sense of humor. She kneeled down beside the casket to open it.

Francis held his shovel at attention. "Are you mad? What if he gets loose? We can't have him roaming about this confounded desert for all eternity. There'd be no getting him back."

"Oh don't be superstitious. Just keep digging," Gulliver said and put a hand on Addie's shoulder. "Go ahead, m'lady."

Addie lifted up the casket lid, ever so slowly, and peeked in. Empty. An empty bed of red velvet. "There's nothing in here."

"But of course there is. Look at it," Gulliver said with a widening grin. "It's a soul, and not just any soul… the soul of old poor Johnny Voord."

Addie slammed the casket shut.

"What do you think about the girl?" Gulliver asked the pirate priest.

Francis heaved aside another shovelful of ash, "Do we have much choice?"

"That's what I thought."

Addie stayed kneeled beside the coffin, even though her every instinct begged her to run. Her bones tried to shake themselves out of her skin. The hairs on her head tried desperately to shoot out of her scalp and be saved. But her legs wouldn't move, her muscles frozen in terror.

"There done," Francis said. He tossed down his shovel and wiped his forehead, triumphant beside a shallow grave.

"That was quick work. You think it's deep enough?"

"If you want it any deeper, you're welcome to dig yourself."

"No, that'll do splendid," Gulliver said and then gestured to Addie. "Stand up."

Addie could do nothing more than obey.

"No need to be frightened." Gulliver cupped a hand under her chin. "I just want to have a look at you." The peg-legged pirate pawed at Addie's cheeks, and with his grubby thumbs, pried open the lids to gaze steadily into those eyes searching, searching...

"Just as I suspected." Gulliver broke off and stepped away. "Vacant."

"Vacant?" Francis repeated. "You're kidding me."

"Null and void, not a wisp in these eyes, my friend." Gulliver took a swig of wine from the canteen, his smile waning.

Addie slinked away, her body wooden stiff with fear. "What's going on here? What's this all about?"

"Heaven and earth, m'lady. Every soul needs a body," Gulliver said. "And every coffin a corpse." The peg-legged pirate seized her arm and held her there. Addie's eyes flashed wide. She looked into the pirate's pudgy face, asking questions, all the questions her clinched throat could not ask.

"I'm dreadfully sorry, m'lady. What must be done, must be done. The dead know no mercy."

Two cold hands grappled onto her shoulders from behind.

"Help!" Addie cried out, struggling to free herself from their grip. She kicked blindly, clumsily, eyes clenched closed in a panicked attempt to conquer her fear, as the pirates wrestled her to the desert, knocking off her spectacles in the struggle.

She floundered, facedown in the ash, like a beached fish, crying and spitting and yelling with her mouth full of soot, kicking the black sand and flailing punches at her blurred, phantom attackers.

"There's no use. Seems we're all alone in the desert here," Francis said. "And don't pretend to cry. We know you have no soul."

"But I do. I swear! Let go of me, you lunatics. Help, HELP!" Addie shrieked and squirmed, lifted into the air by the pirates.

"Francis, get a tighter hold."

"I'm trying," Francis said, hauling Addie by the legs over to the coffin, "Stop wriggling, you squirmy lank. You think this is fun for us? We've been wandering this desert for a thousand years, waiting for this moment of absolution. Do you know what it's like to eat dust and listen to this imbecile drone on about the starless night? Do you think I ever wanted this? Do you think I chose this fate?"

"HELP!" Addie bawled, then choked back her tears when she felt a cold blade caress her throat.

"I wouldn't move if I were you," Gulliver said and gently pierced the tip of his knife into her neck. "I wouldn't even breathe.

CHAPTER ELEVEN

The Trial of Simon Smith

The boy shuffled his feet and fought to scratch an itch under the shackles on his ankles. The leftover charge of three electric shocks made his adolescent body tingle all over. Although he could hardly stand, he tried not to fidget too much, in fear he'd be shocked again. On both sides of the raised stage, the guardians waited with their microphazers charged and ready, miraculous devices which with one blast could throw a three-hundred-pound man onto the cobblestones and leave him there sweating, overheated to the point of incapacitation.

The guardians hoped they would not be required to use their side arms again that day, not out of compassion but because of the grotesque stench discharged from someone shot with a microwave burst at short range. They couldn't have cared less about the accused or the trial. Their feigned conviction in the day's trial was a tired ruse. They picked at their waxy ears and straightened their waistcoats while the young prisoner thought of the many different ways they might execute him. Such is the boredom of virtue.

Councilor Lloyd Saint ascended the short stairs onto the stage, greeted by thunderous applause. He spanned his arms in a silent gesture of embrace and let his red judicial gown drape like wings. A massive video screen projected his image behind the stage, twenty-feet tall, for those in the audience without a clear view and for those tuned into the broadcast from the comfort of their own homes. The applause crescendoed until the Councilor bowed his head to quell the audience, then lifted it again to speak.

"Citizens of the Republic, I come before you to present and bear witness to the just trial of one Simon Smith," Councilor

Lloyd said, starting low and raising his voice at emphasis, a voice that boomed from the speakers overhead. "As an autonomous commonwealth, we hold that certain actions, whether they be forethought or accidental, prey heavily upon the health of our society as a whole. It is for such actions, such injustices named by unspoken truths, that these charges have been brought forth for reconciliation on this day as dictated by the Law of Accord, 99.A.P.03. The charges are as follows..." he unraveled from his sleeve a scroll that dropped in length to the floorboards, "One forth, brought forth by hitherto unmentioned party, the charge of social malignance. Two count, under subhead, Derision of Truth and intent to spread ideas of an unpalatable nature."

Zander listened to the councilor's speech, entrenched in the crowd. He had lost sight of Weber when they came upon the trial in Kensington Plaza on the other side of the clocktower, and passing through, found himself swallowed into the audience. He'd pushed his way closer to the stage with everyone else, mesmerized by the trial underway, like flies drawn to a fresh corpse.

The young prisoner wrung his cuffed hands, careful not to touch the metal bands, when the Councilor approached and addressed him face to face, "Now, Simon, do you understand why we have brought you here today?"

"I understand why you call these trials, but I haven't done anything wrong."

"That is for the court to decide, Simon," Councilor Lloyd said. "We have brought you here to plead your case for the crime of social malignance, derision of said truths..."

"I don't know that word, sir."

"I will not have you interrupt during this trial. You will speak only when prompted," Councilor Lloyd scolded. "The truths to which you are being charged are these. Several of your brothers and sisters have raised alarm to certain things you have been saying. One of your peers specifically heard you singing a song of a perturbing nature, on the morning before the last yesterday. Would you mind singing that song again for the court?"

"I sing many songs, father. I honestly don't remember the one I sung the morning before the last yesterday."

"Let us refresh your memory then, shall we? It had to do with a certain Charlie Bean. Do you remember that one?"

"Yes, father."

"Could you perhaps sing it for us again?"

"Here?"

"Yes, here."

"I don't know if I can."

"Is that because it guilts you?" Councilor Lloyd raised an eyebrow to the audience.

"No, father. I'm nervous, that's all."

"Try if you could, Simon."

Simon summoned up the courage, cleared his throat, and recited his song:

> "*By the river stream, I heard him scream,*
>   *little Charlie Bean.*
> *He waded his feet, in the water too deep,*
>   *and so began to dream*
> *And as he started to sink, I heard him think...*
>   *In a turquoise world, nothing's pink.*
>   *And everything's not as it seems.*"

"Now Simon, who exactly is this Charlie Bean?"

"Dunno, I just made her up. Made the whole thing up. I do it all the time. You want to hear another?"

"So Charlie Bean doesn't exist?"

"No, I don't think so."

"And so you really didn't see her sink into the water, did you?"

"Of course not."

"Then why would you say you did?"

"It's only a funny little ditty. Makes no sense. It's not suppose to."

"So then you admit that the story is untrue?"

"Not untrue. Just not real."

"I fail to see the difference. Simon answer me this: if I were to tell you that your friend was drowning, would you not feel sad?"

"Naturally."

"And why?"

"Because I feel bad whenever a brother or sister is hurt or in pain of death."

"And when you are sad, do not your brothers and sisters feel for you in your sadness?"

"Yes, they do, as I for them."

"And when people are sad, are they not in a worse state than when they are happy?"

"Yes. Of course."

"Would you liken their worsened state to that of illness, which makes one sluggish and of bad temperament?"

"I would."

"And when one is ill, do they perform their work better or worse than if they are healthy?"

"Worse naturally. They are in a worse state."

"And that is because they are sluggish and of bad temperament?"

"I suppose."

"And if one man does not perform his duty and privilege in society, does not the whole of society suffer?"

"Yes, father."

"Then we are in agreement that by you singing what you believe to be an innocent silly song, you are, in fact, harming society by making your brothers and sisters ill with sadness for Charlie Bean."

"But Charlie Bean isn't real."

"Which brings us to our next point of contention, why would you say or sing of things that were not real?"

"Dunno, father."

"But don't you understand that your portrayal of something unreal as real is to speak falsehood."

"I guess."

"And when you speak falsehoods, do you realize that you are fooling your peers into believing something that is untrue? And when people believe in something untrue, are they better or worsened by their belief?"

"I dunno, father."

"Well, consider this: if I were to tell you that nourishment was bad for your health, would you not eat?"

"I suppose I wouldn't."

"And if you did not eat, would you not eventually become sickly?"

"I suppose I would."

"And if you disregarded my advice and ate and were nourished back to good health, how would you feel?"

"I would feel tricked."

"And if I gave you some similar advice later, would you believe me?"

"No, I would not."

"Then by speaking falsely, you instill disbelief in those peers who discover you have spoken falsely and lead those who believe you are speaking the truth into danger. Therefore by speaking falsely, do you not do harm to yourself and others?"

"Well, when you put it that way—"

"Now Simon, what really perturbs me is the nature of your song," Councilor Lloyd said to the young prisoner. "Take the last line of your little ditty, as you so fondly call it: *in a turquoise world, nothing's pink and everything is what it seems.* What exactly does that mean?"

"It means no thing, father. I just liked the way it sounds"

"But other people, could they not interpret your words in many ways and come to their own conclusions as to the meaning."

"But it don't mean anything."

"And if you were to explain that to them, or if they were to try to derive meaning out of something that has none, would they not feel confused, either as to the meaning or as to why you would say something of nonsense?"

"Yes, but father..."

"Please don't interrupt, I'm not finished. And when you confuse your peers, are you not causing them mental discomfort?"

"Yes, but—"

"And when one is in mental distress, are they able to be more or less productive?"

"Less, but—"

"If your confused brothers and sisters were to ask others about the meaning of your nonsense, would not they become confused as well?"

Out of the corner of his eye, Zander noticed a face glaring his way in the crowd. It belonged to a tall man with dark features and elfish ears. The stranger, with a simple gesture, scratched the side of his nose and looked off to the right twice in quick succession. Zander turned discreetly and saw a familiar face in the crowd, in the back of the audience, the guardian from the café earlier, pretending to be engrossed by the trial. When he looked back, the stranger had disappeared, and in his place, a squat man in a top hat gleamed with joy, hooting at the trial.

Zander didn't wait to see if the stranger would resurface again. He waded through the audience in search of Weber.

"Then you would agree that confusion, like a flu, is contagious?" Councilor Lloyd continued his lecture.

"Yes, I guess, I dunno."

"And like a flu, confusion may infect a whole populace in time?"

Simon broke down sobbing and let his shackles spread apart for only a second, but one second too long to avoid the consequences. Electricity blitzed his nerves and surrendered the prisoner to his knees. The boy trembled there, forced to grovel before the Councilor.

"And so by you spouting nonsense, do you not spread confusion, sadness, and disbelief to the Republic? The Republic that has done nothing but serve to lift you up, care and provide for you? Is this what we, your fathers and mothers, brothers and sisters, deserve?"

"No, no, I'm sorry." Simon said. "I didn't know. I swear."

"Ergo it is for this crime that you will be judged."

"But father, please. I meant no harm."

"One's actions speak for one's intentions. Now I ask you, brothers and sisters, do you believe Simon should be punished for his crime? Or are you willing to forgive his indiscretion and receive him back into society?"

There was no pause on the part of the audience. They resolutely shouted his fate, "PUNISH HIM."

"And how shall he be punished? How shall we guarantee that..."

A gentle touch on the shoulder startled Zander. "I've never seen you take such an interest in the trials before," Weber whispered at his side. "There's nothing we can do here and we have no time for this anyway. Come, we are already late as it is."

He pushed his way through the crowd and Zander trailed close behind, stealing glances at the trial on stage.

"What will happen to him?"

"Confinement perhaps, or exile to the yards, or public service if he's lucky," Weber said. "Maybe we'll see him wailing the accordion bellows tomorrow. But I fear the worst for that one. The crowds tend to be less and less forgiving, especially on the eve of the Centennial here."

"But he's only a child."

"Old enough to know better," Weber said.

They shouldered through the audience and exited from Kensington Plaza under the nearest passageway, winding south through the warren of cobblestone streets with the roar of the trials fading to a distant cry.

CHAPTER TWELVE

Shallow Grave and the Unforgiven

Crammed inside the dark casket, Addie pounded her fists against the wood. Her world had been reduced to stale air and darkness except for the slight cracks in the coffin hood that let her know she wasn't six feet under yet. She pounded again and this time the pounding thundered back. Pound, pound, pound, three crooked nails tore through the velvet lining and spiked the side of the coffin. Pound, pound, pound, three more on the other side. Pound, pound, pound the nails hammered through the wood, inches from the top of her head and shoulders, so close she could feel the sharp points tangle in her hair.

Addie dared not move a muscle. She dug her fingers into the seams of the coffin as it jostled forward. "Over this way." The coffin swayed back and forth, rattling her inside like a mummy in a crate. She conjured a scream and punched the lid again with all her strength.

"Stop that. Be a good corpse and keep still."

"HELP!"

"Do you have the book?"

"No, I thought you brought it."

"Damn it, Francis. You're the priest for Christ sake."

"Don't you yell at me, you worthless sot. Just improvise something. Johnny never cared for the good book anyway."

"Alright, ok. Ahem... oh lords of the dirt, scum of the sea, seraphs on high and friends down below, we are gathered here today to bid the passing of Jonathon M. Voord, captain of the once Bobbing Bulfinch. He was a man... whether good or bad, that is still to be debated. Let the Eye in the sky pass judgment as it will.

Born a nameless bastard, died a legend of the wet divide. Fear was not a word he knew nor could spell properly. His blade never quivered unless he were short of drink. He never met a storm he didn't want to wrangle. Never saw a sea he didn't want to taste. A dauntless philanderer of the unknown, whose sheer gusto could billow any tired sail. He touched us all, as sailors, as our captain, and killed a few of us, but usually the malcontent and not without good reason. I'll never forget the look in his one good eye when we'd finally happen upon shore: *Once 'gain, shore be till. Praise be the larkys.* None of us really knew what this meant but—"

"Get on with it. My arms are getting tired."

"Alright, alright, ahem... in the dear memory of our dear dearly departed, I have written a poem:

Oh captain, whose captain, once captain, no more
sailed a lot of water and stopped on many shore
as you rot in silt at the bottom of the sea
we mourn for you poor Johnny
Francis and me."

Silence...

"Can we chuck her in now?"

"No!" Addie banged.

"Quiet you. Death is a silent thing. Can't you hear us mourning out here?"

"We should have killed her. Why wouldn't you let me kill her?"

"Because it doesn't work that way, Francis. She needs to be alive. *In the dying breath, life to life, death to death, so the soul will come unto rest.* How many times do I have to tell you?"

"Now?"

"Yes now."

The coffin lurched back and craned her neck.

"Heave... ho."

The coffin was released thump down in the shallow grave. Dazed and aching, Addie clawed at the casket's velvet insides.

"HELP! This is a mistake," she screamed. "You're

deranged, the both of you. I do have a soul. My mother even took me to church, every other Sunday. I know I have a soul. I swear it, I feel it! LET ME OUT!"

She heard no response. Only murmurs of Latin and the kicking of ash, which rained on the coffin.

"God or goddess or magical cosmos or whatever is up there. I know I've never been very religious, but I pray to you now. I'm not ready. Please!"

A flicker of light shined through the cracks in the wood and she imagined for a moment that the giant Eye had taken pity on her, granted her a reprieve. This hope soon dissipated when the soot filtered through and left her in darkness again.

The pirates' feet shuffled off. A rub of the hands, a brush of the legs.

"Fine job, Francis."

"Took long enough."

"What's done is done. *Oh now the gruesome fate of old poor Johnny Voord, took them down one by one with his rusty sword...*" And so on into obscurity.

Addie staggered short breaths so she could preserve what little oxygen she had left. Panic and despair had rendered her helpless. This was it, she told himself. This was the end. Nothing but darkness. There was no God. She sobbed uncontrollably and waited to swallow her lungs.

There are a few common thoughts one has while they are waiting to die, clutching a wound or choking on their death bed. The first thought is about their life lived: the happy times, the tragic, old faces you'll never see again; the friends at your funeral, all the things you never did, the places you would have like to have seen, your mother, father, sister, brother, dinnertime, your first love, last love, that kiss, this caress, all the itty bitty bad things you've done and if they add up to a mortal sin. Then the afterlife, trees, reincarnation as an ant, karma, heaven as the angels (always singing), clouds, bright lights, the fires of Hades, eating flesh off the walls of Hell, firebrands, eternal pain; all those who have passed before you and who you might meet in either destination. And as your eyes get weak and your hands stop trembling and that pain in your chest seems to have exploded and bled to your knees, you have the final thought that you forgot while thinking about death—that is to live.

Addie screamed to high heaven for an angel with talons to tear her from this unjust fate. She scratched in fever at the velvet lid, butting her bare heels into the wood at the foot of the coffin. She stilled when she heard the rustle of feet returning, then voices.

"See? It was nothing."

"Do you think the girl is…"

"If she isn't, she will be soon enough. What does it matter? We've done our part. We've made our peace with the devil."

"I suppose it doesn't."

"Oh come on, don't you get all sappy on me. You've buried men alive before. This is no new thing."

Listening to the mumbles outside his grave, Addie was suddenly struck by a fire, a rage the likes of which she'd never experienced before, all the fear and worthless defeat channeled into pure animosity, bursting as her veins thickened. A fierce light shined through the layer of soot, through the cracks, and touched her bare forearm with a burning sensation. The half-map, half-hieroglyphic symbol drawn in ash on her skin started to faintly glow in the coffin dark. Something had come over her, something vicious, something savage, stretching its strange fingers down her arm and through her body into her pounding chest.

She gritted her teeth and kicked the casket.

"Did you hear that?"

"Probably just a death spasm. You know how awkward suffocation is, Gully."

Gully, Addie mused in her grave. The name seemed immediately familiar, although she couldn't understand why. Gully. The mention of the name alone brought her blood to boil. "HO GULLY! Ya bastard, open up this damn box!" She grasped her throat, wondering where the voice had come from for it certainly was not her own.

"Did you hear that?"

"Yes, Gully. I'm only deaf in one ear you know."

"Don't call me that. You know it reminds me of the captain."

Her hand clenched a fist, harnessing the anger into a pure rage that pulled her under, and with a shudder, the dead Captain Voord surfaced in her place, "AAGGHH!"

"That sounded like the Captain."

"It is yar Captain, you idiot," Voord reborn cried out.

"Don't play games with me, m'lady. You know how fragile we are, mourning and all."

"CUT THE CRAP, GULLY," the dead captain shouted and drove his fist in splintering crack through the lid, out of the sooty grave. "Get me out of here at once or I swear I'll take that peg leg of yours and drive it through your skull."

"Captain? I didn't think, I didn't know... This isn't how it was supposed to happen. Francis, grab the other side, the other side! Captain. Oh Captain, my Captain."

Voord braced his hands against the casket lid and threw his whole weight upward, booted and jammed the wood with a series of swift jars until at last the nails pried loose. The pirates stumbled backward with the cracked lid in their hands.

For a moment, Addie came back to breathe the cool desert air. She lay in the exposed coffin, paralyzed in a semi-catatonic state, looking straight into the starless sky as the Eye vanished with a wink. The pirates' befuddled faces cropped into view.

"It looks like the girl," said Francis.

"Of course it does, you idiot. But look at her eyes,"

Gulliver reached in so he could paw at Addie's face again.

"There's no time to fool around here," Francis said. "Close him up again."

Before they could get the lid on straight, a hand shot upward and grabbed Gulliver by the throat. The dead captain burst from the coffin and shoved the peg-legged pirate into the dunes.

Voord, in possession of Addie's gaunt physique, rose from the shallow grave and stepped out onto the cool ash in confusion. There was no sign of shoreline nor sound of wave in the distance, no faithful stars in the sky for guidance, no way of knowing which lost isle among the seven seas he'd been shipwrecked. There were only the familiar faces of his former cabin boys, grown older now and far uglier than he'd remembered.

Francis approached the possessed girl against his better judgment and looked into her eyes alight with red fire. He held outright the silver cross that he wore around his neck and recited incantations under his breath.

Gulliver hoisted himself out of the ash and onto his one good foot. "Good to see you again, Captain."

"Traitors," Voord snarled at his former shipmates. "Worthless, weak kneed, yellow bastards, the both of ya. Ungrateful, irreverent. Didn't I treat ya good? Fed and buttered the lot of ya, kept ya under the drink from port call to storm, gave ya a job, a life, something for you scum to be proud of. Where's me ship, anyhow?" He swung around, peering out and about the ash dunes. "Scoundrels! Where am I? What have ya done with me ship? Where's the old Bobbing Bulfinch?"

Francis and Gulliver looked at each other, as if they both expected the other one to respond, and then at their captain now glaring from the eyes of young Addie.

"Sunk," Gulliver said finally and lowered his head in shame.

"Sunk? These are strange waters for a ship to sink."

"It's rotting at the bottom of the Serpent Sea, Captain," Gulliver lied. "Been a long time."

"And me?"

"Sleeping with the ship." Francis itched his nose. "A wave washed you overboard."

Voord bit his lip and bared his teeth. "That's funny 'cause I remember things different." The dead captain picked up the shovel from the black sand and slid a finger down its pointed spade. "Dead am I? Like a lost shore tale of the sea." he readied the shovel in his hand like a sword. "What do you think, Gully? Can a dead man still get his revenge?"

The shovel smashed Francis upside the head and knocked him to the desert ash. The pirate priest moaned, half-conscious as his fractured skull gushed blood, as Voord raised the shovel so he could bash him again and again and again. The butt of the shovel smacked Gulliver in the jaw when he tried to seize him by the arms. Voord ignored the pirate's feeble pleas and continued the brutal bludgeoning until the last life drained from the priest's bloodied cheeks.

"Please, Captain. It weren't our fault," Gulliver pleaded. "We fought for you, but we were only boys. We struggled to save you. They put us in the lockhold, chained us…"

"You squirrelly liar," Voord said, staring him down. "I remember the look on your face when I had to walk the plank."

Gulliver started back. He fumbled for the hammer in his belt and swung. Voord knocked it from his grip and pushed the peg-legged pirate onto the desert ash.

"I had more faith in you, Gully. You really disappointed me, boy."

"You don't understand," Gulliver said, crawling away on his back like a crab. "We feared for our lives. You steered us right into that storm, just like a thousand others before, just for the thrill, just to see us squirm, just to test our faith—"

Voord pinned him to the desert with the shovel.

"We tried to do you right. We have suffered you for a cursed eternity, carrying your damned casket, trying to make reparations, put you to rest…"

The dead captain condemned him with his borrowed eyes. "Only the guilty bear a conscience."

Gulliver squealed like a live pig on a spit when Voord thrust the shovelhead into his chest. Screams filled the desert air, pleading, screaming, pleading. Voord leaned harder, drove the shovel farther in.

The joy that vengeance delivered was brief, a vague emptiness came afterward. When the screams lulled to a low gurgle, he wrenched out the bloody shovel and tossed it aside.

The rage soon subsided to weakness and Addie shuddered awake. The desert spun in whorled blurs. Her head ached like a cracking egg, as if some strange monster were trying to break out of her skull.

Gulliver convulsed in the bonedust at her feet, attempting to hold his exposed ribs together as the blood gurgled out from a spaded cavity in his chest. They stared at each other a moment, in distant recognition. The pirate's eyes then peeled back into their sockets and lost their light.

Addie gawked at the corpse, mortified and dumbstruck. She then turned and found Francis likewise motionless beside the casket.

"Dead. They're both dead," she said out loud, even though there was no one alive to hear her anymore. "Perhaps they killed each other."

At first, she considered giving the morticians a proper burial, then remembered the burial they'd attempted to give her. She kicked Gulliver's corpse, then kicked it again. A trail of blood led from the body to a shovel discarded in the ash. A pair of sickly red handprints marred the handle. She looked at her own hands. Her fingers dripped with blood. She slowly backed away from the corpses.

For a counted hundred paces, she walked backward, eyes fixed on the corpses, expecting their bodies to leap to life at any moment or better yet disappear. But alas the pirates simply lay there, dead beside the coffin. She surveyed the macabre scene one last time before running off into the desert as fast as she could.

She ran so fast the wind began to whir and stir the desert from its long sleep. Ash swirled into the air. Clouds of black dust rose up in an impromptu storm. The desert shrieks, that had once been hissing howls, now yowled in her ears. *Murderer, dirty murderer...* She looked at her bloody hands, running through the tempest of ash. Self-defense. That's what she would have told the judges. Fair play. They'd buried her alive and she'd killed the pirates with the same shovel they'd used to bury her. A reversal of misfortunes, that was all. She hoped the Eye in the sky would appreciate the irony. But how had it happened? Perhaps they were playing dead. She never took a pulse. Best not to know. And then, just as sudden as it had come, the storm parted, curled away in a gust of wind to reveal... two corpses and a coffin.

Addie followed the rivulets of blood that coursed through the ash from their mangled bodies. She found her broken spectacles in the disturbed ash and put them on. The corpses came into focus in gruesome detail, their legs splayed out, their arms flopped in the ash like dolls, their skin pale, faces frozen with vacant expressions, blood pooling from the cavernous crack in Francis's skull, from the ripped flesh in Gulliver's torn chest.

Alright, so they are definitely dead, she thought. But what of it? They were dead and she was free. So what if she may or may not have had a homicidal blackout? Survival is a savage game, everyone knows that. She was alive, that's what mattered most.

Addie knelt down and brushed her hand over Gulliver's vacant eyes, closed the lids. A snort and whiny came from behind. She turned aside to meet the humongous snout of a black horse impatiently digging its hoofs into the black sand.

"Where did you come from? You're a little late, you know?"

The horse said nothing nor did she ask it any more questions when it bowed its neck to let her mount its back. On the horizon, the sliver of a rising sun bled purple into the black starless sky. She saddled her legs on horse and gripped tightly onto the mane as they rode off in silence, leaving behind the cursed coffin and the murdered pirates to be claimed by the boney hands which would soon rise from the ash.

CHAPTER THIRTEEN

Into the Great Machine

Zander and Weber wound through a labyrinth of narrow cobblestone roads, skirting south, the sky ever darkening with grey clouds. The deeper they burrowed into the labyrinth, the quieter the streets became. Brick walls towered high into the foreboding skies. Every city block blended into the next, same barred windows, same steel doors, same mundane facades. The only thing that changed were the plaques on the buildings... ABODE F212, ABODE F214, ABODE F217... and so on.

Laundry dripped out to dry, crossing the gaps between tenements. Every few blocks, they would catch a glimpse of the tenants: a woman at a window observing the silent streets from above, young men in overalls walking home with their tool belts hung proudly over their shoulders, old men with hollow faces who smoked clay pipes on slab doorsteps.

This was the lower ring of the Residence, a derelict quadrant of the city which the Smiths called home. Although the labyrinth seemed to wander and split without end, the Residence had a mechanical intricacy understood only by the Smiths, like a tightly wound gear. The streets had no need for names. The laborers had memorized every brick just as they'd memorized the interwoven guts of the Great Machine.

What has been written about the Great Machine is far too little. Despite the vast libraries dedicate its evolution and innumerable functions, the thousands of volumes stacked on shelves in the Institute come nowhere close to the number needed to accurately account for the Great Machine's every grind and squeal, which is 7,355,3401,513,288,332 pages as calculated by the machine itself.

Simply put, this mechanical marvel, housed in the Great Factory, is a machine within a machine within smaller machines ratcheted to a massive vertical axle that rotates and produces everything known to the Republic.

On raised gangplanks, the runway Smiths feed the crushers raw materials via conveyor belts, black ribbed tongues that draw the copper, steel, sand, and various plastic compounds into the machine's many mouths. At the bottom, the shipper Smiths catalog, label, and box all the products that the machine manufactures. On scaffolding that runs the length of the towering axle and its layers of machines within machines, the mechanic Smiths tinker and tighten the great gears for optimum efficiency. And then at day's end, they shuck off their gloves and come home to the quiet Residence, still deaf from the grinding noise.

"Odd, isn't it?" Weber said, thinking out loud.

"What's that?"

"These streets, how quiet it is out here."

"Elseboro is much like this," Zander said, "Drab but peaceful in an industrial sort of way. Most of the workers there couldn't bear to live in the Republic. They are so proud, it would almost be below them."

"Did you talk with many of the laborers?"

"Yes, only small talk though. There were a few people who knew of Sherborn's involvement in the resistance. But they didn't regard it with any importance. Politicking, they called it. No use for politicking, they'd say."

"Content to be slaves, huh?" Weber scoffed. "Shuffle for the commonwealth? Good riddance. We don't need their support anyway."

"They're decent people, Weber. They simply feel that what happens in the Republic doesn't concern them."

"Doesn't concern them? Maybe I could have understood that once upon a time. But not now, not after witnessing firsthand what they do to these children at Academy," Weber said. "This concerns us all. It's not natural that we harbor our emotions inside. It is not right that we are told love is a policy, anger a conspiracy, ambivalence a sign of illness. For the sake of society, we have been dehumanized, ridiculed, reduced to listless idiots. And what kills me is that I'm part of the process. The social conditioning. You don't know what it's like to tell these children that their make-believe is harmful to society at large. You don't have to scold these poor kids for playing with the blocks instead of putting them into slot a or b or c. You don't know what it's like to explain to a child that daydreaming is a disease and furthermore evidence of a serious mental disorder."

Weber fell quiet, listening footsteps on the wet cobblestones of a side street. The footsteps trailed off, lost in the rain.

"They scare these kids so much that they are afraid to learn, afraid to ask questions," he whispered. "Receive the message, repeat the message, that's all they're taught. They'd rather be locked in the seclusion room than ask one of us teachers a question. They're afraid to show their minds, taught that it's a sin and, well, that just makes me sick, brother. Yet at the same time, I recognize the brilliance of the system. The difference between willing slave and dissenter is simply knowledge, and when that knowledge is controlled by the state, what else is one to believe except that this is the way things are supposed to be."

Zander let the statement stand so that the argument wouldn't boil over, even though they both knew the situation was more complicated than could be summed up in a list of grievances. Besides, how could he possibly explain what he had seen? The tilling of the Elseboro fields, the foundries, the hard day's work, never a complaint, everything in order, same here as there. When food is on the table and the job's done and there's a warm body beside you in bed, who's to complain about a life divined by machines? Naturally, this was all just politicking to the laborers. As difficult as it was to accept, he both acknowledged their ignorance and envied it.

In the deserted silence, they came to a steel door, iron-boned like the many others they'd passed along the way except for this one had a small peephole, the height of a child. Weber pressed the buzzer.

"Give me that fossil you've been hiding in your jacket," he said. Zander pulled the revolver from his belt and handed it over without any questions asked.

Something stumbled and cursed behind the door. An eye squinted through the peephole.

"Do you know what hour it is?"

"I keep no pace with the clocks. The hour is now, and never before the after," Weber replied without a second's hesitation.

"What are you doing here?"

"Let us in, George. We're already late as it is," Weber said.

"I'm aware of that. Tell me the riddle."

"What's the answer?"

"The answer is 'ash.' Now what's the question?"

"Ash? Is this an old one? Come on, let us in."

"What is the ancient world, what will be the new, and where we will all return," Zander recited from memory.

The bolt slid and the door cracked open just wide enough so they could squeeze inside.

"That was a depressing one, George. Do we have to go through these goddamn riddles ever time?"

"Hey, I don't make the rules and you never saw me here, alright?" George said, bolting the door shut behind them. "Who's this? Nobody told me about any guests."

"He's from before your time," Weber said.

George blocked off the stairwell that spiraled up from entryway in a series of angular turns, "Hey, hey no one told me about this. I gotta check and see—"

Weber whipped out the revolver and stuck it against the

doorkeeper's chest. "Like I said, we really don't have time to debate this."

George slinked out of the way. "Look, I've got no problem here. You ring the buzzer, I come. I don't give a damn what you and your friend are up to."

"We appreciate it. I'll put in a good word for you."

The doorkeeper grumbled and let them pass up the warped-metal stairs, still suspicious of Zander. He recognized the face, although it wasn't until Zander and Weber had reached the first-floor landing that he realized where. Three years ago, the same face had been plastered on posters throughout the city, printed in fresh ink on the front of the *Republican Guard*: 'Wanted for Murder.'

This was not the whole truth, of course. The real reason why the Order had hunted day and night for the rebel's somber face was not for the sake of justice. It was to retrieve something of immense value, something so dangerous in fact that Zander never let it leave his person. The satchel that now rested snug in his jacket.

The stairwell wound up and up, past open doors. On the 3rd floor, three young men slapped cards in a round of Split or Miss. On the next, a woman at her slit window counted rain drops. The fifth, sixth, seventh, and so on, were couples in bed, at the dinner table, unwinding on their brown couches. The ubiquitous blue light of tube screens flickered inside, tuned to the daily news, or the Institute channel which announced the scientists' latest experiments and discoveries, or the 24-hour dials that broadcast random scenes from the gridwork city on loop, captured by the Orbservers roving cameras.

Even though open doors meant open ears, nobody gave a second glance at the strangers who climbed the stairs in haste. At last, the stairwell ended at a fireproof door.

"Watch the stairwell while I fix this," Weber said and handed Zander his revolver. He withdrew a spool device from his pocket, pressed a button to pop out its pick pins and skewered the tweezer prongs in between the door seam, probing the lock. Zander examined the rusted revolver before tucking it back in his belt. Slim chance it still worked, although the antique gun granted him a measure of comfort nonetheless. The lock released with a metallic snap and the door swung shy out onto the roof. They cautiously trespassed outside.

In the shadows of smokestacks and spires, the Republic stretched in curious patterns. The labyrinth of the Residence spanned out in rings of spider-web streets that separated the three classes, identical brick tenements clustered and crowded together. These gridwork streets straightened outward and carved the city into sections within the colossal outer wall. Avenues and byways cross-stitched a perfect square round the inner-city, further divided by river channels that sliced the Republic into its four quadrants.

Out and beyond, the Old Quarter and its hallowed clocktower, the Academy, and even farther, the Institute of Progress distant in the hills. To the west, the shops along the boulevard, the plemetic high-rises of the commercial sector. To the north, the warehouses and factories of the manufacturing center from which the Great Factory rose above the rest of the cityscape with its triplet of almost-regal smokestacks, candy-striped and coughing grey trails. River canals teased through the city in blue streaks and swirled around the Citadel due east, its capitol spires gloomed, ever-seeing on high.

"It's incredible," Zander said, admiring the view.

"Ah yes, a beautiful monster, isn't it?" Weber said. "Oh New Rome, New Rome, how we dreamed you'd be a happy home." He checked his platinum watch. "We're late, but I guess the gang is running behind as well. They probably had to handle some last-minute business."

Zander walked over to the roof's edge. "So do you want to

tell me what we're doing up here?"

"Better that Phaedrus tells you. I wouldn't want to ruin the surprise, you know how he feels about surprises. Let's just say there's a little preparation that needs to be done before tomorrow."

"Tomorrow? You mean the Centennial?"

Weber remained silent, but he didn't need to say another word. It made sense now, the urgent letter he'd received in Elseboro, beckoning his return. He hadn't been called back to help plot and prepare for the revolution. He had been called back to deliver the plans necessary for its successful execution.

"You can't be serious?" Zander said. "Tell me this is not what I think it is. I only arrived this morning, and you're telling me we're going to commit suicide on some fool's errand tomorrow?"

"Look," Weber said. "None of us know all the details. Phaedrus has been waiting for you to arrive before he divulged the master plan. Besides, this is what you wanted, Zander. This is what we've always wanted. Why else do you think we would have risked bringing you back?"

"I can't shake this feeling," Zander said. "I thought that by coming back here everything would fall into place, clear the path for a fresh start. But it hasn't. It's tainted somehow. I feel something terrible is bound to happen."

"When did you become so superstitious? Take it easy. I know this is quite sudden, but Phaedrus says—"

"Since when did Phaedrus become lion, king, and god, huh? And what's happened to Leyna? I'm beginning to question why I was sent away in the first place," Zander sighed out at the cityscape.

"You came back for a reason," Weber argued. "You could have stayed cozy in the dust-colored country, but you returned to us. Now why is that?"

"I'll tell you why," a voice interrupted from afar. A

shadowy figure appeared from behind a top house on the roof and walked into the thin dusk light. "He's come to finish what he started."

Out of the darkness came a man whose grin Zander could never shutter out of memory, not matter how hard he tried. Phaedrus. He didn't know what to expect from this reunion, a reunion that dragged the past out of the dirt-swept closet, kicking and screaming. He had both anxiously awaited and dreaded this moment.

Phaedrus never ceased to make him uneasy. The intimidation rested solely in his surly grin, crooked and snarling half his face. There was something to be admired and feared in the sheer audacity of his mad mind. Certainly, he was no picture of the feared rebel that the sainted teachers at the Academy forewarned their young pupils of. For one, he had no fangs nor could he fly. He stood shorter than most, and in the tweed jacket he always wore with a derby bent over his head, he looked more like a history professor than the leader of a dreaded uprising. He seemed perfectly sane and tame at first study, yet in that grin there was nothing to be trusted.

"Callo, callay, my squeamish friends," he said. The wide-eyed rebel sauntered over and embraced Zander. "Thought you'd never see this sour face again, did you?"

"Hello, Phaedrus," Zander said. "Where is everyone?"

Phaedrus snuffed his nose, screwed his eyes and shot them toward the sky. "Around. Look at you. You're shaking. What are you so bothered about?"

"It's been an exhausting day, that's all, and Weber tells me you have designs on the Centennial celebration tomorrow."

"Did he? I assure you it's nothing to be nervous in your shoes about," Phaedrus smirked. "Looks like we've got a bunch of nervous neds here, eh Harry?"

A burst of laughter came from a nearby chimney where a frumpy man sat with his legs hanging off. He smiled playfully when he realized he'd been spotted. "Seems as though they need a little frajoy, frajay," he said and shimmied down the brick stack like a lumberjack.

The joyous fellow was Purple Harry, easily recognizable by his meaty eyes and gaunt stance. More animal than man, Purple Harry was like a feral cat, instinctive and spastic, so light of mind and skinny that he bounced like a marionette when he walked over, shook a round of hands, and chuckled again, "Long time no see, chief."

"The others are waiting for us nearby. Figure we'd keep low till we want to be seen. Never can be too careful these days," Phaedrus said and pulled his derby down over his wild eyes. "There's much to tell, too much perhaps. But all in good time, tick, tick. The night's still a baby yet."

Part Three: Tangled Corridors

Welcome to Hell, the 666th fathom of Oblivion, a sweltering hole of fire and brimstone where sinners come to die and die again in the searing flames. Unbeknown to the theologians of the overworld is the beast that fuels Hade's eternal flames. Contrary to popular opinion, the fires of Hell are not born from God's wrath or the sadistic fury of Lucifer, Mammon, Beelzebub, Mephistopheles or any of the other countless devils. Rather, the flames are snorted from the nostrils of a sleeping giant known as the Krell. Suffice to say, it's an ugly reptile, fatter than the sun and far older. Its scales are larger than most earthly continents, teeth taller than the Himalayas. Its tongue could drink a whole ocean in a single lap, like dew off a leaf.

The Krell lies far below the scarred mouth of Hell, down the throat, in the belly so to speak. It sleeps and snorts and sleeps until it will awake hungry and devour the universe again. But for the time being, the monster is no threat. It's still plenty full from the last time it devoured the universe. Make no mistake, however. These nasal flames that rise up to scar the mouth of the netherworld are just as ferocious as the beast that snorts them. They are the teeth that circle Hell's jaws, as it mashes and salivates, insatiable and unscrupulous in its appetite...

CHAPTER FOURTEEN

What Fire Knows (or Hell's Dirty Secrets)

The terror of the Hell resembled a twisted amusement park. A seemingly endless procession of drooling idiots wound into the horror, pushing, shoving, wailing, whining, stinking the stink of everlasting sweat, panting in heat, cursing their fate. Yet it soon became obvious, as Norman and the other sinners shuffled along listening to the horrendous shrieks ahead, that there wouldn't be any fun at the end of this line.

The fire crackle, screams, and demonic hissing swelled together in a symphony of agony, entombed in the throat of Hell. It was anyone's guess who belonged to the giant hands that stuck out from the throat's fleshy walls like tree branches. Nor was it clear why these enormous arms and hands were holding spatulas, dice, mallets, or why one giant hand was holding a burning Ferris wheel that dipped sinners in and out of a flaming bowl of pudding cradled by another.

Every now and then, huge fists would burst through the flesh and sinew to drop naked bodies into the fire by the handful. Winged demons would then swoop down like cavern bats from the fiery canopy to snatch these sinners and deliver them to the end of the line and beginning of the Hall of Flames, a fancy name for what is, in truth, a flaming forearm.

Stacked like dominos in a row, the sinners dragged their scabbed feet along this bridge of flesh and bone, slicked with blood, walled by fire. It was hard to tell where the line ended, or whether it ended at all, since the fire incensed a delirium both mental and physical. Regardless, every minute or so, the doomed would move another grueling step forward. This would inspire a few hopeful faces to light up, perk onto their tippy toes, and peer down the Hall of Flames as it squealed on and on into further fire.

Most of the damned, however, were wise enough to keep

their heads bowed and not let an eye stray one glance. By now, they knew the fire's ruses, how Hell deceives, how inferno knows the souls it devours. After all, to look into the flames of Hell is to know true misery. It is a sickness that pervades every pore, where one is never dead but perpetually dying in a slow roast. The sinners knew full well that, even if they melted to their bones, they'd still take that step onward into the fire.

Hell stank. Stank like fire, stank like burning flesh, stank like... Norman couldn't place the oddly pleasant aroma that mingled in the mélange of revolting smells. Then, with a sniff, it plucked a note of olfactory familiarity. Coffee, he thought. Smells like coffee. That aromatic fuel of the workaday world, nectar of the nocturnal. The smell was a homesick comfort in the swelter of Hell's inferno. Had he been able to see where the strange aroma was coming from, he might not have found the smell so pleasant.

Flames nipping at his elbows, Norman remained in submissive tow with the sinners' row. The sinners wept, buck-naked and miserable. They complained, they repented, they repeated their sins over and over to count them out. And then there were those, like the sadistic couple ahead of him, who feasted greedily upon whoever happened to be their partner in line. A skinny bone-legged man sunk his teeth into the neck of a young woman, moaning.

"What's that, lover?" the woman asked over her shoulder. Matted, maggot-infested golden hair rode down her raw sweaty back like yellow snakes, squirming all the way to the curve of her hips.

The bone-legged man grinned, his mouth dripping blood. "Nothing, scrumptious."

Norman checked to make sure his own backside wasn't being chewed. He buckled to his knees in revulsion when the young woman turned with a fierce smile and savagely bit a strip of flesh off the skinny man's shoulder.

"Tastes like duck," she said, tugging at his hair. "Did you ever have duck?"

"No. I was a vegetarian actually until I ended up down here," the skinny man said. "Oooh, that tickles."

Norman wiped the vomit from his lips and rose to his burning feet. Although he wretched at the sight of this depraved feast, the wicked temptation of flesh and flame was powerful, the sexual hunger coming from the naked writhing bodies. Carnal pleasure turned carnivorous.

The deranged lovers weren't the only sinners trying to forget their doomed eternity in the netherworld. Everyone was trying to distract themselves from their misery with either violence, groaning, or idle chit-chat.

"I disagree," a vengeful mistress gabbed to the narcissist behind Norman. "The maggots are the worst. I mean, they burrow right under your skin and you don't even notice."

"Look on the bright side, the heat is slimming," the narcissist said. "I find it all somewhat lackluster, to be honest."

"What do you mean?"

"I imagined Hell a bit different. Maybe I have a grandiose imagination, but this doesn't really do it for me. I mean, where's Lucifer, what about those dogs with three heads? Where are the legions of fallen angels?"

"Is this your first time through?"

"My third, actually."

"This is my eighth, and honestly I don't know what's worse, the intolerable suffering or the immense boredom."

Norman turned around in line and interrupted the conversation. "Do either of you know where in Hell we are?"

"We're on route to the Lip, the doomed plunge, the ledge that precedes the vat of Boiling Agony!" the narcissist said.

A period of awkward silence delayed Norman's inquiry a moment or two.

"That was slightly melodramatic."

"Forgive me for my old theater ways. I'm only trying to lighten the mood," the narcissist laughed without any company. "You've got to hold onto your sense of humor down here, you know? Humor's our last salvation, my friend. Keeps you sane in this eternity of madness. They may scorch our flesh and broil our brains, yet they'll never be able to stop us from laughing at it all." The narcissist raised his chin and scratched underneath with his black-nailed thumb at the maggots nestled in the fleshy rot. "You're new to Hell, I gather."

"I suppose that's one way to put it," Norman said.

"Then you don't know about the vat?"

"No, I'm afraid I don't."

"You must understand by now that the nexus of this rung of Hell is, to be frank, a mug of coffee. A giant mug held aloft by an enormous burning hand. See, there's the thumb and we're almost at the handle right now and up there, that's where a vast pool of black coffee boils and boils awaiting our descent."

"A mug of coffee?" Norman said incredulously. It sounded like a practical joke, but then again, after having met God, it all strangely made sense. "What kind of coffee is it?"

"That's slightly irrelevant," the vengeful mistress cut in. "What is relevant is the immense heat of the coffee as it seers off your flesh and pulls you under."

"But what does it taste like?"

"You don't want to know."

"Cream and a couple sugars?"

"No, black boiling deadly coffee. Coffee of death."

"And you have no idea what kind it is?"

"It's decaf espresso."

"That's horrid," Norman shuddered.

"It's the absolute worst," the narcissist said, picking at a bubbling scab behind his right ear. "Hell isn't supposed to be a cup of tea, you know. Heaven is."

There was an odd pause, a moment of envy, a flash of self-pity, a silence to contemplate what they were missing.

"Why aren't you basking in the heavenly tea, anyway?" Norman asked.

"I was…" the narcissist replied with great shame in his eyes, "…a writer."

"I didn't know writing was a sin."

"It isn't traditionally," the writer said in hushed tones. "I wrote a couple short stories that portrayed God as senile and temperamental. Just a little scathing humor, poking fun, but I don't think the Almighty took it lightly."

Norman refrained from telling the writer his own experience with the Father-all-powerful-Genius-of-Creation. He wondered how many souls had been cast into the mouth of Hell because of God's touchy temper or misfiled paperwork.

"And what about you," the writer asked the vengeful mistress. "Care to tell us why you've been damned eight times over?"

"You don't want to know," she said.

"Oh, but we do." The writer gave Norman the old nudge-nudge. "Right? And don't leave out any of the juicy details."

"Don't look at me with those scandalous eyes," she said.

"Oh, I apologize wholeheartedly. I humbly beseech your forgiveness," the writer said. "Let's shy away from any disagreement, shall we? The climate's disagreeable enough. And we're all friends here, aren't we? Not that we'll ever see each other again after the dip." He let out a short chuckle. Nobody else laughed.

"And what happens after?" Norman asked.

"You drown, necessarily, and either escape to purgatory or suffer another excruciating walk through the fire. Depends on how many sins you've committed."

"Supposedly, you suffer a lap of misery for every sin," the vengeful mistress elaborated. "But who knows what counts as a sin nowadays? It's hopeless. We're doomed forever."

"Oh don't be such a cynic," the writer chided her. "Just like a woman to expect the worst."

"And what would you know about women?" she scowled.

"I'd be more than happy to show you if you ever cared to give me the time."

"What are you going to do? Romance me in flames while the Nephs jeer and the flesh drips off the walls? Caress me with your raw bubbling hands?" she said. "Can you kiss while the Hydras hiss?"

"Don't hate me because you're beautiful," the writer quipped. "Hell hath no fury like a woman's scorn."

"Your literary charms won't work on me. And I don't hate you because you are an egocentric delusional child whose thin soul reels at the horrors of Hades," she said. "Maybe you haven't noticed, but this is it. This is eternal suffering without absolution, this is everafter in an oven and it's not cute or entertaining. And I hate because there is no other feeling. Nothing but hate and misery and degradation. And when I look at you, I think of nothing other than clawing off your face with my nails and gorging out your baby blues."

"So you do like me?"

"Never have I met a man so oblivious to his own suffering. It's as if you revel in it. You're demented. You belong in this place."

"Such a puritan!" the writer said and shined Norman a black-toothed grin aside. "Denies her own passions to prove a point."

"Get over yourself."

Norman, with nothing pithy to say, left the couple to flirt it out, moved by the novelty of love in the netherworld. He smiled at the thought and gazed off into the hypnotic flames ahead. Was it possible? Love in Hell, love in the infernal squalor of this eternal damnation. Would they journey together through the torments that awaited? Maybe this was their chance at redemption. Perhaps they'd grow wings and fly off, propelled by the power of their amour, out of the throat of Hell, chased by winged demons stabbing at their heels, onward to salvation above, as in the unfinished Faustian fable. Maybe…

"Aargh!!!!"

The scream shook Norman from the trance. He reeled back just in time to dodge a belch of fire.

"Mr. Writer?" he hollered into the fire, as it tapered and tamed. The vengeful mistress, in his place, stood on the bridge of flesh and bone, the sinners' row winding for miles behind her through the flames. Norman extinguished his eyebrows, "What happened to the writer fellow?"

She slanted her eyes and cracked a corner smile. "Whoever are you talking about? Honey, I do believe the heat is getting the better of you." The flames flickered in the gloss of those eyes, her pupils burning from tawny brown to amber red. In her stare, he heard laughter. "Best keep your head straight. The worst is yet to come"

When he turned to face the Hall of Flames ahead, Norman saw the further horrors of the Hell unveiled. There, out of the dizzied dance of fiery doom, puckered the Lip, the giant rim of the gigantic mug of decaf espresso. A thin mist shrouded the fiery passage where the line of sinners tangled up onto the rim. Beyond the supernatural steam, the vat of Boiling Agony burbled.

The pace quickened. Soon, he could count the heads ahead. Fifteen, thirteen, then twelve. Every step forward in the queue was preceded by a cry, shriek, or scream for mercy: 'Please, please no, no, NO!!! AHHH!!!' splash, sizzle, 'Please!', gulp, 'Lord have mercy on my soooou…', bubble, bubble. Ten.

The mug, in all its harrowing glory, slowly revealed itself through the steam, suspended there in middle of the throat. The Furies, in flight, shrieked and licked their lips; the lesser devils stroked theirs horns, perched on the many titanic hands that stuck out from the fleshy hollow. And round the jutting porcelain lip, the Nephs egged on the death march.

There is little record in scripture or in folklore of the Nephs, grotesque creatures born from Hades' fire. These spectators of Hell have however been portrayed time and time again in many artistic interpretations of the netherworld. Hieronymus Bosch, the renaissance Dutchman, painted the sickly creatures with frightening accuracy in his triptych of *Earthly Delights*.

The Nephs are not demons in the literal sense, yet they are far more vicious than the Furies, the Fallen, or the Mansa beasts. They are the damned without a prayer, beyond absolution. Once men of flesh, now vile half-demon, half-human hybrids with heads like giant newts, dead eyes, and tiny dagger teeth that spike out from their frog jowls. They are the unforgivable, doomed to hiss and growl forever, crawling naked up the throat for a glimpse of the sinners row. Sometimes they wear cloaks. But only when visiting the overworld.

Thousands of these vicious creatures stomped their flat three-toed feet to the primordial rhythms that rumbled out of Hell's digestive tract, while thousands more climbed their way up the throat, up the mug. They tore their brethren off the lip, desperate to see the doomed sinners drop, plop, and fizzle. With every splash, the Nephs would erupt in a howl which rang the rim, sang off the tonsils of Hell and called the roaring fires to rise. Sibilant cries of joy, cackling, heckling, all the while chomping their jowls in a chant of demonic cant: "Squeal, squeal, writhe and squeal. Squeal, squeal, writhe and squeal."

And squeal, they did.

"No, no, mercy, no! Ahh!!!" Splash, bubble, bubble, sizzle, fizz... one after another the sinners gurgled in the black bath.

Five, Norman counted and climbed into the mist, maybe two more beyond that. So seven. A gigantic hand broke through the flaming canopy and shook what appeared to be a giant-sized sugar packet over the mug. 'DAMINO: Pure Sinner' it read as big as a billboard. The huge hand ripped off a corner and out poured hundreds and hundreds of helpless bodies. The sinners screamed in vain, as they fell, plop, plop, plop, plop, plop, plop into the scalding espresso, bobbed, gulped, yelped, and eventually drowned. A burning red pitchfork, half a mile long, plunged into the black bath after the shower of sinners, and stirred the damned into a whirlpool of espresso and bones.

Three. The time was drawing nigh for what was to be his own demise. On the edge of the lip, a murderer cringed before the black bath. Winged demons circled, ready to execute the final judgment, their falchions brandished. In a gracefully flying swoop, they delivered the murderer his just deserts, slashed him hara-kiri and kicked him into the mug.

The carnivorous lovers stepped up to the lip next, not least bit concerned with their impending doom. While the skinny man nibbled voraciously on her ear, the young woman waited, arms akimbo, tapping her foot in anticipation of the thrilling splash. The winged demons swooped down and sent her giggling into the scalding espresso. The skinny man, who up until then had been sadistically nonchalant, panicked when he saw his beloved bobbing in the bubbling black sea of bones.

"You first," he screamed and pushed Norman out onto the precipice. Norman wobbled before the black bath, disoriented by the mist. The devils flew down over, faster than the flicker of a flame, pierced the cannibal through the chest and flung him into the mug like a piece of bad meat. He met his fate with a splash, screeched, fought, sizzled, gulped, yelped, yapped, sizzled, and finally melted under.

The vat of Boiling Agony belched. Norman held his nose.

"Well, this it," he said flat. "Might as well make the best of it."

Norman stuck his toes out over the lip and prepared himself for the drop. The thunder of stomping feet ceased when the Nephs sniffed the scent of something peculiar in the flesh-rot air. A thousand demented faces turned toward the sinner before the black bath, hissing through their daggered teeth, staring with their sickly red eyes. Winged demons circled overheard, agitated by the intense hissing, batting away the Nephs that came too close to the doomed candidate, waiting to deliver justice themselves.

Before any of Hell's devils or demons could strike, Norman closed his eyes and completed his last glorious feat, his own personal finale. With the divine grace of an albatross, he leapt off the lip, through the supernatural steam, did a flip, two, three and then swan-dived into the scalding coffee. It was an Olympic sight, proud and near perfect. If the Nephs had scorecards, he would have received at least a 6.66. And as he drowned and melted to blood and bones in the black boiling bath, he had one final thought before complete dissolution, that the bitter taste of decaf espresso wasn't as awful as he'd imagined.

CHAPTER FIFTEEN

Jackals in the Night

The rebels chased the setting sun. The soft light through the clouds shed an amber glow over the low-slung sprawl of brick tenements, plemetic high-rises, and factory warehouses with a thousand windows like dead reflective eyes. As the daylight waned, the rebels scurried across the rooftops, with their heads crouched low, like mice in the attic.

"Where are we headed? What's the plan?" Zander asked. "Since I've arrived, I've heard nothing but riddles from both you and Weber. Where do we stand?"

"On the top of the world, my friend, in more respects than one," Phaedrus said, running alongside. "You've come at the crucial hour. The resistance is rolling along faster than you or I ever imagined. It's true what you said earlier. My reasons for bringing you back are more practical than sentimental. Truth is, I need you, Zander."

They crept backs-bent, hidden behind the long-toothed roof hem. Out and beyond, dusk slowly seduced the Republic. In bedrooms, in breakfast nooks, in silent studies, the lighted windows went dark. Yet before the citizens of the Republic flipped that final switch and kissed each other goodnight, they would perform their final and most important duty of the day. They would wash their hands once, twice, thrice. They would fill a glass of water and lay it by the bedside. They would uncap the small bottle printed with their IDR. And with prayer for health and prosperity, they would swallow a single red pill.

This was their nightly ritual. Although never expressly explained, it was assumed the pill was protection against whatever phantom remnants of the plague still carried in the breeze. However it was not out of fear or coercion that the good people of the Republic took the pill every night without fail. It was out of love and gratitude for the great commonwealth. It was an act of conviction, of commitment to a better tomorrow. An act that gave them a sense of joyous connection with one another, knowing that at the same time their brothers and sisters were making the same pledge. There was nothing more noble, nothing more selfless than to obey and be saved.

The rain returned with the coming dark, the rising moon seemed to follow their every move. Zander couldn't help but look over his shoulder in a quiet panic, thinking every stir in the night was danger waiting.

"Any news from Sid?" he asked.

"He continues to relay reports from the inside," Phaedrus said. "Correspondence has been scattered lately. We actually were forced to cut off contact with Sid for awhile so that he could maintain his cover. He did send us notice last week of a few new interesting projects at the Institute, specifically a protocol for security that relies on the populace itself. Radio transmitters imbedded in articles of clothing like shoes, belts, gloves, etc. There are already enough willing spies, as you well know. Eyes and ears at every corner. My biggest fear is that if we don't act soon, they'll strike before we have the chance."

"Safe to assume that the Order has not forgotten the incident?"

"Not in the least, yet the assumption is that you are dead. They even faked a hanging in your honor. A young man, about your age, squealed like a pig with his head in the noose. There's nothing to fear, old friend. Like all lies of the Republic, they soon become true. By now the Order has convinced itself that you truly are dead."

They paused at the roof's edge between one tenement and the next. Phaedrus bounded over onto the other side, crossing a short gap with a cat's cradle of laundry lines strung between the windows a hundred feet down. Zander hesitated before the gap, then jumped across. He rushed to catch up.

"But what's this about the Centennial?" Zander asked. "This is not what we planned."

"Plans? It's too late for plans. That's exactly what they'd be expecting," Phaedrus said. "Tomorrow, we'll throw a match in the powder keg and conduct the fire. Have faith in chaos, my friend. It's saved us thus far. I trust you brought the satchel with you?"

"It's safe," Zander patted the inside pocket of his jacket, "provided you let me know how you intend to strike the match."

"All in good time. But for now, just trust me. I haven't done you wrong yet, have I?" Phaedrus tipped his derby and hurried ahead to Weber and Harry who were already scaling the next roof.

The future loomed in silhouette as they climbed higher into the night. The tenements rose in steps to the plemetic towers of Westchester Avenue and the outskirts of the Old Quarter. The clocktower chimed to mark the hour, scaring crows from their roost. By the sound, Zander measured his position on the unfamiliar roofscape. Southeast. The Citadel spires loomed over the city with roving spotlights. The Institute, divided by miles of wired fence on the eastern hill, radiated a perverse industrial glow over the sleeping machines in the Great Factory.

"Look at it all, dear friend," Phaedrus said, admiring the cityscape. "The precious perfect world asleep, with not a single sweet dirty dream or even delicious nightmare. Blank, nada, nil."

A shuffle from the shadows cut their sightseeing short. Zander drew out his revolver and scanned the foggy rooftop. Harry and Weber were nowhere to be seen. Faint laughter carried from somewhere nearby. The revolver trembled in his hand. His eyes pierced through the dark.

"Slow down there, chief," Phaedrus said and gently pushed down the barrel of the gun. Stepping into the moonlight, he whipped off his derby and called out with his hands cupped, "Callo, calloo!"

In the next moment, faces swarmed from the darkness. Shadows grew eyes and hands, hooded black cloaks and black leather boots, rifles slung over their shoulders. The armed gang grinned, stalking closer. Harry and Weber reappeared, rushing back to the call like frolicking lovers.

"Callo, callay," Phaedrus greeted the gang. "Any trouble with the royal collies?"

"Nothing of any alarm," one of the cloaked men said.

"Too busy scratching themselves, eh?"

This received a healthy chuckle from the black-clad greeting party. Zander let his revolver droop by his side but kept his finger in the trigger. It was true what Phaedrus had said. Their numbers had grown, although he recognized only a few faces in the dark hoods.

There was Neale, standing a foot taller than the rest. Quiet, crafty, and ever aware. A former reporter for the *Republican Guard*, he'd once cobbled together snippets of propaganda for the daily press. The facts the reporters pieced together in their cubicles were delivered by the all-seeing Orbservers, which flew through the Republic constantly collecting data. This information was then sorted by the council, redacted, and submitted to the reporters to be refined into easily digestible blurbs. Little did the Republic know that imbedded in his briefs about babies born, Heroes honored, scientific breakthroughs at the Institute and lengthy progress reports, Neale wove a secret code, every third word and known only to the rebels.

Sprockett, unmistakably with his eye-patch, lingered near the back with Elsa, his partner in crime. Always the dark pair, they wore the same expression of stoic disinterest and identical straight-ironed short black hair. They were wanted criminals, both ex-programmers for Control 6, who'd slipped the grid after embezzling 20,000 skid from the state bank five years ago. With Sprockett as the brains and Elsa the quick draw, they would slip in time and again to hack at the Republic's security network and garner funds for the resistance when need be.

Then there was Angus, cheery and fat-cheeked, a top-salesman with a winning smile who sold worthless trinkets out of a junk shop tucked off Anderson Boulevard. Secretly among the boxes of whiz-cracks, miniature dolls, and yo-yos, he stored a hidden trove of another type of trinket: .22 caliber pistols, 12-gauge shotguns, a catalog of rifles and an ammunition stockpile.

The rest of the rebels seemed vaguely familiar, like faces stolen from a forgotten dream. They shared the same blank expression of recognition, unsure exactly who this stranger was that Phaedrus had brought for their night of mischief.

Zander could feel their uneasiness. Somehow he'd become the intruder, where once he'd commanded the room, hidden in the abandoned bomb shelters beneath the city, where once a band of misfits with the same faces and different names listened intently to his delicate plans on how the revolution would evolve organically like a plague, and how the power of the idea was greater than the power of any weapon.

It was Neale who first realized who this stranger was standing at Phaedrus' side. He walked over and gave his old comrade a brotherly hug.

"Hello, Neale," Zander said. "Been a long time."

Angus let down his hood. "So this was the big surprise? Man, I can't believe this. You've finally come back."

Several others came forward to greet him afterward, including Sprockett and Elsa who said nothing, yet in their sinister silence, let Zander know they were glad for his safe return.

All in all, it was an awkward reunion on the foggy rooftop in the quiet night. In their handshakes and polite smiles, there was a skepticism. The new recruits surely had heard of Zander, either through the folklore Phaedrus had spun around his disappearance or from the ghost stories that still passed in hushed whispers throughout the Republic. Yet there remained a mistrust of this dead martyr come back to life.

"Well, since we've got all us jokers here, let's get this party rolling," Phaedrus said and snapped to Angus who slumped a hefty bag off his shoulder. "The game is simple tonight, gents. Eris is with us and the time is nigh to trace the sky." He knelt down and unzipped the bag to reveal its bulging contents: dozens of white mason jars. The rebels unloaded and distributed the jars. Zander sloshed the white liquid inside, an acrid toxic smell stung his nostrils when he opened the lid.

"What are these?" he asked Weber privately. "Some sort of chemical bomb?"

"Far more dangerous," Weber smiled through his glasses and handed him a brush. "Paint."

Zander thumbed the brush bristles. Paint... tracing the sky, another prank. A black cloak was thrown at his feet. "Here. You don't want to be left out of all the fun, do you?" Phaedrus said. "Now swell chums. Shall we?"

By the time Zander slipped the black cloak over his jacket, the rebels were already off and running over the rooftops. In mad dashes, they dipped their brushes and painted the message of revolution in their black boots and long midnight cloaks. They attacked the slanted roofs in wild white strokes, the chimney tops, the hatch houses with cryptic slogans: MECHANISM UNKNOWN, BEWARE THE GHOSTS, NOTHING IS WHAT ANYTHING WAS. They leapt between tenements with instinctive grace, slopping paint— QUESTION THE ANSWER—leaving behind a trail of white-slashed slander that traced their path into the inner-city.

While the rebels raced on, possessed by moonlight, Zander lagged behind, frustrated by what had become of the resistance, their delicate revolution unraveled to this nonsense, and with it, the promise of a new tomorrow. A promise he'd safeguarded in dank cellars, moving from one hole to the next in Elseboro so he could avoid the weekly inspections. A promise he had staked his life on, splattered to the wind on the whims of a madman and his fledgling cult.

Phaedrus. No wonder Leyna had left without a word. She could see what was happening. Phaedrus. Although he wanted to be angry, somehow the sight of his manic partner, charging the rebel brigade into the night with his wide eyes and devil's grin, made him feel at home. This gang of misfits was his family, the only family he knew now, for better or worse. An old feeling returned. Zander tried to brush it off.

The clocktower came into view, as did Concord Square cluttered with empty stages for tomorrow's festivities. Garish lamplights in the streets below shone obscure on the guardians with their LR-5s cradled in their arms. They maintained their post, nodding off and on, more might than sight. In mechanical hums, the true eyes and ears of the Republic made their rounds. Orbservers on night patrol zipped by in flight, analyzing every darkened corner, nook, and alley of the deserted streets.

Phaedrus hushed the rebels with a single gesture of his finger to his lips. The rebels pocketed their brushes and skirted from shadow to shadow along the darkened rooftops. Ghosts. Phantoms. That's what the rebels were to the Republic, and true to the myth, they moved just beyond sight.

The guardians yawned and adjusted the straps on their rifles, the Orbs whizzed past in tandem, and the rebels slinked by on high.

For the commonwealth to admit the resistance existed would be to admit failure, admit holes in the Order. The council instead preyed on the rumors and used the myth of these ghosts to their benefit. Tomorrow, their raid on the rooftops would be denounced as the work of phantoms come to haunt the benevolent Republic on its historic day, a reminder from the world that had perished with the plague.

The rebels moved in a conspicuous pattern. Slash and dash. Calculated in their mayhem. From the shoulder of the clocktower, the Citadel revealed itself beyond the fog. A network of canals separated the island capitol from the rest of the city, centered in concentric circles that mimicked the clocktower dials. It was here that Sprocket paused so he could survey, with his one good eye, the course ahead and the distant roving lights of the Citadel.

"What's the good word?" Phaedrus asked.

"Three drones flying due south, two more headed east," he pointed to the robotic orbs zipping out like pinballs from under the clocktower arch. "We've rerouted their patrol to bypass the garden in such a way that our breach should go unnoticed by Control. The watchtowers scan a quarter-mile circumference around the Citadel, which makes getting over there a little tricky. But if we time it correctly, we should be fine."

"Agreed, my friend," Phaedrus said. "Scout ahead. We'll join you there in a second."

After Sprockett had vanished into the dark, the rebels collected themselves in the shadows of the clocktower where they silently traded swigs from a bottle of moonshine and loaded their rifles.

Zander stayed cool and tried to figure out where they were headed. This is madness, he thought. Suicide. He watched the Citadel spotlights roam from afar. Inside, the Grand Muse and his council advisors slept, secure in the clean-lined corridors of the fortress capitol. Zander was glad the rebels seemed to have no intentions on storming the Citadel, which put his greatest fear to rest.

Phaedrus slapped him on the back, conscious of his disapproving scowls, and attempted to smooth matters out. "Remarkable bunch, aren't they? Such fire, such life."

"Very excitable," Zander said. "Better than any circus I've seen."

"We're just trying to liven things up here a little. Got to give them the taste of danger to keep their spirits alive."

"I'm not amused, Phaedrus. We're out here pulling pranks the day before you intend to pull the pin on the revolution. A revolution, mind you, we planned together. But a revolution I don't understand anymore. So forgive me if I find this a bit foolish."

"It's simply a red herring. This night of pranks has become tradition for us, and not to get all sentimental, but we started it in your memory," he said. "Just like the old days. Remember the Witching Hour?"

How could Zander forget their first real experiment together? It had been a test of the system. Introduce the radical element and see how the Order reacts. The plan was simple: let loose a hundred stray black cats in Allister Commons during the summer solstice, just to see what would happened.

The chaos that unfolded was more than they'd anticipated. Superstition brought people to tears and violence, thrashing to get away from the furry black omens. They stampeded through the streets, blindly running, the guardians left helpless to do anything except shoot at the black cats and claw at the stone walls themselves.

But that had been back then. There had been an innocence then. Murder in the name of a cause always changes the situation.

"We've set a precedent here," Phaedrus said. "The guardians are expecting this. If we don't pull this prank, they'd be immediately suspicious."

Angus popped out of the dark and put his arms over their shoulders. "And what are you boys talking about here? Planning the revolution without me?"

"There you go again with your bloody plans," Phaedrus said and walked off.

Soon the rebels were on the move again, over the city, across the rooftops, heading east into the Old Quarter with its odd mix of government buildings, museums, and public offices, the outer edge of which was fronted by the ivy brick walls of the Academy.

The rebels crossed unnoticed onto the slanted roofs that enclosed the civil courts and the offices of the bureaucracy—the Office of Vital Records (births, deaths, marriages), the Department of Trial and Error, the Office of Common Sense, and Zander's former employer the Office of Preservation.

The rebels treaded softly, grins washed away. Ahead the Academy stood silent, locked in brief recess for the Centennial tomorrow when its best and brightest pupils would compete for the honor of becoming heir to the Grand Muse's throne. It seemed fitting that the school bordered on the manufacturing sector, Zander thought, the mass production of generic wares beside the mass indoctrination of the Republic's next generation.

The roofs spanned out in a horseshoe ring over the Academy walls and made a crescent awning that hung over the Savior's Garden. The memorial garden was a place of solace and reflection dedicated to the victims of the plague and the world that had died with them. It would be here that the elders of Republic would come before the festivities tomorrow to pay penance to their ancestors.

The rebels breached this holy sanctuary, descending from on high, dropped ropes and shimmied down the Academy's stone walls into the garden. Hedges lined a paved walk where a series of statues depicted the suffering and triumph of the new society over the old, and in the center of the garden, a giant statue of a scientist welcomed the rebels with open arms.

The statue wore a flowing uniform, same as the waistcoats worn by the guardians, carved to mark every wrinkle and seam. Its arms were grossly disproportionate to its body and forever frozen in a wide embrace, as if hugging all of creation. From behind a pair of stony goggles, the giant smiled upon the rebels like a father might his children.

E.S. Benedict, it said in the marble base beneath his carved feet, Hero and Saint.

Gazing at the statue, a flush of memories came back to Zander, as if he were remembering them for the first time. A scattered childhood, a herd of children suited in numbers, scientists in white labcoats giving instructions in a metallic room of colored boxes and puzzles, ceremony after ceremony pending his release as an adolescent, the stench of the dormitories, his induction into Sainthood, the years of apprenticeship in the filing room at the Office of Preservation, watching, waiting, mimicking his mentor's methods for keeping the records of marriages away from the records of births.

"Glory be the Republic," Purple Harry hollered, reaching out from behind the statue to paint a manic smile on Benedict's stone face. He hopped down from the pedestal and rejoined the mayhem underway.

The rebels, like rabid dogs, slopped their brush tongues along the garden walls, statues, the Mourners benches. They drew sporadic Xs on the paved walkway, along with the words, SIT DOWN, STAND UP, ROLL OVER, all the way to the gated entrance into the Academy. Their brains were scrambled in a full-moon fever, sizzling with the thought of revolution, each one madder than the next.

Zander let down his hood and observed for awhile, paint jar in hand. There was a certain brilliance to the twilight raid in its brazen foolishness. Unknown to the ever-present wandering eyes of the Republic, these phantom men painted in a wild delirium, splashed their defiance in dripping white paint.

He expected the side gates to break wide open at any moment, for infrared eyes to flare yellow in the dark as a guardian patrol surrounded the garden with their LR-5s charged and ready. But the guardians never came. Not a sound, rustle, or whisper could be heard beyond the rebels' laughter.

Along the garden path, he passed a rebel who was writing in broad strokes on a set of granite steps, a single word per step. TRUTH... IS... the rebel stopped so he could mull it over. Zander studied the broken sentence, and without thinking, gently dipped the bristles in his paint jar. He finished the lingering phrase... TRUTH... IS... RELATIVE.

"Relative, eh? I suppose that makes the mark," the man grinned underneath his hood. Another disciple of the great Phaedrus, Zander thought. Amazing how that grin breeds.

"I didn't even see you there. You truly are a ghost like they say," he said. "Zander, right?"

"That is one of many names," Zander replied.

"Name's Stub. Wonderful celebration, isn't this?"

"And what exactly are we celebrating anyway?"

"Why the same as any other day. The succulent sins of life. The primal call. Free will and rebirth in every new moment. Bhava, blink," he said. "I've been anxious to meet you. Phaedrus raves about the old days. I must confess you were the one who inspired me to join the cause."

"Really? How's that?"

"The Millhouse Raid, I guess. I'd been an admirer of the ghosts before, yet that raid put everything in perspective. I myself was returning from my humbles at the barbershop when I heard the first glorious bang. It shattered my world to see those guardians on the run, the windows smash with that magic touch, the song of the sirens. It woke me up, it did. Woke me to the possibility of life without the Republic."

"That was a mistake," Zander said. "Many innocent citizens died that day. It didn't need to happen."

"Maybe so, but it saved many others. Me, for instance."

Zander wished he could fade into the background, anything to get away from this man's misplaced veneration. He searched for Phaedrus among the mayhem yet saw him nowhere, and then far off, he noticed several shadowy figures on the rooftops, headed toward the manufacturing sector.

"Excuse me a moment," he said to his admirer. He broke away and walked over to Weber who was defacing the statue of a dying mother with long soliloquies.

"Where'd Phaedrus head off to?"

Weber looked around and shrugged the comment off, "Gone already, is he? So rude, he's always disappearing without saying goodbye." He cricked his neck and yelled, "Angus, yank that bottle away from Harry before he drinks it all."

Purple Harry slugged from the moonshine bottle whilst singing from on top a bench:

"The world is a grand affair,
a song of joy and sorrow, hope and despair
and many die before they lose their hair
and many cry while others stare
but ah, we all get our turn.
To rage and burn
to sit and brood
to dance a jig in the nude
to love and lose and pick and choose,
Our poison, pleasure, pain, or leisure
and all that does entice
while we the fools delight in vice of paradise."

Angus snatched the bottle from his waving hands. The

bottle passed among the rebels, smeared with white fingerprints as it made the rounds. Weber took a slug of the moonshine and thrust the bottle into Zander's hands.

"Something to loosen those dead nerves of yours," he said. "Drink and be merry, my brother. We have a long night ahead of us."

The bottle smelt worse than the paint fumes, but Zander drank from it anyway and sat trading gulps of moonshine with the gang. Across the memorial garden, Neale had climbed halfway up one of the hanging ropes so he could paint OBEY high on the brick wall for everyone to see. A group of rebels delicately painted the leaves of a small magnolia tree white and sang, "Damn the Heroes, damn the Saints. Damn the Smiths, and let us paint, our fate upon the shadowglass."

Zander slugged from the moonshine again as he felt that old feeling return again. It overcame him in waves, as if he were thawing from a prolonged freeze. A righteous indignation, a reckless anger against the commonwealth and everything it stood for. A surge to cry fraud at the tenements of new man, the innocents asleep in their cozy beds, unable to rest before checking their alarm, once, twice, thrice. Why not scream? Why not howl? he thought. And so what if this rebellion was a return to the madmen past, to primal mankind, to the dangerous mind that bled on instinct and intuition, not holy logic and superstition.

He thought of all the happy unassuming citizens of the Republic who dared not question, who would never set foot outside the boundaries of their instruction. These were not the same people who had been granted free reign of the earth, whose color and comment had once animated all that was great. Their freedom traded for security and mime.

This was not a city, this was not a civilization. This was a mockery. A vain attempt at humanity. Mice in a machine. So why not howl? Why not scream? Why not show these machines what it means to be alive? A drunken grin crept across his face as he watched the rebels dance on.

"Funny, isn't it?" said a voice from behind. The voice floated tranquilly on air like an echo in his brain. He turned to meet a hooded man who sat cross-legged on a nearby bench. He assumed the stranger was one of the rebels at first, dressed in a dark hooded cloak. But the haunting iridescence of his blue eyes told him differently.

"What's that?" Zander asked. "What's so funny?"

The stranger let down his hood, unveiling his bald misshapen head. He smiled with transparent grace. "The dance of life. The twists and turns. Oh Marcus, what a mess have you gotten yourself into."

Zander checked to see if perhaps the man was addressing somebody else, but the rest of the rebels were occupied elsewhere in their righteous slops of paint.

A breeze brushed through the memorial garden, the painted trees burst buds of white petal snow that fluttered aloft in the strange wind. He looked at the stranger who refused to shake his gaze off of him. His sedate face seemed eerily familiar, like a gravestone in the cemetery of his buried memories. In the stranger's lap, a small blue candle flickered and trembled on extinction.

"Marcus," the stranger said calmly, "this will not end well."

"I'm sorry, you must be mistaking me with someone else," Zander said. When he stood from the bench, the gravity of the drink spun his head in circles, the mayhem whirled round and round, laughter echoed off the ivy brick walls, paint slashed the bricks.

"You're lost in the fathoms, Marcus. You're not supposed to be here."

Zander felt the iridescent eyes at his back and turned to find the stranger still staring. "Who are you and why are you pestering me?"

"You know who I am. You have always known."

"Look, you've got the wrong man."

"Do I?" the stranger said. "Have you forgotten already?" A snap of his fingers sent flashes through Zander's mind like cars on a moving freight train... the moon and sea of stars over an ancient metropolis... a well hidden in the hedges... tea time down in the hollow... a bonedust desert with endless dune horizons... The memories fought to surface themselves as Zander fought to straighten his thoughts.

"Marcus, you don't belong here," the stranger said, "You need to—"

"My name is not Marcus, you lunatic," Zander said. He turned away again, woozy and nauseous, his vision blurred. He made it only a few steps before he was forced to sit down on the bench. The vagrant memories resurfaced in sudden fragments, half-resolved, half-diluted.

"Is this a prank? Who put you up to this? Phaedrus?" He wheeled his eyes through the rebel brigade, still hard at work, painting the garden white.

"I wish I could tell you everything you need to know, yet I fear this would only further unhinge your mind," the stranger said. The voice seemed not to come from his lips but rather from a haunted chamber in Zander's own skull. "The story is simple and simply told. But pay attention to know what will unfold, the truths of old..."

CHAPTER SIXTEEN

The Story of the Jargon King

The stranger began the story in a whispered tone, waving a finger through the blue flame of the candle in his lap. Zander held his throbbing head in his hands and listened, watching the stranger tease the fire with hypnotic repetition.

"Twice upon a time and long ago, the Jargon King of Blah sat high upon his royal throne. Every day, he would snore away the idle hours, his belly too full and too heavy to lug around, jiggling with the sleepy chuckles that erupted from his dreams, because life was grand and he was king. A god unto his people.

"His noble lords and ladies would loiter about his throne room and wander the vaulted corridors of the palace, chatting about ontology, philosophy, politics, ethics, religion, and everything else that didn't affect their sheltered lives. Outside the palace walls, life was not so jovial and carefree. Outside the palace walls, the king's subjects were starving. Peasant people, hard-working folk, farmers of one kind or another.

"By strict law, every uneducated person in the Kingdom of Blah was forced to farm. But they didn't harvest your typical crops. No rice, no wheat, no potatoes, or substance that one might call 'food' per se. They raised crops of a different variety. Words, the intellectual food of civilization. Cultivated across the countryside, crops of nouns, pronouns, adjectives, verbs, adverbs, conjunctions, prepositions, and the occasional sprout of punctuation, prospered in fields of grammar. This literary harvest was then heavily taxed by the king and his lords, which left the farmers with little more than scraps to live on.

"One terrible winter, there came a time of great strife and famine in the land of Blah. The peasant farmers, who were by far the majority, could hardly survive on the puny words they were allowed to keep. They were so thin their lungs hardly had enough breath to speak. They tried in desperation to invent new words like snork, dussleworp, vuggle, frast, and nubble. But none of these words ever ripened into parlance.

"Meanwhile, the nobles gobbled and gagged on huge lengthy words, sometimes eight syllables long. The Jargon King was the greatest glutton of all, yet no one dared question his appetite nor his power. It was presumed that he'd been ordained by the gods to rule because of his deep understanding of the harvest, his profound knowledge of the crops. This knowledge however hadn't come from heaven's manifest; it came from a very special book, an empowering tome that he'd swallowed for safe keeping, a Dictionary.

"During the worst days of the great famine, a young peasant boy named Ivan heard rumors of this secret book and plotted revolution. He was a natural idealist; he believed that no one should starve and that no one should have too much or too little. He believed that words should be distributed equally among the people and that all history hitherto had been the history of class appetites.

"So he united the farmers against the Jargon King and raided the palace. The peasants, as a people of short words, had plenty of weapons—an onomatopoeia artillery and whole SHA-BAM! of them at that. They subdued the palace guards with a WHACK, SMACK, CRACK attack. The mob broke through the gates with a SMASH, CRASH, BASH. The noble infantry were pulverized with a WHAM, BAM, SMASH, CRASH, BANG, TWANG, CLANG.

"During the commotion, the Jargon King was giving another one of his nonsensical yet verbose speeches to the nobles of Blah: 'Now you must comprehend that such flagellation leads to a causal situation in its pityriasis sense and state, then our aluminiferous reimpression will not blastogenesize, but rather cerebriate in an omniscient transcendence into marsupial acquiescence.'

"The Jargon King then burped, the famous closer of all his speeches. The nobles responded with a huge round of applause, which soon turned into pleas for help when the peasant mob finally busted into the throne room. SMACK, POW, THWACK... the peasants bludgeoned the bourgeoisie till their egos burst.

"Ivan barged through the riot and confronted the Jargon King himself. His majesty simply sat on his throne, unaffected by the coup d'etat at hand, as fearless and as pompous as ever. 'The chaotic association of antidisestablishmentarianistic parties is futile against the jurisdiction under the sovereignty of totalitarianistic subjugation!'

"Ivan's refute was simple and to the point. He punched the Jargon King in his jellyfish gut with a gigantic BAM! to which the plump tyrant belched up that sacred book and key to his power, the Dictionary. He toppled backward over his throne and choked on his own tongue.

"Thus the Jargon King met his end. The peasants rejoiced and unanimously proclaimed Ivan the new king of Blah. They had complete faith that he would fulfill his promise, share the yearly harvest, and disperse the wealth of knowledge by ripping out pages of the Dictionary so that they could be given to every man, woman, and child. This had also been the young king's honest intentions, until he began to study the book's contents.

"Day and night, he absorbed each word and its denotative brilliance, its connotative currency. The more he learned, the less he thought or cared for the peasant people who had delivered him to the throne. And as Ivan sat on that grand throne, revered by his people as a god, given every luxury a king could ever want, he started to wonder, 'How could I possibly share these words with these ignorant fools? They wouldn't understand their beauty, their truth, the way they roll from the tongue and taste like honey. They don't even know the proper syntax and grammar associated with correct speech and formulation of sentence structure. They would probably just sloppily throw them around in sentence fragments, hanging subordinate clauses. They would bastardize these amazing words and this holy book.'

"With this thought, Ivan swallowed the Dictionary, which then swelled his gut with word after word after word. And so it still swells today. And so he still sits on his throne, surrounded by a select counsel of educated nobles who gobble his words and deliver him the hoarded crops from the fertile fields of Blah. And, of course, his jellyfish belly occasionally jiggles with laughter, mocking the stupid, illiterate, simple-minded nature of the poor starving farmers. So lives on the Jargon King…"

Zander lifted his head from his hands. The garden hedges and stone paths wobbled before his eyes, blurry at first and then stabilizing in a foggy focus. Throughout the memorial grounds, the rebels continued to paint every last brick, every last block of granite, every last square of the paved walk with dissident graffiti, although in more leisurely manner than before, a lethargy brought on by drunken stupor. Their laughter grated his eardrums and added to the dull, indistinct pain in his temples left over from the heavy moonshine.

"What a depressing story," Zander said to the stranger.

"Indeed," the stranger said, "but it does have a poignant moral to it."

"And what's that?"

"It's a four-fold truth," the mysterious one told him. "1) History is hilarious and never ceases to repeat itself. 2) There's no such thing as a revolution, only a reshuffling of the deck. 3) Ignorance is a luxury for the rich and a yoke for the poor. And the most important: 4) As the ancient proverb says… knowledge is power."

"But what does all this have to do with me?" Zander asked.

"You pursue the truth, although you've always known it.

You seek perfection, although you know it doesn't exist. You want a peaceful resolution to everything, although you know that life is a constant struggle and necessarily so. There's nothing I can do to change your fate. You don't belong here, Marcus. But here you've come. Perhaps to better understand. I will only give you this advice. Accept your world, your life, your fate as it is. The silence within will lead to your salvation. Only then will the contention resolve itself."

"What contention?" Zander demanded to know. "What are you talking about?"

"Just be careful," the stranger said. "And weigh your passions wisely."

The mysterious one folded his hands, smiled that serene smile and bowed his head. The blue candle in his lap snuffed out, and with it, the stranger vanished from the bench. Skinny trails of smoke twirled and tore in the light breeze with no sign that the candle nor the stranger had ever been there.

Zander scanned the garden to see where he had gone. He rose slowly from the bench and stumbled along the hedged walkway, searching his brain for those distant memories that had surfaced at the stranger's bidding. A faint alarm sounded outside the garden walls, somewhere in the city, however the rebels hardly noticed the disturbance since they were so absorbed in the twilight mayhem. That is until a gunshot shattered the night.

The mad dance came to a halt. The rebels froze in awkward poses with their brushes about to slash—everyone except for Neale who stood near the garden entrance, his rifle aimed at the granite stones where a blasted Orbserver shot sparks and smoldered.

CHAPTER SEVENTEEN

Death in the Coliseum

A white wing of togas arched round the Coliseum amphitheater. Here, the people of the desert kingdom of Nault sat on their day of leisure, packed row after row on stone benches that scorched in the midday sun. They twitched with excitement, prone to random fits of violence while they swilled wine by the bottle, munched on grilled lizard sticks, and counted down the minutes to showtime.

As always, the Emperor sat impatient in his royal box, a crowning jewel that jutted out above the rest. As always, the souvenir hawkers sold gladiator toys for the children, shorn hands, feet, swords of the fallen, and other spoils of the game. The audience cheered with open mouths and dumb eyes, overcome with joy for the beginning of the Light Season. Armed, dangerous, and blinded by enthusiasm.

Although the Coliseum was hardly a calm reprieve from the horrors of the black ash nightmare, Addie was relieved to be anywhere besides the cold desert. She had ridden the black horse at lightning speed over the dunes and toward the rising sun. As the sun disintegrated the black starless sky, she'd witnessed an army of skeletons called to life from underneath the desert. Their boney hands surfaced from the black ash to pull out their skeletal bodies and chase after the horse by the thousands as she rode on. Along with the skeletons, tremendous giants awoke to stalk the desert and feast on these animated bones.

Addie had kept her eyes closed and trusted the horse to guide the way, holding on for dear life, listening to the wind whip by, the sound of the skeleton chatter, the thumping giants. She opened them only for brief glimpses what lay ahead, as her trusty horse raced under the colossal legs of these enormous beasts, as the skeletons rattled their bone fists on the chase, as huge hands swooped and grabbed the awakened dead by the handful for breakfast. She opened her eyes again, once the sounds had faded off and her horse had slowed. She opened her eyes to behold the Coliseum.

When she finally arrived at the gates, the guards out front gave her grief for not having a) a ticket, b) a toga, and c) a convincing smile. But they thought it better not argue with this barefoot rider, marked with weird ashen symbols, demanding that she should be let inside with a series of equally confusing hand gestures. And so Addie said a tearful goodbye to her horse and entered through the gates.

The only trouble now was finding a seat. The rat-a-tat-tat of drums rumbled through the amphitheatre stands. The audience jumped from their stone benches in applause, from the highest ring down to the front row. Still, it was unclear what all the excitement was about. The oval field was completely empty, a sandy arena with metal grills along the rounded sides. Maybe they have incredible eyesight, Addie thought as she hunted for someplace to sit. Maybe they're cheering on a battle of dune mice or lizards or something.

Little did Addie know she was about to witness the battle to end all battles, the contention to end all contentions, the philosophical fight-to-the-death-match-of-all-time-only-one-can-survive: Sir Real versus the Hippocritus.

~

"Wake up! Time to face the devil," the warden tossed a bucket of water in the prisoner's face. Norman squealed awake, shaking the dirty water out of his eyes, and discovered himself chained in a dungeon underground. Flickering torches shown weakly on the other prisoners along the chamber wall, framing their misery in the weak light; more hung in further reaches of the dungeon, forgotten in the dark but heard in the echoing moans, groans, and rattle of chains by which they made their presence known.

"That a boy," said the fat face sneering. The warden put the bucket down and fiddled with his chains. Norman dropped onto his knees, unshackled, and rubbed his burning wrists, dizzy from his long sleep in the dank dark dungeon.

"Thank you, thank you sir. I think my arms were about to fall off—"

The warden booted him onto the sawdust floor. "I didn't say you could speak, you filthy dog. Up, up on your feet." He kicked him again, this time square in the chest.

"I'd have an easier time getting up if you'd stop—"

A punch to the jaw smacked Norman flat on his back in the sawdust.

"Don't be smart with me, dog," the warden said. He bent over, clutched him by the head, and cinched a metal collar on his neck. "Today you die, boy. Today you die."

"Again? Isn't once enough?" Norman said.

The crack of a whip jolted him onto his feet.

"Now come along, we must get you fitted. Not that it'll matter much," the warden smirked with all four of his rotten teeth. He snatched a torch off the wall and yanked on the collar chain. "I said come along, you filthy dog." Norman followed in jerks, guided by the warden down the dungeon hall toward flames bobbing in the darkness.

~

THAT'S RIGHT! THE SHOW'S ABOUT TO BEGIN!

The voice boomed over the din of drums. On the left side of the arena, a trick door in the field split open and out came the announcer on a rising pedestal. He slowly ascended with his arms toward the sky, as if he were willing it to rise. His outrageous hair, bright orange and maddening and twice the size of his head, curled in waves like cosmic fire. The announcer brought a bullhorn to his jumbo lips and shouted: LADIES AND GENTS! I WELCOME YOU TO

WITNESS THE BOUT OF THE CENTURY... A DEATH MATCH OF GRUESOME PROPORTIONS...

A hush from the audience held the pause for all it was worth.

SIR REAL VS. HIPPOCRITUS!!!

The audience went wild for the start of the grand show, spitting wine and smashing bottles onto the field in a sign of approval. The announcer and his flaming supernova hair rose to meet their eyes like the morning sun.

IN THE LEFT CORNER, THE MOST FEARED MAN IN THE DESERT OF ALCAZARA... A VILLIAN WHO WEIGHES HIS HONOR IN OUR DEAD... A DEVIL WHO RECKONS BY THE SWORD... SIR REAL!!!

The south gates swung apart. Out in chains came a man reviled by the Kingdom of Nault. Sir Real, the boldest knight to ever grace the desert of Alcazara, reduced to this humiliating entrance. When the guards escorted him onto the field, he raised his head to see the thousand cruel smiles that heralded his death.

Sir Real, with his shining armor, handsome complexion and sandy blonde hair, had never lost a battle and was only taken prisoner by the knights of Nault because he'd taken an ill-advised nap in the desert a little too close to enemy lines. Legend surrounded the hero. The greatest giant slayer that ever lived, they said. Sir Death, they called him. A brutal fighter in the unending war between the Kingdom of Nault and the Kingdom of Blithe, two sandy outposts in the ash desert.

Nobody could remember why they were fighting over the hundreds of miles that lay east to west between the two kingdoms. All that mattered was the death tally and who was winning. But with the coming of the Light Season, the knights had returned home and the war was put on hold once again, since both kingdoms preferred not to tangle with the strange desert monsters awakened by the sun.

The Coliseum erupted in an uproar of boos and hisses when the guards unlocked Sir Real's collar and backed away. But Sir Real did not unsheathe his sword nor slash it around like a fool. Instead, he removed his helmet, flung his golden hair, and boldly saluted the Emperor in his royal box.

A few gasps escaped from certain women in the audience who hid their tears while their husbands chanted for the knight's death. Rumor had it Sir Real had a dozen of lovers on both ends of the desert and young sons fighting on both sides of the war. But the men of Nault cared little about this. They chanted for blood because that was the game, because that was the thrill: to see the clash of mortal men and their blades, to see the animal of man come alive.

IN THE RIGHT CORNER, OUR DEFENDER... A BEAST WHO INSPIRES FEAR... A BEAST NOT TO BE TRUSTED... A BEAST WHOSE BLOODTHIRST IS NEVER QUENCHED... HIPPOCRITUS!!!

Even before the north gate let loose the gladiator, the Coliseum quaked with foot-stomping, a cacophony of joyous screams. The stomping built in momentum until the metal gate cranked open and out lumbered a huge purple beast clad in armor.

Truth was nobody knew whether he was man or beast. He stood seven-feet tall with peeling purple skin, the face of a hippopotamus, and hands so large they could squash a man's head like a melon. It required thirty knights to capture him in the desert, tie him down, and carry him back on the slat of a catapult. They attempted to tame the beast at first, then quickly decided he would be best kept in the Coliseum rather than out in the desert where he was liable to start thrashing anything that moved. Two hundred dead gladiators later, Hippocritus had grown to like the game.

PLAYERS, TAKE YOUR POSITIONS.

Hippocritus came face to face with his disturbingly handsome contender in the middle of the field. Sir Real winked at his secret damsels in the audience.

TO THE DEATH...

Addie snuck down the aisle to an empty seat beside a young woman in a toga who covered her face in anxious anticipation of that first clash of swords, watching the field through her fingers.

"Do you mind if I sit here?" Addie asked. The young woman turned with an expression of mortified bliss, her eyes glazed over, hand over her mouth, biting her palm in anxious exhilaration. Addie didn't press the question.

ON THE COUNT OF THREE...

The gladiators posed ready to fight with their hands at their hilts. Sir Real put on his helmet and soaked in this noble moment before the duel, unbothered by his beastly purple opponent who growled with bloodthirsty rage.

ONE...

Hippocritus was ready to pounce and kill.

TWO...

Sir Real was ready for a cup of tea and another nap.

THREE!!!

They drew their swords together. SHING—Hippocritus unsheathed a huge rapier and slashed it about in the air. SHING—Sir Real gallantly pulled out his blade and judged by the tremors in Hippocritus's hand where the strike would come. He thrust it forward to parry the blow, and heard the amphitheatre explode with laughter. The sword he held was not his trusty sword of Alganor, anointed by the priests of Blithe and handed down by the king himself. Instead he was pointing a foot-long dagger at the beast.

He looked down at the puny sword and then up at the towering purple gladiator, just as the beast swung.

FIGHT!

And off went Sir Real's head flying toward the stands.

~

"There," the warden said and made sure the chain-mail armor was on snugly. "That should work."

Norman wobbled his head. The gladiator helmet jiggled loose at his ears.

"He needs a size smaller. I told you he's a 35b," a second warden said. "His small body makes his head look big."

"I told you to be quiet," the first warden said. "I don't pester you when you're dressing them." He tilted the helmet and readjusted it straight on Norman's head.

"It just looks silly," the second warden said. "He'll get his head cut off."

Blood-curdling applause thundered from the stadium above.

"Sounds like the first contender already did," the first warden said. "Besides, his skull is larger than it is wide. I need the helmet big enough so that it will touch his shoulders like it should. It's going to be wobbly. There's no way around that."

He held out his hand and the second warden passed him a sword. The first warden checked its gleaming edges, how the shiny blade threw firelight off its sharpened point. It was spotless; not a smear, stain nor streak of rust marred the blade, even though the sword had spilled its fair share of blood. These gladiator swords were the wardens' pride and joy. They spent painstaking hours at the whetstone, sharpening the edges of even the puniest daggers, just to ensure the most gore.

Norman almost felt honored when the warden laid the huge sword in his hands. It was without a doubt the shiniest thing he'd ever seen. In the gleam of the blade, he gazed at himself, suited in armor.

"It's a little heavy," he noted, weighing the sword in his open palms.

"You get a better swing that way. Trust us," the first warden said and yanked on the collar chain. "Come along now, dog. Chin up and make the Emperor proud."

~

WOW, LOOK AT THAT HEAD FLY! I BELIEVE, YES, THAT IS A RECORD-BREAKING DISTANCE THERE...

Ecstasy surged through the audience as Sir Real's severed head flew into the stands. A young boy, hoisted on his father's shoulders, caught it in mid-air. He hugged the knight's head tight with glee, soaking his white toga with fresh blood, and then plucked off the helmet so that he could play with its golden hair.

Meanwhile on the field, Sir Real's beheaded body ran in circles like a cut chicken. He lunged sporadically with his tiny dagger at where he assumed his opponent was, while Hippocritus waited offside for the perfect moment to make his grand finale.

The audience cheered him on, shouting and stomping and yelling at the top of their lungs: "Let him have it, Hippo! He doesn't need those legs. Cut 'em off! Split him down! Make him round!"

The armored beast answered this request simply by walking over and knocking Sir Real to the sandy ground. A horrendous shriek of delight from the audience sent Hippocritus into a fit of blissful fury, which he exerted by hacking and plunging his sword into the knight's corpse over and over, as though he were churning butter.

WELL FOLKS, LOOKS LIKE THIS MATCH HAS TURNED INTO A GRAND EXPOSITION OF CARNAGE GALORE!

Hippocritus threw kisses to his ravenous fans from a safe distance when the lions were released from their cages at chain's length to clean up the arena. The lions roared onto the field and tore the decapitated body to shreds, paying little attention to the gloating victor. Hippocritus bowed toward the stands and the Emperor perched in his royal seat.

The Emperor clapped once for the victor, as is right and honored, before delicately taking a grilled lizard stick from his royal guard and enjoying a dainty bite.

Never had Addie seen so much blood, she felt sullied by simply witnessing the carnage. Her stomach had lurched with each churn of the beast's sword. A throbbing came again at her temples, as if something were trying to break loose.

"He really split him one, huh?" said a spectator seated nearby.

"That was the most revolting thing I've ever seen," Addie replied.

"Right you are, sister," the man said. "You can almost taste it. That's the life of the game. Wait till you see the next round. Heard it's a newbie. Fresh as your liver. You want to take a seat?"

"No, thank you. I have a fine view from here."

"Smart. Yes, very clever."

"Leave her be, Crito," said the man beside him. "Can't you see she's trying to enjoy the show in peace? No one wants to hear you babble on. Keep it shut. The next round is about to begin."

"Ignore him, sport. Looky here." Crito opened his toga and displayed a row of severed fingers that dangled from the fold. "Collector's items. This one here is from the famous Battle Rouge. Good and fierce, that fight was. I had to pry this little digit from the lion's mouth."

"It's all lies. He's a dirty grave robber."

"Your jealousy is unbecoming, brother. These are priceless little treasures, the real raw deal, and that's what I'll cut you for them."

"Thank you, but I'm not interested," Addie said.

"See I told you she wouldn't be."

"Well, of course not, with you spoiling all the fun."

The argument that followed gave Addie ample opportunity to sneak away from the finger-seller and his friend. She didn't get far however since it was nearly impossible to squeeze through the togas in the crowded stands, the spectators chanting for more gore. In the swell of cheers, she missed the introduction of the next contender. She only heard the final quip.

TWICE THE SLICE IS TWICE AS NICE, EH FOLKS?

The audience applauded when the lions were hauled from the field by their chains. Addie watched the guards escort the next contender out onto the field, a skinny gladiator in a helmet so big it half-blinded him. There was something familiar about the awkwardness of the young man in armor. But it wasn't until the gladiator tipped up his helmet, in awe of the arena and its crazed spectators, that she spotted the unmistakable look of fright on the face of her long lost friend.

Chapter Eighteen

Mechanical Shadows

The rebels escaped to the rooftops with sirens sounding. An electronic wail cranked out from the emergency beacons in volume, rising from a low-pitched whine to an ear-piercing squeal, over and over again. The black-clad gang raced against time into the fiendish night, out over the Old Quarter and onto the factory warehouses, seeking shelter in the manufacturing sector.

Their every move was now being tracked from afar by the roving lights of the Citadel spires. The guardians would be waiting, they knew, their sights set on the phantoms' mad dash back into the outer city. It was only a matter of time before they were dodging laser blasts in the shadows.

"They'll be waiting," Weber told Zander, ducked down behind the hulking machinery on the warehouse roofs. "We're lucky we skinned out of there alive. They won't be far behind."

Zander pulled his revolver from his belt. "What can I do to help?"

"Just keep your finger hooked in that trigger and wait for the signal."

The guardians marched down Piston Row, their shoulders arched, their LR-5s scanning the rooftops. Dozens of scope beams drew invisible red lines along the roof hatch houses, boilers, ventilation shafts, massive tube fans.

Red emergency beacons flared and blared this message in the streets: *Everything is under control. Stay in your homes. This is only a test. Take one blue pill and one red pill and pay penance to the Order. Glory be the Republic.*

The emergency beacons cast streaks of pulsing light across the river where the warehouses connected with a row of factories laid out along the canal. The rebels blindly sprinted and jumped from one warehouse to the next, sobered by the cat-and-mouse game afoot. Now and then, the night clouds would drift to block the moon and shroud the roofscape in darkness, later to betray the cloaked gang with spells of light.

Movement on the warehouse roof ahead froze the rebels at once. They wrapped themselves in their cloaks and dove into the dark. Weber and Angus, huddled behind a water tower on the far end, leveled their rifles at the warehouse ahead. Out from a pair of defunct factory boilers, Neale covered their trail with his rifle sighted on the roofs behind.

Zander, leaning flush against the serrated metal of a ventilation shaft, checked his revolver and spun the wheel. Where was Phaedrus? He noticed that Sprockett and Elsa were likewise missing, presumably off with the maniac on some mission unknown to him.

He listened to the alarm sirens and watched the search lights cut through the darkness, remembering the first time he'd met Phaedrus. Quiet at his desk, the wide-eyed rebel was no one remarkable among the archivers in the Office of Preservation. No evidence of his scheming mind except for that wily grin which would slip out on occasion when he'd find something of interest in the piles of time-ruined history books, reports, letters, and other miscellaneous papers on his desk. Simply another subservient worker, skimming off and cataloguing pertinent information for the records, typed out in file after file on his grapho-machine. Then one fateful day, he'd surprised Zander on his way home, to his once quiet life, to his quiet home, to his love Scarlet who would later betray him to the Order.

"Zander, right?" he'd asked with a gleam in his eye.

"Yes?"

"Mind if I walk with you?"

They walked for three blocks and talked casually about the archives, polite conversation with a few grumbles about this or that inefficiency in the office bureaucracy. Phaedrus was not afraid to grin anymore. Derby tucked over his feral eyes, he probed Zander with questions and let his mouth curl until that crooked smile finally broke loose.

"You're different from the rest. I've noticed that about you," he'd said. "There's something I want to show you. Something I think you might be interested in seeing, as a lover of history, that is. A little keepsake, that I kept for myself. You won't tell, will you?"

Zander cursed himself for being curious, for meeting him the next day after work let out and walking into a world of conspiracy that would change his life forever. But then again how can one refuse a mystery?

Shots rang out. Zander stayed hidden behind the ventilation shaft. Someone returned fire carelessly, LR-5 blasts shattered off an exhaust fan, spitting flecks of steel. He poked his revolver around the corner and saw a guardian patrol emerge on the warehouse roof ahead. Their high-collar uniforms ran stripes down to their steel-toed boots. Their infrared goggles made a faint hum as the guardians scanned the darkness with yellow piercing light.

The rebels observed their movements from the shadows, ready for the inevitable. Zander, crouched and motionless, remained calm and weighed the options. The roof's hatch house was only a few yards away, although the steel door into the warehouse would undoubtedly be locked. But that didn't mean all hope was lost. While he calculated a number of different scenarios on how to get inside, the hatch house door broke open on its own and another patrol breached its way onto the roof, armed and cautious.

The blaze of gunfire lit up the night. Zander rolled out and blindly knocked off a shot in the direction of danger while searching his brain for a way out. Two more shots rattled back, hitting a chimney and shattering a window in the hatch house. Then silence. The air scarred by the smell of burnt metal.

He looked out when the moon vanished behind the clouds again. Yellow infrared eyes probed the darkened rooftop, like fireflies in the dark. The patrol lieutenant signaled to the other patrol on the neighboring warehouse and sent a few of his own patrolmen over to check out the factory boilers near the roof edge.

Zander traded glances with Weber by the water tower, who made motions with his darting eyes toward the hatch door and then mouthed something he couldn't quite make out in dark.

"This is Guardian Patrol 565. Lay down your weapons or prepare to face the consequences."

Weber laid down his rifle and came out the dark end of the water tower. The patrol charged their LR-5s and targeted the rebel, laser scopes dotted his hooded cloak. Weber walked boldly toward the armed patrol. "Don't shoot, I surrender. I'm alone."

The lieutenant unhooked his side holster and unleashed a microphazer burst at close range. Weber crumpled onto his knees, convulsing in shock and sweating out of every pore.

"Really? Do you want to lie to me a second time?" the patrol lieutenant said. "Where are your friends, heathen?"

Weber trembled in a ball, barely able to stutter out the words. "I'm alone. I swear. My rifle is there. Please, I'm unarmed."

Zander watched the lieutenant shoot Weber with another blast and cringed in sympathy. None of the rebels moved from their hiding places. He was impressed by their patience. Not until the cuffs come out, he told himself. Never show your face until you have to. As he lay in wait, twin red electric eyes floated up to greet him, swaying back and forth in front of his face. He brought his revolver to its robotic head just when the Orbserver locked in on his retina.

The gunshot knocked him backward, the mechanical orb

fell in a fit of sparks. In the next moment, the clouds unmasked the full moon and illuminated the rebels in hiding.

The patrol had little time to react. When the guardians turned their LR-5s, the rebels rose and returned the favor. The cloaked gang emerged, from front and behind, and cocked their rifles at the patrol near the hatch house. Neale poked out from the boilers with a few other rebels to surprise the guardians who were searching the far end of the rooftop. Angus and Purple Harry came out from the water tower to hold off the other patrol on the warehouse across the way.

"Drop your weapons now," the lieutenant said, his microphazer angled at Weber, close enough to fry his brain.

Zander whipped round the ventilation shaft and pointed his revolver at the lieutenant only feet away. "Stand down."

The patrol turned their sights on him.

"Stand down," he demanded again, his revolver trained at the lieutenant's forehead. "Tell your men to back off or I swear I'll shoot."

The guardians on both rooftops struggled with what to do next. Their sights roamed from the rebel to rebel and then back toward Zander who now threatened their chief in command.

"Shoot," the lieutenant told his men. "Don't be afraid. Glory will save—" He stiffened, feeling the cold muzzle of pistol dig into his temple.

"I believe the gentleman told you to stand down," a shadowy figure whispered over his shoulder.

The lieutenant dropped his microphazer, and with a gesture, instructed his men to hold their fire. Their LR-5s took aim at the new threat. Scope beams illuminated a young woman in a black leather jacket with the collar flipped. Zander hardly recognized her at first. But there she was, out of the shadows, out of his memories. Leyna, in the flesh, pressing her pistol behind the lieutenant's ear.

She kicked the microphazer and sent it skidding across the rooftop toward Zander. The patrol looked at their white-faced leader for the order to act.

"Not so proud now, are we?" Leyna said. "Well, my faithful Heroes, this has been real swell, but it's late and of course we wouldn't want to be out past curfew…" She glanced at Zander who looked over at Weber, still on his knees and sweating in temporary paralysis, who made eyes at the hatch door ajar and then at Purple Harry giggling nearby.

The moon disappeared behind the clouds again and left the rooftop in darkness. A microburst blast threw the lieutenant onto the roof floor as a series of flaming jars lobbed through the dark and crashed in front of the patrol boots, spreading blue fire across the rooftop. The guardians shucked off their infrared goggles, blinded by the blaze, and fired wildly into the smoke, choking on paint fumes. By the time the flames had petered out, the phantoms were already gone.

The rebels rushed past row after row of boxes stacked high on shelving inside the warehouse, past odd piles of scrap metal and rusted generators, then out of the storage room and down the main stairwell. Weber held onto Zander and Leyna, his arms hung over their shoulders, his cloak drenched in sweat and eyes half-peeled. It wasn't until they were halfway down the stairwell that laser blasts came chasing after them.

The gang raced down the final flight and burst out into the blare of sirens on the streets outside. They scattered and ran with the barbed wire, through the gaps between factories, over the canal and toward the Residence. Like ghosts, they disappeared down narrow passageways, dodged through the labyrinth of streets under the cover of darkness, under the red glare of the emergency beacons.

Ducking into an alley, Zander and Leyna lowered Weber off their shoulders and watched the guardians hustle by.

"Leyna, I…" Zander started but found himself at a loss for

words.

"Not now. Later," Leyna said. "Weber, you alright?"

Weber leant against the alley wall, breathing uneven, and moved his fingers until he felt the sensation come back, "Yeah, I'll be fine."

"Good, get to work on that door then," she said.

Leyna and Zander scanned the outer street from behind the trigger while Weber lumbered over to a side door that blended into the brick walls of the alley. He fished the lockpick spool from his pocket and peeled back the bottom corner of a public advisory poster for the Republic's 'Many Eyes for Safety' campaign tacked beside the door.

Underneath the poster was a broken electronic panel, its wires exposed in a jumbled connection to the circuit-board hardware. Weber insert the spool prongs into the nest of wire with surgical precision and fiddled with the circuitry. The light turned green.

Slipping inside, they made certain the door was properly sealed and waited in the dark, listening to the patrol boots outside. Weber flipped the wall switch once the sound had faded. A track of shoddy recessed lights flickered on overhead, leading underground. He limped down the tunnel corridor without waiting.

"Are we sure no one has followed us?" Zander said. "Where the heck is Phaedrus anyway? That was complete foolishness out there. We almost got ourselves killed over a stupid prank—"

Weber simply turned and shoved him against the tunnel wall, "Don't play games with me. Don't you screw with my head. How did they know where we were, huh? How have you been communicating with them?"

"Calm down," Leyna said. "You're still in shock."

"No, I won't calm down," Weber said, gripping Zander tighter. "You just slipped into the Republic unnoticed, easy as that, huh? How convenient. What deal did you make, Zander? You traded us for amnesty, didn't you? Didn't you, you traitor? Come on, at least be man enough to tell me the truth."

"I've been with you this whole time. How could I have possibly given us away?" Zander said.

"Back off, Weber. Just cool it," Leyna said. "You don't know what you're doing."

"You don't understand, Leyna. He's been communicating with them somehow. We hacked into Control 6 yesterday and redirected the orb routes. Nobody knew, yet somehow they tracked us down to our exact location. So where is it? Huh?" Weber threw Zander against the wall harder, hand pinned at his throat, and searched his face for the unspoken answer. "Speak, goddamn it. I'm not playing around here. You have a transmitter on you, don't you? Where is it?"

Weber sloppily tore at his friend's cloak in a desperate search, until he found a red needle mark on Zander's right arm under the sleeve.

"What is that? When did you get shot?" he asked.

"I went through standard inoculation right after I got off the train," Zander said. "What of it?"

Weber eased his grip and backed away, shaking with an angry laugher. "Why didn't you tell me about this earlier?"

"I didn't know it was important. I thought it was simply routine."

"Routine? Yes, it is routine!"

"Honestly, Weber. Look at me. After everything we've been through together, you must believe me. I'm not a traitor."

"Yeah?" Weber cocked his rifle and jabbed it at the mark. "Only you've been running around with a goddamn tracking device in your arm."

Zander looked incredulously at the tiny needle mark. His friend grabbed him with force again, clamping his arm against the concrete wall. Weber pressed the rifle barrel hard into the needle mark, "Look, we don't have time to discuss this. Just close your eyes."

"What are you doing?" Zander pleaded. "Slow down. Talk to me."

"You've been stung. Trust me."

"Hold on," Leyna said, rummaging in her jacket. "Hold on a second…"

"I'm sorry," Weber turned his face and slowly pulled on the trigger. Zander shut his eyes in anticipation. There came a loud scream and the gun went off. He opened his eyes and found Leyna holding his arm with a wide-nosed syringe in her hand.

"Ouch, that really hurt. You didn't have to hit me," Weber said, rising from the damp floor. "Why didn't you tell me you had an extractor?"

The needle sunk into the skin with ease and suctioned there with a tremendous burning, which caused Zander to howl out in pain despite Leyna's gentle pace. Weber scrambled over and covered the patient's mouth.

Blood gradually filled the syringe. Leyna gripped his hand, "This will only take a second." There came a slow painful draw when a pin-sized electronic device spit up through the needle into the blood-filled syringe. She tapped the side of glass cylinder and let go of Zander, who slumped against the tunnel wall in agony.

The tiny transmitter floated innocently in the blood. The electronic rod was no bigger than a fingernail, as thin as a strand of hair.

Leyna squirted blood out of the syringe and plucked out the miniscule device from the nozzle. She snapped the transmitter in half and laid the tiny pieces in Zander's hand as he clutched his mined arm.

"Welcome home," she said.

CHAPTER NINETEEN

The Unknown Hero

The flimsy helmet left only a thin line of vision ahead. Blood tarnished the sandy arena, scattered with half-gnawed chunks of the once noble Sir Real. The lions in their cages chewed grizzle off the bones they'd grabbed before being hauled back into their cages. Centerfield, the fat blur of Hippocritus leant against his sword and dug it into the sand.

Norman could barely walk weighted down in pounds of armor and chain mail. In the ears of his helmet, he heard nothing but muffled yells like a flock of tin seagulls. The sinister stares of the Coliseum followed his slow movement across the field from above. They were waiting, he knew. They were waiting for him to die.

Having already died once, life and death now seemed trivial. He'd die and die again. The fear had vanished with the mystery. What will be, will be, Norman thought. If it's a show they want, then so be it. He pulled the huge sword from its sheath and let the heavy blade drag, cutting a line in the sand behind him. He only hoped that, when he did die, he'd get the chance to meet God again—so he could punch him in the nose.

NOW, NOW, SETTLE DOWN. YOU WOULDN'T WANT DROWN OUT ANY LOVELY SCREAMS, WOULD YOU? the announcer chuckled into his bullhorn. PLEASE WELCOME OUR CHALLENGER. DON'T LET HIS LOOKS FOOL YOU. HE'S A HARDENED CRIMINAL WHO SPITS IN THE FACE OF GOD, DREDGED FROM THE BOWELS OF HELL ITSELF.

Addie hurried down to the front row, where a bunch of hecklers chugged wine and spat over the rail. Through a gap in their smelly sweat-drenched togas, she watched her friend clad in armor march toward certain death.

Spit trails splattered red behind Norman like an omen of

what was to come. He tipped up his helmet to see the fat-faced gladiator wink his way and show off his two enormous buck teeth in a bloodlust smile.

LADIES AND GENTS, LOOKS LIKE OUR CONTENDERS ARE READY TO TUMBLE, RUMBLE, AND SLASH. IN THE LEFT CORNER, OUR DEFENDING CHAMPION HIPPOCRITUS. AND MEANDERING ACROSS THE FIELD, A FIERCE FIGHTER NOT TO BE UNDERESTIMATED, THE HEATHEN.

Addie squeezed upfront and yelled, "Run away, Norman! Run! Stop, you idiot! Don't walk out to him!" But her constructive criticism was drowned out by the roar for blood.

TO THE DEATH, GLADIATORS.

LET'S SEE THAT BLOOD SPILL…

Hippocritus waited with his sword still sheathed in the killing field. He shook his bulbous purple head at the clumsy gladiator half his size when he approached. Norman stopped before the giant contender, wiped the sweat and sand from his face.

"Come on, hero," Hippocritus barked, his mammoth hands straddled on the hilt of his sword. "Come closer, you coward. I want to see what your insides look like, spilled out all over the sand."

Norman wiggled his helmet. "What's that? I didn't catch that last part."

The armored beast yanked his massive sword from the sand. "I said I want to cut out your heart and watch it slowly stop beating in my bare hands."

"Sorry, I can't hear a damn thing in this helmet. You were saying?"

The giant gladiator slashed the air in front of his nose. "I said I can't wait to see you grovel, see you writhe in the bloody sand and beg me to end your miserable life."

"Hold on. Let me take this thing off so I can hear you right." Norman removed his oversized helmet and held it under his arm. "Alright now, what's that you wanted to tell me?"

The beast's huge nostrils flared.

"Done talking, then?" Norman threw his helmet to sand like a gauntlet. "Can we get this over with then? I have an appointment to keep."

"You think you're brave, don't you? You vulgar waste of life. I could split you from here."

"Let's see it then, you ugly son of a bitch. I'm ready." Norman flumped his sword in front of him and struggled with two hands to lift the heavy blade a mere inch off the sand. "Just give me a second."

The beast's sword came down past his shoulder, chipped a metal joint, and tore the entire left sleeve of his plated armor off.

"Hey, now," Norman screamed. "That's not fair. Let's do this like gentlemen here."

The second strike barely missed his forehead when he bent down to retrieve the useless metal sleeve, after which he received a swift boot to the face. The armored beast grabbed his fallen sword from the sand and tossed it out of reach.

The audience exploded in heckling laughter round the Coliseum. Norman looked up at the blood stains that streaked down the beast's bulging armor, the colossal sword glinting in the high sun ready to strike again, and felt his courage in the face of death bleed away. Although he couldn't hear his friend's pleas from the sidelines, a tiny voice in the back of his head summed up the argument. Before the beast could lunge again, he took off running.

"Come back here," Hippocritus yelled, chasing after him. "Now you're going to get it, you little coward."

The Emperor in his royal seat sat unamused by this

aberration. His highness put down his chalice, handed a half-eaten lizard stick to the nobleman at his left, and motioned down to the royal guards waiting in the arena wings.

Norman bolted past the lion cages, across the bloody sand, toward the steel-enforced gates at the north end of the amphitheatre. His only exit loomed ahead, the gates under the Emperor's royal box, from which the royal legion ushered forth and formed a human barricade.

"Die, coward, die!" the audience howled from the stands when he arrived at the blocked gate. The spectators drenched him in spit and pelted him with broken wine bottles as he pleaded with the guards. A few hundred feet away, the armored beast slowed so he could catch his breath and strutted in for the kill.

"Look, obviously there's been some mistake," Norman told the guards. "Look at me, I am not a gladiator. Don't even believe in violence." The royal legion refused to bat an eye in acknowledgement. They drew their swords and forced him back onto the field where the beast lay in wait.

The giant gladiator swung at his head again. Norman dodged the slash and dashed away in no particular direction, weaving like a fishtail rocket across the arena.

With no fresh blood on the field, the novelty of the chase wore off after the fifth lap around the oval arena and the violence turned inward. Fights spurred among the spectators. Drunkards on their fourth bottle smashed heads, toppled vendor carts down the amphitheatre stairs. A gang of children kicked an elderly man who'd flopped onto the stone steps clutching his heart.

Addie followed the chase from the stands, shoved her way through the tangle of togas and flailing punches. One of the drunkards snatched her arm when she attempted to squeeze by.

"What's the rush, stranger? And where's your toga anyhow?"

Addie looked down and suddenly realized how out of place she looked in her torn-sleeve turtleneck and blue jeans. She ripped her arm free from the man's grip.

"What's your problem?" she said. "I'm just trying to get a good view like everyone else."

"Problem is you're ruining the fight for me and my friends here," the drunkard said. "And we just can't have that, see?"

Addie ignored the threats and pushed past the drunkard. On the field, Norman was losing ground. Hippocritus circled closer for the kill with each lap around the arena. There was nothing she could do, she knew, but hope, better yet, pray her friend could fell the beast by some absurd stroke of luck. She was so preoccupied by the chase that she didn't notice when the drunkard's friends moved in and blocked her path down the aisle.

The drunkard latched his sweaty hand on her arm again and held on so tight she could feel the bruise form under the skin. Adrenaline burst through her veins. She could feel the sickness of fear, anger coming to rise.

"I was talking to you," the drunkard leaned in so she could yell in her face. "Where do you think you're going?"

Addie lost her spatial bearings, her head woozy, her knees weak, as the fear gave way to a righteous anger. She couldn't tell which way was up or down or where her feet met the ground, until she looked toward the bright dusty sky and saw the Eye blink open high over the Coliseum.

The gawking apparition passed unnoticed by the tussling spectators. Its pupil swelled with a fiery brilliance. Addie felt her body flush with sudden heat as a burning sensation traced the ash-drawn symbol on her arm and illuminated the mystic markings. And in a jolt, the old soul of Captain Voord roared back to life.

A solid crack to the jaw knocked the drunkard into the aisle, smashing his face against a stone bench on the way down.

He lifted himself on all fours and spat out a wad of blood and teeth. His friends huddled in faster than Voord could move. They drained their wine bottles dry, smashed the glass on the stadium rail, and stalked closer, accompanied by a gang of onlookers, incensed by the smell of violence.

Mutiny, the dead captain thought. Stranger on a strange ship here. He locked stares with the drunkard who angrily wiped the blood from his beard and rolled up his white sleeves. Voord caught the man's fist as he threw out, and head-butted him square in the nose.

The commotion in the stands distracted Norman on his eighth lap around the arena, gaining and losing ground from one moment to the next. A crowd cheered on a fight in the audience, in section XIV as demarcated on the stone. From afar, he could barely make out the stranger in blue jeans.

The mob twisted Voord's arms and restrained him for the battery of punches. With each blow, the dead captain neither winced nor cried out, but let the pain hardened his contempt. His nose dripped crooked. The fifth punch stole the wind from his lungs. The sixth knocked his nose back into place. A kick from behind knocked the mob away long enough for Voord to wrench out of the hold and charge at the drunkard.

Off the side rail they fell with a bone-cracking thunck onto the field. Although the fall had clearly broken the man's skull, that didn't stop Voord from continuing to beat the drunkard in the sand where he lay. His fist came up and then down, up and then down like piston, bludgeoning the drunkard's face into the sand. The cheers died down in pockets with every punch until the entire Coliseum fell silent.

HEH HEH, LOOKS LIKE SOME FANS ARE A LITTLE OVERZEALOUS TODAY.

The royal legion advanced into the arena and marched with caution toward the dead captain come to life.

FOR THE BENEFIT OF THE FIGHT, I MUST

REMIND THE AUDIENCE TO REMAIN SEATED
WHILE THIS SITUATION IS KINDLY HANDLED BY
THE ROYAL GUARDS.

Voord glowered at the armed men that soon surrounded
him, confused by their odd costume, the gold-plated armor,
matching plume helmets, ornate shields, and shin-high boots.

"More of you, are they?" he said, rising from the beaten
corpse. "Who out of the lot of ya wants to meet the Lord of
Death first?" He made a quick round of eyes. Not one of the
guards took another step forward.

The royal legion parted like a wave when Voord
approached, storming through their ranks. He narrowed in on
the beastly gladiator halfway across the field. Lost in a
shipwrecked fantasy, the dead captain saw none other than his
mortal foe Dreadnought in Hippocritus's massive build. He
likewise mistook the skinny gladiator being chased by the beast
for his former cabin boy Eliot who'd drowned years ago off the
island of Gaul. Guess they're all coming back from the dead
today, he thought.

The giant gladiator whirled round to see a young woman
in a strange black tunic snatch the discarded sword from the
sandy arena.

"Hands off that cabin boy, Dreadnought," Voord
threatened him with the blade. "Looks like I'll have to send
you to yar grave a second time."

"A lady with a sword. I'm shaking in my boots,"
Hippocritus laughed. "Who do you think you are? This is no
game for little girls."

"Oh, how soon yar forgotten, Dreadnought?" Voord came
face to face with the armored beast. "Leave the boy and face
me, yar scallywag."

Hippocritus looked toward the Emperor's seat for
permission. On high, the Emperor nodded and returned to his
lizard stick in anticipation of this new contention.

HEH HEH WHAT ACTORS! THIS IS ALL PART OF THE SHOW, FOLKS.

The royal guards hauled the drunkard from the field by his limp legs.

A QUICK ROUND OF APPLAUSE FOR THE ACTOR NOW BEING DRAGGED OUT FOR DEAD. AND NOW PLEASE WELCOME OUR UNKNOWN HERO, HAHAHA, ANOTHER VETERAN GLADITOR OF THE GAME, I ASSURE YOU, AS HE TAKES ON OUR FAVORITE BEAST OF BLOOD, HIPPOCRITUS!

The clash of swords on the other end of the arena alerted Norman to the fact that he was running from no one. Hippocritus traded blows with another contender, his fallen sword in hands of his long lost friend.

"Addie?" he cried out. "What are you doing here?"

Voord swung and missed the giant gladiator. "Shut yar yap, cabin boy and stay away."

The blades clanged and tangled. Hippocritus made a narrow swing at Voord's head. "Clever but you're no match for me, squirt. I'll wear you down and then slice you up the middle."

The dead captain dodged another swing and parried a stab at his torso, "You and yar sea tales, Dreadnought. How 'bout I cut out yar tongue and take it with me this time?"

Hippocritus ducked a chop at his neck, countered with a side swing that nicked the young woman's shoulder.

"Cat scratches won't kill a man," the dead captain traded hands with the sword and felt the blood run cold down his arm. "You're going to have to do me one better than that." He fended off a series of slashes, faked left and jabbed his sword into the meat bulging out from a slit in the beast's armor.

The audience's unexpected applause startled Hippocritus more than the close hit. The beast screamed with renewed fury. Back and forth, they clashed swords across the field,

Hippocritus nearly slicing open the dead captain's chest one moment, Voord clanging his sword off the beast's armor the next.

Norman stayed away from the duel, confused as to what he should do. He marveled at the fiery rage in Addie's eyes and winced at every strike of the blades, the thunder of the swordplay. He knew he had to do something, but was at a loss for how to aid his friend. Then he spotted the blood trails that trickled down the beast's leg from an exposed wound under the slit of his armor. The sparkle of a broken wine bottle in the sand called him to action.

The sheer force of the next assault knocked loose Voord's grip. His sword flew out of his hands and skittered across the sand. The dead captain dodged two slashes upside the neck and tripped backward. Hippocritus stomped forward, pushed him to the sandy ground, and held him there with his metal boot on his chest. Voord wriggled under the weight of his foot. "Just like you to kill an unarmed man, Dreadnought."

"Sorry, squirt. There can only be one great gladiator," the armored beast said. "And for the record, his name is and will always be Hippocritus."

Voord felt the fear flash through his nerves, his ribs crushed. In panic and exhaustion, Addie once again returned to see the beast's two-toothed grin and the gigantic sword raised high over her head. Up in his royal box, the Emperor nodded in approval. Hippocritus howled as a sharp pain jabbed in his side. The beast swung in a wide-arch behind him, barely missing Norman who backed away with the broken wine bottle in his hand.

The dead captain shuddered awake, rolled, and swiped up his fallen sword. Jumping to his feet, he swung long and the blade cleaved straight through. The beast thumped down onto the field. His head dropped beside his massive body and rolled a few feet away.

The audience gasped and there was not a sound after.

Addie heaved and wheezed and wondered how she'd ended up in the middle of the arena. Then in her hands she saw the sword slicked with black blood, the vanquished Hippocritus lying next to his purple head.

Norman stood on the other side of the beast's colossal body, taking alternate looks of disbelief at his long lost friend and the slain gladiator between them.

"That was incredible. You were incredible." he said. "I just... I don't know what to say. Where the heck did you come from? How did you get here?"

The spectators gazed from the stands, mouths agape, at their beloved beast of blood beheaded on the field. Their whispers collected in a tremendous murmur across the amphitheatre. The Emperor rose from his seat, spat out the final bite of his lizard stick, and motioned to the royal guards.

WELL, GREAT... the announcer faked a chuckle. LOOKS LIKE WE HAVE OUR WINNER. THE UNKNOWN HERO! THREE CHEERS FOR THE NEW CHAMPION OF THE ROYAL COLISEUM.

The whispers became boos and hisses as the crowd threw anything they could find out onto the field, even an unfortunate grilled-lizard vendor who happened to be parked too close to the front row. The unknown hero had proven himself the villain in the cruel game.

Norman stepped over the beast's carcass to greet his old friend who was squinting up in a daze at the thousands of angry faces.

"I can't believe this," he said. "What are the chances? Really, huh? Man, it's good to see you."

Addie winced, feeling the pain in her wounded shoulder. "Please, just be quiet a second, alright?"

The lions in their cages started to growl and bite at the bars when the royal guards turned the mighty cranks that lifted the grates on the sides of the arena. After the last turn, the guards scuttled away and ran out through the north gates under the Emperor's royal box.

WHAT A SHOW TODAY HUH, FOLKS? the announcer said, brushing back his extravagant orange hair. ONCE AGAIN OUR THANKS TO CRIMSON STEEL, FINE SPONSOR OF THIS DEATH MATCH AND THE ROYAL GUARD.

Unexpectedly, the pedestal descended.

HAVE A SAFE RIDE HOME, WATCH OUT FOR THOSE PESKY SKELETONS, AND REMEMBER TO TIP YOUR CHARIOT DRIVER.

The lions rushed from their cages and clawed at the retracting pedestal, gnashing their teeth at the fresh prey that descended like a sacrificial offering. The announcer tried to remain calm when the pedestal halted just above the arena floor and refused to descend any farther. He called out to the royal box, to the Emperor who simply ignored his cries for help. When he finally turned to run, it was too late.

The chase ended in a curdling shriek when the lions pounced and dug in their claws. The ravenous animals devoured the announcer with remarkable speed, bullhorn and all, mashing and crunching his boney flesh, tufts of orange hair stuck in their jaws.

Once they were finished, the lions scratched the sand beneath their claws and leered across the field at Norman and Addie, now alone on the stark, blood-splattered field.

"Addie?" Norman said, pale and trembling.

Addie dropped the gladiator sword, "Don't talk. Just run."

CHAPTER TWENTY

Underground Murmurs

Half a mile underground, the tunnels leveled out, the low ceiling giving way to wider chambers that reeked of death. The recessed lights overhead guided the rebels into the sealed catacombs through which the passageway dovetailed. For nearly an hour, they had navigated the underground tunnels, en route to the secret headquarters, and talked little. Weber limped ahead, groggy from the blast yet determined to walk it off. Zander and Leyna lagged behind and waded through the awkwardness of their reunion.

Much had been left unsaid between them, too much perhaps to even broach the conversation. And whenever Zander would ask her about how things had been, she would simply dismiss his questions with a terse reply. Through her coldness, she let her anger be known, although at odd moments, he would catch her glance his way with a look of tender sadness.

They walked together and listened to the compounded silence, the hollow drips, the muffled sirens above. It was a mystery how many corpses were piled on the other side of the walls since no record of the dead survived, neither for the thousands of bodies deposited in the vault during the plague nor for the original occupants of the ancient ossuary. The lone reminder that the passageway had once been part of the necropolis was the dank stench of saturated decay from the hidden chambers behind the cinderblocks.

Zander knew every curve and bend of the tunnels, where one passageway terminated or where another circled around and reconnected with the previous one. The architects of the Republic had created this series of secret passageways under the city during the Antriac War—the uprising after the plague in the beginning days of the Order. The architects knew what would happen once they'd completed Benedict's vision of a new republic. The political climate was too volatile to let any faction of the populace know more than the Order. And so from the city's abandoned medical basements, they roped underground tunnels that segued into the catacombs and emergency bunkers pocketed under the city to escape underground.

It had been nearly three years since Zander had last set foot in the dank tunnels, or run from an armed patrol for that matter. He looked at the broken transmitter in his hand, no bigger than the tip of his finger, wet with blood.

"Clever, isn't it?" Leyna said, breaking her silence. "A simple injection and they can track anyone, anywhere."

"It's so small though, it's remarkable," Zander said. "How long has this been going on? Were we always being tracked?"

"No... well, maybe." Leyna brushed a few red strands of hair out her face and talked ahead of her, as if to the cinderblock walls and the corpses entombed within. "The injections started a few weeks after you left. The official lie was that a band of dissidents had plans to unleash a new mutation of the plague. Thus the need for mandatory inoculation. They stuck everybody with those little buggers, registering their ID numbers before receiving two injections. The Order has synched the transmitters with Orbserver surveillance and has supposedly been tracking people's movements ever since. But monitoring suspicious activity isn't their only endgame. They're also using the devices for specific indoctrination tests."

"What kind of tests?"

"Psychological tests so they can better understand behavioral anomalies among the citizens. It seems they've been experimenting selectively with the pills to see how certain people react to crisis, such as infecting a subject with a simple virus and timing their indoctrinated response."

"Rats in a cage," Weber turned and said, "with transmitters in their arms and chemicals in their brains. I'm sorry I overreacted earlier, Zander. I'm the one who should have known they'd inject you as soon as you arrived. You, alright?"

"Don't worry about it. Just try not to wave a gun in my face next time," Zander said.

"Of course, they don't need transmitters," Leyna said. "I've been on your tail since you left the café. I don't know what this prank was about tonight, but you nearly blew the whole operation."

"What do you care?" Weber said. "You're not part of this anymore. You have no right to judge—"

"Oh, spare me. What would have happened out there if I hadn't been following you?"

"And where have you been all this time, might I ask?" Weber stopped to confront her. "We thought the worst, we had no idea where you went."

"I have no obligation to you or Phaedrus," Leyna said. "My only loyalty is to the resistance."

"Oh, is that so? Is that why you keep running off and hiding whenever the heat gets too intense?" Weber said.

"You make another comment like that and I'll smack you so hard you won't get up next time."

The argument was silenced round the next bend when a faint noise came murmuring from somewhere farther down the tunnel. They followed the sound to a metal door with a thin light present under the doorframe.

Leyna pressed and held a buzzer while speaking into a grate in the door. "Cor igni verum."

A crackle came over the intercom, "Who comes to town?"

"The merrymakers," Leyna replied. A buzzer sounded and the door swung inward.

In the antechamber before another door, a rebel hugged

his rifle in a military stance. He nodded, after giving the visitors a silent inspection, and pulled the next door open.

Inside the headquarters, the thrill of victory hung in the stale boxed air. The rebels drank and chatted enthusiastically, crowded within the concrete bunkers. Their faces were galvanized with a mischievous glow from their rooftop skirmish with the guardians. A coat rack, laden with hanging rifles, stood near the door beside a pile of paint-smeared cloaks.

During the beginning years of the resistance, the rebels had lucked out when they discovered the pre-plague bomb shelter long forgotten in the tunnel network and intentionally omitted from any blueprints of the city-state. It was in these bunkers that the rebels had taken refuge after the botched sabotage of the hydro-grid, which was what had presumably instigated the raids. Their safe houses in the Western Quadrant and Allister Commons were compromised after the disappearance of Trevor and Gidget and the daylight arrest of four other members, whom the rebels assumed were tortured into confession.

Thus began the systematic kidnapping and execution of anyone suspected of involvement with the resistance. The guardians conducted comprehensive searches of every registered tenant in the Residence, rammed down doors, hauled the suspects away in black hoods, never to be seen or heard from again.

The handful of rebels who survived the raids sought shelter underground, out of necessity at first, believing that they could wait out the Order, as they had many times before, and then reemerge to establish their foothold again. But the risk of being seen was too great and the bunkers soon became their de facto home. His home, Zander thought, and although the notion seemed estranged, he was relieved by the immediate comfort he felt walking through the threshold into the noisy bunker.

Despite its drab confines, the headquarters had an almost playful ambience, especially in what the rebels fondly called 'the living room,' littered with junk furniture and a collection of antiquities from the distant past: a typewriter here, a phone booth there, a record player drifting raspy jazz, a stuffed bulldog with the fluff torn out its mouth, dusty books cramped on several shelves.

Neale slouched on the couch with his pant leg rolled up to his bloody thigh where a LR-5 blast had burned clean through the skin. One of the new recruits stitched the wound and dressed his leg in a bandage.

"Well, thank god." Neale lifted his head to greet the three stragglers. "What took you so long?"

"We had a slight security problem to handle," Zander said. "What happened to your leg?"

"I caught a lucky shot, but it's nothing to worry about. The bleedings almost stopped," Neale said and wiggled his toes.

"He's an idiot, is what he is," said the new recruit, wrapping gauze around his thigh. "He ran straight into a firefight and nearly had his leg blown off."

"Yeah, I fired off a few rounds before they got me though," Neale smirked. "I left a few guardians bleeding on the cobblestones and another one crying for help." He laughed at this and awkwardly stopped because of the pain, "Ouch, be careful."

"I'm glad to see you're alright. You better not pull any stunts like that tomorrow," Zander said. "This is not about taking shot for shot, kill for kill. This is not a war. We are out to change minds, not take lives."

Neale looked at him sideways from the couch. "No offense, Zander, but you haven't been around for awhile."

Zander had nothing to say to this nor was there anything he could say. Obviously the rules of the game had changed. This was inevitable. He knew everything would change the instant he'd pulled that trigger three years ago, on the run after his successful infiltration of the Institute. He knew it the instant the bullet flew, as if in slow motion, out of the revolver barrel and straight up the underside of the guardian's jaw. He'd been cornered by a night patrol on a dead-end street near Sector 3, forced onto his knees, sickened by a long-range microburst. He'd simply turned and fired a single shot when the guardian moved in to shackle his hands. And in that act, the idealism the resistance once possessed had been lost for him, the noble cause subverted under a more sinister tenor.

Now, with Phaedrus in charge, the game had taken an even darker turn, this much was clear. Yet he could see in the rebels' faces, crowded at tables, on couches, in armchairs strewn about the living room, that there was still a lustful hope for change.

They questioned, argued, and joked with one another, swapping stories. They talked loudly and full of verve, about philosophy, about poetics, about painting, about music. The lost arts of the old society. These were their treasures. And in corners of the room, the rebels scribbled down their thoughts on yellowed pages, the rebels dipped nails in buckets of paint and scratched graffiti in the concrete walls, the rebels read books that hadn't been opened in centuries, in search of a truth other than the Republic.

These were the new idealists, men and women who'd forsaken all guarantees, who'd come from every level of the bureaucracy, disillusioned with the life unexamined. Former laborers and engineers from the Great Factory, retired teachers from the Academy, merchants, public servants, researchers, and even a few defected scientists from the Institute. It always began the same: a whisper and an invitation from a friend, quiet attendance of the meetings, seduced by the clandestine affairs, driven by their hardened convictions. Then the choice: to disappear from the great civil machine completely and live underground or lead a double life, knowing the dangers that came with either decision.

Perhaps they'd all gone a bit crazy from the constant fear, from their righteous self-delusions in the name of the cause, from their fervid desire to unmask the Republic's false society. But what did it matter if it kept the heart pumping? Zander thought. And what more is the questioning mind than madness?

The only relatively quiet area of the headquarters were the bunkrooms, although not because anyone was sleeping. The silence was for concentration's sake. Leaning against bed posts inside, the rebels sat on the floor and relaxed over a game of cards. Angus shuffled the deck, cut, and dealt to the players. The rebels fumed over their cards and guarded piles of gun shells for betting.

"The game is nine card neat," Angus said. "Three cards down, five cards up, one wild. No cheating, biting, stealing, or placing cards in obscene places. Bet before you take a card, and please don't throw your ante carelessly on the floor. We don't want anybody blowing up a good hand here."

Spindles of recording equipment spun through an open door off the living room, tinkered with by Phaedrus and Elsa who were listening intently into headphones connected to the circuit board. Sprockett, hunched over a long table inside, positioned miniature green toy soldiers on a rough-drawn map of the city and explained tomorrow's strategy to a group of rebels gathered there. Phaedrus threw off his headphones when he spotted Zander and Weber, and came out of the surveillance room. He then noticed Leyna standing beside Zander, fiery and proud with a smug look of defiance, just as she had so long ago. His elation died with it.

"Glad to see you made it back safe and sound," Phaedrus said. He grabbed Leyna by the shoulders and kissed her mockingly on both cheeks. "So good of you to return. You know how we worry. And for a moment there, I thought you didn't like us anymore."

"I didn't come back on your account," Leyna said.

"Well," he said with an arched eyebrow. "All's for the best, eh?"

"So the ball is set in motion?" Weber asked. "Did they take the bait?"

"It's better than we could have hoped. Those charges will keep the patrols busy till dawn. But let's pray our little snafu tonight doesn't snag our plans for tomorrow," Phaedrus said and motioned for them to follow him into the surveillance room.

With a nod from their leader coming through the door, Elsa punched a button, which stopped the spindles. Sprockett excused the rebels hanging around the map table. Silent and serious, the conspirators smiled in greeting to Weber and Zander. Their faces soured when Leyna walked in afterward.

"What do we have here?" Sprockett said. "Good to see you, Leyna."

"Good to be seen," Leyna said. "How's that one eye holding up anyway?"

Sprockett ignored the insult and fiddled with a toy soldier in his hand.

"What are we going to do now about the approach?" Weber asked. "The rooftops are quashed as a vantage point."

"True. But just for the approach. We'll hit them high and we'll hit them low. They won't know what to do," Sprockett said.

"The Order truly believes they averted disaster tonight," Elsa added. "All radio chatter indicates that they're treating this as a callous prank, a blip on the radar. But they will be reinforcing patrols at the Institute and along the hydrodam perimeter, as expected, which should strain their resources for the festival itself. Beyond that, directives from Control 6 remain unaltered for tomorrow's security."

Zander stepped over to the map table and analyzed the plotting: a couple toy soldiers on the clocktower, six near the manufacturing sector, a dozen more scattered in different quadrants of the city.

"What's happening with this division here?" he asked, pointing at a cluster of soldiers positioned on the outer stretch of the commercial sector.

"Never mind that for now," Phaedrus said. "Let's take a look at those prints that I'm sure have been burning a hole in your pocket, shall we?" He brushed aside the miniature green soldiers to make space on a corner of the table.

Zander pulled the leather bundle from the inside pocket of his jacket. He snapped open the satchel and unfolded the architectural plans of the Republic, stolen from the Institute three years ago. He laid out the blueprints.

"These are difficult to read at first," he began. "But I've marked certain landmarks to clarify exactly what we're looking at. If you see here, there is a second network of interconnecting tunnels, far older than the sewer lines that skirt alongside the canals. Supposedly, the architects used these tunnels to build the newer water network that ties in with the Citadel aqueduct and provides drainage for the hydroelectric dam. It's safe to assume that these tunnels are in fact the old water network that runs parallel with the new. It weaves through the city in a confusing gridlock, but it should suffice to safely get us under the clocktower for the main strike."

"And what about the Citadel forum?" Sprockett asked.

"It's accessible, albeit tricky," Zander told him. "The tunnels empty out into the canals between the Old Quarter and the capitol. From there, we'd have to find a way to cross undetected onto the other side. Possibly the aqueduct bridges, although I'm almost positive they're armed with rotary guns, plus we'd have to get onto the Citadel roof in order to cross. I imagine there are pipes that cross the gap and connect underneath the capitol complex, however I've seen no indication on these plans nor Citadel blueprints themselves."

Leyna leaned in and said, "Are you going to tell him about your grand swoop now?"

Phaedrus looked at her, annoyed. He turned to Zander. "Yes, I suppose it is unfair to leave you in the dark any longer. We're not just attacking the clocktower and security network, and I've scratch plans for the assassination of the Grand Muse as a primary objective. It's not needed anyhow, with the heir being chosen tomorrow. Instead, we're going to do the next best thing. We're going to kidnap the heir philosopher king."

"Wait, when? After the ceremony?" Zander asked. "He'll be heavily guarded. There could be serious casualties if we attack the parade."

"I may be crazy, but I'm not a fool. We'll swoop in during the Master's Game, when anxiety will be at a fever pitch and no one will be expecting it."

"How? We don't even know who will be selected."

"But you see, my dear friend, we already know who's going to be selected. It turns out that the games are staged during the Centennial to give the impression that the young heir is the best, the wisest, the most promising prospect of all the Academy graduates. We now know, thanks to Sid, that this is a farce. They select the heir long before the tournament, take him aside and school him accordingly, educate him on the inner-workings of the Republic in preparation for the throne.

Therefore this young child is not just a symbol of what the commonwealth stands for. He knows more than you or I, or most of the council for that matter. He is a living breathing resource that could help us bring the Order to heel. And under our guard, we can use him, just as the Grand Muse would, to lead this society toward a new era, free from the shackles that have kept us chained."

It made sense, quite suddenly, like the bang of a gong. In

the madman's words, there rang reason. Zander studied the map and looked back at Phaedrus who'd perked his famous grin.

"You're a lunatic. You know that, don't you?"

"It's now or never, my friend. We can take the pill and dream away another day as slaves. Or we can make our stand now."

The grin fanned out around the table till the conspirators all sported the same devilish smirk. Except for Leyna. She simply shook her head. "He's only a child. You're putting his life in grave danger."

"I know what's at stake here. He'll be shaken at first, but then, ah then, he'll see," Phaedrus said. "Now pay attention because this must be exact if we are to avoid any unneeded casualties."

The rebel leader then delved into the logistics of tomorrow's mission, its careful precision, the specific teams and which of the members present at the table would be assigned to what task. It was a long-awaited briefing that lasted over two hours, during which Zander offered his expertise on how best to navigate underneath the city so they could secure their positions for the main strike. There was respectful but passionate debate on how they would execute the primary maneuvers, a constant shuffle of miniature soldiers on map, of pen jotting, of chin scratching, of hand wringing, until a final scenario was agreed upon.

"Well, I think it's time we let everyone know about full details of the attack tomorrow," Phaedrus said in closing. "Zander, these blueprints change everything. Your sacrifice alone has made this possible. You truly are a prince among swine."

The manic leader slapped Zander on the shoulder and sauntered off, already occupied with the next thought, the next step. The rest of the conspirators followed him out the door except for Zander who stayed behind at the table with Leyna. His mind remained static on the blueprints, laid out on the city map, excited and nervous, unable to believe this was truly happening. He leafed through the blueprints again and again, mulling over the options. It could work, he thought. But what was the best angle? How would they get the heir alone? Did they even have enough men for operation?

"He's lost it," Leyna whispered. "It's been awful since you've been gone, Zander. This idiocy tonight has been a long time coming. The man's lost his mind."

But Zander was already lost himself in the fantasy of revolution. Kidnapping the child would not be easy. They would need more than a distraction. What if... He moved two toy soldiers from the clocktower and repositioned them inside the Citadel.

"What they have planned for tomorrow is a death wish. We're putting that boy's life at risk and the lives of thousands of innocent people. You must stop him."

"But it may just be the start we need," Zander said without taking his eyes off the blueprints. If we glitch the power grid, we could cut through there, he calculated on the map. By the time he looked up again, Leyna had disappeared from his side.

CHAPTER TWENTY-ONE

Stranger in the Dungeon

When being chased by a lion, there are a few simple rules to keep in mind. First, discard any meat in your pockets: sausage links, pork loin, rib-eye slab, hunks of lamb, etc. The strategic hurl of a mutton chop can significantly slow down your predator, not for long, but long enough to postpone becoming the beast's tasty lunch for at least a short while. If you don't have any spare meat on hand, you might want to consider lining your pockets with juicy cutlets in the future, in case you get chased by a lion again. That is, if you're lucky enough to survive round one.

Second, don't scream. This only adds to the thrill of the chase for the lion bearing down upon you. Likewise, refrain from bobbing and weaving or waving your hands in the air or hollering that you are going to die. As we learn from rudimentary geometry, the fastest route between two points is a straight line, unless you're dodging pits of poisonous snakes.

Third and most important, whatever you do, don't look back.

"Don't look back," Addie yelled to Norman as they ran side by side through the corridors of the dark dungeon. "For the last time, keep moving."

They'd escaped the Coliseum by chance. After witnessing the announcer's gory death, the reunited friends had raced toward the dungeon gates at the same time the prison wardens had come out to see what all the fuss was about. This was lucky for them but not so lucky for the wardens who were knocked flat on their backs, trampled by the chase, and mauled to death by the pursuing lions. Curiosity is almost always deadly.

"That was incredible," Norman said. "Did you see the size of that thing or whatever it was? And then you come slashing and screaming out of nowhere like a warrior."

"Really, Norman," Addie said. "I don't want to talk about it."

No longer in control of their legs, they bolted through the underground dungeon that tunneled under the Kingdom of Nault. Prisoners hung from the walls, illuminated by torchlight, chained and helpless. One minute, they'd lift their heads in confusion to see Addie and Norman dash by. The next, they were torn from their shackles and eaten alive by the lions who snatched them in passing, like a laundress picking clothes off the line.

Beastly chomps and growls filled the dungeon, pierced by the prisoners' screams of terror. Norman stole a glance over his shoulder. Furrowed yellow manes and knitted teeth grimaced back, a mere arm's length behind. Like a sailor trying to buoy the boat, he reached inside his pockets where he felt a strange weight, pulled out a string of sausages, and tossed the meat over his shoulder.

The first lion slackened the chase and snatched the flying sausages before the second lion could. The tug of war that ensued only gave Addie and Norman a few yards reprieve, but at least the snack had bought them time.

"I'm not even going to ask where that came from," Addie said.

"Strange how coincidence works in this place, wherever we are. Things tend to simply appear out of thin air," Norman said. "So you came down the well after me, huh? Did you see God?"

"No, and as long as you pick up the pace, I hope not to."

"I saw God."

"Oh, was Marcus with him?"

The tunnel swerved deeper into the dungeon, the light from the outside getting dimmer and dimmer, the growls louder. Along the stone walls, the torches silhouetted the hanging prisoners in ghostly shadows.

"No, I assumed he was with you," Norman said.

"He was until we climbed down the well after you," Addie said. "I just spent an eternity roaming a desert of ash, tangling with pirates, and saving your sorry ass from a bloodbath. Before today, I'd never killed man, and now I'm a freaking gladiator. What's happening to us, Norman?"

Just then, a stranger in a hooded cloak appeared in the hollow darkness ahead. He stood perfectly still, as if he were made of stone, with his hand posed forward, flat out to stop the stampede. As the duo fast approached, knees kicking, the lions' breath hot on their backs, snarls in their ears, Addie and Norman waved wildly at the fearless apparition in the path of their escape.

The cloaked stranger remained undisturbed by the deadly chase headed his way. He slipped off his hood, revealing an unshapely bald head, and kept his hand outstretched, "STOP."

Addie and Norman met the stranger eye to eye, and as if by the force of those eyes, as if by some magic cast from that hand, ran smack into an invisible barrier. The lions slowed before their fallen prey, with teeth gnashing and claws out, and leapt in for the kill. Addie and Norman dove onto the sawdust floor, covered their heads, and played dead. The cloaked stranger snapped once, shooting an echo through the tunnel.

Addie huddled in a ball in the sawdust, listening to the screams, the unmistakable sound of claws tearing into flesh.

"No, please... ouch, damn it! Get off me, get off, GET OFF!"

When she finally peeked out from under her arms, Addie was surprised to find a pair of tiny yellow kittens scratching at her friend's face. She was so baffled by the sight she didn't even bother help to Norman fend off the little beasts, which still seemed intent on ravaging their prey despite their cuddly size.

"Well," the stranger said. "This has been quite a day for

you, hasn't it?"

"How'd you—" Addie peered down the dungeon corridor to make sure the lions were truly gone. Broken chains dangled in the dark with torn arms, half torsos, and shorn hands. The prisoners that were not yet dead moaned in agony. These moans continued on into the dungeon where more prisoners hung, saved from the lions' wrath but completely miserable nonetheless.

Norman successfully tore the ferocious kittens away and rose from the ground, his cheeks scored with cat scratches. "Who's this?" he asked.

"Allow me to introduce myself," the stranger held out his hand. "The name is Alexander."

"I have a strict policy about not shaking hands with sorcerers," Addie said.

"You seem shaken." The stranger moved a single step forward. The whole dungeon seemed to shudder when his foot hit the sawdust floor. "I assure you there's no reason for alarm. I've come to help."

"No reason for alarm? Really, huh? Only seconds ago, we were about to be mauled to death by lions, before you appeared with your voodoo fingers," Addie said, shaking one of the tenacious cats off her ankle. "Which I appreciate, don't get me wrong. But it seems everywhere I go, someone's always trying to kill me. So I believe it's safe to assume you've come for our souls. Just back off, sorcerer."

"Oh, don't be so dramatic," the stranger said. "You're already dead. And I'm as much a sorcerer as you are Addie and he is Norman."

"What's that supposed to mean?" Addie said.

"Perhaps, I've said too much," the stranger folded his hands into his cloak sleeves. "Obviously, you are frustrated and tired. It's been a long journey in the elsewhere, this I understand. However we must move quickly. The Nephs are soon to follow."

"It's a trick, Norman. Don't listen to him," Addie said. "Trust me, he's come for our souls."

"But you don't have a soul," Norman said.

"She acquired a dead sea captain's soul in the desert of Alcazara by accident," the stranger said.

"What? Stay away from us. I'm warning you," Addie said, although the statement was less than convincing since she was distracted by the kittens that had redoubled their efforts to tear apart her leg, digging their claws deep into her jeans. "I'm a ruthless killer, just ask Norman what happened to the last guy."

"Keep your voice down," the stranger said.

Norman rubbed the tender scratches on his face and gazed at the stranger's bald head, awestruck by its shininess, noting its smooth, hairless, eggplant-like shape. The stranger then held out a hand, palm forward, and gave him something else to look at... Marcus dashing across the industrial rooftops of a sprawling city, a clocktower in the distance, the foggy night... the visions warped in a swirling spiral on his flat hand.

"The Nephs are coming, and there's nothing I can do to stop them," the stranger said. "They've given up on Marcus and they are coming for you."

"Marcus?" Addie said, nabbing the tiny kittens by the fur on their necks and flinging them aside. "What about Marcus? You know where he is?" The kittens landed and scurried in the sawdust, prowling, looking for their next angle of attack. The yellow cats hissed in anger, Addie hissed back.

A very different kind of hissing sound then came from somewhere deep in the dungeon, like a thousand serpent tongues licking the darkness, soft at first and then the sibilance gained in momentum, in volume. The cats perked their ears and promptly scampered off into the dark.

"And now you've awoken the dead," the stranger said. He listened intently, as if trying to count how far away the sound was. "Come, we have no time to argue."

"We're not going anywhere with you," Addie said. "We're going to find our own way of—" She stopped mid-sentence when she saw the images of Marcus that persisted to swirl and shift in the palm of the stranger's hand... gunfire lighting up the night sky, sirens flashing red, uniformed soldiers on the march... Addie approached the looking-glass palm, like a moth drawn to electric light.

"Your friend Marcus has traveled to what is known as the 336.84th fathom, time-stamped 2433 A.P. on earth. He's in serious danger, embroiled in a revolution that's doomed to fail. And unless you find him soon, I'm afraid there's no way he'll ever be able to come back."

"Fathom of what?" Addie asked.

"Of Oblivion," Norman said. "I've been through this before."

"That's right," the stranger said. "And you'd be wise not to wander too far."

"Hold on," Addie said. "Do you two know each other? What's going on here? I'm not going anywhere without an explanation."

"Hmm, how can I put this gently? How can I explain this to you?" the stranger thought a moment and then shrugged. "Did you ever wonder whether you're just a figment of somebody else's imagination?"

Addie and Norman looked at each other, "No."

"Well, you are. Sorry."

"So none of this is real?" Norman said.

"On the contrary," the stranger said. "I assure you that all this is very real. It's just that the two of you aren't wholly real. In fact, everything you're saying, every mannerism, every itch, every twitch is simply Marcus's subconscious interpretation of what you'd say, how you'd act in any given situation."

Addie closed her eyes to prevent herself from looking at

the stranger's hand any longer. "Stop it, I don't believe you. He's trying to fill our heads with this nonsense, Norman. He's trying to confuse us."

"See, that's just Marcus's projection of what you'd say, how you'd react under these circumstances. You are not Addie. You are not you. You are a manifestation and animation of Marcus's fractured mind."

"Why are you telling us this?" Addie asked. "Can't you see we're having a heck of a time as it is?"

"I'm telling you this because it's the truth."

"Well, that's not a very nice thing to tell someone you've just met, is it?"

"I'm telling you this because you're in trouble," the stranger said.

The hissing swelled, louder and louder, accompanied by the clamor of footsteps in the dungeon's dark reaches. The stranger closed his hand. "There's not much time. The Nephs are getting closer by the minute. You must trust me for Marcus's sake. Come this way."

The stranger whisked his hood on and stormed off down the torch-lit corridor, knowing Addie and Norman would soon follow. The dungeon sloped its sawdust tongue through the fragile dark, the dimensions of the chambers uncertain, constructed of crooked stone blocks. The prisoners wailed from their chains as they passed by; the deeper they ventured into the dungeon maze, the more indecipherable their pleas became, so starved, so crazed by the eternal dark, that the prisoners had lost all humanity, sputtering and yowling like rabid dogs.

"Pay no attention to them," the stranger said, wending through the twisted, tangled corridors, "This way." The hissing, which had faded momentarily, returned with force, along with the pounding of footsteps on hard stone. The stranger wrenched one of the torches from its steel holder and waved its flame against the dungeon wall in a ritualistic pattern, straight across, up and down, around in a series of circles, smaller, smaller. The stones gave way when he pressed lightly upon them and pushed an entire section of the wall inward.

The stranger extinguished the torch. He ushered Addie and Norman into the crevice and whisked his cloak in front of the narrow entrance, shielding them from the source of hisses that swept through the dungeon at tremendous volume.

"They'll pass," he assured them. "Thankfully, the Nephs can't see much since their eyes have been scarred from the flames. Instead, they sniff out the smell of fear on their prey and strike. Stupid creatures really, though utterly merciless. It's rare they come out to hunt, but it seems Marcus has called all hell to rise."

A flicker of cloaks rushed by outside, passing in the dim light. Their horrific faces were half-veiled in the cloth, brushing by in the darkness, although a single glimpse was enough for Norman to remember. He quaked in sudden recall of his brief eternity in the netherworld, the thousands of Nephs he'd witnessed clawing up the throat's fleshy walls, the chomps of their frog-jowls, the intense hissing.

"What do they want from us?" he asked.

"They are mercenaries come to do Oblivion's dirty work," the stranger said. "Damned souls without a prayer, sinners who have taken the oath after so many laps through Hell and been granted some measure of freedom by denouncing the very existence of God. The transformation is an ugly process, a grotesque peeling from human into these vile monsters. In the end, the last laugh is on them, of course. While allowed to roam, they are slaves to their urges, namely to hunt and kill. And now they are coming for you."

"But we're not real, right? What do they want from us?" Addie asked. "Can't they just leave us alone so we can live out our obscure imaginary existence in peace?"

"Real is always relative," the stranger said. "The true Addie and Norman, that Marcus once knew, died long ago and returned to Oblivion, as is the fate of every soul, to be reborn. You two are rogue factions of Marcus's mind taken on a life of their own. You see, his mind has undergone a sort of rebellion, one which you both are part of. A tri-fold split of his consciousness, traveling in and out of the myriad realities and alternate universes spun from the ethereal realm of Oblivion, the great nothing, between here and there, somewhere and nowhere, anywhere and everywhere. Are you beginning to understand?"

"No," Addie and Norman said.

"Fine. Let's try this then. Imagine, if you will, a giant sphere with billions of tentacles stemming from a point at its center, what is commonly called the collective unconscious," the stranger held out his hand and twiddled his fingers in the air. "These tentacles are individual consciousnesses swimming in the waters of the Oblivion like the feelers of a jellyfish. When awake, they are erect and unmoving in a finite depth of the water, a single fathom, experiencing a single reality as a straight line of time and space. When dreaming, the tentacle retracts and flops between fathoms in a subconscious state, experiencing transitive universes in eddies. Upon physical death, the mind is released from the paralysis of conscious life. The tentacle wrangles about like a fish caught on the line and warps between different fathoms as it is slurped back to the source. This is a natural reaction, of course. Since it's unaware of what is happening, the conscious mind reacts irrationally and resists. However, no matter how hard they struggle, everyone succumbs to the pull in the end."

The stranger collapsed his twiddling fingers and clenched his hand.

"And so you see what the problem is," he said. "Marcus's mind has split into three separate strands of consciousness, which have become entangled in the fathoms. The Marcus you know, the proverbial ego, isn't even aware of who he is, where he is, or why he is there. He's probably more clueless than you are, the worst of which is that his ego has actually latched onto another consciousness in a parallel universe, like a snake swallowing the head of another snake. There are very few rules in Oblivion, although the grand mind knows it can't have a rogue consciousness causing a pendulum rift. That is why the Nephs are coming for you. That is the reason why I'm here. I must lead you back to Marcus before you are erased."

When the hisses eventually drowned out in the distance, the stranger looked out into the dungeon corridor and ducked into the crevice again.

"They're gone. Not far. But they've gone for now," he said.

The stranger snapped again to ignite a flame on his index finger. The well-behaved flame danced on his fingertip and illuminated the crevice, revealing that this corner of the dungeon was not accidental. He held the flame before a red button, burrowed in the limestone wall, and pressed it gently. The wall shuddered and a hidden pair of doors opened into the chamber of an elevator.

"Cool, another elevator," Norman said. "Does this one go to God, too?"

"Yes. I mean, no, it doesn't matter," the stranger corrected himself. "Just go to the 33rd fathom. I know this must be very confusing. But trust me. The more this seems like nonsense now, the more sense it will make in the future."

Addie stepped into the elevator and marveled at its size. The chamber soared 20-feet high, scaled with buttons on an immense panel, "Why so many?"

"There's a button for every fathom projected by the overmind," the stranger said. "No fooling around, though. The 33rd fathom is where you must go if you want to spare yourself the complicated misery of cognitive dissolution. You must find Marcus before it's too late."

The hisses returned with the sweep of cloth and feet once more.

"And what's going to happen to you?" Addie asked the stranger.

"You are coming with us, right?" Norman said.

The stranger slipped on the hood of his cloak. "I'm sorry. You'll have to make your own way from here."

The hissing intensified and surged back. The stranger popped inside the elevator and pressed the 33rd button. It whirred and purred as the doors closed on the lost travelers inside. Addie stuck out her hand to stop the elevator from closing. "Hold on, what are we supposed to do once we get there?"

"Look up through the screams and Time will tell," the stranger said. He then turned with the flail of his cloak, and disappeared in the dark. The doors sealed shut. The elevator rose, the buttons blinked in succession, ascending from the 19th fathom at turtle speed.

Chapter Twenty-Two

Eve of the Revolution

The moment the news was announced, everyone hustled into the living room, out from the bunkrooms, out from the concrete corridors and subterranean recesses of the bomb shelter. The rebels laid down their playing cards, plunked their paint brushes in tin cans of rainwater, slapped their musty books shut, removed the needle from the spinning record with an abrasive scratch that silenced the music. Phaedrus was finally ready to speak about Operation Discordia.

Sitting on moldy couches, broken chairs, pressed against the bunker walls, the rebels circled round to hear what their fearless leader had to say. The long table had been brought out into the main room of the bunker. Phaedrus stood over the city map and plotted toy soldiers. Zander, against his wishes, had joined him there, under the scrutiny of so many curious faces and furrowed brows.

"Well, my friends, we've made it," Phaedrus said. "Safe and sound and not a moment too soon. There's a rumble in the siren-spooked streets tonight. The whisper of revolution. The return of the phantoms. And as the citizens toss and turn restless in their beds, disturbed by the howls outside, the Order is in a panic. While you planted phantom messages in the garden, the bait was set. Twenty explosive charges centered around the perimeter of the Institute and an anonymous tip on where they might be found.

"Right now, these duds are being dismantled and the guardians are claiming victory for their prevention of such a catastrophe. This sets in place our simple game of cat and mouse. Tomorrow, while the auxiliary patrols stand guard at the Institute in fear of losing their precious research, we'll strike from every direction." He stabbed his finger at the manufacturing sector on the map. "The factories will be the second distraction. A simple explosion. A failed sabotage it will seem as we shake their confidence and take hold of higher ground for our attack on the Centennial."

He strutted to the other side of the table and pointed at the island Citadel. "And when the time is right, we'll kidnap the heir philosopher king."

The rebels clapped and hooted at the news. Phaedrus cleared his throat with bravado and motioned for the crowd to quiet their applause so that he could continue.

"There is much to be said and I'm not quite sure how to say it. I know you encountered some trouble out there tonight. That's nothing compared to challenges we'll face tomorrow. Challenges that we wouldn't be able to overcome were it not for a great man who is among us today. A man who has returned to fulfill the vision of this revolution. A man who stands before you now, Zander Saint," he said, putting his hand on Zander's shoulder. "During those sobering days after we were forced underground, it was Zander who stepped forward to fill the vacancy left by Trevor Smith, one of the founders of this resistance, a martyr for our cause against mechanized oppression.

"From then until now, our rebellion has grown broader and stronger. You people have all come for different reasons. Some of you have come enticed by the danger at hand, to feel what it truly means to alive, to be vulnerable and choose your own destiny. Others of you have come frustrated that you must hide your true passions, that your wants and needs are shunned as evil and destructive by the Republic's false society.

"We are united by a belief, that there is more to life than numbers, than the piston's push or the gear's grind. We take aim at the ideology that has enslaved our minds for generations, that has been ingrained us ever since we were toddlers sorting blocks under observation. I speak of the ideology of productivity and perfectionism with technology as our all-holy savior. The gospel of machines, right and wrong, black and white, 1s and 0s. Everything in its right place. Everything in order."

Overheating from the speech, Phaedrus paused a moment, his cheeks flush, his forehead running sweat. He thanked a rebel who quickly produced a handkerchief and patted his forehead with the cloth.

"Our cause is above all else a human cause in pursuit of liberation from this mental prison," he said. "We are awake and we are righteously indignant. We fight for truth in an age of hypocrisy. We are not the advocates of anarchy. We are the defenders of its principle. And tomorrow we will strike at the heart of the Republic."

The conclusion of his speech let loose another uproar of applause, the rebels rising from their seats and letting their praise echo in the concrete vacuum of the underground bunker. Phaedrus grinned at the resistance he and Zander had fostered, the audacious men and women who'd left behind their seemingly perfect lives to stand and be heard, to fight in defense of free will. The applause carried on, until Phaedrus excused himself with a graceful bow and dip of his derby cap.

With tomorrow's strike spelled out in detail, the rebels returned to their leisure with renewed enthusiasm. They talked loudly, clinked bottles, and held aloft the jovial spirit brought on by the rousing speech. There was little discussion out in the open about the grave undertaking they would perform at daybreak. This was the way Phaedrus wanted it, of course. The record spun again and the music resumed from the gramophone horn, the stakes were raised among the card players in the bunkroom, the rebels drank and laughed and rejoiced as if it were their last night on earth.

Purple Harry, juggling a pocketknife in his hand as he talked, regaled a circle of rebels with stories of the old days, the tricks they used to pull on the guardian patrols. Another group of rebels surveyed the city blueprints on the map table, giggling at the heavy breathes that came from the surveillance room where Sprockett and Elsa had convened to discuss the Centennial strike behind closed doors.

Only Zander remained unaffected by the celebratory mood. He roamed through the crowded living room, silently processing and planning his measure of the attack. He was accosted by many rebels on the pass, who insisted on shaking his hand and offered bottles of bootleg mash in appreciation, in adoration, which he graciously accepted with simple thanks before swiftly moving on.

He was grateful when he found Weber hiding out in a far end of the room, seated in a pre-war phone booth, reading by himself.

"Zander, my friend, my brother," Weber said between sips from a moonshine jug. "Why the sullen face? This is a time of celebration." He slugged again from the jug, his cheeks rosy with an inebriated glow, and sloppily handed the bottle over. "Listen to this, you must listen to this." He adjusted his square spectacles on the bridge of his nose and read aloud from the nameless black book in his lap.

"*Think. Stand to be beheld, contemplateaued, wrenching the words into the machine. Try. Do not be afraid. There is nothing but paper memories, burning pages for the ages, held out of view...*"

Zander was so overwhelmed with anxiety about Operation Discordia that the words passed through his ears as mumbles. It could be done, he thought, it can be done. It would have to be precise, the timing, six teams synchronized and acting not a second too soon.

"What are your thoughts on our numbers?" he asked. "What if we've miscalculated..."

"Numbers? Didn't you hear what the man said? No more

numbers tonight," Weber grinned with drunken glee. "Now listen for a second, this is important:

"*Tired and tongue tied, holed up and choking. Nothing to be desired and yet every one strays, every thought betrays the cold heart, stoic, perceiving every wish like a distracting melody...*"

The sight of Leyna across the living room shook Zander from his obsession with the framework of tomorrow's mission. In a corner, she chatted with Angus and the invalid Neale who sat upright on a couch and drank from a bottle of mash to kill the pain in his stitched leg. Her black leather jacket flipped at the collar. Her wavy red hair, fiery and untamed. Her hazel eyes gleamed with a soft light whenever she'd laugh at one of Angus's jokes. Dreaming in her hair, Zander suddenly forgot all about the revolution afoot.

Weber turned the page and clumsily traced the text with his finger as he read:

"*I am less than I preach myself to be, the Farce goes on to trace the tributaries of a great river, that is to say the conscious flower blooming madly at the eve of innocence.*"

Zander sighed overcome by a foreign feeling as his heart dropped to his stomach. Why did I ever leave? he thought. He wondered what would have happened had he met her before the resistance, when he was simply content to live and work and contribute to the great commonwealth. Would they have fallen in love or simply traded glances in the market square, never to see each other again? Would they have settled into a quiet life and lived out their years together?

It's love or revolution, he thought as he suffered the emptiness. You can't have it both ways.

He remembered the day he'd first met her. The resistance had been reduced to a dozen or so loyalists back then, and in the door came Leyna. So young, so passionate, so resolute in her righteous anger. She'd come with a friend and was filled with a passion that made one feel electrified in her presence, talking about the revolution and what needed to be done.

It would be much later that Zander would find out the reason she'd come, a reason she shared in common with many of her female comrades. The Republic had taken her infant son, as they did all children, so the child could be reared by and for society at large.

The commonwealth severed the maternal attachment at birth and became the sole guardian of the child, rendering the parents anonymous. These children were then raised by specialized teachers at the Academy where their aptitude was tested toward the three paths: the Hero, the Saint, and the Smith. On occasion, the Order would permit itself to discard of a defective offspring, in order to spare the child a life of hardship and save the commonwealth from bearing the burden of a miscut cog. And so being a mother in the Republic meant many wandering minds and broken hearts.

Before the birth of her son, Leyna had been a upright citizen of the commonwealth, engaged in civic policy for the health bureau by educating the lower wards of the Residence on the importance of cleanliness in every aspect of life.

In the days prior to her birthing appointment at the Institute, she had been overjoyed by the prospect of giving back to the commonwealth that had given so much to her. Everything changed once the doctor delivered her son, after those eight excruciating hours of duress, screaming in pain, her wrists strapped to the hospital bed. She only caught a glimpse of her child before they sedated her and ushered the baby away. She never forgot his face, though.

When she awoke, she felt as if she had been torn apart. She screamed at the doctors to let her see the child, to hold her son in her arms, to look once in his eyes. She scratched the doctor's face when he refused and nearly strangled him in a fit of rage. This earned her six weeks in rehabilitation, and six more weeks under observation.

When they finally released her, she returned to work as if nothing had happened, yet unraveled inside. The spell of the Republic had been broken. The commonwealth had taken a piece of her, a piece she was not willing to give. She joined the resistance a year later, driven by a desire for change and a yearning for revenge.

"Zander?" Weber broke from his reading when he noticed Zander staring off absently. "Are you even listening? Pay attention. This is the best part, I'm telling you: *It is a fluent suffering, as if I could pretend to have tasted the pains of the best men, heroes and saints, basking in the streetlight vigil.*" He shut the nameless black book, laid it down, and smiled at it reverently. He beamed from his stool in the phone booth, waiting for a reply. "Well? Brilliant, right? Simply brilliant."

Zander chugged from the moonshine bottle and searched the living room for Leyna who'd once again vanished into the crowd. "Yes, it's clever."

"Clever? It's more than clever," Weber said. "It was written by Robin Dupont, the original merrymaker. They hung him from Anderson Bridge fifty years ago for writing love poetry. How utterly trivial is that?" he shook his head in disagreement with the world. "You know what he titled it?"

"No. What's that?"

"Ballad of the Wild Heart."

"Well, it's titles like that which probably got him strung."

"The wild heart, Zander," Weber said. "The entire poem is a righteous cry of defiance, an homage to Art and furthermore his love affair with Art. He had no choice, just as we have no choice. He was compelled, as we are compelled, to release his passion, his art, his spirit on the world. He once said that in order to save himself he had to write."

"That's ironic," Zander said. He spotted Leyna leaning against a brick wall near the bunkroom. Her eyes narrowed in a side-long gaze and seized his own.

"I've been writing myself. Phaedrus has asked me to document our efforts for posterity's sake. That way, whether we succeed or fail tomorrow, there will be some note... Zander? Where are you going?"

Zander walked toward Leyna, feeling his heart pound in his chest, feeling the vibrations from the clomp of her high boots on the concrete floor as she met him halfway. Zander handed the moonshine over after a slug of the foul liquor to calm his nerves.

"So we're really going do this?" she asked.

"We? Does that mean you're onboard?" Zander said.

"I'm still here, aren't I?" she said. "I realize there's no stopping him. We want the same thing, but I'm worried, Zander. This feels reckless. After all our careful planning..."

"It's now or never. Phaedrus is right about that. The Centennial. We will may never have an opportunity like this again. Do you think we can pull this off?"

"It's not a question of what we can do. This pack of wolves will do anything they are told. The question is what is emancipation and what will be its cost, especially since we would be putting a child's life in danger."

"I'm not thrilled about the idea. But that boy may be the answer we've been looking for. We need the young heir. A ransom for change."

"He's only twelve years old. He didn't choose this."

"It's a risk we must take," he said, searching for her eyes for understanding.

"Is it?" She stood so close he could smell the lavender in her hair. "I've heard that line before. The night before you left on a train three years ago. Do you know what you're risking this time?"

"I was a fool to leave. You were right," Zander said. "It's so strange seeing you again. I've missed you, Leyna."

"Don't say these things. Don't look at me that way."

"If not now, then when? Who knows what's going to happen tomorrow?"

"Stop it." She cut him off and looked into his eyes with cold indifference. "You're a ghost to me, Zander. This is how I was able to go on."

Phaedrus called out from across the living room, advancing toward them, "Zander! There you are, my friend. Where have you been hiding?"

Leyna slipped away and wandered back into the crowd. Zander watched her go.

"Forget about her," Phaedrus said. "I need to talk with you about tomorrow," he led Zander over to a quiet corner near the record player, "I'm reassigning Angus to your team. Neale is hurt too badly to be crawling around in the sewers, and besides we'll need him as a sharpshooter."

"Sharpshooter? Do you really think we'll need a sharpshooter?" Zander said.

"Who knows what will happen out there. The situation may become unpredictable once those charges detonate. It's better to be prepared."

"Well, let's keep the shooting to a minimum. We don't want this turning into a bloodbath."

"Why are you telling me this?" Phaedrus said. "Everything's going to fine, but we can't get ahead of ourselves here. We'll have to judge the situation as it arises. Have faith, my friend."

"Faith?" Zander balked. "Luck is what we need."

Phaedrus looked around to see if anyone was eavesdropping on their conversation, "Keep your voice down. This is what I've been meaning to talk with you about. You have your doubts, that's fine. But I must know that I can rely on you. I can't do this without you."

"I do have my doubts, however they certainly don't

outweigh my convictions," Zander said. "You can count on that."

"Good, good," Phaedrus said and then spoke softly. "You know I trust you. I've always put my complete confidence in you, I don't need to remind you of that. As for Leyna, she's been acting very peculiar as of late. Disappearing for days, outbursts of anger, open dissent. I have serious concerns about her true commitment to the cause."

Zander glanced across the living room at Leyna, who was talking again with Neale on the couch. "You really think she would betray us?" he said. "She's been with us since the days we used to strike the markets. She came to us, remember?"

"I know this, I know," Phaedrus said. "I simply can't read the woman and her recent behavior shows how volatile she is. So I'll put this in your hands and ask you once and for all. Can she be trusted?"

"Look, I understand that there's been tension between you and Leyna during my absence, but this needs to stop," Zander said. "She is as much a part of this as you or I."

"Okay, old friend. But hear me now, I expect you to keep an eye on her. That's the last word."

Zander looked at Phaedrus, and for the first time since his return, he saw a twinge of fear in the rebel's wide green eyes, his grin fallen flat. This profound seriousness was so comical, coming from the prophet of nonsense and mayhem himself, that he couldn't help but laugh.

"When did you become such a nervous ned?" Zander smirked. "There's no reason for any unease over this. Everything will go according to plan. You just worry about making sure the big bang goes off without any hiccups. The world awaits us tomorrow, hungry to be awoken."

Part Four: The Awakening

There are grave consequences for any traveler, be they psychonaut or transmigrator, who would dare trespass through the fathoms of Oblivion without invitation. These foolhardy explorers are only asking for certain disaster if they were to open any number of doors along the corridors of a transitive fathom, or say, take an express elevator to the wrong floor. For every detour, there is an instinctive correction, a contraction of the collective organism. For every infraction, there is ample retribution.

The stories are never-ending, all warnings. Take the case of Seiko Pasha, for example, an eager young Buddhist monk who used to meditate on rare wildflowers in the foothills of Nepal. Pasha was well on his way to supreme stillness and the threshold of Nirvana (the fathom that will remain unnumbered) when he made an unfortunate miscalculation. Upon opening the mind's eye behind the mind's eye, he found himself of the sixth plane of enlightenment, which is more or less colorless waves that glide to every horizon. Little did he know that this vast plane was also riddled with holes.

Pasha, in his impatience to reach Nirvana, ran toward the blinding light of perpetual peace and fell through into the 209.24th fathom of Oblivion—a sluggish reality populated by amorphous blobs that wander about in symbiotic heat, gyrating to mate and mating to gyrate. Pasha was quickly slurped inside their jellied bodies where he spent an eternity stuck in gelatin. The young Buddhist luckily lost all memory of the mishap and went on to exist in harmony among the gelatinous blobs and their blubbery songs of the wild for 5,381 years.

An innocent case with an untoward end, the simple result of faltered virtue. The consequences are far more severe for those less noble in their intentions.

In the 335.23rd fathom of Oblivion, the exalted Glen Norfolk of Grenoble, renowned scholar and amateur occultist, once attempted in vain to breach the doors of perception by eating the delicate sofa plant of the Andean cloud forest while being zapped with 200 kilovolts of electricity. While he did not unlock the universal mysteries he was hoping for, he did find his surrendered flesh shredded by voracious wombats in the burrow caves near the lunar sea of Xanto 4, in the 693.45th fathom of Oblivion.

The traveler need not suffer any pitfall within the fathoms themselves to incur the wrath of Oblivion. Many who have glimpsed the surreality of the subconscious from simple dreams and nightmares come back with their synapses tangled, no longer able to put their pants on straight come morning.

If this should happen, one way to untangle the psyche is to dive again into the unknown and hope, say pray, the problem rights itself. That said, there's no failsafe way to straighten the mind once it's lost its way, at least not without fraying the thread of the consciousness itself. Even the momentous splash of birth and slow emersion of death can prove troublesome if the traveler is not ready for the journey, or better yet, the arrival.

This is why the Watchers roam. There are the shepherds of Oblivion in a sense, though impartial to the myriad paths of fate. Perhaps you've seen them, flitting by in their long dark cloaks late at night, gone when you shake your eyes for only a second.

They come to guide the way but never intervene, to explain but never extrapolate. For in the end, everyone is in control of their own mind and must make that choice to return and surface. In other words, to awaken. And so it is in the 272nd fathom of Oblivion that the Watchers come to learn the secrets that the collective unconscious hold…

CHAPTER TWENTY-THREE

The Paradox of Professor Dodgeson

The elevator ascended fathom by fathom at a lethargic pace, the buttons flickered on the wall panel as if operating on exhausted energy. Addie and Norman watched the numbers rise on the panel, 20, 21, 22, waiting for the moment when the button for the 33rd fathom would switch off its yellow bulb and release them from this tedious limbo between universes.

"Frayed threads of Marcus's mind. Should have figured," Addie said, mothering the wound still fresh in her shoulder. "What complete nonsense."

"Being and nothingness," Norman said. "It is what it is."

"And what's that supposed to mean?"

"We are and are not. If perception tells us what is real, why would it be so farfetched that our mind can skate the planes of different realities?"

"Because there needs to be solid footing," Addie said, watching the dial rise past the 23rd floor. "Reality has rules. Order as a dice game is a paradox unto itself."

"But paradox is just the logical mind's inability to reason a given perception," Norman said. "As perception changes, so does our reality. Therefore if the mind is caught between the subconscious state and a concrete universe, of course everything would seem in flux and paradoxical, almost chaotic. But chaos, after all, is only an unperceived order in seemly erratic minutia."

"This is giving me a headache," Addie said. "Even if what you say about paradox is true, and I'm not saying it is, how does that explain how one man's mind can skid off into the unconscious, split, and realize several parallel universes at once."

"You mean what are we doing here?"

"Yes, exactly."

"I don't know," Norman said and pressed the button for the 1st floor. The 33rd floor button flicked off, the 1st floor on. The elevator jerked and began a slow descent.

"What are you doing?" Addie said.

"I have some unfinished business with God," Norman said. "It'll be quick, I swear. Then we'll go track down Marcus."

"What? No way. If Marcus is on the 33rd floor, then that's where we're going."

"And if we do find Marcus, what happens to us then, huh? What if we really are figments of his imagination?" Norman said. "I'll tell you what then. Then we'll cease to exist."

"We don't know if that's true."

The elevator passed the 20th floor.

"Look, I won't be more than five minutes. I'm just going to stop in and punch God in the nose. Then we'll be off, I swear."

Addie interrupted the descent with a quick click of the 33rd-floor button. Up they went again. "This is not up for debate. Let's stick with the plan here. We'll find Marcus and figure things out from there."

"Fine, be that way." Norman leaned back against the elevator wall.

"Good. I'm glad you're listening to reason here."

19th, 20th, 21st, 22nd...

At the 24th floor, Norman made a sneak attack at the button panel. Before Addie even realized what was happening, he lunged out, jabbed the button, and splayed his body spread-eagle in front of the panel.

"I need closure. You don't know what I've been through. You don't even have to come. You find Marcus and I'll meet up with you there."

"Are you crazy?" Addie tried to sneak in a hand, and it was swatted away. "Move, Norman."

"No."

21st, 20th, 19th...

"Move, damn it."

"No!"

That's when Addie smacked him across the face. Harder than she had intended, but it was a knee-jerk reaction to being trapped in an elevator with a madman. Norman rubbed his stinging cheek.

"Sorry about that, we must stay together on this," Addie said and lightly nudged Norman aside so she could press the 33rd button. An elbow to the ribs knocked her flat against the panel, pressing four or five buttons above the 33rd floor. Addie wheeled around to punch him, only to be tackled onto the floor. As the elevator rose again, the two friends wrestled about the elevator, kicking and swearing. By the 27th floor, they reached a standstill in negotiations holding each other's heads half-nelson on the floor in an awkward stranglehold.

The elevator shuddered with a grinding noise and shook herky-jerky like a mechanical bull. Smoke puffed inside when the grinding came to a halt and the elevator doors started to twitch. The button for the 27^{h} floor pulsed on and off in the aftermath.

Addie wriggled out of the stranglehold and got up from the floor. "Now look what you've done."

"What I've done?"

She jabbed at the 33rd button with no response. "We're stuck."

"I can see that, Addie. You broke my nose, you jerk."

"Shut up a second. We need to think this over."

Norman shoved her against the wall and pushed the 'Open Door' button. The doors pulled apart in a cranky manner, unveiling a long white hallway through the sliver, and then stuck halfway.

"Great," Addie said. "What'd you do that for?"

Norman didn't bother to answer, he was so angry. He

wrenched the sliver wider with his bruised fingers so he could squeeze out. The hallway was lined with school lockers, gaudy maroon metal boxes that spanned the length of the bright-white hall, interrupted periodically by classroom doors.

"Wait," Addie yelled from the elevator. "This isn't the right floor."

Norman flicked her off and strutted down the gleaming hallway. The sterile hall was so quiet that the click of his shoes on the checkered tiles made him feel as though he were a burglar who'd broken into the inner sanctum of a top-secret laboratory. Florescent tube-lights snaked along the ceiling of the empty hallway, which split at crosses into identical hallways, bordered with the same maroon lockers, the same wooden doors at intervals.

Norman inspected everything with childish curiosity as he ambled down the hall, touching the doors to see if they were real and rapping his fingers along the lockers as if he were a schoolboy back at Warren Elementary.

Addie broke from the smoking elevator and rushed after her friend, worried that the tiles might crumble and fall beneath her feet. "What are you doing? We need to get out of here."

"Sometimes it's better to act than react if an elevator may plummet at any moment with you inside," Norman said. "This is weird, isn't it?"

"Not as weird as I expected," Addie said, squinting under the bright lights.

"Yeah, that's why it's so weird," Norman said and tugged open a random locker for a peek inside. It was empty, except for a small black cloak that hung from a hook off the locker door.

"Here you go," he said, passing the cloak to Addie. "Put this on."

"I'm not stealing. Put that back. Stop touching

246

everything."

"Don't be such a pansy. Put it on. I'm tired of looking at your battle scars. What is that symbol drawn on your arm anyway?"

"It was a map," Addie said and slipped on the cloak. "I don't want to talk about it."

The cloak fit surprisingly well, despite being a bit short in the sleeves. Perhaps the students here were sorcerers in training, she thought. Little bald sorcerers with tiny flaming fingers. She wrapped the cloak around her and followed Norman down the hall.

They read the names of classrooms as they wandered past—METAPHYSICS 203, CARTOGRAPHY 333, FATHOM-WARPING 210. Through the fogged glass, blurred figures were seated inside. Norman stopped at one of the classroom doors, but Addie knocked his hand away before he could reach the shiny doorknob.

"Hey, we don't know what's going on in there."

"Sure we do," Norman said and pointed at the sign overhead: NONSENSE 111.

"And why would we want to go in there? Haven't you had enough of this already? Come on, let's find the stairs. We're losing valuable time here."

Norman stuck his ear to the door and listen briefly, "Maybe we could learn something about all this."

"It could be a trick, a test, the strange wizard guy could be testing us. He said the 33rd fathom. That's where we need to go. I'm not fooling around here. I'm not afraid to kick your ass again."

"Oh, you kicked my ass, did you? That's funny. Yeah, keep on telling yourself that."

Addie was about to slug Norman in the face again when the tapping of an angry foot intervened. Over their shoulders stood a man in a v-neck sweater, the same maroon color as the lockers themselves. He scowled through a pair of half-lens spectacles and shook his head. A yellow patch on his sweater announced his title in stitched yellow letters: *Headmaster Lewis.*

"Trying to make the slip, eh?" he said. "Fat chance, Lilly and Timmy. Aren't you supposed to be INSIDE Mr. Dodgeson's class?"

"Sir, with all due respect, I think you have us confused with someone else," Norman said. "Don't worry. Alexander sent us. We're only passing through. Do you know where the nearest stairwell is to the 33rd floor?"

"Ha, ha, nice try Timmy. Very pawky," the headmaster said. "How dare you try to skip class? Didn't you take Ethics 202: The Definition of What's Right and Wrong."

"No, actually that sounds interesting. Which door is that?" Norman asked.

"You insolent little twit!" Mr. Lewis barked. "Hold open your trousers."

"Excuse me?" Norman said, in defiance at first. He soon caved before the wagging clipboard and loosened his belt. The headmaster plucked a pair of live goldfish by the fin out of a plastic bag filled with water, and dropped them into his trousers. Norman wriggled and shook his legs until the tiny fish slid out of his pants and flopped onto the tile floor, flipping their tail fins in a fruitless attempt to swim away.

"Serves you right. I hope you've learned your lesson, Timmy," Mr. Lewis scolded. "And Lilly, I'm very disappointed with you, associating with this troublemaker." He opened the classroom door and shooed them inside, "Now sit down and get educated."

When the door slammed shut behind them, it sent a shudder through the classroom. The lecture hall was packed with row after row of bald young pupils in identical white gowns, pens at their notebooks, ready for the day's lesson. The pupils glared at the intruders from their seats.

"What do we do now?" Addie muttered aside.

"Well," Norman said. "I supposed we sit down and wait this one out."

Norman and Addie snuck up the aisle and sat in two vacant seats near the back of the class. Down in front, a blackboard spanned the length of the classroom. It was covered with long, tongue-twisting names like Wittgenstein, Heidegger, Kierkegaard, and Schopenhauer, scrawled in chalk. The notes on Confucius, Lao Tzu, and Siddhartha Gautama were separated from the Western philosophers, allocated in the top left corner where they would be safe from any East/West rivalry. Another corner of the blackboard was dedicated to Kant's *Critique of Pure Reason* (a complicated text about the reason behind reason which the class had undertaken the task of deciphering).

In front of the blackboard was the professor's desk and a steel podium. The remnants of a wooden podium lay discarded off to the side like a butchered tree. In a previous class, the professor had cut the podium in half with a chainsaw so he could demonstrate how the extreme makes an impression. Needless to say, the students never forgot that lesson.

Minutes ticked by and yet the professor had not arrived. Addie and Norman fidgeted in their seats while the rest of the students tapped their pens, waiting for class to begin. Even from as far back as they were seated, the skulking shadow of Mr. Lewis could still be seen through the window on the door. There was nothing else to do but wait.

The clock struck three and off went the school bell. The door flew open and in stumbled the professor, an obvious eccentric in the way he walked, talked, and carried himself. He was unshaven, hair tousled and wet for some odd reason, his clothes wrinkled and loose. He wore an untucked blue dress shirt under a small corduroy jacket, and a purple tie knotted with a sailor's hitch. His khaki slacks were almost wrinkle-free, although splotched with large ink stains from the professor's mistrust of pen caps.

After he'd exhausted several minutes pacing and scratching his head, the professor suddenly sprang alive. He ran over to his desk and flung down his folder full of papers, spilling them everywhere, then spun around to face his students.

"Hallo, hallo!" he greeted them.

"Good evening, Professor," the class responded in unison.

"That it is, my friends," he chortled in his joy. "And how are my maddening minds this eve?"

"Very well, Professor."

"Good, good... I propose we start this evening with a bang," the professor said. Quicker than the sweat off a fly, he whipped forth a tiny pistol from the breast pocket of his jacket and fired a shot into the air... BANG!

"Oh dear, how'd this naughty little gun get into my hand?" he chuckled to himself, tossing it aside on the desk, "No matter. Samuel, can you give us the shimmy on what happened in class yesterday?"

"You rambled for half the class," said a boy slouched in the front row.

"Naturally," the professor said.

"And then I dozed off a bit."

"Naturally."

"And then you started guzzling sand out of an hourglass and told us time was an illusion."

"That sounds about right. But what was the basic idea behind all that gibberish?"

"Chaos?" a spectacled fellow replied nearby.

"More specific."

"Pure drivel?" another bright lad said.

"Yes... now you're burning..." the professor smirked from ear to ear. "Broil the brain. It is very complex philosophical concept we're dealing with here. Rebecca, you're always my most attentive. Tell me what was the basis of yesterday's class?"

"Honestly, Professor Dodgeson, it sounded like more of the same nonsense to me."

"PRECISELY!" the Professor vaulted onto his desk and almost slipped on the mess of papers, "Nonsense... the universe is such utterable nonsense and unutterable sense. Why are we here? Did the fathoms always exist? How can something come from nothing? What is the Great Unknown? What's with the giant Eye in the sky?"

The professor leapt off the desk, fluttering his arms like a strung pigeon, and landed in a bandy crouch. He remained in this position so he could survey his students' shock.

"May I present to the jury..." he slipped a hand into his corduroy jacket again and pulled out a wooden mallet. "Exhibit A: a mallet. A very simple object, yet a complex symbol of paradox. The shape is concise for its purpose, a handle and a bulky head. That purpose is hitting things. Now the mallet differs from the hammer by the mere distinction that it's not stylized for a specific purpose, thus more in tune with the universal. When used like so..." He pounded the desk, THUNCK, with the mallet. "It symbolizes order, such as it would be used in the courtroom. When used like this..." The professor then took the mallet, bashed himself straight in the head. He fell onto the floor and recovered moments later as if nothing had happened. "It is a symbol of nonsense, chaos, anarchy, cartoon mayhem and masochism. Thus the paradox arises, order vs. chaos, sense vs. nonsense, structure vs. anarchy, all contained within the symbol of a mallet."

The professor ripped the bland tie from his collar and threw it at the front row. "Let all formality die at this moment for we are about to delve into the pith of Nonsense which knows no rules or etiquette. For nonsense is the mallet that smashes and breaks open the question between dumb eyes. Do you understand?"

"Of course, Professor," his pupils chanted.

"I don't," said a young woman in the third row.

"Shhh, Valerie. Just humor him," the boy beside her whispered beneath his breath.

"No, I won't, Philip," she said. "Professor Dodgeson, I don't understand. How can nonsense make sense if by definition it is the absence of sense?"

"She speaks! How curious?" the professor said quietly stealing over to her side. "Nonsense is never nonsense unless compared to sense. Now you must understand I use 'sense' for lack of a better word. I mean 'sense' as a sort of common knowledge, a conventional reasoning. Nonsense doesn't conform to this reasoning and thus it's deemed nonsense or 'without sense.' Therefore sense and its logic are convinced reality, the stencil which we lay on the world so we can give it order. But what's more important than the 'what' of Nonsense is its action… its bombastic effect on this convinced reality."

He pulled out a spinning top from yet another jacket pocket and twirled it on his palm. The toy top stayed there, levitating up on its point, and spun its many colors.

"Consider this toy here as Oblivion as we know it, the myriad universes and innumerable fathoms. And in each and every one, it's a ricochet of matter and energy, molecule against molecule, changing and forcing form, that creates the great mystery. While spinning, we see the true color. When stopped…"

The spinning top came to a standstill in his hand.

"We see each singular color, each singular facet. This is the eye open and dissecting what is seen. Of course, we can only see one side at a time through our limited perception. And here is where the real power of Nonsense comes in…" The toy top once again flipped up onto its point and began spinning, the colors more crystalline now with an unnatural luminance.

"…Its power to spin, to break perceptive constructs and show every side at once, perhaps just for a glimpse, just for a moment, to release the cinch and understand the paradox as whole, our ricochet universe."

"But how?" a student on the left spoke up.

"Through its unique method of abstraction, the absurdist reduction," the professor said, clasping the top in his fist. "The act of Nonsense is a form of spontaneous creation wherein the universe is framed with skewed margins and broken tiles in order to examine our paradigm. To uncover the truth through a corkscrew lens, a vantage point from which we can weigh our perceptions by recognizing the whole of existence as unutterable sense and utterable nonsense."

"Oh, well, I'm even more confused now."

"Good. This wasn't meant for textbooks. It is meant for reverie, for fantasy, for myth, for the subconscious riddles that seem out of place. There, it can dig for the answers through all the imperial garbage, picked apart by monkey minds and their machines.

From murky birth to clever feet, thick with flesh, the babble at every stony crawl is a reflection concave, the alphabet an algorithm to the mystery as it both unravels and reinvents the tangled paradox of a circle as a straight line wound round itself. And we, the curious hairs of anima, scratching at the sun, never cease to amuse each other with the funny things we say."

The professor chuckled and gave a warm smile out at the lecture rows. His pupils looked at him, either in utter confusion or with blank faces of total indifference.

The school bell chimed.

"I guess that's all for today. Class dismissed," the professor said. "Don't forget to read section IV from the Great Moltarius' *Lost Dogmas of the Moltar* for next class."

The students hurried for the door, shuffled in their gowns, and emptied out of the classroom. Addie and Norman slyly rose from their seats and walked down the aisle toward the door, unsure whether the headmaster was still waiting outside.

"Hey wait a minute," the professor skipped over and caught them before they had a chance to sneak out. "I don't believe we've met. You two aren't enrolled in my class, are you?"

"No, we aren't. We just stopped in to listen," Norman said.

"Well, I hope you do come back," the professor said. "Next week, we'll be studying how the attraction of..."

"Not likely," Addie said. "We're on a mission to track down the subverted ego of our friend, who has imagined us to life as split entities of his own psyche but is in danger of having his entire consciousness dismantled because he's latched onto another mind in a parallel universe. Any idea where the stairs are?"

The professor scratched his chin. "That is a predicament, isn't it? In that case, you better take this." He handed Norman his trusty mallet. "Stairs are down the hall on your right."

"Thanks, I guess."

"You are very welcome," the professor smiled and ushered them out. "Remember. If you ever do find yourself between a hail storm or avalanche, it never hurts to duck."

Addie and Norman thanked the strange professor again and continued on their journey in search of the stairs, moving with the flock of gowned students through the sterile school halls, careful not to run into the headmaster again and suffer another lecture.

CHAPTER TWENTY-FOUR

What Comes to Rise

Pennants waved on high, flapping boldly in the breeze. The emblem of the Republic, in every color imaginable, was strung out in rows from tenement windows, from lampposts, from shop awnings, from office buildings, from flagpoles erected for the occasion. In Concord Square, the pennants flapped from the clocktower ramparts where the crows roosted, scared by the mounting cheers and cannon-blasts of confetti that broke in the air. The pennants flapped from raised stages where the tournament games were underway. The pennants waved, dipped, and fluttered in the wind from the canal bridges, flew proudly over the shops along Anderson Boulevard, were held up into the air by the hands of young and old alike, as flags of the great nation, as a proclamation of their love for the commonwealth.

From the crow's eye, it looked as though the city had exploded overnight in a kaleidoscope of color, the streets teeming with thousands of people, moving en masse like an amoeba that had wriggled out of the thaw. The day had come, the Centennial, the long-awaited crowning of the heir to the Grand Muse's throne.

Throughout the great city, the best and brightest of the Academy graduates competed in a battle of wit and brawn for the coveted title. Among the contenders were aspiring pupils such as Wallace and Carlo Proto who raced against the clock to solve chemical equations on gigantic chalkboards for the amusement of everyone in Archers Plaza. Or Alison and Derrick Proto who parried blows on gangplanks across the western canal while teams of physicians waited with nets to scoop whoever lost out the rushing water. Or Melvin and Jane Proto who answered questions rapid-fire with wires streaming from their heads, electrodes hooked to their brains, their thoughts projected onto a massive video screen in the background.

Throughout the great city, criminal minstrels riled on the games with a romping tune from the sidelines. They whomped their accordions and made sure not to squeeze a wrong chord, or slip into a censored key, lest the guardians take notice. This was their penance, after all, for the crimes they'd committed against the commonwealth, their chance of proving their devotion to the Republic by playing the bellows blind-folded while everyone else rejoiced in the anthem of the streets.

Throughout the great city, people wandered with the fanfare from stage to stage, bit their nails and gossiped about who had the best chances, privately weighed the contenders' strengths and weaknesses. They'd dressed in their best for the festival, wore their most practiced smiles, cheered at every turn of the games and clapped for both the winners and losers in polite support. In every third square, aligned tic-tack-toe across the Old Quarter, the scientists demonstrated the newest advances to come out of the Institute, a hodgepodge of odd gadgets, robotics, and bio-experiments, the latter of which mostly involved the resuscitation of lost species of flora and fauna.

Throughout the great city, the guardians waited, entrenched in the masses, wary of what the festival might bring after last night's charade. Their microphazers hummed on standby, their stern faces connected with every passing smile, every wandering eye. Their apprehension went unnoticed by the good people of the Republic who reveled in the excitement of the day, building on the strike of five when the Citadel gates would open and the finalists would take their seats at the Master's Game.

Beneath their feet, beneath the celebration, beneath the great city, the rebels moved in stealth through the abandoned sewer pipes that snaked underground. As they crawled ahead with flashlight helmets shining off the limestone, Zander thought of Phaedrus' last words to him that morning. To listen close for the signal and not act a second later.

While they maneuvered through the sewers, Phaedrus and Neale led three teams of rebels into the manufacturing sector, toward the Great Factory and the annexed printing presses of the *Republican Guard,* where the Orbservers buzzed in and out through gaps between the factories, delivering tournament information to an outpost of Control 6 situated inside. Zander prayed they would be able to flip the switch in time to return and create the distraction needed for the kidnapping of the newly-crowned heir, the next philosopher king, the next Grand Muse.

"Where are we now?" Angus asked, the same question he'd asked at every curve and bend of the sewer. "Are we getting close?"

Zander unfolded the blueprints and traced his finger along the path traveled. Drips of water from the cracked ceiling splotched the parchment. "We should be under Pistons Row, near the river crossing."

"I can hear it," Leyna said. "I hear rushing water. Over there."

Weber wiped the sweat and filth from his brow. "That might be coming from the pipes next to us."

"Could be," Zander said and neatly folded up the blueprints. "We'll know when we get there."

The rush became stronger, strong enough for the vibrations to tremor the rounded pipe enclosure as the rebels crawled carefully through the water-logged sewer. Pieces of confetti and trash swam in the shallow stream they splashed through. Soon they could hear muffled footsteps and voices above, garbled by the rush of the stream.

"Listen," Leyna held Zander's arm and whispered, "I think

the Grand Muse has begun his speech."

The sermon blared from speakers in every sector of the city, a break in the festivities to reflect on the progress of mankind risen anew. In the Old Quarter plazas, the Grand Muse's image flashed on enormous video screens, broadcast from the capitol steps inside the Citadel, surrounded by his council advisors and parliamentary elite. He held out his arms, his purple cloak draped like unfurled wings, and called the Republic to attention.

"By the testament of this day, I hereby call upon you loyal citizens of this great city to celebrate the birth of a new era, an era to be define by our new philosopher king," he began. "Let this day give us pause so that we may remember the tenements of our society, this new Republic, free and just..."

Along with the Grand Muse's voice, the ticks of the clocktower reached the rebels' ears, loud enough for Zander to judge their distance from the heart of the Republic. Another few minutes and they would be there. The faint ticking set in percussion the gravity of the speech.

"Through normative principle, we aim to preserve and sustain a society free from the trappings of cognitive malignance that the old world suffered. After the Scare of 2309, we as a race had been reduced to an order of rodents, living in the ruins of a world that had both exploded and imploded. We cowered in safety zones, afraid to breathe the air. We resorted to violence and anarchy.

With the advent of the cure, we were slowly able to regain control and rebuild ourselves as a functional society. We rose from the ashes to embark on the greatest reconstruction of all time. In brief, we died in the scare only to be reborn as a new people, carried from our deathbeds to new life and prosperity by the light of reason."

The rebels shut off their flashlights as fresh light filtered through the street grates and shimmered off the wet limestone.

Ahead the sewer pipe forked around the ancient foundation of the clocktower, its wooden beams still rotting in place. Zander breathed a sigh of relief when he saw the foundation glisten there. A relic of the old world, now being damned above.

"...It was reason that faltered when the button was pressed during the plague, when the air we breathed became the poison that annihilated nearly every form of life on our dear planet. Although it has been a hundred years since, we retain the visceral image instilled in us as a reminder. The dead limbs of the trees, the black grasses, the animals, domestic and wild, charred corpses, frozen in terror, the entirety of indigenous life obliterated, sick and dying beyond the revival.

"We had little at our disposal in those days, except for our reason and an understanding of what must be done. As a collective force, we rebuilt this devastated city, as our sanctuary, our new home. We chiseled stone, erected the Academy, our capitol, paved roads, built bridges, constructed the Great Factory and everything we hold dear. In short, we rectified our losses."

Zander waded closer and shined his flashlight on the rusted steel foundation barred with rotten wood. He turned to call Weber over, but he was already at his side, holding the welding torch steady. They exchanged no words when he lit the flame.

"In the beginning, evil forces sought to undermine our efforts. Anarchists who feared the power of a rational evolution of our society and provoked violence against the allies of the new Republic. These delusional villains, whose chaotic modes of thinking dared question the very integrity of our great work, doped and deluded many of our youth, riddled their minds with lies in order to pervert our truth in the light of reason. Their resistance to our pragmatic ways incited riots and chaos. For our sake, for the future of humanity and all that is sane and good, we rid ourselves of their kind, the same kind who brought the plague upon us."

The rebels peeled away layers of rotten wood so they could break through to the steel foundation. The metal bubbled like a scar, under the torch flame.

"We have come to terms with the evil that is still fostered by the fascination with the irrational, the traitor of reason and the plague that creeps unseen. Today, we stand a happy and harmonious people, free of this old-world dissonance. And so we stand and profess these truths as a reminder of who we are…"

With a series of kicks, a steel block cut in the foundation broke inward, exposing a jungle of wires that dangled in a crawl space underneath the clocktower. The rebels crouched inside.

"First, that knowledge is power and should be used to further society, not undermine its base. This understood, it is necessary that knowledge be controlled in order to sustain a healthy prosperous society. Therefore, all education must be solidified and administered by the commonwealth."

Beneath the foundation, the rebels lit the ceiling of the crawl space with roving flashlights, looking for the hatch denoted on the clocktower blueprints.

"It was common back in those days, before the rebirth of new man, to raise children with fantastical beliefs, a mythology that warped these young malleable minds. Prophets of doom and glory, creatures with magical powers, mystical tales which championed insurrection against any authoritative force and honored immortal heroes for their defiance, simple parables which engendered a perverse morality and nonsensical understanding of the world. Where these myths may seem harmless at first, we know now their devastating influence on the nubile mind and how these false stories undermine the pragmatic practice and thinking of a just society."

A chorus of applause erupted from above as the rebels hoisted themselves up through the hatch and into a forgotten cellar of spider webs and dust.

"The detrimental effect of these parables is evidenced by the fact that for thousand of years, many educated and esteemed individuals, as well as common people, lived and died by the beliefs propagated by these myths and such fantastical concepts as the fires of Hades and clouds of Paradiso. These ideas drove millions to madness, to sacrifice themselves and others in the name of the ideological dogma prescribed by their cherished religions.

"Wars raged on for centuries, with one religion subverting its power upon the next. These wars were without end and are reputed to be the impetus for the plague that left the old world in ruin and nearly destroyed mankind. Therefore we profess that no beliefs shall be fostered that would speak falsehood against the tenements of practical society."

The rebels waited for the next word while Weber scouted another chamber upstairs. He poked his head out of the trap door in the ceiling. "All clear."

Zander turned off his flashlight, and with a gesture, informed the rest to do the same, "Any sign of the guards?"

"I hear footsteps somewhere overhead," Weber said. "This looks like an old mechanic's workshop. A stairwell continues up from here, but there's not much else besides rusted tools and old boxes."

The rebels climbed, one by one, up into the strange workshop. It was here among the counters cluttered with mechanical odds and ends, screws, hammers, springs, smashed alarm clocks, that the rebels quietly loaded their pistols. Zander flipped out his own revolver and checked it once again, clicking the chambers so that the holes aligned with the last two bullets. Out of superstition, he didn't bothered to load the missing rounds. The gun had proven its luck thus far.

"Remember," Zander said and pointed toward the door at the top of the stairwell with his pistol. "These are our last resort. It's essential we make this as quick and quiet as possible." The rebels nodded and strapped on their masks.

Outside in Concord Square and the adjoining commons, the crowd applauded every crescendo of the Grand Muse's speech, every roll of rhetoric in a fever of national pride. From the video screen, the Grand Muse smiled down upon the masses, just as Saint Benedict had done a century ago.

"Second, we profess that every man and woman must have their place in society," he said. "Nowhere in the Republic shall a man, woman, or child be without a home, a role to serve the greater good. The commonwealth shall provide for all who are willing to work toward a progressive future. Depending on their aptitude, everyone shall be assigned a niche in the greater fabric of our society to be decided by the Academy. No position shall be more auspicious than the next because we are all merely hands working toward the same goal—the prosperity of mankind."

Inside the control room, the guards peered through the plate-glass of the clocktower face into Concord Square, obscured by its many moving hands. They shifted their attention from the sea of people in the square, to the indicator lights on the electronic panel, and back to the Grand Muse projected on the video screen. After the emergency patrols last night, it seemed only natural they'd be tired when a sudden fatigue began to take hold. The power flickered briefly on and off.

"Clegg, you want to check the cables over there. That's the third time that's happened..." the guard heard a noise and turned to find his partner had collapsed on the floor. His vision then became spotty and black, only catching glimpses of the grey cloud pouring under the doorframe and a strange amber glow that burned a line along the edges of the steel door. Before he had time to comprehend what was going on, the gas hit his brain like a breaking dam, and down he fell.

On the second collapse, the rebels kicked down the door

from its melted hinges and burst into the control room. They breathed cautiously through their gas masks and scoped out the mechanical wizardry inside, waiting for the gas to dissipate. A modern control panel underlined the clock's glass face, but the rest of the room was from another time. A series of cranks, wheels, and cogs circled a ten-foot column in the middle where cobwebs spun up the clock's gear-riddled heart and soared high into the beamed ceiling. A glass triangle beneath the antiquated machine showed a hanging pendulum that ticked the clocktower's pulse.

Zander removed the headset from one of the guard's helmet and listened in. Radio chatter came from the earpiece.

What's going on tower? We registered a power glitch a few seconds back.

He whisked off his gas mask and spoke without taking a breath, "Everything's fine. The generator is just being funny again."

The rebels moved about the control room without a second to waste. They mimicked Angus's silent demonstration, and ever so meticulously, molded the putty, stripped the wire, and set the explosive charges in place like careful presents.

Roger that. Be advised the games are finishing up now and we anticipate procession in T-minus thirty, over.

There came a loud clang from across the control room. Zander quickly covered his hand over the headset microphone. "Be more careful, damn it."

Angus ripped off his mask and cursed at a metal pipe protruding from the clockwork. "I can't see a damn thing in this mask."

What was that, over? Everything alright?

"Nothing, over," Zander spoke into the headset. "Everything is fine."

A pair of eyes shot open and glared upward from the floor. The guard lay there paralyzed but awake, twitching, his throat emitting a hoarse hacking sound, choking from the gas fumes.

We're getting some kind of weird interference. Do you hear that, over?

With a sickening crunch, the sound ceased and blood trickled out from the guard's mouth. Weber removed his boot from the guardian's throat and knelt down beside the second guard so he could injected a syringe full of sedatives into his arm. Zander struggled to transmit the next message over the headset, his stomach turning cartwheels, "Like I said, generator is a little funny today. Over."

Well, remain vigilant there. We still don't know what those pathetic ghosts have up their sleeves today. Over.

"Yes, sir. They are unpredictable, that's for sure."

Zander released the transmit button and glared at Weber in disbelief. "Look what you've done."

"What? What do you want? Shut up alright. Just help me clean up the blood before it gets on his clothes."

Zander stared in shock at the guard's dead body and crushed throat. This is how it starts, he thought. Then it all adds up and the numbers don't matter anymore.

"Zander! Help me out here."

The blood pooled out from under the guard's head, swelling in a red puddle on the wood floor, which Weber desperately tried to contain with his sleeve.

"Zander!"

Leyna touched Zander's jaw and turned his face so she could look at him straight on. "What's done is done. Get a hold of yourself." She then let go and bent down to help Weber wipe blood from the corpse's mouth.

"...We profess that without the vigor and fortitude of every citizen, there would be no Republic." The Grand Muse held the pause for all it was worth. "Society can't stand in dissonance, cannot hope to prosper and flourish as a harmonious commonwealth, cannot sustain itself as a republic, without every facet of the diamond aligned by a common purpose. Every man must be just unto himself to create our just republic, must know his place, must perform his role for the benefit of all. Every man is our society and our society is every man..."

Weber snapped the last button on the uniform and put the helmet on his head.

"How do I look?" he asked with a smirk.

"This isn't funny, and keep that collar turned down. It has blood on it," Zander said, tightening the straps on his own uniform. He adjusted the armored vest, its high-shouldered sleeves, buckled the holster belt, and examined his reflection in the clocktower glass.

Once their uniforms were properly fitted, Zander and Weber joined the rest of the rebels who were still busy rigging small-charge explosives. The rebels tried not to think about the murder that had taken place in their presence moments ago. Leyna wrung her hands clean with a rag and gazed out the plate-glass of the clockface, out onto the assembly in Concord Square.

Angus called out from the backside of a mechanical pillar deep in the clockwork, "You have to take a look at this." Intense electronic waves washed over Zander and Weber when they walked over to inspect the curiosity. Behind the pillar, a steel box hummed in the machine, surrounded by the rotating wheels.

"What do you think this is?" Angus asked.

"There's only one way to find out," Zander said and hunched down beside him. He opened the metal hatch to uncover the innards of the machine and source of the waves. A mesh of wires connected to a black device inside with green indicator lights next to a handle switch and keypad. It simply read LASKA in bold letters. Beside it, a darkened indicator showed the second setting for the black box: STRACH. "What is that?" Weber asked.

"I don't think we really want to know nor do we have time to philosophize about it," Zander said and closed the hatch. The smell of burnt gas lingered; he straightened his uniform and glanced once again at the dead guard and his unconscious partner, stripped naked in their undergarments, with fuses running past their bare feet.

"Listen everyone, we have little time as you can see by the hour on the glass," Zander said. "The plan remains the same. Carry the guards downstairs and follow Leyna's lead through the sewers to the cross-pipe passage I showed you earlier. There, you'll for wait the second team to join you before surfacing for the rendezvous. Angus, you stay behind and place three more charges directly at the base of this pillar here and do it fast. We have a crowning to attend."

CHAPTER TWENTY-FIVE

In Transit

The black staircase twisted like a corkscrew up a white shaft, unattached except for the bough platforms that connected with different floors. Holding tight onto the sinuous rail, Addie kept her mind off the steep climb by counting the steps between fathoms. She wouldn't let herself look down the winding stairs, out of fear and out of a strange temptation to simply let go. What did it matter? she told herself again and again. What did it matter if she fell? She was less than real, a fractured piece of the cracked mirror of someone else's mind. Even though she recognized the fleeting nature of her spectral existence, she still couldn't do it. Because no matter who she was, no matter what she was, the compulsion of *being* was real.

At least they now had a purpose. Red and green lights flashed over the arched doors at each floor level. 31.07th, 32.08th, 32.09th. Not far, she thought. Whatever happened when they did find Marcus, she would handle then.

A few steps above, Norman ascended the staircase with an almost cavalier stride and studied the wandering cracks in the white walls, a scrawling railroad map which he imagined to be the network of all consciousness. A breath of cold air swirled up the shaft and caught him off guard.

"Hey, watch what you're doing," Addie said, pushing him back onto the stairs. "Pay attention. This is dangerous here."

"Ah, don't be such a baby," Norman said and continued the hike.

The sight of the mallet tucked in his friend's back pocket reminded Addie of the mortician pirates and brought to her attention the queasy rumbling of something inside her body, something alien. If she concentrated, she could feel it, a burning sensation that circulated through her arteries, like a parasite coursing through her blood. Addie wrapped her cloak closed and controlled a sudden urge to yank her friend off the stairs.

"What did that last door say?" she asked.

"32.09 or 32.10," Norman said. "I forget. We'll come to the next one in a moment."

The door on the next level read: 111.32.

"How is that possible? We've jump 80 fathoms in one floor."

"Maybe it's backward for some reason."

"And what sense would that make? Is every door going to read backwards from now on?"

"Did you learn nothing back there?" Norman slowed his gallant ascent. "You must allow your mind to follow the logic outside of reason."

"Not more of this. Not from you at least." Addie wiped sweat from her forehead, only to discover it had turned a slimy green. "And why is my sweat green?"

"What did you expect? We are ascending from one plane of existence to another. You should be happy that your face hasn't melted off."

"Has it??"

"Not yet. But you never know. It's hard to judge the rules when they keep on changing," Norman said, huffing up the stairs two at a time. "But this feels good, this feels right."

"We may have just missed where we were supposed to go. Maybe this is the express stairwell."

"Don't get paranoid. The number changed, not the direction."

The next floor proved this point. It read 112.32 written on the door, same flashing lights, same scenario.

"Why did it change?" Addie asked. "What's the point?"

"Why should it stay the same? You assume it should read one way because it did before, but now it reads another, backwards. Regardless, it still tells us we are on the right track."

"With only 900 more floors to go."

"That's assuming the math is the same, an assumption based on what you've been taught. You assume the floor after 999.32 is 001.33. But we don't know if that's true. And that, my friend, is the problem with reason."

"And what's that exactly, oh wise one? Please enlighten me."

"The problem with reason is that it is based on assumptions, a given set of rules deemed as infallible. It's a system for analysis," Norman explained. "The problem comes when the initial assumption, call it proposition A for argument's sake, is only partially true and leads to conclusion B, which may be more or less true than the original proposition, but is logically connected and therefore given some measure of truth. As further conclusions are linked by reasoning, the truth in the initial assumption is stretched. The illusion of truth is created by these so-called logical proofs and often the argument only serves to validate an erroneous perception inherent in the original proposition."

"Whoa, slow down," Addie said. "So you're saying reason only validates misconceptions."

"If the proposition is a misconception, yes. If the proposition is true, the logical conclusions may also be true or false depending on how far that proposition is stretched." Norman said. "Take science for example. Science essentially lays out a set of rules to interpret the world. Through these rules, scientists code the universe by means of mathematics and apply this knowledge to further applications, namely technology. With reason as their guide, they interpret data, or 'physical truth,' and draw a logical proposition from that data. Sometimes their propositions are correct and experiments lead to anticipated results, and sometimes they aren't, which baffles many scientists as they look to see what's wrong with their initial assumptions.

"Now here's where the importance of the irrational comes in. The history of scientific breakthroughs have been, for the most part, accidental. They come not from testing a theory for its conclusion, but from scientific frustration, moments when the scientist acts on his irrational whim, his gut feeling based on his knowledge, and sees a conclusion outside of the anticipated result that makes sense intuitively, if not logically. Then when it turns out to be true, the illogical conclusion is either reasoned backwards for proof or thrown away as paradoxical. 'The world is round complex.' Remember only 500 years ago, all science was based on the fact that the world was flat until Copernicus found a whole lot of puzzles in the night sky."

Addie climbed faster so she could keep pace with Norman who raced up the black stairs to the acceleration of his argument. "That's completely idiotic. You are generalizing the whole of scientific thought as a simple logic game, and reducing eons of ingenious, painstaking work to a series of divine revelations. Reason is the greatest power we have and science proves this by piecing together a logical argument of how the universe operates, an argument that can be tested with empirical evidence. Reason reveals to us truths we would not otherwise understand. It's the light in the tunnel of darkness that is the unknown."

"I'm not denouncing reason in its entirety. I'm just denouncing that notion that reasoned logic is the end all, be all of thought. Much happens inside and outside the mind that we cannot understand by looking in the tunnel, especially when the truths we find are only shadows on the wall," Norman said. "In the world of science where reason is a tool to devise a network of rules for interpreting the world, it has immense power. Outside that arena however, reason is often used in rhetoric only to validate a given opinion or perception through a logical argument as its proof. Consider: Proposition A (true) is stretched to conclusion B (partially true) which is stretched to the conclusion C (totally false). But if one follows the argument, they are convinced. It's intellectual trickery."

"Kind of like this whole discussion."

"Perhaps," Norman said. They arrived at the next floor, simply marked: 33. "Perhaps not."

They stepped off the staircase together, onto the cantilevered platform that led to the fabled 33rd floor. The arched doors were perfectly grey with an enormous '33' split down the middle by the door seam. A button protruded on the left side, beside a flashing red light.

"What did I tell you? Huh? How's that for trusting your gut?"

"Yes, yes, it's very impressive. But your argument is still flawed," Addie said. She reached over and clicked the button. The red light changed to green. The number 33 separated when the doors slid apart and unleashed a fierce light. A maelstrom of images howled in the doorway, bleeding color, blurred shapes, brushing by too fast to be understood. Without another moment's hesitation, they walked through.

In the next instant, the grey doors sealed and they were ejected in a chrome tube. Addie and Norman instinctively grabbed onto the metal bar overhead and watched wires in the darkness rush by the horizontal windows that framed what appeared to be a tram car.

Seconds later, the tram burst out into the sky, over a sprawling city that emerged in clumps and clusters, high-rise towers that loomed high in black glass and descended toward factories along a riverbank. The tram shuttled forward and screeched on elevated tracks, racing between these towers, over low-slung brick tenements in an urban gorge with ring-road streets further divided by a series of canals, which from afar looked like etchings in a woodblock.

For several minutes, Addie and Norman didn't say anything to one another and simply marveled at the city outside the tram window and the chrome car in which they now found themselves. The tubelike tram was immaculately clean and completely empty, except for a newspaper on the bright blue benches that ran the length of the car. An electronic screen hung from the ceiling and scrolled the tram announcements... WESTCHESTER AVENUE NEXT STOP... MELVIN AND CARLO PROTO JUDGED FINALISTS IN CENTENNIAL... REMAIN ALERT... WESTCHESTER AVENUE NEXT STOP...

Addie picked up a discarded newspaper off the bench. *Republican Guard,* it said along the top. The headlines in bold all talked about the importance of something called the 'Centennial' and laid out instructions about the day's festivities, where certain events would take place, how to prepare and so on. She leafed through the pages, more fascinated with the novelty of this newspaper, its unusual typefonts and authoritative language, than what was printed. Closing it up again, she noticed the date on the upper left-hand corner of the front page.

"2433 A.P.," she read aloud. "What do you make of that?"

"Sounds like the future," Norman said without looking away from the window. Outside, industrial warehouses whisked by as the tram curved and followed the bend of the canal. The tram took a sharp turn over the river and wound along the outskirts of an obviously older part of the city. Stone edifices seamlessly blended into one another with slanted roofs that crisscrossed in a mesh-like fashion. Along the rooftop hem, colored flags were strung out in the breeze as decoration. Now and then, splotches of smeared white paint marred the roofs. Someone had clearly attempted to remove the graffiti and only succeeded in smudging whatever was written. Norman spotted the word 'LEARN' far off, written in huge letters across a ventilation shaft on one of the roofs.

"This city is huge," he said. "Where is everyone anyway?"

Addie nudged in beside him and searched the cityscape until she found what she was looking for. "There," she said and pointed at where the tracks curved over a series of plazas anchored by an old clocktower.

"I don't see anything," Norman said. The cobblestone streets below were deserted, except for random specks of people walking here and there. When the tram neared the first plaza, these specks multiplied into a sea of people that flooded the city squares and appeared to be moving eastward. Extending as far back as the eye could see, this parade marched toward the clocktower, in the direction of a fortress citadel surrounded by canal rings and attached to the inner-city by a succession of bridges.

"Do you think Marcus is down there?" Addie asked. "How are we ever going to find him in that mess?"

"That's a very good question," Norman said.

The tram arced round a corner with a sudden jostle, and entered the darkness of an asterisk-shaped station. THIS IS… WESTCHESTER AVENUE. TRANSFER HERE FOR THE SECTOR-5 EXPRESS… GLORY BE THE REPUBLIC… the metal doors slid open into a glass-enclosed antechamber, raised between the elevated tracks.

"Well, should we get out here?" Norman asked.

"What does your all-holy intuition tell you?" Addie said and whisked on the hood of her dark cloak.

"Simply that we should keep moving."

CHAPTER TWENTY-SIX

How the Games Began

Through the clocktower arch, through Kensington Plaza, through a pathway cleft in the burgeoning crowd, the Centennial procession came. The fanfare swelled to match the cheers of the citizens of the Republic as the parade advanced in slow, deliberate increments. Flying out in front, a dozen Orbservers guided the commemoration, buzzing and scanning with a high-pitched whir that sounded as if their engines were propelling the parade. Next, a regiment of guardians marched in ceremony, LR-5s cradled in their arms, a gesture of the Republic's strength. Most of the guardians were on their third and fourth shifts after the midnight hunt for the rebels. But their stony faces and rigid shoulders masked their exhaustion.

The emblem on their grey uniforms was replicated on the flags held up on curved poles over the parade, the enigmatic symbol of a snake wrapped around a sword-shaped syringe rising from a laurel crescent, framed by stars in a knitted circle. GLORY BE THE REPUBLIC.

On mechanized floats, the councilors, Institute scientists, and Academy graduates waved down at the exuberant audience, which sang back to them in praise, in passing. GLORY BE THE REPUBLIC.

Accordion minstrels whomped and jangled the Republic anthem from the sidelines, accented by trumpeters who blared from atop the floats. GLORY BE THE REPUBLIC.

In the middle of the parade, the Grand Muse in his purple robe posed with two young graduates, Melvin and Carlo Proto, who'd won their place at his side. The boys mimicked the royal wave and tried not to let their nervousness or contempt for each other show. In a matter of minutes, they would be behind the Citadel gates. There it would be decided. The two finalists did their best to act calm, waved enthusiastically at the parade voyeurs and smiled up at the king whenever he'd lay a hand on their shoulders, while inwardly calculating their strategy for the Master's Game.

Alongside his majesty's float, Zander marched in a line with the guardians that shepherded the procession. He blended in surprisingly well, in his borrowed uniform. His collar tight at his neck, arms stiff with one hand under the LR-5 barrel and the other holding the butt of the rifle.

Through the visor of his helmet, he counted the guardians ahead and behind... thirty on either side, fifteen in front, maybe another regiment already inside... and watched the Arch of Truth approach. He'd occasionally steal a glimpse of the young finalists and the Grand Muse on the float. But only for a second. How easy it would be to kill him right now, he thought. He imagined himself doing it, turning and firing a single precise shot at his crowned head. The temptation consumed him as he straightened his shoulders like the soldier he pretended to be. Let the game play out, he told himself. The time will come soon enough.

Radio chatter crackled over the headset in his helmet.

Sector 5 clean, you are cleared for entry.

Bridges clear.

Arrival in T-minus six minutes and thirty seconds.

Gates ready.

Copy that. Reaching the Arch now.

The procession tightened into a narrow chain when it passed under the Arch of Truth, a massive stone monument erected in memory of those who perished in the Antriac War. Spectators hemmed the canal bridges on the other side and stepped aside into neatly packed rows so that the procession could proceed unhindered.

Faces whisked by in the crowd, the elders of the Republic—the finest Smiths and Saints, retired Heroes with badges of honor pinned on their guardian uniforms, many of whom were old enough to remember the Consecration of the Order fifty years ago when the Grand Muse had been one of the young contenders on that float. They considered themselves blessed to witness the parade firsthand while others viewed the broadcast from crowded plazas throughout the city. This was a privilege granted for their exemplary service to the commonwealth. When the gates opened, only they would be permitted inside the Citadel to see the Master's Game unfold and take part in the time-keeping. The elders held silver pocket watches in their wrinkled hands, small replicas of the clocktower face with its many moving markers, set to start and stop with the click of a knob.

Once the procession had traveled over the third bridge, the elders filed in behind the parade and accompanied the floats over the last canal to the Citadel gates. There was something monstrously beautiful about the fortress capitol from up close, majestic and terrifying. Its flat plemetic walls, those windowed eyes of Control 6, the watchtower spires... Zander stopped himself from staring at the imposing structure so that he wouldn't draw any unneeded attention. He kept his head locked in march formation. The gigantic iron gates swung outward with a salute from the entrance guards, just as the head of the parade arrived.

In Concord Square, video screens broadcast this historic moment for the audience that mobbed the plaza, their open palms held out in worship to the Centennial parade and the Grand Muse on screen, so overcome with emotion that their eyes brimmed with tears.

"Some sort of celebration, don't you think?" Addie said.

"Yeah, I don't know," Norman whispered by her side. "Strange, right? Why are they smiling so much?"

"Yeah, something is definitely off here," Addie said. "This seems all too friendly to be anything but trouble."

Addie and Norman watched the broadcast from the middle of the public assembly, surrounded by these awestruck citizens of a future unknown, whose fanatical smiles, whose curled mouths of bright white teeth fell agape to see their king and his contenders for the throne delivered through the gates to the Citadel forum. Flying orbs zoomed over the mob of onlookers—heads tilted, palms forward—and bled red beams into the exposed retina.

"There are those things again," Norman noted.

The accidental tourists had been greeted by an orb patrol the second they'd stepped off the tram escalator into the northern end of the Old Quarter and were swept south by the steady flow of parade attendees. The orbs had tailed their movements through the congested streets for several blocks, past the shuttered shops and offices, past the accordion minstrels on the sidelines who greeted them in musical salutation, through the arches of the ancient arcades and under the banners that declared 'Long Live the Muse,' before the orbs had lost interest and promptly zipped out of sight.

The odd flying machines weren't the only ones that had taken notice of the two misfits among the Centennial celebration. During their short time in the mysterious city, they'd encountered many looks of disapproval and reactionary scowls from passersby who'd interpreted their lack of proper attire for the occasion as a lack of respect for the commonwealth. But thankfully the sheer magnitude of the assembly had once again allowed the travelers to regain their anonymity, crammed in the public square among the countless men in dark woolen coats and countless women in sky-blue dresses.

"We're too exposed here," Addie said, hiding her face under the hood of her cloak. "I feel like people are staring at us and not in a good way."

"Don't be so paranoid. Relax, okay?" Norman said. "Besides, we have a great view from here. Do you think Marcus is somewhere in the parade?"

"Could be," Addie said. "If only we could get over there somehow."

The tail of the procession slipped beyond the high walls of the Citadel and the gates swung closed. Behind the fortress walls, the capitol guards scrolled through the names and faces of the 'Missing and Wanted' in their digital ledgers, as the Republic elders ushered into the colonnade courtyard. The parade floats disbanded at either end of the courtyard and its grand forum, between the outer columns and passed the rounded marble steps that ascended to the stone pavilion and hallowed entrance into the capitol complex.

The Grand Muse stepped down from his royal float to take his seat on a throne between the main pillars that fortified the pavilion. The councilors of the Order then filled into rows behind the throne, facing the elder congregation and a trapezoidal stage that rose like an anvil in the center of the courtyard. A giant chess board was positioned under spotlights on the stage. Pawns in formation, rooks locked in their corners, queens aligned, knights lying in wait, bishops standing tall for the Master's Game.

Once the last of the elders had settled into the courtyard, the Grand Muse rose from his throne with his arms outstretched in a symbolic embrace of the elder congregation.

"Dear citizens," he began. "We've come to this final hour wherein we shall see who will be elected as the next great philosopher king of our Republic. Let history show that on the centennial anniversary of our great commonwealth we stand stronger than ever and ready to brave whatever the future may hold as one holy and united people. This, my friends, my sons, my daughters, my colleagues, is the dawn of our golden age and may another hundred years pass with such prosperity. May

I introduce to you our two young candidates for the throne, whose youth will keep us young and whose wisdom will lead us onward." The young graduates came out from the pillar shadows and stood beside the Grand Muse. "Melvin and Carlo Proto."

The elders applauded with heavy hands and heavy hearts as the contenders marched side by side up the ramp toward the lighted table and shook hands before taking their respective places at the game board.

Melvin had been the obvious favorite since he beat Sarah Proto at the chalkboard in the preliminary rounds by solving the chemical equation for ergotamine in a matter of 23.35 seconds. Carlo Proto was a relative unknown. There had been no talk of his Academy achievements, no report on his mental physique or intellectual prowess in the *Republican Guard* during the months of tournament training. Yet he had triumphed again and again against all odds to win his slot at the Master's Game.

Zander remained alert among the guardians in the forum wings that flanked the courtyard. He imagined himself at that table, imagined himself as one of the young contenders there on the stage. The Republic seemed an immaculate marvel to a boy of twelve, so exact, so perfect in its daily devices, the future so brilliant ahead.

Whatever happened would be on his hands, he told himself. No matter how hard he tried to shut it out, the vivid memory of the clocktower murder replayed over and over in his mind, and each time, he saw the blood pool wider and wider out from the guard's crushed throat, then the somber look on Leyna's face, her soft touch before she knelt down on the floor to scrub away the evidence.

The last time he'd seen that look was the night she'd rinse the blood off his own hands. The mission had been risky from the outset: to break inside the Institute and find the root of the rebel's suspicion, a history of the atrocities committed by the Republic for sake of its perfect society. Sheltered by the shadowed shoulders of the Institute's hydrodam, which churned the north river in its turbines and supplied the electric lifeblood of the city, he'd scaled the barbwire fences and colossal stonewalls of the Institute, cut through a skylight dome in the roof, and repelled into the darkness.

After bypassing security with a duplicate keycard forged by Sid, he'd gained access into the maze of vaults underneath the research labs. What he discovered was much more than he'd been searching for. Deep in the laboratory vaults, he discovered files that contained both the architectural blueprints of the city as well as documented proof of the commonwealth's attempt to create a just society, free from indecision and dissention.

Saint Benedict knew that, while they had successfully saved mankind from the plague, they couldn't stop there. They needed to find a cure for the disease that had led mankind down the path of self-destruction. The disease of the free man, the free mind, the iconoclast.

Zander had escaped from the Institute with relative ease, and in the foolish pride of his success, stumbled across a guardian patrol on his way through Sector 3 in the dark of night. His first shot smarted blood, and in the same instant, a microburst blast buckled his knees. Shaking on the ground, he turned his revolver just in time to meet the face of the guardian who'd rushed after him.

When he returned to the rebel headquarters underground, he found Leyna awake in the bunkrooms among the snoring rebels. She had been waiting for him, unable to sleep. Zander couldn't speak nor did she ask him any questions when she helped him rinsed the blood off his hands.

"This is the reality of change," she'd said. "You're a good man, Zander, in a world that's difficult to understand." She kissed him softly on the lips in sympathy, but her lips stayed. He held her arms in a close embrace and felt as if his soul were breaking. He then brushed back her hair and put his broken soul into those lips, that moment.

They never spoke about that night afterward. Phaedrus planned Zander's escape the following week after wanted posters cropped up throughout the city with a reward for his capture. And now this. This whirlwind of hijinx, danger, and conspiracy with Leyna somewhere in the midst of it all.

Zander pushed away the feeling and focused on the mission at hand. He studied the royal escorts near the Master's stage without making direct eye contact. Twelve. More guardians would be waiting inside the capitol complex, he knew. Searching the helmets and uniforms on the opposite side of the courtyard, he spotted Weber in disguise and exchanged a fleeting glance of recognition. He looked toward the clocktower, barely visible over the Citadel walls.

Tick.

At the Master's table, the young candidates scratched at their mops of hair and met eyes with quizzical affection over the chess board. Melvin had won the honor of playing white because of his high marks in mechanics tournament earlier. Carlo seemed unshaken by this advantage and touched his black pawns one by one in an intimidating manner.

The five o'clock hour chimed from across the canal bridges. Melvin and Carlo sweated under the spotlights. With a punch of the time clock on the table, Melvin slid out his queen's pawn in the center of the board. The elders clicked ahead the knobs on their pocket watches in unison.

The Master's Game moved in the flash of hands, black to white across the stone table, a checkered dance. Little hands moving the pieces in complicated patterns which excited ohhs and ahhs from the elder congregation. The boys were hardly cognizant of the weight of each move, how every swipe, hook, and fork brought them one step closer to deciding who would be heir to the throne.

Carlo moved his bishop out through a crack in his pawn defense and smiled across the table when he punched the time clock in the center.

Click.

Melvin mused for a couple seconds, picked up his queen, put it back down and thought again, sliding out a knight to threaten the advancing bishop.

Click.

Carlo advanced his queen to the open field.

Click.

The black queen met the white bishop center field.

Click.

Carlo itched behind his ear and studied Melvin for his reaction. Melvin gave none and kept his eyes on the board, ignoring the roll of whispers below the stage.

Click.

The young contenders resembled giants on the video screens in Concord Square, the Citadel cameras zoomed in on the board, focused solely on the match of wits. Whenever the cameras would pan over the elder congregation for their reaction to the game's twists and turns, Norman would scan the courtyard audience for Marcus, as he had been instructed. Addie, meanwhile, steadily searched for their lost friend among the thousands of faces amassed in the public square.

"Any sign of him?" she asked.

"Nah, not yet," Norman said, stretching on his toes so that he could see over the many top hats in the assembly. "I don't get it. What's the point?

"The point is," Addie said, "that our only way out of this twisted freak show is to find that son of a bitch."

"No, I mean chess. I've never understood why people are so fascinated by the game," Norman said. "There's no spontaneity, no life. Just combinations of clever moves."

"It's never the same game, that's the beauty," Addie explained. "Yes, every game begins the same way. Yet through a series of seemingly arbitrary moves, the puzzle takes shape. Then each player puts forth their own design and changes that puzzle with every turn. A logical quagmire to undo, to push toward your favor."

On screen, Carlo took the first pawn of the game with his bishop, which evoked resounding cheers. Click.

"Doesn't seem like a spectator's sport, that's all," Norman said.

"Well, that depends on what's on the line," Addie said. "The fate of this crazy world as we know it could be in the hands of those two young boys, the equilibrium hanging in the balance as white faces black, good confronts evil…"

A wild applause broke out when Melvin swiped Carlo's queen in a single move and punched the clock. The audience in Concord Square likewise clicked their pocket watches ahead in syncopation.

"Is that bad?" Norman asked.

"Depends on what really does hang in the balance."

A patrol of Orbservers flew out from under the clocktower and made another round over the crowded square. After a preliminary inspection from afar, the orbs zipped toward the two foreigners in the assembly. Norman, with the instinct of a cat, grabbed the mechanical fly when it passed over. The robotic orb sputtered and grinded its internal circuitry in confusion.

"Don't touch that thing," Addie said. "Stop fooling around. Let it go."

Norman yelped in pain when the orb sent a burst of electricity through his palm and zip out of his hand.

"It bit me," he said, watching the orb zoom toward the soldiers in grey uniforms under the clocktower pendulum.

"Maybe we should get out of here."

But it was too late for that. The public assembly was so densely packed that they barely had enough room to breathe, let alone wriggle their way out in time. An envoy of soldiers barged through the mob and pulled their guns from their holsters when they singled out the presumed troublemaker by his long dark cloak.

"See what you've done now?" Addie said, pushing Norman forward in vain. "I should let you be arrested, you moron…"

In swift succession, the first soldier kicked the hooded foreigner behind the shins and knocked her onto the cobblestones, the second put his knee on her back so that she would stay there, and the third, with the same enthusiasm and expertise, unhooked a pair of electronic cuffs from his belt and charged the pulse.

The Orbservers returned to the Citadel, zigzagging over the crowded plazas, over the canals toward the fortress capitol, and reported to Control 6. And from their mechanical eyes to his majesty's ears, the information filtered through. The Grand Muse listened from his throne to updates from every sector of the city and observed young Melvin calculate the next attack with a rook between his fingers.

Nothing would ruin this day, he'd made that vow. The callous nature of the rebel's raid last night on the Savior's Garden had mortified the council. That morning in secret session, the vote had been unanimous to authorize emergency directive B4. Any dissension in the ranks or among the populace, and the guardians were advised to shoot on sight. If worse came to worse, they'd mask the incident and turn the city to paralyzing fear with the flip of a switch. This was nothing he hadn't dealt with before. The Republic knows no flaws.

Sector E-5 clear…

Orbs report 20-19 in 5.3 rounds…

Sector E-7 is a negative... strays in Sector A-6

ID checks out, over...

Roger that, Command is all green...

Interspersed in the radio traffic came repeating morse code of the Orbservers in alert patterns.

Check those level 8 again. We've got a slight variation in the pulse near Sector B-9...

North or the sound end...

South... Copy back...

Clocktower W, how's your sight...

"Commons is clear, over," Zander spoke secretly into his mike of his helmet. He released the transmitter and watched the Orbservers scramble back and forth, high above the courtyard congregation, zipping between the Citadel spires.

Domestic disturbance in Sector D-3, but we're handling it...

Roger that. Keep your sight clean... There must be no mistakes today...

Click.

Carlo bit his lip and bounced his eyes, scanning the board. In a single move, his world had collapsed. His queen lost. He made no whimper or whine, although tears joined the sweat that streamed down his face in silent despair. Melvin hid his pride well and folded his hands while planning his opponent's demise. Carlo's small hands twitched over each piece with indecision. He finally moved his knight out from behind a regiment of pawns.

Click.

Patrol 122, over...

Good ahead, C4.

We've got trouble... We've got trouble near the left bank of the Factory...

You're breaking up... Say again...

Trouble in Sector F-7... A series of alarms have been

disabled...

Are you positive? Verify again...

Command, are you seeing this?...

Negative... We have green and functional on screen, over...

Get the screen fixed then... This is a positive... I'm send over the visual now...

Zander stayed calm while running through the scenarios in his mind. The radio traffic continued. No gunshots. Just sterile panic in the voices of the guardians on patrol, hunting for the phantom rebels whom they now knew were inside the Great Factory.

We've got a definite breach here... There's no doubt about it... The door is broken in... Are you still not picking up any disturbance on screen...

Negative... All is green... Where are you seeing this...

Report, where is the breach...

We have visual...

Where?

Visual, one spot... Moving in...

Click.

Melvin watched his opponent's fingers twiddled over the black king as if he were casting a spell. Then his fingers calmed. The conviction in Carlo's face drove the fear into Melvin, whose own smirk had broken loose into a full gloat. Carlo hooked his knight to check the white king.

Click.

Melvin, without a piece to defend, moved his king one space to the left.

Click.

Carlo checked him again, sliding in his bishop to claim the lone pawn.

Click.

Melvin greedily swooped across the board to take the

bishop with his queen.

Click.

As soon as he'd removed his fingers from the piece, Melvin knew the next move. He'd seen the fatal flaw in the last second, but he couldn't resist the temptation to take the undefended piece. Carlo, with an even bigger smile, simply moved his knight to check both the white king and queen.

Click

Melvin moved the king out of the way and winced when the knight claimed his queen.

Click.

Zander looked at the hands of the clocktower over the Citadel wall, worried that the game might end before the strike. Weber shot anxious glances across the courtyard from the opposite wing. But Zander ignored them. He knew better. He listened and waited.

There's nobody here... floor two clear...

Floor three is negative... En route to basement level...

Production is clear, but there are boot marks in the sawdust...

What's happening? Command sees nothing... I repeat Command sees nothing... We need everyone on full alert... Re-check all sectors and double patrols...

Tick. The clocktower markers read 5:21 through a space in the skyline carved by the Citadel spires. Zander counted down the minutes while the rest of the guardians between the columns frantically listened to the reports over their headsets. Tick.

As the radio alerts persisted, the ranks began to move outside the Citadel. The guardians assembled into small teams, adjusted their rifles on their shoulders, and heaved their way through the plaza crowds. The citizens of the Republic were so mesmerized by the Master's Game on screen that they hardly noticed the guardians on the move nor did the public assembly in Concord Square pay any attention to the domestic situation being handled by the guardians in the audience.

"Who are you? Where are the others?" a guardian screamed at Addie on the ground and ripped off the foreigner's hood so he could see her face.

"We arrived only a short while ago. I don't know what you're talking about," Addie shouted at the soldier whose knee was digging into her spine.

"Let's try that question again, traitor. Where are the others?"

Norman wrestled with the soldiers behind him and then felt the cold snap of steel on his wrists, an electro-pulse through the skin. "She's telling the truth. We're from out of town and thought we'd just drop in for the festival," he lied. "Please, let us go. We'll explain everything."

Tick.

Carlo inched up a single pawn to defend his bishop.

Click.

Melvin plucked his own knight to counter the attack. With confidence, he pinned the knight down so he could corner the black bishop and defending pawn.

Click.

We've got confirmation on that movement... They're on the run...

Stay steady, Patrol 122... We have reinforcements on the way...

Click.

In a brilliant turn, Melvin made his victory known. He moved his bishop in to check the black king and slammed the piece down triumphant. "Mate," he said.

Carlo, in awe, checked his options. After a moment's calculation, he bowed his head and punched the game clock. Click.

The elders threw their arms into the air for this pivotal

moment in the Republic's history. The Grand Muse rose from his throne and slowly descended the steps toward the stage so he could inspect the board himself, as the congregation began to sing. GLORY BE THE REPUBLIC.

The clocktower's rusted hands ticked the final seconds till the half. Zander took one last look through the Citadel spires where the clockface held the hour. Tick. Tick. Tick...

The first explosion sent a quake through the forum courtyard that trembled the base of the columns. Yet the sound was almost inaudible as the elders cheered on the victor of the Master's Game.

The Grand Muse lifted Melvin's hand. "Citizens of the Republic, lift your hearts to our new philosopher king."

A second explosion deafened the applause within the courtyard walls. Smoke rose from the heart of the Republic, the Great Factory, the Academy, pluming with dances of fire. The elders turned their heads, distracted by the sulfuric smell, to see the distant flames over the Citadel walls.

The screen is still green... This can't be right... What's going on?

We have multiple explosions... the Factory is... We need medical help now... we have three men...

The guardians in the forum wings hurried to form into emergency patrols before heading out into the city. Zander tapped twice on the stone column beside him, and across the courtyard, Weber tapped three times in response, slowly. On the count, they advanced from opposite ends of the forum and filled the void left by the guardians rushing out. Zander knocked shoulders with a guardian when they tried to shove through a gap in the congregation at the same time. They locked eyes briefly. Zander dodged past and continued on his way to the raised stage.

Come in Command! Come in Patrol 363!

The capitol guards swiftly escorted the Grand Muse and

his new apprentice from the stage when a third explosion struck somewhere inside the fortress itself and jostled the chess pieces on the board. The imposters moved with the guards, running up the steps toward the capitol pavilion.

Move out, move out, move out. We have multiple explosions, multiple contacts, they're heading east...

The iron gates swung open once again, this time to the sound of sirens. The emergency patrols rushed out of the Citadel with their eyes turned toward the sky, watching the smoke trail from outlying rooftops in the east, north, west. Red beacons lit up in every street, in every square, in every sector, when another series of explosions erupted throughout the city and forced the unassuming citizens of the Republic to witness the chaos begun.

CHAPTER TWENTY-SEVEN

Prisoners of War

After the fourth round of explosions, the screens went black, and left the thousands of people huddled together for the Centennial celebration to face the fact that they had no idea what to do next. Flames rose in pockets above the Republic, spreading smoke in a cloudy haze. Black here, grey there, tongues of red and orange which lapped the sky. In the Old Quarter plazas, red emergency beacons pulsed erratically, embedded in stone arches and mortared brick. The loyal citizens searched for signs in the sequence, listened for that booming voice over the sirens to give them instructions.

They had come from every quarter of the city, every borough, to partake in this joyous occasion, knowing that when the festivities ended they would go home and begin again tomorrow for the next hundred years. And now the screens were black? What did that mean? Something had gone terribly wrong, they could feel it, a collective severance.

No one moved at first, just whispers and empty questions, others remained silent and continued staring, expecting the video screens to flash back on as if it had all been a test. But this illusion soon evaporated when gunfire erupted from the rooftops and swarms of guardians came running through the streets, firing their LR-5s up into the shadows.

We need back up in Sector 5-A... We've got five men down...

They're on the move again... rerouting to intercept...

Sector 4 is breaking into disorder... We're in the dark... Get over here now...

Copy that... Teams en route to higher ground...

This is Command... All patrols not engaged are to secure the commons... I repeat, secure the commons... We need to isolate the threat before we let anyone out....

The guardians formed blockades at every exit of Concord Square, under the north wall arcades, along the riverbank, in front of the clocktower and behind it so that the crowd in Kensington Plaza would be prevented from entering.

"Look, you don't understand. We're not part of this," Norman said and screamed as a 600-volt jolt from his cuffs shot through his body like an electric eel. The soldier shook him upright and forced the prisoner onward through the mob of people.

Another soldier kept tabs on the other prisoner whom they assumed was the leader of the two. Addie concentrated on holding her cuffed wrists together since she'd learned rather quickly, and painfully, what happened if she didn't. She remained silent and schemed of some way of escape. But there was nowhere to run, at least not fast enough to avoid being shot in retreat.

By now, the guardians had divided the assembly into two halves and positioned soldiers down the middle with their LR-5 rifles aimed at the rooftops, waiting for the rebels to come out of hiding at any second. Marcus, this is all Marcus's doing, Addie thought. She didn't know how, but a strange feeling told her it was true.

"Listen to me for a second," Norman said. "This is a mistake. We come in peace."

"Really? Then tell me why you were carrying a weapon then?" the soldier said, gesturing with the mallet.

"That was gift from a very distinguished professor in a parallel universe. I can explain everything if you just give me a second, if you just take off these cuffs. Where are we going?"

A third soldier pushed past the baffled faces in the crowd to let the prisoners through, and spoke softly into his headset, "Copy that. We'll dispose of the threat and proceed to the Sector 5."

Addie then noticed a man in a dark cloak similar to her own on the clocktower ramparts but said nothing. The clocktower teased the final seconds to six, the hour of remembrance. Tick. Tick. Tick. She noted the time before the last second split.

It exploded before her eyes. The clockface shattered outward in a million jagged shards. A remarkable, fiery glitter of glass like a crystal flower which bloomed and disintegrated in the same moment. Broken markers, glass, and flaming stone showered on Concord Square as the mob dispersed, hurrying to get away from the falling debris. The Orbservers fell from the sky in mid-flight and smashed like metallic marbles on the cobblestones.

The chaos that followed was surreal, as if time had been suspended in the clocktower explosion. Everyone shoved past one another to get to safety, eyes peeled upward. The stampede knocked over the guardians that separated the square, and joined the two halves of the assembly. The crowd rushed toward the riverbank only to meet the armed soldiers on the bridge. The guardians removed their microphazers and shot them in self-defense, one after another, like spastic birds. The citizens collapsed onto their knees and shook with heat, sweating and praying.

When Addie and Norman lifted their heads from the ground, they discover one of their captors dead and the other soldiers attempting to stop the mob that came clawing through the smoke. Remarkably the clocktower itself still stood, its archway crooked with the pendulum barely clinging on. In the midst of the mayhem, there were those citizens who didn't react at all, necks bent back, unmoving, as if they didn't hear the screams, the sirens, the gunfire. They only gazed upward, paralyzed there, trying to divine some meaning from the smoldering hole in the broken face of the clocktower.

Norman parted his wrists and felt no shock. The electronic bands had turned red.

"I suppose you're right, Addie. Chess is a dangerous game," he said, bending over to pluck the mallet from the soldier's dead fingers. A nearby guardian turned and unhooked his gun from his holster. The mallet proved faster than his quick draw and smashed him upside the head.

"This way," Addie yelled, shouldering through the angry mob. "Come on, move. Get over here."

Norman marveled at the power of the mallet and what he'd done, and then he dashed away just in time from the falling blocks of the clocktower arch when the keystone finally gave way and the pendulum came crashing down.

What are our orders, Command? Come in, Command.

We've lost... we've lost all visual communication... the Orbs...

We need... We see nothing... We're in the dark... Get over here now...

We're clearing the courtyard now... standby for orders... all guards on red alert... report to Command...

Zander had to act quickly. The metallic corridors traversed in a sophisticated maze that protracted itself through the capitol complex. Cameras nosed out from the ceiling and tracked the movement of the Grand Muse and his entourage. If they ventured too deep, escape would be impossible, he knew, with or without the young philosopher king as their hostage. The more imminent danger, of course, was the probability that a camera would soon zero in on his retina and alert security to the intruders' presence.

The royal escort had been reduced to five guardians and the two imposters waiting for the perfect moment to attack. The other guards had departed with the councilors on separate routes. The plan was to reconvene in the central auditorium once security had swept the Citadel, level by level, room by room, hall by hall, for explosives. As they hurried past the lithographs of Saint Benedict and scenes of Inoculation framed on the walls, the Grand Muse cursed under his breath and marshaled Melvin and Carlo along with his hands on their shoulders.

Command, come in Command… They're on the roof again… We need…

Watch A, what do you report?

A few broken loose from the containment in the square…

Watch B is sighting movement in Sector F-5…

"What's happening?" Carlo asked. "Was there an accident with the fireworks?"

The Grand Muse ignored him and turned to his guards, "Order them to flip the switch."

"Your majesty…"

"Flip the switch and do it remote if you must. I will not have our ancestors' blood and sweat undone by these cowards. Tell them to flip the switch now."

"It's gone, sir. There is no switch."

"What are you saying?"

"They've destroyed the clocktower, sir."

We're losing control… six men down… they're dropping propaganda on the streets… They've taken the press and we have reports of engagement…

Melvin tugged at the king's robe. "When do I get to wear my crown? Can I try it on now?"

The Orbs have gone haywire… come in, Command…

"I want that court secured now," the Grand Muse told his men. "Executive order is in effect."

The guards in front rushed ahead and punched a keypad at the end of the corridor, which unlocked another in a series of magnetically sealed doors. Zander and Weber exchanged nods and moved in. Syringe needles flicked out of their sleeves, pricked the rear guards through their uniforms, and down the escorts fell with a muffled thud, thud on the hard steel floor.

Weber fired twice at the guardians at the end of the

corridor before they could react. They dropped beside the exit as Zander knocked out the remaining guard with a wave of heat from his microphazer and then blasted the cameras in the ceiling. Throwing the stun gun aside, he whipped his revolver out from his belt and pointed it at the Grand Muse, alone beside the shaken young boys.

"A new day has come, your majesty. And there's nothing you can do to stop it." Zander leveled the gun at his crown and cocked the hammer. "The Republic shall be free. By now, your people have awoken from the sleep of machines. They have awoken afraid to know their hands as more than a tool by which to serve the great Order."

The Grand Muse glared in disgust at his would-be assassin. "The Republic is no invention. It is our destiny, a utopia for which our forefathers sacrificed their lives. Perfect and pure. A destiny that cannot be undone."

"Right now, your people are realizing they are alone in an imperfect world, not so easily reasoned to perfection. That society is a contract among free men," Zander said. "Outside, in fear and panic, they are learning to breathe."

From his majesty's side, Melvin and Carlo gazed up in utter confusion, waiting for their king to speak, to dissolve the situation by a simple wave of his hand. But the Grand Muse said nothing and instead closed his eyes in resignation, expecting death.

The revolver trembled in Zander's hand as his finger squeezed the trigger halfway, and then stopped short. He saw the look of terror on the king's face. It was nearly identical to the look on Melvin's face. An innocence, a fear, although he tried to hide it. They were the same, he realized. Had the revolution not intervened, someday the young heir would have grown to become the man of power and guilt before him.

Zander peered through the sights to keep himself from his thoughts, and steadied the revolver. He teased the trigger and then let it ease back again. This man was only a symptom, a product of rearing. Fed power and the idea, he had been corrupted, had become this demagogue with the heart of a murderer and the mind of a saint. A symptom of the great machine whose design is to never end the cycle, a design never to see fire and chaos, to produce, progress, and prosper toward a more efficient future.

This was not a king, not a dictator or tyrant. This was a doll dressed by generations of grinding gears, a man who hardly remembers his past. Zander unleveled his gun and the Grand Muse ran off down the hallway.

"Kill him. Shoot."

Zander aimed the revolver again when the king neared the end of the corridor. "I can't."

Bang. His crowned head jerked back. The Grand Muse fell onto the floor. Weber fired his pistol again. And again. Until he stopped moving. He reloaded his gun, teeth gritted. Carlo screamed and tried to run away, but Weber caught him by the arm before he could get very far.

"Go ahead," he said. "Run, my friend, and tell them that his majesty is dead. That a new king has been crowned today, of a free new Republic. Tell them and don't be afraid."

The instant he let go of the boy, Carlo sprinted as fast as he could out of the capitol complex, his footsteps echoing through the steel maze of halls. Melvin stood perfectly still, abandoned in the middle of the corridor, almost regal beside the pool of blood that rippled out from the fallen king.

Zander walked over to the young heir and crouched down to his height. "You need to trust us, Melvin. I'm not asking for your forgiveness. I'm only asking you to trust us."

An alarm sounded somewhere deep in the maze and triggered the others, from corridor to corridor, alerting one after another to the intruders. "That little bastard," Weber said and stuck his pistol in its holster.

"What did you expect? You just murdered the man he most admired in cold blood, right in front of him," Zander said.

"One must die for another to be born," Weber said.

They grabbed Melvin by the arms and ushered him through the unsealed doorway, onward through the corridors ahead, in search of higher ground for their escape.

CHAPTER TWENTY-EIGHT

Pandemonium

Panic and the unknown. Fear of the unknown. There were no answers and even if the guardians could have responded to the citizens' pleas, they wouldn't have known what to say. Burying all emotion, the guardians held at bay the restless mob in Concord Square. The citizens called out for help, from what they didn't know, and raged from moments of compelled calm to violent fits of claustrophobia on the verge of a desperate madness, collective and contagious. They only wanted to go home, take the pill and sleep off this nightmare. But each time the mob attempted to break through the barricades, the guardians would blast them to their knees. And each time the guardians pulled the trigger and saw their kin fall onto the cobblestones with their faces flushed and bodies shaking, they would question the civil order they'd been commanded to enforce.

When the microphazers proved too slow for the onslaught, the guardians fired their LR-5 rifles into the air and ordered the citizens to stand back, to cease and desist. When this failed, it only took a single blast in the crowd to shake the mob from fear to violence. The guardians stomped forward in a wide flank, their rifles pointed in a human fence, which corralled and compressed the public assembly, arresting anyone who met their advances with resistance.

Addie and Norman observed the rush and push and pull, kneeling in a layer of glass shards and debris, behind a fountain in the southeast end of the square. They cautiously peered over the stone basin and ducked whenever another rifle blast would punctuate the noise of emergency sirens and static from the blacked-out video screens.

"This is unbelievable," Addie said. "Somehow Marcus is

behind all of this. I know it."

"Do you think they're still after us?" Norman said, the mallet tight in his hand in case they ran into trouble again.

"No, they definitely have bigger problems to deal with now," Addie said. "So here's the plan. We'll wait this out and as soon as we see the opportunity, we'll sneak through that exit there." She motioned toward a nearby passageway where a guardian blockade stood their ground against the angry mob.

"And then what?"

"Run as far away as we can from this mess and then figure out things from there."

A succession of explosions along the north wall shattered the gothic statues that jutted from the arcade buttresses. Flecks of stone rained down and drove the citizens again into the armed regiment, only to be shoved away. On the smoky rooftops, the rebels surfaced from the haze and threw bundles of newspapers into the mayhem, then disappeared into the smoke by the time the guardians cocked their LR-5s up and fired.

"I've never seen a war before," Norman said.

"Life amid chaos," Addie said. "And here we are, two ghosts watching the end of a world we never knew existed."

Embers fell like confetti through the air. Newspapers fluttered from the sky like wounded birds, flopping onto the cobblestones. The cloaked body of a gangly man dropped from the rooftop and hit the fountain behind which they were hiding with a fatal splash. The man's jaw rocked in the final moments before death, as he clutched a newspaper in his hand, draped out of the basin pool.

HARRY! The call came from the rooftops over the rattle of gunfire. HARRY! His meaty eyes shot open with the last gasp, the paper released from his fingers. A NEW DAY DAWNS, the headline read, smeared in his blood:

'Remember. Stop a moment and remember. Forget the clock,

the buzzer, the time-code, the machines squealing gears, and remember when you were young and everything was fantastic and forever. Then remember when the progress and prosperity took priority, told you that dreaming was a waste of time, time progress, progress happiness. And then try to pinpoint the morning when you stopped believing in your own mind and adopted the thoughts of society.

Think for a moment, are you happier now? Now that you've given up dreaming for a real life, carefully constructed, having fulfilled all the proper steps to secure the necessities of higher living. Reverent of society and its technological progress and nothing else, in which you function on routine happiness. A modulated life. The perfecter of mediocrity.

We live today in a society that has deemed the imagination a dangerous defect of our mind, the rogue agent in an otherwise logical organ. A society that vanquished art in name of preserving a pure and secure ideological pool. And they were right to think that it was a threat, they were right to burn the books and pens and brushes. Because it is not through logic that we see our soul, our aware reflection. It is not by atomizing God that we find reverence. From one to infinity, we can follow the points, but we cannot touch a nerve, cannot codify a soul, cannot answer the essential questions we've had since the beginning of time.

In defense of the imagination, we call to arms the troubadour, the gifted liar, the lionhearted savant to come forth now and join together to blaze a path for a bold New Republic. A society in which man must be free to think in as many ways as he feels. Imagine a world without chains and you will be free. Imagine a life where every path you take is a path you choose. Imagine. Stop and imagine, imagine, imagine...'

~

Weber kicked out the steel door onto the Citadel roof, into the cool air, sirens screaming in the coming dusk. Spotlights circled the fortress from the ever-watching spires that scraped the burnt sky. ALERT ALERT ALERT. Everywhere the sound of panic hailed, the sound of the revolution begun.

Zander pulled young Melvin alongside, chased by the lights, by gunfire, by guardians in pursuit, toward the aqueduct bridges that crossed on high over the canals to the Arch of Truth. Laser blasts smattered in every direction, from the windowed spires, from the parallel bridge of the aqueduct, as they hurried across the ancient overpass, the clocktower in view on the grey horizon within the inner-city. They took shelter behind the bridge posts when the rotary guns whirred on and unloaded round after round of ammunition.

"We should make a run for it," Weber said. "If we wait out too long, the guardians will close in behind us." He peeked out from the post and surveyed the final span of the aqueduct, noting where the rotary turrets were stationed, silent once again and cooling their engines for the next assault. Off in the distance, a team of rebels emerged on the peaked roofs that swerved out from the Arch of Truth like a twisted spine, the outer ring of the Old Quarter.

"Good thing our rendezvous team is on time then," Zander said. "Let's move, we're almost there."

He shielded the young heir, dashing from one post to the next. Weber covered their path across the aqueduct on the run, unslung the rifle from his back, and sniped at the rotary turrets mounted on the far shoulders of the bridge. Zander pushed Melvin down behind a post when a firestorm unleashed from the rear.

Weber turned and fired at the guardian patrol that had stormed out onto the fortress roof, then hunkered behind a neighboring post. "I'll cover you," he said. "You go on ahead with the boy, escort him safely to the clocktower. I'll be right behind you."

"No, we move together," Zander said. "We can't afford to separate right now."

"Don't be foolish," Weber said. "Protect the heir. Let me handle…"

Melvin, without any warning, made the decision for them. In the bat of an eye, the click of a barrel, the boy was off and running as fast as his scrawny legs could carry him. He dodged the blasts with almost mechanical precision and grace, in a frenetic zigzag across the aqueduct, a fluid ballet of hops, rolls, and sprints, as if he could see the trajectory of the blast before it launched. Before the rotary guns could trim the hair off his head, the boy snuck between their honeycomb barrels at the bridge's end and leapt onto the Arch of Truth.

The rebels captured the boy when he attempted to scale the incline onto the bordering roof. Melvin looked up in confusion at the cloaked woman who came forward and offered her hand. He neither cried out nor struggled to get away when she approached. He buried his head against her body to muffle his eardrums from the raucous gunfire.

"Zander! Get over here," Leyna cried out toward the bridge. "There are more coming out behind you."

"Don't worry about us," Zander shouted. "Take the boy and get him out of here."

Leyna hugged Melvin to her side and dashed away in the direction of the clocktower with the young heir at her hips. Zander and Weber recharged their rifles, and with a nod, exchanged fire on the guardians amassed on the Citadel roof in a synchronized assault.

~

News spread of the Grand Muse's death. They'd found the body facedown in a pool of blood which, in the electric light of the metallic corridor, was shaded the same violet color as his ceremonial robe. When they lifted his crowned head, careful of the hole in his left temple, the Citadel guards wiped off his face and closed the lids over his blue eyes before laying the king on his back. THE GRAND MUSE IS DEAD… the radio was silent for a long time afterward. What more was there to do except remain vigilant, as they always had, and wait for further orders. Orders that never came.

In the radio panic that erupted, the guardians disregarded their formation, and in numbers, advanced into the scrum to stamp out the riots that had broken out in every sector of the city. They let loose a barrage of microbursts and laser blasts into the mob, in hopes this would scare them into submission. But nothing could stop the thousands, the confused, the angry masses who had awoken from the cheap dream of paradise.

The mortal fears, which had once kept them in their yokes, pounding at the whetstone, sharpening the great machine, had broken them from the fiction of a perfect society. It unleashed an aggression, stifled for generations, the feeling of chains, the urge to scream in the middle of the night, the desire to pray, to question, to say NO for once, to defy, to revel in the notion that man is his own society, his own keeper, and should be free to choose, choose, choose. And so the mice in the machine went rabid.

The mob shoved through the barricade at the river crossing from the Old Quarter, bowling the guardians over the abutment, into the rushing canal. The citizens thrashed their way through the streets, kicked down doors and smashed windows with impulsive rage, along the entire concourse of Anderson Boulevard, down Westchester Avenue, through the Residence.

Even the citizens who had remained in a state of shock, staring at the flames in the clocktower's burnt face, were finally shaken from their trance. They observed the pandemonium that had disrupted this happiest of days, read the newsprint on the ground. After one last look at their pocket watches, they smashed the clocks on the cobblestones and rejoiced to see the glass splinter, shatter the tyranny of time.

By the southern exit of the square, the guardians were

grappling with the same debacle, the same melee of citizens clawing at their arms, braving the shot and coming back to tear off their helmets and wrench the LR-5s out of their hands.

Addie and Norman sprinted toward the southern passage at the first sign of weakness and found themselves in an even more compromising situation, tangled in the mindless commotion, pressed in the heaving slaughter. Many anonymous hands grabbed at Addie's cloak, ripping at the black cloth, screaming for help as they wrestled through the mob.

Norman swung the mallet out in front to plow a path ahead, hurrying toward a nearby tournament stage in search of refuge, "Back off! Back off, I say. We're not part of this. We're not even supposed to be here."

He could hear the authoritative shouts behind them, the many voices seize into a singular howl of pursuit as he vaulted onto the stage, as he turned and saw the mob surround the soldiers in a furious tide.

"Thank you for that," Addie said once she'd been helped safely on top.

"No problem," Norman said and handed over the mallet. "Take this away from me. It makes me nervous."

A group of citizens on the stage had ripped the Republic banners down from their posts so they could use the poles as weapons in self-defense. When they became aware of Addie in his long dark cloak, they dropped what they were doing and glared in shock, like animals disturbed in the wild. They gathered up handfuls of smashed pocket watches from the stage and showed the broken treasures to the cloaked stranger and his wounded companion, as a sort of primal offering.

"I saw you running," a woman said. "Are you a phantom? Have you come to save us?"

"No, sorry," Addie said. "We've only come for—" Their conversation was cut short when a fierce round of rifle shots from the rooftops whizzed overheard, picking off the guardians in the crowd.

Addie and Norman looked toward the source of the gunshots, toward the clocktower and the flames still burning in its broken face. A shadowy figure stood on its shouldered ramparts, laughing with eyes that reflected the circus of mayhem all around and a grin that chanted on the devil dance of fire and smoke over the rooftops.

"There he is again," Addie said.

"Who?" Norman said, squinting upward.

"That man on the roof. I swore I saw him standing there right before the clocktower explosion."

"Maybe that's him. Maybe that's Marcus."

"Perhaps," Addie conceded. "But we'll never know. There's no chance of us getting up there now."

"It must be him. Who else would find this amusing?" Norman cupped his hands and called out toward the clocktower. "MARCUS!"

CHAPTER TWENTY-NINE

As the Hammer Falls

Atop the clocktower, Phaedrus whisked off his dark hood and gazed down at the riots through the stone crown of the ramparts. Black smoke billowed from the smoldering clockface and obscured the blind flurry and fury of the thousands driven to madness in Concord Square. It was near impossible in the haze to distinguish between the citizens and the guardians, between the screams of righteous anger and the screams of sheer terror. Even the people caught in the fray couldn't tell who was fighting who or which way to run so that they might escape the violent insurrection.

This was what Phaedrus had been waiting for. This savage play of utter chaos. He had imagined the moment so many times before, yet he'd never envisioned it would be so marvelous, so perfectly unhinged. He chuckled at the way Purple Harry's corpse lay skewed in the fountain basin, with the blacked-out video screen as a backdrop for his theatrical demise. He knew Harry would have done the same if he'd been able to see the odd contortions his body took in death.

This was inevitable, he assured himself. What mattered more than life or death was that the civil machine had been unchained. And soon the city would bow to a new order, a bold new Republic.

"Beautiful, isn't it?" he said to no one in particular. Crouched with rifles on either side of their fearless leader, the rebels sniped through the parapet teeth at the guardians in the square and the patrols that appeared on neighboring rooftops. They'd been surprised twice thus far, both assaults coming from the eastern rooftops with erratic gunfire. They defended their position with relative ease. There had been casualties, of course. Fallen cloaks motionless along the ramparts.

Zander, running toward the distant clocktower, felt the electric heat of LR-5 blasts chase him across the rooftops. He wouldn't let himself check to see where the shots were coming from. Keep moving, he told himself, nothing else matters. After he'd vaulted onto Arch of Truth, he'd only looked back to know Weber was dead, slumped on the aqueduct bridge, bleeding his last. He'd been hit by a lucky round from the rotary turrets when they'd sprinted for the end, and fell. RUN, he'd cried. RUN, Zander told himself, trying not think, trying not to feel the empty sickness. Just run.

He dashed over the rooftops that enclosed Kensington Plaza, toward the burning clocktower where the rebels had secured their roost. When he arrived at its high shoulder, he threw aside his rifle and grappled up the stones. Neale helped him over the parapet and onto the clocktower wall, "Where's Weber?"

Zander ignored the question and ran ahead to join the rest of the rebels.

"Answer me," Neale said, hurrying after him. "Answer me, goddamn it. What's wrong with you?"

"He's dead, Neale. Alright?" Zander turned and said. "That's what is wrong."

Neale shook his head without expression. "He's not the only one."

The rebels nodded when they rounded the clocktower bend onto the ramparts that overlooked Concord Square. He then saw why Neale's reaction had been so indifferent. For the first time, he saw the fires lighting the coming dusk, the plumes of smoke on every horizon, the guardians wrangling with the mob and the strange pattern of corpses strewn among the crushed pocket watches, fallen orbs, and newspapers that decorated the square. His stomach turned at what he saw in the bedlam below, the reality of revolution.

"Callo cally, my squeamish friend," Phaedrus called out

and walked over. "And what do you think of our brave new world?"

Zander refused to look at him. He instead watched the riots unfold from the ramparts, horrified but detached from the feeling because it seemed so unreal.

"We have set them free," Phaedrus said. "Marked a new path for our new Republic. And where is Weber to delight in this moment?"

Zander lowered his head to hide the tears that trailed down his face.

"Oh I see," Phaedrus said, placing his hand on his shoulder. "Nothing is what anything was, my friend, nor ever will be again."

"This is a slaughter," Zander said, throwing the hand off. "A massacre."

"And what did you expect?" Phaedrus said. "They are returning to their beastly natures in order to realize what real humanity is. Change does not come easily, my friend. And to change the world in a day takes a lot of blood."

"The explosions were supposed to be a distraction," Zander said, "so we could instigate the coup, not spur the Republic into all-out war. Two explosions. That's what we planned. And then you decided to blow the city to hell and fire on every last guardian standing."

"So what if I changed the plans? Maybe we did get a little carried away with the fanfare. But we did what was necessary, Zander. For the cause," Phaedrus said. "You never understood. You reveled in the fantasy of revolution yet refused to recognize the pain. All words, all plans, all sketches for a perfect future. That's exactly what they did to build this false utopia. Perfection is the devil's tease. Action is what the world respects, action is what makes time turn on edge. And now maybe the world will sit back and be humbled."

"It didn't have to be this way," Zander said. "We only

needed to plant the seed, the idea that there is something more than the civil machine. Things would have changed. We could have ransomed the child and forced the council to listen, not to us, but to the thousands of citizens calling for change. But not this. What do you really think will happen now, Phaedrus? You know what comes next. The council, as we speak, is weighing its options. They will hunt us down and try to bring the Republic back under control. And when that fails, they will give the order. The executive order to unleash the virus."

Phaedrus looked out into the square, off at the smoke and fire that lit the cityscape, and perked his famous grin.

"That's why they kept the virus. You said it yourself. That day you showed me the pictures of the vault," Zander said. "They didn't keep it for research. They kept it as their failsafe. They'll give the order and then secure themselves in the Citadel so they can wait out the plague and then start again."

Phaedrus faced him without remorse and said, "So be it. Let them unleash the virus. You think I didn't anticipate this? Why else do you think I had Sid smuggle us the cure?"

In that instant, the foggy chaos became so clear and so terribly wrong. Zander stepped back. The virus. The cure. The reality crystallized in that ridiculous grin. The stranger's message returned in flashes: revolution as revolution, a repeating cycle, everything and nothing had changed. The Jargon King. The pendulum. This fight, this so-called noble forge for the freedom of the Republic, a ruse. For power. And yet he knew he was just as guilty. Why else did he fight except so he could participate in this tug of power, so he could affect his aggrandized change under the mask of justice.

"You planned on this," he said.

"Well, not exactly. But you always have to roll with multiple scenarios," Phaedrus said. "Chance and consequence. Unleashing the virus and killing thousands of people is one of the more serious repercussions, I admit. It is unfortunate.

Many will suffer, yet in their suffering they will realize a happiness they did not know or understand under the illusion of a perfect society. That to be human is to suffer both happiness and sorrow, trapped in this skin, agitated by the want of the incommunicable, by the desire to take hold of the force which binds chaos and night to order and light."

"You're a fool, Phaedrus, and a liar," Zander said. "Beyond your rhetoric, this is not about the Republic. This is about exacting a vision, forcing the world to witness your creation. You're just as sick with the lust for power as the king's men."

"Don't be a sorry sport, chum," Phaedrus said, talking down his anger. "Recognize the paradox within you right now. Your moral evaluation of bad blood. Your spite in my smile. This is why this had to be done. Our minds are rusty from rational thought and trying to pin everything in its proper place. But there is no proper place. The lines bleed beyond good and evil. Here today we witness the death of false truths and the birth of the new philosophers and the new philosopher kings. Let the slate be cleaned of everything, all knowledge, all ignorance so that we might start anew."

The soliloquy would have gone longer had Phaedrus not become immediately aware of one missing link in his grand plan. He searched the rebels crowded on the rooftop and turned back to Zander.

"Where is our young philosopher king anyway?" he said coyly. "You haven't done something foolish, have you?"

"What do you mean?" Zander said. "He's not here?"

"I'm in no mood for games, my friend. Where is the boy?"

"Leyna took him at the rendezvous. They should have been here awhile ago."

"Oh really?" Phaedrus said. He snapped aside to Neale and Angus. "And did they stop off for a nap?"

"She's here," a voice shouted. Sprockett and Elsa appeared from beyond the clocktower bend with Leyna and the young heir. They escorted the hostages at rifle point, stiff-armed toward the clocktower summit, "We found them attempting to climb down the industrial fire escapes in Sector 6."

"I guess she was just confused about the plan, right Zander?" Phaedrus sneered.

Leyna avoided eye contact with Zander, holding onto young Melvin's hand. The horrors she'd witnessed had been too terrible to bear during her journey with the young heir over the Old Quarter roofs. Every time she would peer into the gridwork streets, she would witness another scene of monstrous violence. Half-burned faces with laser-seared tracks gouged in the skin, citizens dragged by their feet over the cobblestones with parts of their scalp scrapping off in a trail; a team of guardians huddled around a troublemaker, pushing his face to the ground and kicking him there till his ribs buckled, blasting him till the smell of burnt flesh forced them pull away; a group of rioters who'd knocked up the helmet visor of a fallen guardian, shoving the stolen LR-5 rifle barrel in his eye socket before pulling the trigger.

She couldn't reconcile these atrocities with the ego of her conscience. No matter how many ways she tried to reframe the day's events, she couldn't escape the truth, that she was partially responsible. And under the weight of that guilt, her sanity cracked with faint fissures which left her mind in a state of hostile panic. Her hair was in tangles, her face swollen from tears, her cool demeanor replaced by an anguished hysteria, broken as she held tight onto Melvin's hand.

"Please. Leave him out of this. You have your revolution," Leyna said. "You have your damn revolution. Leave him with me. He needs to be taken care of."

Elsa grabbed the boy from her embrace and brought the young heir over to Phaedrus who then bowed down to his small stature and said, "Well, what do you think, my young king? Would you like to go with her?"

Melvin gave no reply. His eyes shifted left to right and counted the armed rebels on the clocktower perch.

"I've waited so long to meet you. You are, as you know, the most promising candidate that has ever come out of the Academy, the most noble, the most wise. Terrible things have happened today. But tomorrow the nightmare will fade to a new day, my young king. And you will take your proper place on the throne."

Melvin gave the rebel leader a smug smile of his own. "I think I could be comfortable on a throne," he said. "But you can stop with the flattery. You need me, I know this, or else I would be dead like the rest of them."

Phaedrus nodded, somewhat startled by the boy's indignation, and regained his composure. "Alright, you seem to have a very keen head for what's going on. So tell me, what is it that you want?"

"I want what anyone wants," Melvin said. "Power. You're right, I will be king. But you're either willing to come to an agreement here or—"

"Now you listen to me, you little brat," Phaedrus wrenched the boy's arm so hard he cried out in pain.

Zander made a start for the child, but then felt a rifle muzzle shove between his shoulder blades. "Sorry, old chap," Neale whispered in his ear, pressing the gun gently at the base of his neck.

"I don't have to take this insolence," Phaedrus released the boy and walk away. "Kill him. We don't need him now anyway."

"Wait," Melvin said, trembling. "I was... I was only playing. Please... don't kill me. I swear I'll do anything you say."

"Oh, you want to play now, do you?" Phaedrus said. "I think we have a difference of paradigm here. You see this..." He gestured toward the outlying rooftops that enclosed

Concord Square. Here and there, the corpses of fallen rebels were visible in the shadows and smoke, splayed out in their cloaks, their rifles still clutched in their hands. "That's the blood of the men who trusted me, who risked their lives and asked no questions, who put their faith in me and made the ultimate sacrifice to ensure the rebellion would succeed. I need us to be on equal footing. So we can trust one another."

He withdrew a pistol from his cloak and laid it in the boy's hand like a toy. Melvin marveled at the weapon, frightened and excited to have its lethal power in his grasp. Phaedrus wrapped the boy's fingers around the handle and lifted the pistol at Leyna.

"Shoot her," he said. "Then we'll see what we can negotiate."

~

Trapped on the stage, surrounded by a thousand angry faces, Norman hopped up and down and waved his arms at the clocktower, "MARCUS!"

"Stop that," Addie said. "Do you want to get us shot?"

Norman ignored his friend and screamed louder up at the shadowy figures on the ramparts, "MARCUS!" He could faintly discern a child on the clocktower summit. "What do you think they're doing up there?"

"Who knows? It's hard to see from here." Addie scanned the ramparts and paused when she noticed a uniformed soldier among the cloaked men on the roof. "That's odd, why aren't they…"

The thought was interrupted by an eerie sensation, an almost deja-vu precognition of the event that was unfolding on the clocktower. She knew who the soldier was but couldn't explain how, she could even see through the soldier's eyes, as if in a daydream, the armed rebels perched with their rifles there, the young boy raising a pistol in what appeared to be the forced execution of a female hostage. She could hear the soldier's thoughts; she could feel his remorse for the terror and bloodshed caused by the rebellion.

"That's Marcus," he said, pointing to the grey figure among the black cloaks.

"How can you be sure?"

"I just know," Addie said. "He's part of this and he's in serious danger."

"MARCUS! MARCUS! MARCUS!" Norman shouted toward the clocktower.

"He can't hear you. And even if he could, there's nothing he could do for us now nor is there anything we could do for him."

"What choice do we have?" Norman cupped his hands again, "MARCUS!"

Addie resigned from any further rebuttal and quietly suffered the confluence of emotions that the soldier stirred within him, hoping that he would hear their calls, that he would turn and acknowledge their presence on the stage, that, by some private miracle, he would save them from their imminent doom, like the old Marcus had whenever the three friends had found themselves in trouble during their mischievous youth.

The insurrection around them had floundered into an odd carnival of destruction. Half the citizens had escaped through broken blockades and those that remained in the confetti-speckled square were held there by force, lined against the perimeter walls or clustered into desperate, fractured mobs that still scuffled with the guardians.

Over the shouting, the mercy screams, the gunfire bursts, a peculiar yet familiar noise, which he then realized had been dwelling in the background for some time, became louder and more distinct.

"Do you hear that?" Addie asked.

"MARCUS!" Norman screamed and then turned aside,

"Hear what?"

"That hissing, it sounds like it's coming from over there," Addie said, signaling toward the northwall arcades.

As the hissing intensified and overcame the clash and clamor of the riots, a swarm of cloaked figures became visible through the arcade arches. The guardians stationed by the passageway assumed at first that the rebels had finally descended from the rooftops to make their ground assault. But when the black mass neared, the deformed faces and sickly red eyes under the hoods told them differently. Demon jowls unclenched and opened wide in the dark cloth, serpentine tongues flicked behind jagged teeth when they came hissing through the laser blasts that greeted them.

"MARCUS!" Norman continued to scream at the clocktower but soon became distracted by the sibilant noise that echoed off the old stonewalls. "Yeah, I hear it now. What is that?" He turned toward the arcades as the black mass stormed into the plaza in a seemingly endless rush.

Addie watched the Nephs rip through crowd with ease, how their claws and saw-like teeth shredded anything in their path. She felt the fear inch up her spinal column, her heart beat like a tribal drum. Then, another odd sensation, a burning under her sleeve that spread to trace the symbol on her forearm. The fear switched to anger. No way, she thought, this can't be. We've come too far to have this end here. She clenched the mallet and felt the tension spread up her arms, the adrenaline kick into gear.

Over the western wall, over the burning rooftops, a giant Eye tore open in the grey sky to behold the chaos and panic that consumed the Republic. Addie shuddered in its presence, in uncontrollable tremors, as the ash-drawn symbol on her skin glowed an iridescent pale red underneath her sleeve. The symbol sent pulses of heat into her body until it felt as if her heart was on fire. The heat circulated back from her chest, down her shoulders, down her arms to her fingertips clasped round the mallet until the wooden tool itself began to glow. The Eye, unlike before, didn't disappear right away. Instead the strange apparition lingered there, staring out of the burnt sky, as if curious to see what happened next.

Captain Voord returned with a righteous fury, seconds before the cloaked creatures swamped the stage. He didn't think twice about where he was or where the monsters had come from. Swinging the mallet, he snapped into action and clocked every ugly hooded face that came close.

~

Melvin aimed the pistol at Leyna, unsure where to shoot, whether to shoot, or if this were only a test like the many before. When he slipped his little index finger in the trigger, he realized that he had no other choice. He started to rationalize the living being with piercing hazel eyes and wild red hair as simply another obstacle to his rightful destiny.

"Please, I'm begging you, Phaedrus. Don't do this. Kill me if you want, but don't make him do this," Leyna pleaded. "He's my son, Phaedrus. My son."

"What are you talking about?" Phaedrus said. "That's impossible."

And it was. But in her madness, she was already convinced that the boy before her was the child she'd given birth to six years ago, before she'd become involved with the resistance. The child she'd only seen for second, his crying face in the hospital room at the Institute. The baby she'd only held for an instant before the doctors wrested the child from her arms for proper rearing under the guard of the commonwealth.

"Leave my son out of this," she said. "Come over here and kill me yourself, you cold-hearted coward. You have my permission. Watch me die. Watch us all die. We are all guilty for this. We are not liberators. We are murderers."

~

Filtering through the arcade arches, the cloaked demons converged on the stage like piranhas at a feeding. Guardians and citizens alike abandoned the fight during the carnage that ensued and fled from the square as fast as they could. The Nephs didn't bother to chase after them. They'd come for one reason and one reason only. The demons flooded around the stage and hissed wildly at Captain Voord, summoned to life once again in Addie's body.

"Flargin, mar!" he hollered and struck the demons with such power they surged back in shock. With each blow, with each flesh-smacking thump, down the Nephs would crumple into empty cloaks. Then from their sleeves, clusters of millipedes would sliver out and scatter over the cobblestones, over the corpses, over the smashed pocket watches.

"Addie! They're coming at all sides. What should I do?" Norman said, wielding a stripped flagpole to knock away the demons.

"Shut yar yap and keep swinging, cabin boy," Voord told him and then yelled out at the vile creatures. "Back, back, you varmin, you sneeving ugly warfs. Get back to your hell hole."

Every time he swung, the pulsing mallet parted waves in the throng of hooded cloaks and chomping jowls. Soon, this was the only thing that prevented the Nephs from coming close enough to strike when the demons clawed their way onto the stage. The cloaked creatures tore off their hoods, unveiled the bulbous scars and bubbled flesh of their newtlike faces.

Back to back, Voord and Norman swung in a wide arch at their forked tongues. The Nephs swiped in turns with their talon hands, only to meet the blunt head of the mallet and collapse on impact into crumpled infested cloaks. Voord could feel himself slipping, his arms rendered numb. The mallet wavered with each swing less powerful than the last. When the anger finally succumbed to fatigue, Addie collapsed in exhaustion. Norman grabbed for the mallet just before the demons pounced.

~

Nauseous and spotty eyed, Melvin let his finger slide out from the trigger and then slid it in again when he felt a hand on his shoulder. Phaedrus whispered in the boy's ear and helped him hold the gun straight, "She betrayed us. She betrayed us all. She wants you to be hers. To be mothered. To be ordered around like a child and tucked into bed at night. But you are no child. You are the next great king. Successor to the Grand Muse's throne."

Zander watched and sweated. As did Neale who let his rifle droop as he looked on. As did Angus and Elsa and Sprockett and the rest of the rebels, many of whom were secretly appalled, although too scared to intervene. Melvin lowered the gun, overcome with nausea, and simply gazed at Leyna in a daze. Zander elbowed Neale in the face and he rushed toward the child. The rifle fell onto the rooftop and misfired into the air. A dozen guns cocked at his back before Zander could wedge himself in the line of sight between the young heir and Leyna.

"Stop this, Phaedrus," he said. "Let her go. She's done nothing wrong."

"She's one of them, Zander. She's always been one of them," Phaedrus said and faced the boy again. "Kill her, my young king. Prove yourself."

"You're mad," Zander said. "This is savage. Leave it to a jackal to throw all his friends to the vultures." He looked young Melvin in the eyes and walked straight up to the wobbling pistol. No one stopped him. The boy simply stood there with the gun outstretched. Zander snatched the pistol by the barrel from his young hands and waved the butt of the gun in Phaedrus' face.

"This was never about him or her or any of us," Zander said. "It was about the idea, to free us from the clock, the time stamp, the machine. In defense of the imagination, Phaedrus, in defense of everything that makes us human and sane, faults and otherwise. Where did you get this murderous heart from? Or was I a fool for believing you were once a great man? Stop this. It's over."

MARCUS! MARCUS! MARCUS! The faint calls reached Zander's ears, the voice drowned by a low hissing below. He looked over the ramparts and saw the deluge of black cloaks in Concord Square, circled around a stage in the northeast corner. A boy was swinging a glowing mallet to ward off the hooded creatures and yelling up at the clocktower. MARCUS! MARCUS! MARCUS! Over the mayhem, over the city rooftops, over the fire and smoke, a giant Eye blinked from the burnt sky. MARCUS! MARCUS! MARCUS! A flood of strange memories and half dreams flooded his head as he felt his brain pulse.

"Zander!"

MARCUS! MARCUS! MARCUS!

The shot didn't make any sense at first. He felt it hit and couldn't believe it. The pain where the bullet had buried in his abdomen. The ultimate burn as the blood ran cool down his side underneath his uniform. Zander stared at the gun in his hand, and then at Phaedrus, his former friend and partner on the clocktower precipice overlooking the city turned graveyard of their sins. It didn't make any sense. The Eye in the sky. The lame pistol in his hand, handle gestured at Phaedrus; his empty holster and young Melvin beside him, holding his own revolver. A thin trail of smoke lazily drifted from the barrel.

"Zander!" Leyna cried out, running toward him. Time slowed as the blood rushed from cold to warm.

MARCUS! MARCUS! MARCUS! Off the clocktower he fell clutching onto the pain. Time wounded down, down, down. The air felt weighted. He thought he heard the chimes of the clocktower when he fell past its blasted face. He looked up to see the horror on Leyna's face. Her lips parted in a scream.

The Nephs, like wolves on the hunt, instinctively rushed at the fallen body when it hit the cobblestones, incensed by the smell of their prey. The hooded demons disbanded from the stage, which granted Norman enough time to shake Addie onto her feet. They jumped off the platform in a mad dash toward Zander who bled unconscious before the clocktower. They cleft their way through the cloaks with the mallet and arrived at the body.

Zander's eyes shuddered awake to see a girl in a cloak huddled over him.

"He doesn't look like Marcus," Addie said.

"It is him," Norman said. "I can't tell you how I know... I just know."

"Damn it, Marcus," Addie said, pressing her hand on the gunshot wound in Zander's abdomen. "This isn't funny, you know? We didn't come this far to watch you die."

Zander shut his eyes again.

Norman swung in a circle and held the mallet high over his friend's body so she could keep the demons at bay. But still the Nephs crept closer. He swung again to drive them away, but there was nothing they could do, he knew. He laid his hand on Addie's and saw his dying friend's eyes move with sudden life under the lids. "Look, he's dreaming in death."

"Let's hope so," Addie said. They gripped his chest together and applied pressure over the corkscrew bullet hole that oozed blood through his grey uniform.

Leyna. Leyna. Leyna. Melvin's innocent eyes. The jackal's grin. The hissing, the sirens, the racket of the revolution in the distant streets as he bled. As he bled. He opened his eyes again to unveil the universe laid out in the stars, lying on the playground mulch. He heard voices but couldn't move. His blood rushed warm. Addie and Norman were more distant now.

"It will be sad to see him go."

"It's inevitable. Somehow I feel this had to happen."

The stars twittered and the moon howled and then the sky went black. He thought of everything, briefly in the movement of the moment. Of love, of life, of death, of all the foolishness in between. He suffered this nostalgia as the sky closed in on itself. He swore he felt Leyna's hand brushing back his hair, her tears wet his chest as he surrendered. As he bled. As he bled.

The Absent Door

The old man awoke, in the flutter of an eye, the pulse of a heart, to the first light of dawn. The room settled and came into focus. Sunlight lanced across his oak desk and seeded the wood grain with an almost holy effulgence. Time accelerated as his bleary eyes adjusted to the wavering light, then steadied. The silent dawn dispelled the darkness from the room with a radiant breath. Through the window glass, the sun rose over the jagged teeth of the hungry world and slowly dissolved the moon.

The peace of the moment was almost too much to embrace as the old man realized he had returned. He remembered nothing from the journey, besides his death and how he bled. Like burning photographs, the memories came back to haunt him, clear and then disintegrating into an absent understanding. The chessboard on his desk was locked in checkmate, pieces shuffled off to the side, the black king cornered by the white bishop and fellow knight. It seemed the mouse had beaten him in his sleep or perhaps he'd played out the moves while unconscious.

How much time had passed, after all? Hours? Days? Months? It didn't matter. Nothing mattered beyond the feeling he had surrendered to upon awaking, the feeling that he'd been reborn.

The pocket watch still lay cradled in his open palm, all three markers stopped, the second hand forever frozen like the rest, at the 27th notch. It saddened him that the watch had finally broken, yet at the same time he felt relieved. Why, he didn't know.

He latched the silver lid over the clockface. He laid the pocket watch aside on his desk and looked about the room that defined him. White walls, glaring white, flaking off to whiter white, notched with a history of holes and nicks where pictures had once hung. Had they always been here? He couldn't recall. The curve of the walls also seemed different, rearranged perhaps in his absence, the books, papers, and bird feathers scattered in a different pattern than the way he remembered.

The old man reached out for his mahogany pipe to mull the thought over. It was strangely absent from his desk. He then noticed the left drawer was slightly ajar. He rummaged through the random junk collected in his desk, searching for his pipe—matchbooks, buttons, coins, postcards, a thimble and spool of thread. Then his fingers came across something familiar in its shape, something his fingertips remembered by the touch, even though he'd lost all recollection of ever placing it in the drawer.

He pulled the object out, a wooden frame with a picture behind the glass. It was a photograph of himself when he was a schoolboy.

That's when he realized they were all there, the pictures from the barren walls. From the depths of the drawer, he pulled the framed photographs out. First, his wife Helena, her black hair cut short, smiling by the astronomical clock in Prague during their travels in Eastern Europe. Then came the photographs of his battalion during the War, the 33rd Division: Patrick, Henry, and Nigel hunkered down on a dusty rooftop in a burnt-out city. Of their son William as a young boy, before the tragedy, before he'd drowned off the rocks near Glenswell, stolen out by the tide. Of his old friends, Addie and Norman, on a road trip many years ago, parked on the side of a highway road in the middle of nowhere where nothing mattered because nothing mattered and that was a beautiful thing.

Laying the pictures out on his desk, the old man studied each of these moments caught in frames and started to remember in the dawn's profound silence. He held the photograph of himself as young man close to his face, then put it down beside William's picture and noticed the uncanny resemblance, the lightness of his fingers as he let go.

He wiggled his fingers before his eyes and felt their movement on air. In the palm of his hand, he traced his fate in the etched grooves and saw a life lived. Of all the simple faults, of all the crossed mistakes. A life between the lines.

These hands. The hands his wife had kissed in bed, soft kisses that made him feel like a king even on his worst days. The hands with which he'd slaved at the pulp mill, like his father before him. The hands that wrote in fever the long letters to his love from overseas, the hands that pulled the trigger, that leveled the rifle with the sulfur of war in his eyes. The fingers that touched his lover's face to know her face, amazed to be alive.

The hands that his mother had held on those lazy days in the park, that she had squeezed three times to tell him that her love was unwavering, just as her mother had, and her mother's mother. The hands he sobbed into, that dripped with sorrow, when she passed away. The hands that shook his grandfather's when he would say, look me in the eye, son... that's my boy, now you never forget.

The hands that he never forgot from that day, from passing acquaintances to the governor's ball, the hands he had forgotten, on trains, in restaurants, at parties, the hands he'd just remembered, the hands his son held as a baby to understand. The hands now wrinkled, now worn, that he moved, finger by finger, to know he had returned, before his eyes, like the first time, the first time, amazed to be alive.

With these hands, he lifted himself out of his armchair. His knees trembled yet the floor remained steady. The room was silent and the city outside his window slept except for the birds. The sparrows chirped, waking with the sun, heard but not seen in the bushes and forgotten gardens of the city. They called out to him alone. He unleashed their voices by throwing open the glass door to the new day.

The sun shined a narrow streak toward his roost among the skyscrapers when the old man walked out onto the balcony. He wrapped his fingers around the railing, wind breezing through his thin hair, and gazed off and beyond. The world asleep, tranquil, on the verge of some great dream shared by a billion roving minds in the collective unconscious of Oblivion, who would all awake and forget.

A new day where hands would meet and the reflection of passing eyes on the cluttered streets would betray their innocence. A new day of money in the market, of slipping on pants, of pulling up socks, of feeding, of breathing and recognizing what it is to breathe, of brushing back the hair in the mirror, of hailing cabs and riding subways by the bar, of that touch on the chin on the kiss goodbye. Of sharing a laugh, a thought, a heartbreak with friends, and the scribbled sweat of madmen who dared write about it all, sore from the pen, from the pain of travesty, of love, of honesty, of happiness suffered.

For once, the old man understood. The sun blinded off the skyscrapers, off the windows coming to rise. He knew. The world is not broken, he told himself, but whole as the pendulum swings.

The thought lay vacant and a sudden calm swept over him, an acceptance of everything laid out under the sun and the dreaming minds that passed through. Acting on impulse and reason. Free to choose, right or wrong. Free to choose, taking the weight of consequence to carry in memory. Creating the drama day by day, with virtue only the patience unto tending one's private universe. Accepting what comes to pass, tragedy and beauty intertwined.

When he returned to the room, he was greeted by the pictures on his desk and smiled at his life lived. He eyed his bed in the corner and thought about sleeping a little longer so he could search for his loved ones.

A glimmer of light shimmered from the far end of the room, the sunrays catching the antique mirror in the broom closet. It was half unmasked, the sheet hanging loose. The old man was more curious than afraid now. He walked straight toward the looking glass and whisked off the sheet.

In the doorway stood a young man in brown suede jacket, reflected in the shadowland of the antique mirror. His teenage face was gaunt, inquisitive brows and eyes burning green, messy mop of brown hair. It was his reflection, the old man knew, or rather the reflection of the misfit youth he'd once been, alone in the void. And as he admired the lost boy, remembering the forgotten years and how that face had changed, he suddenly noticed a stranger standing behind the young man in the shadowland. A pale figure in a black hooded cloak who watched as he watched.

The stranger smiled when he realized he had been seen. "It's been a long time, Marcus."

The old man turned around and found the stranger in his room. He met him eye to eye, trying to place the familiar face.

"You've been here a long time," the stranger said, not moving, simply staring on and on as if he were gazing through him.

When the old man turned back toward the looking glass, away from the stranger's unsettling gaze, he found that the young man in the jacket had disappeared. Only the hooded stranger remained. He watched the stranger's lips move, reflected, "It's time to go."

In the absence of being, the old man was swept by the calm again and tried to imagine the many ghosts of his former selves in the mirror glass. His heart ticked down, he faced the stranger again. He knew what came next.

"Come," the stranger said and held out his hand. "Let me show you the way.